THE LIGHTHOUSE PROPHECY

THE LIGHTHOUSE PROPHECY

BROOKWOOD MYSTERIES
BOOK 3

JORDAN JACE

EPub ISBN: 978-1-967657-49-0

Print ISBN: 978-1-967657-50-6

To Alice—my partner in love, words, and wonder.

Thank you for believing in every story, and for sharing this beautiful journey of writing together.

CONTENTS

Prologue ... 1

1. A Beacon at Dusk ... 19
2. The Etched Spiral ... 36
3. Visitor with a Claim ... 58
4. The Candle Maker's Warning ... 80
5. The Keeper's Logbook ... 99
6. Storm Over the Water ... 115
7. The Charter Fragment ... 129
8. A Rift in the Fog ... 145
9. A Candle for Sight ... 161
10. The Council's Reproach ... 168
11. The Sea Captain's Compass ... 182
12. Damien's Buried Memory ... 188
13. The Night Watch ... 205
14. Print Shop Blueprints ... 218
15. Damien's Daughter and the Flame ... 224
16. The Lighthouse Keeper's Letter ... 237
17. The Apothecary's Disappearance ... 252
18. The Jazz Melody Returns ... 267
19. The Burned Page ... 279
20. A Secret Shared ... 286
21. The Hidden Cellar Door ... 297
22. The Green Flame ... 303
23. The Lantern Ritual ... 318
24. Council Confrontation ... 330
25. The Mirror Room ... 345
26. Damien's Vision ... 357
27. A Long-Lost Medical Journal ... 370
28. Lighthouse Legacy ... 382
29. Reclaiming the Flame ... 389
30. The Light Stays On ... 396

Epilogue: The Winter Bell 409
Afterword 415
About the Author 419

PROLOGUE

The wind along the Brookwood coast carried the scent of brine and saltgrass, threaded with a silence so deep it pressed against the eardrums like a held breath. To those who had lived in the town long enough, silence was never only silence. It was memory lingering, waiting to be stirred.

Marley Taylor pulled her scarf tighter around her neck as she stood on the cliffside path, her eyes trained on the dark column of the lighthouse. The structure rose against the winter sky like an accusation. Even in ruin, even with its lantern room blackened and its once-white walls weathered to gray, the tower commanded attention. It had watched this town longer than any living soul, bearing witness to the arrivals and departures that defined Brookwood's story. And now, after the stilling of the bridge, its presence felt different—charged, as if the sea itself leaned toward it in anticipation.

Behind her, Damien Hawthorne struck a match against the cold iron of his lantern and coaxed a reluctant flame to life. The glow cut through the twilight, settling against his profile, sharp and brooding. Marley had come to recognize that expression: skepticism layered over unease, the mask of a man who wanted the world to be rational but who had already seen too much to believe in coincidence.

"You're certain about this?" Damien's voice carried, low but edged.

Marley did not answer at once. She kept her gaze fixed on the lighthouse, its silhouette stark against a sky bruised with indigo and violet. She thought of the envelope slipped to her days before, the word scrawled across its front: *Illuminate*. Inside had been the prophecy, brittle parchment whispering of shadows and truth, of a light that would rise when echoes ceased. She had not shown it to anyone but Damien, and even then, she sensed the words had unsettled him more deeply than he admitted.

"Yes," she said finally. "The bridge was never the end. It was a beginning. This is where it leads."

Damien exhaled, the lantern light flickering against the hard set of his jaw. "And what if the prophecy is nothing but an old story? People love dressing fear up in mystery. Maybe the echoes made them restless enough to invent a sequel."

"Then explain the light." Marley's voice sharpened as she turned toward him. "You heard it too—the bell. You saw the flicker in the lantern room last night. That wasn't invention."

He didn't argue. His silence was concession enough.

The cliff path narrowed as they drew closer to the lighthouse, the crash of the sea below growing louder, insistent. Each wave broke against the rocks with a rhythm Marley could almost mistake for words, a chant too old to translate. She thought of her aunt Clara, of Annabelle whose voice had finally been freed, of the Green Healers whose mark had appeared again and again in the town's buried history. The spiral was never idle. It pointed. It revealed. It warned.

Her notebook weighed against her coat pocket, its pages already dense with scribbles. Words were her way of keeping fear at bay, pinning chaos to the page. But tonight, she hesitated to write. Tonight felt less like a story she was documenting and more like a story demanding she *live* it.

The lighthouse loomed above them now, its base circled by a waist-high wall of stone long battered by storms. The iron door at its foot was streaked with rust, sealed once by the county but now—impossibly—ajar. The sight struck Marley like a hand to the chest.

Damien cursed under his breath. "That should be locked. No one in town has a key."

Marley reached for the door before she could think, her fingers brushing iron chilled by decades of salt air. It groaned as she nudged it open. The dark throat of the spiral staircase yawned inside, twisting upward into shadow.

She stepped back instinctively, her pulse tripping. "It wants us to climb."

Damien held the lantern higher, its glow cutting shallow into the stairwell. Dust spiraled in the beam like restless motes. "Or it wants us to fall."

The irony was not lost on her: he, always grounded in caution, always weighing risk; she, drawn forward by some inner magnetism she could neither explain nor deny. Together, they had walked the bridge when others dared not. Together, they had endured whispers and revelations that altered the town's very identity. And together, now, they stood at the base of another sentinel, summoned by a prophecy neither of them fully understood.

Marley touched the envelope through the fabric of her coat. The parchment's words seemed to burn hotter the closer she stood to the tower: *When the echoes still and the bridge releases its hold, the light shall rise. Shadows will resist, but truth will not remain buried.*

She whispered the line aloud.

Damien flinched, lantern shifting in his grip. "Don't recite it here."

"Why not?"

"Because..." He hesitated, shaking his head. "Because it feels like an invocation. And I'm not ready for another haunting."

Marley studied him in the lantern's glow. Beneath his skepticism, she saw what he wouldn't say: that he believed enough to fear the words might already be working.

The sea wind surged, whipping her scarf against her cheek. Far off, a sound rose—a low toll, so deep it vibrated through the ground beneath their feet. The bell. Not the chapel's, not the buoy's, but something older, rooted beneath the lighthouse itself.

Damien's eyes snapped toward her, wide despite his efforts to remain composed. "You heard that too."

Marley nodded, her throat tight. "It's beginning."

They stood in silence as the bell faded into the sea's roar, leaving only the stairwell's waiting mouth before them. Marley's hand tightened around the doorframe, the metal rough against her palm. The choice hung heavy: to climb or to retreat, to step into prophecy or to let it wither in shadow.

She looked at Damien. His face was pale, but his gaze steady, fixed on hers. The man who had once refused even to acknowledge the echoes now stood ready to face what came next, fear and reason colliding in the furnace of loyalty.

"If you climb," he said, "you don't climb alone."

The words anchored her. Whatever lay ahead—memory or haunting, truth or ruin—they would meet it together.

Marley drew a long breath, the salt air sharp in her lungs, and turned her face toward the spiraling dark. Somewhere above, a flame waited. Somewhere above, the light would rise.

And so they began.

THE FIRST STEPS rang like coins dropped into a deep well, each metallic note swallowed by the spiral. Marley kept one palm to the inner wall as she climbed, fingertips skating over chill iron and old paint, counting the turns without meaning to—one, two, three—because rhythm steadied breath and dulled fear. Damien's lantern threw a soft ellipse of light that rode up the steps ahead of them and then slid back over their shoulders with every rise, a tide of gold cresting and falling.

Half a flight in, the air changed. It grew colder, yes, but also denser, like a place that remembered a thousand held breaths. She stopped without deciding to, and Damien almost collided with her. His free hand caught the rail, knuckles white until the lantern light eased the bones back into flesh.

"Sorry," she murmured.

He shook his head, listening. She was listening, too. And she heard—

"Call him home..."

It was the voice of a child, the syllables nothing more than the soft pressure of air, as though spoken into her open palm. The words traveled down the stairwell, rounded the curve, and brushed her ear a second time, as intimate as a secret. "Say it. Ring it. Call him home."

Damien's breath hitched. He had that look she knew by now—the one that said a truth he didn't want had just arrived and taken a chair in his chest. "That," he said, and his voice came out rougher than he meant, "is what my daughter said in her sleep." He didn't look at her as he spoke, only into the lantern flame as if it might deny him. "Word for word."

Marley pressed her fingers against the inner wall again. Under the paint, under the scabs of rust, the tower seemed to hum—not with electricity, but with attention. The sound gathered at the crown of each step like dew. "We keep going," she whispered, because stopping would confess more fear than she wanted to show the dark.

They climbed. Dust drifted in the light as if the room had its own low gravity, each mote moving not randomly but with the small intent of ash returning to a fire. The stair treads complained and then adjusted to their weight, as though remembering another pair of feet, another ascent. When they reached the first landing, Marley caught the faintest glint beneath a blister of paint at knee height. She crouched. The lantern followed.

There it was: the spiral. Not drawn, not painted, but carved shallow into iron and then hidden by years of coats. It was no sailor's whorl, no idle graffito. It was the same mark she had seen in Clara's journal, the same she had traced in the ledger where Annabelle's name had been pressed into ink. The same sigil that had appeared on the parchment with the sketch of this very tower. Green Healers. Guardians. Witnesses. All of them had pressed this sign into the town's bones until the bones themselves held the shape. Marley set her fingertip to the groove and felt the smallest shiver as though the mark had temperature. "It's here," she said, not triumphantly but with the hush of someone finding a pressure point on a living body. "The same spiral."

Damien didn't deny it. His rational mind went quiet in these moments, and the man beneath—the father, the widower, the builder who knew that structures stored intent—took the lead. He thumbed the edge of the carving as if measuring tolerance. "It shouldn't be," he said, which was his way of saying *it is*.

Marley stood and they kept on. Above them, the darkness wasn't absence so much as thickness, a fabric you could imagine lifting if you had two more hands and less to lose. Somewhere higher, glass creaked as if shifting in its frame. The lantern flame bent in a draft and then corrected itself. The tower breathed.

"Illuminate," a voice said.

Marley's head snapped up. It wasn't the child this time. This voice was older, low and sure, worn by use. She felt it on the back of her neck before the word formed in her ear. **Illuminate.** The same word inked across the envelope that had found her at the café. The one that had carried the prophecy she shouldn't believe but couldn't stop believing anyway. The spiral under her palm seemed to pulse once with the syllables, as though the tower itself acknowledged the command.

Damien lifted the lantern. "Who's there?" The echo made him wince. He swallowed. "Who are you?" He wouldn't give it personhood by asking *what*.

Only the sea answered, climbing the stones from below in slow bruising beats.

They passed another landing, then another, the steps tightening in radius as if the tower's spine cinched to hold its head. Marley's calves burned. She cataloged the pain because it kept her anchored to this body, this breath, this moment. The prophecy's lines rode with her, bright and black all at once: *When the echoes still and the bridge releases its hold, the light shall rise. Shadows will resist, but truth will not remain buried.*

"Shadows don't just leave," Mrs. Bennett had warned at the festival, her flour-dusted hands closing around Marley's wrist with surprising strength. "Shadows cling." The words came back now like a scent in a long-closed room. The black beyond the lantern's radius didn't feel empty; it felt occupied, politely, by whatever had arrived first and never bothered to move on. Shadows clung to the curve of the wall, to the undersides of steps, to the places her gaze didn't land. She didn't look too hard into any of them. Not yet.

The last turn opened into the lantern room, a round with glass and iron for ribs and the lens at its heart like a sleeping eye. Salt had drawn dendritic maps down the panes, branching into delicate trees that caught the lantern light and made it meaner, more fractured. The great Fresnel lens rose taller than Damien, a cathedral of prisms. Even cold and dust-veiled, it carried authority—machined devotion to the idea that light could be shaped until it behaved like will.

They stood at the threshold without crossing it. Marley felt the line like a seam in a floorboard—this far, and then a different world. There was no smell of gas, no faint tick of wiring. The room felt both new and ruinously old.

"Look," Damien said, and lifted the lantern just enough to pour a wedge of gold into the lens's core.

At first it showed only themselves—two figures distorted into a dozen by glass, multiplied and winnowed, some versions of them closer than others. Then a third shape rose where there should have been none.

Green.

Not a person; not yet. Only the color, but it was the *kind* of green that meant plants with a purpose. Apothecary green. Grove green. A shawl maybe, a skirt, a ribbon you only remembered when you woke. The color passed across the inner facets like a thought trying on faces and not choosing one, then went.

"Did you—" Marley began.

"Yes." Damien's answer grated. He did not want this and it did not matter.

A flicker, then. Not the lantern's. Within the lens itself. The faintest spark skittered across the prism's core like a caught insect, then stilled, then skittered again. It brightened—no more than a breath—and went dark.

Marley didn't know she had stepped forward until her knee bumped the metal ring. The tower had trained her to keep her hands to the rail, but her body disobeyed. She leaned in, breath fogging a slice of the inner glass. The flicker returned—a nerve twitch, a small animal waking inside something enormous. A warmth spread against her face that could not have come from Damien's lantern.

"Impossible," he said. The word had no force in it. He set the lantern on the deck, the better to see with nothing but what the lighthouse provided.

The thing inside the lens gathered itself. It did not ignite the way a match does, clawing up the stick with hunger. It *cohered*. A pearl from sand. A syllable from breath. It became a bead of flame no bigger than a thumbnail and then held, refusing to gutter, refusing to grow, as if listening for permission. Marley swore it pulsed in time with the sea.

With each gentle flare, the shadows at the circumference of the room bucked and flinched and then flattened again, like fish scattering from a boat's keel. "Shadows cling," Marley said aloud before she could stop herself, and the little flame brightened in answer as if it recognized its enemy by name.

Below them, deep as bedrock, the bell tolled once. The sound traveled the tower's stones into their bones and took a seat at the small of Marley's back. It did not *ring* so much as *arrive*. She felt Damien's hand find her elbow, not to pull her back but to anchor himself forward. They stood together with their weight toward the lens, the same posture as people leaning into wind.

"That's not the chapel," Damien said. "It's under us."

The bead of flame swelled—as if the bell had fed it—and a beam formed, not a full sweep, not the grand turn of a lifesaving arc, but a single blade of light that tested the room, touched four panes in slow succession and then withdrew. Where it went, dust rose and memories recommended themselves to the glass, faint negatives coming up in a basin of developer.

Marley saw—she didn't see; she *knew*—the outline of a ship hewn from light alone, a hull without mass sliding along a horizon that wasn't present, sails hoisted on nothing, moving against no wind. The image did not ask to be believed. It treated belief as irrelevant. It showed itself because it had business here. Then it was gone, and only the bead remained.

Her notebook found her palm. She had not planned to write in this room. The page opened as if the tower turned it. She wrote:

The light does not guide ships—it guides truth.

The words steadied her. Naming a thing did not make it safe, but it made it held.

Damien leaned nearer the lens, close enough that she wanted to tug him back and didn't. He did not reach for the glass; she was grateful for that. His reflection multiplied the way her own had, his face rippling into versions of itself—stubborn boy, worn man, father at the foot of a bed. He swallowed. "If this works the way the bridge worked... it will show the town what it's been hiding." He said the last word like it had weight. *Hiding.* Not *forgotten*, not *lost.* Deliberate, not accidental.

"What if it doesn't stop at the town?" Marley said. The question surprised her as it left her mouth, but the tower's hum made it feel earned. "What if it wants us, too?"

Damien's answer was to let his hand fall from her elbow to her wrist and then to lace their fingers without looking down. A practical grip, the kind you make before crossing a spinning log. The pulse in his palm beat fast. So did hers. They steadied each other to the same tempo until both could claim the beat as their own.

The flame breathed, small but certain. Each pulse sent that thin blade of light out to find a pane and then return, as if the tower were testing the strength of its own gaze. The bell below did not toll again, but its one note stayed struck in the stones. Marley could feel it in the nerves of her teeth.

Out at the edges of the room, movement. The shadows weren't content to be named. They resolved and then withdrew, resolved and withdrew, always just beyond the reach of detail. She thought she saw a woman's profile and then it was only her own reflection bending. She thought she saw a shawl and then only an illusion made by salt trails. She thought *Aurelia* and faltered, surprised to find a name waiting on her tongue. *Aurelia Ward.* She had never said it aloud. She had only read it once in a fragment of town history that had no business existing, a page that insisted the lighthouse's truth began with a woman the records had erased. If the tower carried anyone's memory in preference, surely it would be hers. The green that had crossed the lens earlier suggested as much.

"Do you smell that?" Damien asked.

Marley did. Not smoke. Not oil. Lavender. Pressed-bloom lavender, the kind that survives years inside the fold of a letter and brings the whole day back when you crack the paper. The scent threaded the cold air without warming it. She thought of the old lighthouse log with its dried sprig between pages, the one that had closed on a line about the healer's oath rising if the light faltered. She didn't realize she had reached for the envelope in her pocket until the parchment's crackle answered her. The word written across it—*Illuminate*—felt less like instruction now than inevitability.

The bead of flame, finally, asked a question. She could feel it, absurd as that was; a pull in the chest that felt like the tower's attention bending toward her. The little light brightened and held and then brightened again, patient, as if waiting for permission it had already been given in another century.

"What if it wants a vow?" she said.

Damien's hand tightened. A vow had cost them before. A vow had freed Annabelle and broken other things they hadn't meant to touch. He knew it. She knew it.

"No vows," he said, gently, not as command but as protection. "Not tonight. We look. We listen. We *see*." He let the last word sit between them because it was the only promise they could keep without binding themselves to forces they didn't understand. Seeing was dangerous, but it was honest.

The flame dimmed as if considering, then swelled in assent. The thin blade of light extended once more, thicker now, tasting each pane like a fingertip along a row of spines. Marley dared a step forward, bringing their joined hands with her, until warmth licked the back of her knuckles and she stopped. She thought of ship captains steering by a beam they never thanked because gratitude doesn't move a rudder. She thought of towns deciding who counted and who did not, and how light might be the only archive that refused to collude.

The beam gathered itself tighter, and in its next pass, the glass did something it had not done before: it held. For a breath, and then two, the light stayed on a single pane and pushed through it, out and down and over the sea. Marley's skin answered with gooseflesh. The tower's bones exhaled. The bell's old note lifted, not tolling, but rising as if the struck metal had found its own voice in the stone.

"Marley," Damien said. Not a warning. A witness.

She could not answer. She watched the blade cut the night once, a clean incision that made a line on the water where no line could exist. Far below, something like a crowd shifted—the sea, perhaps, or the town waking.

The light withdrew, not fading but coiling, as if the lighthouse were drawing breath for the next thing. The first thing had happened; that was clear. But the *true* thing—the one that would not be a test or a flicker, the one that would announce itself to everyone who had not climbed these stairs—gathered itself now in the small bead at the lens's heart the way a storm gathers on a horizon that looks, to the untrained eye, perfectly calm.

Marley found the rail with her free hand and held on, not to steady herself but so she would not reach further than she should. Beside her, Damien kept his eyes on the light, his grip firm, his skepticism set aside like a coat on a chair he meant to retrieve later. The shadows along the wall bucked once more and then pressed flat, waiting.

Beneath them, in the stones, the struck bell-note rose a

fraction of a tone, asking—without words and without mercy—if they were ready to see what had always been there.

The bead brightened.

And held.

THE BEAD of flame brightened until it seemed to inhale the entire room. Its light fractured through the Fresnel lens, painting the walls with a thousand shards of gold and green. Each refraction bent around Marley and Damien, wrapping them in shifting halos that turned their faces into living icons, witnesses inscribed into the tower's story. The shadows resisted, clawing the edges of the room, but the flame pushed them back with each pulse, insistent, inexorable.

Marley's chest rose and fell too fast. She gripped Damien's hand tighter, needing the reassurance of his body anchored beside hers. He had become more than her skeptic, more than the town's reluctant protector—he was the tether that kept her from floating into the pull of forces she barely understood. The flame did not simply illuminate; it beckoned. It wanted them to see, to understand, to accept a burden carved into stone long before their births.

Then, without warning, the beam surged outward. It swept across the sea in a full arc, clean and deliberate, the way it must have turned decades ago when ships relied upon it. But this light was different. It did not just illuminate the water—it pierced it. Marley gasped as the beam carved a visible path across the black surface, a silken ribbon of green and gold shimmering where no human craft should have power to draw.

Along that line, a figure began to rise.

At first, she thought it was the reflection of the town's cliffs. Then the outline curved upward, catching the flame. A ship. Its hull gleamed faintly as if built of fog and memory, its sails full though no wind touched them. The vessel's prow turned toward Brookwood with a slow inevitability that stole her breath. It was neither entirely spectral nor entirely real—it was an echo made visible, the kind of truth only light could reveal.

Damien swore under his breath, his grip on the railing white-knuckled. "That... that's not possible."

"It isn't supposed to be," Marley whispered, but her voice was thick with awe. She wrote furiously in her notebook, though the words looked pale against what her eyes drank in: *A ship built of light, summoned by a beacon that should not burn.*

The bell tolled again from beneath the tower. This time not once, but three times. Each toll shook the floorboards beneath their feet, resonating through their bones. The flame in the lens flared with each toll, brighter and steadier, until the room itself seemed to dissolve in brilliance.

Marley blinked hard. When her eyes adjusted, she saw figures gathered in the circumference of the lantern room. At first, they looked like shadows refusing to retreat. Then they clarified.

Women. Seven of them.

Their outlines shimmered in translucent greens and whites, robes like woven fog. She recognized two from Clara's journals, another from a sketch in the ledger. One— tall, her hair a braid of silver—felt at once strange and familiar. Aurelia Ward. The erased co-founder. The "Beacon of the Grove." Her presence radiated authority that made even the light seem like it deferred to her.

The circle did not move, but Marley felt them breathe as

one. And then Aurelia lifted a hand. Her eyes, piercing even through haze, met Marley's. The words came soundless, carved straight into marrow: *One must hold the light. One must pass it on.*

Marley staggered back, nearly colliding with Damien. He steadied her, his own face stricken. "Did you—"

"Yes," she breathed. "I heard her."

The figures began to fade, their edges dissolving into smoke, leaving only the pulsing flame in the lens. But the message hung heavy in the room, undeniable.

Damien's voice broke the silence. "This isn't about ships. Or storms. This is legacy. It's about what they started, and what we're supposed to finish."

Marley nodded, her throat tight. "The bridge taught us to listen. But the lighthouse..." She trailed off, then whispered, "It demands we see."

As if in answer, the flame surged once more, filling the lens until the entire room blazed like a sun. The beam swept the town, lighting rooftops, alleys, and the chapel spire. Windows flared awake as townsfolk stumbled outside, faces upturned in awe and fear. They had seen it now. The lighthouse no longer whispered—it proclaimed.

The spectral ship dissolved into mist, but the beam remained. For the first time in eighty years, Brookwood's coast was crowned with light.

Damien's voice was low, reverent, and afraid. "We've woken something larger than the bridge. Larger than us."

Marley turned to him, heart pounding. "Then it's not just Annabelle's story anymore. It's Brookwood's."

The flame held steady, unyielding. Shadows writhed but could not conquer. The prophecy was no longer parchment or whispered warning—it was alive, breathing through the stones, through the sea, through them.

Marley set her notebook against the rail and wrote the final words of the night:

The lighthouse does not warn—it remembers. It does not shine for ships, but for truth. And it has chosen to burn again.

The bell sounded one final time. Not a toll of warning, but a resonance of beginning.

Outside, the town gathered along the cliffs, whispers rising like tidewater. They would call it miracle, omen, curse—Brookwood had always named its mysteries with what comforted them most. But Marley knew, as did Damien, that they stood at the threshold of something greater.

The bridge had been about echoes. The lighthouse would be about prophecy.

And Brookwood's story was only beginning again.

1

———

A BEACON AT DUSK

The sea stretched in black velvet beyond the cliffs, broken only by the restless gleam of moonlight tracing the waves. Brookwood was quieter than it had been in years—no murmurs of the bridge, no restless hauntings calling neighbors from their beds. Yet in the hush of nightfall, something stirred again.

Marley Taylor had returned to her favored perch on the coastal path, notebook in hand, pencil already smudged by the habit of nervous fingers. She had grown accustomed to listening for silence as though it could speak. Tonight, however, it wasn't silence that drew her—it was light.

The lighthouse, abandoned for nearly eight decades, stood dark against the horizon. Its windows had long since lost their glass, its white paint reduced to weary gray, and its lantern room should have been nothing more than a shell. Yet, just after dusk, Marley saw it. A flicker. Then another.

Three quick bursts. Two long.

The pattern repeated. Not random, not the falter of a failing bulb. It was deliberate, calculated—as if someone, or something, inside the tower wanted to be seen. Marley's pulse quickened. She flipped open her notebook and began counting the sequence aloud, softly so as not to disturb the stillness around her.

"Three... two... three... two..." She scratched the markings onto the page, mapping the rhythm with hash marks.

Damien Hawthorne stood a few paces behind her, his coat collar raised against the wind. His lantern hung unlit at his side, unnecessary under the pale spill of the moon and the strange flash of the tower. He was trying, she could tell, to dismiss the phenomenon before it had time to take root. His hands were stuffed deep in his pockets, jaw tight, the line of his shoulders betraying the unease he would never give voice to easily.

"You're really going to stand here every night cataloging a bad wire," he said at last, voice steady but clipped.

Marley didn't look up from her notes. "A bad wire doesn't repeat the same sequence every evening, Damien. This is a signal. Three short, two long. Morse code. A pattern like this means something."

He exhaled, the kind of sound he made when skepticism wrestled with memory. "Or it means a storm fried the grid years ago and what you're seeing is metal settling, light bouncing off the water. Our eyes invent patterns all the time."

Her pencil paused mid-stroke. "But you see it too, don't you?"

His silence stretched, telling her more than any dismissal could. He had seen it. The flashes had burned into his eyes just as they had into hers. Still, he shook his head. "Even if it is real, it's just... a glitch. Some leftover wiring sparking against salt air. It doesn't mean prophecy. It doesn't mean ghosts. And it definitely doesn't mean the lighthouse woke up because the bridge finally went quiet."

Marley closed her notebook slowly. The tide struck hard against the rocks below, sending spray that climbed almost to their boots. "That's exactly what it means," she whispered.

The light flashed again—three short, two long.

MARLEY RETURNED the following evening with a thermos of coffee, her scarf knotted tightly against the cold. She had not slept well. The pattern had danced behind her eyelids until morning, her dreams filled with a blinking rhythm that chased her through corridors she didn't recognize. She hadn't told Damien how unsettled she was; he would have reminded her that she already had a history with haunted bridges, whispered voices, visions from beyond. He would have reminded her that obsession made her vulnerable.

But obsession was also how she had uncovered truth.

The lighthouse blinked again as dusk bled into night. Three. Two. Three. Two.

Her pencil scratched furiously across the page. She had started a chart now, columns of nights, rows of sequences, cross-referenced with the tide and moon phases. Patterns always hid in data if you collected enough of it. She believed the flashes meant something. Whether warning or invitation, she wasn't sure, but the sea never moved without purpose, and neither did its sentinels.

Footsteps approached on the path. She knew them before she turned—Damien, steady and reluctant. He lowered himself onto the bench beside her, the one carved years ago with initials that had long since weathered away. He carried no lantern tonight, only his presence, which for Marley was equal parts comfort and conflict.

"You'll catch a cold out here," he said, but softer than his usual tone.

"Then you'll nurse me back to health," she countered lightly, her eyes never leaving the lighthouse.

He huffed a laugh without amusement, watching the horizon. When the flashes came again, his jaw flexed. He leaned forward, elbows braced on his knees. "It doesn't unsettle you?"

"It unsettles me completely," Marley admitted. "But that doesn't make me want to look away."

The silence that followed was thick, threaded with the pulse of waves and the insistent rhythm of light. Damien rubbed the bridge of his nose, weary from more than just the day. "You think it's a code."

"I know it's a code."

"And if it is?" His gaze shifted to her at last. "What then?"

Marley hesitated. She thought of the prophecy in her coat pocket, the envelope marked *Illuminate*, the brittle parchment that had promised shadows would resist but truth would not remain buried. She thought of the Green Healers' sigil etched into journals and ledgers, the whispers that had led her to the bridge, and how each clue pulled her deeper into the town's forgotten legacy.

"Then it means the lighthouse isn't finished with us," she said simply.

Damien didn't argue. But he didn't agree either. His silence, though, was louder than denial.

The lighthouse flashed again—three short, two long— and for the first time, Marley swore she saw something in the space between the beams. Not shape exactly, not shadow, but intention.

She scribbled the word into her notebook with a hand that trembled: *intention.*

The light kept speaking. And she promised herself she would learn its language.

By the third night Marley had a system.

She staked the same perch on the coastal path twenty minutes before dusk, spread a wool blanket on the bench to keep the cold from seeping into her hips, and set a thermos, pencil tin, and small metronome on the plank beside her. The metronome wasn't for rhythm—she could keep time well enough—but for certainty. She set its pendulum to a steady sixty beats per minute, then used the ticks as a scaffold to measure each burst of light. Between ticks and pencil scratches, the sea did its old work—pushing and pulling, indifferent to the two figures sitting above it and insisting on meaning.

Three short. Two long. Pause. Three short. Two long.

She built columns on the page and began recording exact intervals in seconds: 0.3, 0.3, 0.3—1.2, 1.2—2.0 pause— then repeat. The pattern didn't waver, not once in the hour she sat there. If it were a fault in the metal or a trick of swelling wood, it would drift. The eye invents order sometimes; time does not. Her faith wasn't in magic. It was in measurements.

Damien arrived without announcing himself and set a paper sack of dinner between them. The smell of the café's stew lifted gently into the salt air—thyme and beef and something slightly sweet that meant Evelyn Grant had been generous with carrots again. Marley offered a tired smile and kept counting under her breath.

After a minute, he asked, "Morse?"

"If dots and dashes can be made of light," she said. "Three shorts would be S. Two long, M." She wrote the letters in a margin, then boxed them as if that might keep them from changing. "S M. Or..." She hesitated. "Or maybe it's not letters. Maybe it's the kind of signal ships used to swap—units, intervals, marks. But it's *something* and it's precise."

Damien watched the tower without pretending not to. When the pair of long flashes came, his jaw worked once before he got hold of it. He took the metronome in his hand and listened to its ticks like a man who wanted to be convinced that clocks still mattered. "I checked the county records again," he said. "There's no line powering that tower. Nothing's been connected since the forties, and that was torn out. If there's a light, it isn't coming from a grid."

"Then it's coming from the lighthouse," Marley said simply.

He half smiled despite himself. "You hear how that sounds."

"I do." She capped her pencil, then uncapped it again because the light resumed and she refused to miss a beat.

He let the smile go. "You still have the envelope?"

She didn't touch her coat pocket as if the gesture might prove too much to the night, but the parchment felt present against her ribs all the same—the brittle sheet with a single sketched tower and the Green Healers' sigil tucked into its base, the word *Illuminate* scrawled across its face like a dare. *When the echoes still and the bridge releases its hold, the light shall rise. Shadows will resist, but truth will not remain buried.* She had read that line enough times that it floated up now without ink or paper, not as comfort but as pressure. The bridge had gone quiet. Everyone knew it. The town had even begun leaving the chapel doors unlocked at night again. Whatever had haunted Brookwood's river no longer asked to be heard; in the empty space it left, the lighthouse had cleared its throat.

"Yes," she said. "I have it."

"You think this"—Damien gestured toward the tower—"is *that*." He didn't say *prophecy*; he didn't have to.

"I think they're connected," Marley answered. "If not cause and effect, then an order of operations. Listen, then see. Echoes, then light." She heard how that sounded, too—and how close it cut to faith.

Another sequence flashed. She marked it cleanly and then pressed the eraser into the page as if weight could keep numbers from slipping into mere superstition.

They ate without talking for a while. The stew lost its steam quick in the wind. When she finished, Marley slid her notebook across the bench. "Look. First night, forty cycles. Second night, forty-one. Tonight, same intervals, but the pause has shortened by a tenth. It's tightening."

"Or your fingers warmed up," he said, but softly enough to make it a kindness rather than a dismissal.

She pulled a folded tide table from the notebook pocket. "Moon's four days off full. Tides are running higher at dusk. If the lighthouse were reacting to boats"—she angled her chin toward the empty horizon—"fine. But there's nothing out there. Nothing moving. It *starts* at dusk, as if a time were chosen, not triggered." She hesitated, then said the word she knew would taste strange in his mouth. "Like a vigil."

Damien's gaze didn't move from the lantern room. "Vigils are for the living," he said at first, but then added, "and the stubborn dead."

Marley watched his hands. They stayed in his pockets even when the temperature dropped, not because of cold but because he knew better than to reach for what he could not fix. She'd learned his tells as if they were their own code—how the muscle at his temple gave him away before the rest of him conceded what he'd seen; how he angled himself between her and a precipice without drawing attention to the fact; how he cataloged risks even when he pretended to catalog reasons.

"You could admit it unsettles you," she said gently.

"It unsettles me," he said immediately, and surprised them both. He cleared his throat. "But being unsettled isn't the same as being sure. We've already paid for false certainty once."

She knew what he meant by *we*. It stretched back through the bridge, through Annabelle's voice carried on fog, through found objects and old vows and a night when truth had rattled the town's bones so hard that whole families went to the square the next morning just to look at one another in daylight. She had been there for every step of it. So had he. And they had learned to move together—even when fear and reason tugged in opposite directions.

Marley thumbed a fresh page and drew a line down its center. On the left she wrote *phenomena* and on the right *likely explanations*. "Help me," she said. "If I'm pointing at a ghost, point me at a wire."

Damien's mouth tilted but he played along. "Phenomenon: discrete patterned flashes. Explanation: kids with a drone."

"Kids with a drone would go for spectacle," she said. "And they'd get bored by the second night."

"Fine. Phenomenon: no power on record. Explanation: a concealed battery or generator."

"Where."

He didn't answer, because they both knew the county had welded the door shut after the restoration grant failed twenty years ago. And after that, salt and time had welded it again. He shifted tactics. "Phenomenon: you're already looking for meaning. Explanation: confirmation bias."

"I'm always looking for meaning," she said, and made it not an apology but a claim.

The light flared its three short, two long. He didn't try to outtalk it.

When the hour ended, she packed slowly and felt the ache in her shoulders let her know she had done a day's work even in stillness. Damien walked her back toward town. The path cut through saltgrass and then between two houses whose windows kept their own quiet watch. At the turn where the café came into view, he stopped.

"Let me run something down," he said. "The restoration committee filed a packet when they tried to get money to stabilize the tower—schematics, notes from the last keeper's quarters. If there's any mention of a clockwork or residual mechanism, it'll be there. I'll look in the morning."

The offer cost him—she could hear it in the careful way he kept it practical. Admitting he'd look was admitting he expected to find something. She reached out and touched his sleeve, a mirror of the way he had steadied her on the stairs a week before. "Thank you."

They paused at the café door as Evelyn dragged a mop across the floorboards in slow, satisfied arcs. The café owner glanced up, took in their faces, and softened. "You two keeping the night honest?" she asked.

"Trying," Marley said.

Evelyn nodded once, then looked past them toward the black seam of sea. "I cooked with my grandmother by lamplight the night the beacon died," she said. "Brookwood slept worse for years after." She wrung the mop, voice lower. "Careful what you wake. Shadows don't just leave—they cling." The same warning she'd pressed into Marley's wrist at the festival; it landed differently now that the tower had started to *speak.*

Back in her small apartment above the bookshop, Marley taped the night's chart beside the others on a wall that had become what Damien teasingly called the *lighthouse room.* She didn't mind the joke. Rooms acquire names when they earn them. Pins held tide tables, a sketched coastline, and a copy of the café's hand-drawn calendar so she could track human rhythms alongside the sea's. On the desk, the envelope sat under a paperweight like a patient she wasn't ready to examine too closely—*Illuminate* bleeding through the old fibers where the ink had sunk. She touched it once with two fingers, not to open it but to mark her place in a story she had not started and could not set down.

She made tea she would forget to drink. She marked one more note on her chart: *Pause shortened again by 0.1s.* Then, in the corner of the page, small, almost embarrassed, she wrote: *Maybe not S and M. Maybe S... and M answered.* She didn't know why the thought arrived. She only knew the light felt less like a broadcast and more like a conversation —call, response.

Sleep came at the gray edges of dawn and brought with it the old things—stairs that never ended and a lens that watched even with no flame in its heart. She woke with the word *see* in her mouth as if she had spoken it aloud to someone who had been listening.

Morning brought Damien's message: *I'm at the office. Found the committee box. Old restoration notes are a mess. There's a mention of a timing drum. Coming by with copies.*

She read it twice and then swept the charts into a neat stack so that when he arrived the room would look like a place to work rather than a place to worry. He came up the shop stairs with a cardboard banker's box held in both hands and the air of a man who had already lost three small battles with himself before breakfast.

He cleared a space on the table and began laying out folders—schematics, grainy photographs of the lantern room before the lens had been shrouded, minutes from a town meeting where someone had scrawled *cost overrun* in the margin. He tapped a yellowed sheet. "Here. Last keeper's note." He read aloud, almost reluctantly. "'Clockwork disabled October 1942. Lens to remain. Lamp assembly removed. Watch maintained until spring closure. If the light falters, the healer's oath must rise.'" The last sentence wasn't in the keeper's hand. Different ink. Different slope. Someone else had added it, and the town had filed it anyway. He didn't look up as he said quietly, "Your people."

Marley brushed the edge of the page with the back of her knuckle, the way you touch a relic at a museum you can't afford to be caught loving. Lavender lifted, faint as a rumor, from the paper itself, or else from her memory of the lighthouse log where a sprig had been pressed and forgotten until someone opened to the page again. She didn't say *Green Healers* because the room felt too small to hold the words. "It's there," she said instead. "In the record."

Damien took that in without letting it win. "It explains the *idea* of a signal, not the existence of one. A timing drum without a lamp is just gears trying to remember work."

"Maybe remembering is enough," Marley said. "Maybe that's what this place is doing. Remembering, out loud."

He leaned back and crossed his arms, less like a skeptic than a man bracing for a wave he couldn't stop. "You think the light is answering the bridge," he said. It wasn't a question.

She nodded. "And I think it's waiting to see if we'll

answer back." She tilted her chin toward the envelope on the desk. "*Illuminate.* Someone wanted us to climb. Someone wanted us to measure. Someone wanted us to *see.*"

He didn't ask who *someone* was. Some questions conceal themselves inside too many answers. Instead, he flipped open a folder with a blueprint of the tower and traced a finger along the spiral staircase. He didn't seem to realize he was doing it—but she did. The motion was careful, almost reverent. When he reached the lantern room at the top, his finger paused over the lens the way a person hovers before touching a scar. The air between them tightened like a string.

"Tonight," he said finally. "If the pattern holds again, I'll go up with you. We'll time it from inside."

She let out a breath she hadn't noticed she'd been rationing. "Okay."

But he wasn't finished. "No vows," he added, and the words were gentler than the warning they meant. "No names. We look, we note, we come back down. We don't give the tower anything it can keep."

Marley glanced at the charts, at the careful columns she'd built to keep awe from becoming a trap. "Deal."

He gathered the papers back into their piles, readying his retreat. Before he reached the door, he turned. "If it *is* Morse, S and M"—he rolled the letters in his mouth like he was testing them for hidden barbs—"maybe it's not letters at all. Maybe it's the start of a phrase. Something someone used to say." His eyes flicked to hers, intention clear. "Like a reminder."

She knew what he meant before he said it, because the memory they didn't speak belonged to both of them now— the stairwell whisper, the child's voice curling down the iron spine as if coughed out of stone: *Say it. Ring it. Call him home.*

"It isn't the chapel's bell," Marley said, and the hairs on her forearms prickled at their own agreement with the thought. "It's under the tower."

Damien nodded once, rough, as if the gesture cost. "Tonight," he repeated, and left.

When the door closed, the apartment filled again with the ordinary sounds of morning—pipes sympathetic in the walls, a gull insulting a rival on the gutter, the shop counter bell a floor below as someone stepped in for a secondhand book. Marley should have gone down. Instead she stood at the window and watched the line where water met sky until it stopped looking like a horizon and started looking like a ledger—left column sea, right column air, the lighthouse a narrow mark between where the town kept the sum of its debts.

She turned back to the desk and pulled the envelope into her hands at last. She slid the parchment free. The sketched tower felt less like a drawing than a recognition. Down at the base, the small circle—spiral inside a ring— seemed to throb faintly under her thumb. She read the line again, because she could not help herself: *When the echoes still and the bridge releases its hold, the light shall rise...* She let the rest move through her like breath. Then she set the parchment down and wrote beneath it in her own hand, not for the town, not for Damien, but to remind herself what work was required of her: *Listen with numbers. See with patience. Don't name more than you can carry.*

Dusk would come, as it always did. The pattern would either hold or it wouldn't. Either way, she would be there on the path with her metronome and her pencil and the steady idea that the world—even when it was strange—could be learned by attention. She did not know what S and M would mean by nightfall. She only knew the lighthouse had chosen to speak in a language she could learn. And for all his caution, Damien had agreed to climb—because unease, like faith, was a kind of assent.

On the wall, the charts breathed in the draft, paper making a sound like quiet surf. For a moment Marley let herself hope that the pattern was not a summons to disaster but an invitation to stewardship—that the light wanted keepers again, not ghosts. She put her pencil beside the metronome, reset the pendulum to a fresh minute, and listened to the tick until the room became a clock.

Three short. Two long. A pause.

Whatever it was, it was waiting.

THE NIGHT CAME DOWN FAST, the way it always did on Brookwood's coast—sky blackening from indigo to slate to something thicker, more consuming. The wind carried salt spray in fine needles that clung to Marley's hair and dampened the edges of her notebook pages. She sat again on the bench with her chart pinned under a paperweight, her thermos steaming at her side.

Beside her, Damien stood with his lantern unlit, hands in his pockets. He had promised to climb tonight, though his posture told her he would rather be anywhere else. Still, he was here, which meant something. It meant he had chosen to be unsettled rather than absent.

The first flash came as predictably as a clock striking the hour.

Three short. Two long.

The pattern traced itself across the sea, bright enough now that Marley swore she saw ripples catching the gleam, reflecting it back in small, fractured lines. She wrote quickly, though she had memorized the rhythm by now. On her wall of charts, she had left a space for tonight's entry, certain the sequence would not break.

Damien exhaled slowly, the kind of breath he used to steady himself before walking into a courtroom. "It's exactly on schedule," he muttered. "Like someone turned on a machine."

"Or like someone lit a candle," Marley said softly.

His eyes flicked toward her, unsettled. "Don't romanticize it."

She ignored him, tapping the metronome once to reset the ticks. "I'm not romanticizing. I'm recording. And every record points to intention. This is no accident."

The light repeated, steady, unwavering. Three short. Two long.

Damien shifted his weight, gaze fixed on the tower's dark silhouette. "If it's Morse," he said slowly, "and you're right about it being S and M..." He hesitated. "That could mean something. Initials, maybe. Someone's name."

Marley's pencil stilled. "Or a reminder," she said, echoing his words from that morning. The memory of the stairwell whisper slid into her mind again: *Say it. Ring it. Call him home.* She shivered.

The silence stretched between them, filled only by the pulse of the sea and the insistent rhythm of light. Then Damien straightened, decision hardening his frame. "Let's go."

Marley blinked. "Up the tower?"

He nodded. "If we're going to face this, we don't do it from the bench. We do it from inside."

THE CLIMB WAS SLOWER than she remembered. The iron stairs groaned beneath their weight, each step echoing in the hollow cylinder. Damien's lantern swung in his hand, throwing uneven slices of gold against the walls. Dust floated like restless spirits in the beam.

Marley kept one hand on the railing, her other clutching her notebook tight against her chest. She had thought she was ready, but her heart beat too fast, each pulse a warning she couldn't ignore.

Halfway up, Damien paused. "Listen."

She froze. The tower breathed around them, the kind of silence that wasn't empty but weighted. Then, faint and curling down the stairwell like a ribbon of smoke, came a whisper.

"Say it. Ring it. Call him home."

Marley's breath caught. Damien stiffened, his knuckles whitening around the lantern handle.

"It's the same voice," he said, low. "The one my daughter spoke in her sleep."

The words pressed into Marley's skin like a brand. She wanted to deny it, to tell him it was imagination, but she couldn't. She had heard it. The tower had spoken again.

They climbed faster.

AT THE LANTERN ROOM, the door resisted before yielding with a long, reluctant groan. The air inside was colder, sharper, threaded with salt and something older—like lavender long pressed between forgotten pages.

The Fresnel lens loomed at the center, fractured and veined with dust. Marley approached cautiously, Damien just behind her. The glass caught the lantern glow and split it into fragments, scattering their reflections across the room.

Then the flash came. Not from Damien's lantern, but from within the lens itself.

Three short. Two long.

Marley's hand flew to her notebook. "It's inside," she whispered, her pencil racing across the page. "Not outside. The signal is coming from here."

The light pulsed again, steady and deliberate. This time, shadows along the wall writhed, stretching and contracting as if recoiling from the beam.

"Shadows cling," Marley breathed, recalling Mrs. Bennett's warning.

Damien stepped closer, face pale. "This isn't a glitch. This isn't—" He broke off, gripping the railing as the flame within the lens swelled. It grew brighter, more insistent, until the whole room bathed in green-gold light.

Marley's breath came shallow. She scribbled one final note: *The lighthouse does not guide ships—it guides truth.*

The bell tolled beneath them, deep and resonant, vibrating through the stones into their bones. Once, then twice. Each toll matched the pulse of the flame, until the rhythm of the prophecy itself beat inside their chests.

Damien's voice shook. "It's not just a pattern. It's a summons."

Marley met his gaze, her fear matched by certainty. "Then we've been called."

The light swept across the sea one last time, brighter than before, carving a line of illumination so clean it felt like truth itself had been laid bare. Down below, Brookwood stirred— the town waking to a mystery it could no longer ignore.

The pattern held. Three short. Two long.

And both Marley and Damien knew: dusk would never fall the same way again.

2

THE ETCHED SPIRAL

The keeper's quarters felt closer to the sea than the lantern room ever did. Maybe it was the way the wind threaded through the cracked sash and rattled the warped panes, or maybe it was the smell—salt and old rope and the ghost of whale oil that had soaked so deep into wood it would never completely leave. Morning fog pressed its face to the window and peered in like a curious child.

Marley eased her palm across the desk where a keeper once wrote out weather, tides, arrivals, and absences. An ink stain lived beside the blotter like a small permanent eclipse. The chair creaked when she tested it, softer than it looked—as if, even now, the room preferred the presence of a watcher.

"The floorboards," she said.

Damien set the pry bar he'd brought from his truck against his thigh and followed her line of sight. Near the east wall, where the quarters stepped down two inches, a seam in the wide-plank floor was not like the others. The joins all ran true except this one, which held the barest crescent of a gap—as if a board had swollen, been lifted, and set back slightly wrong.

He knelt and pressed a thumb to the edge. "Whoever lifted this was careful," he murmured. "But they didn't re-seat the tongue."

Marley did not crouch yet. Some part of her wanted to acknowledge the threshold before crossing it, and in Brook-wood thresholds had proven to be real things—places where stories and structures negotiated custody of memory. She glanced to the window. Outside, the lighthouse's shadow fell short in the pale fog, not long and accusing as it did at dusk. Even so, she felt watched—in the way of houses that are not empty.

"Ready?" Damien asked.

She nodded. "Lift at the joist, not the grain."

He slid the pry bar gently under the lip and levered. The board rose with a sigh, reluctant but not resistant, as though exhaling after too long a silence. He set it aside. Beneath lay a run of joists and the subflooring darkened to near-black with age. And there—on the face of the beam—carved shallow but unmistakable, lived the spiral.

It was not the whorl of a bored boy's pocketknife or the painter's idle flourish. The groove was fine and sure, cut with a narrow chisel and patience. A circle; within it, a spiral that traveled inward from the cardinal point like a tide pattern trimmed down to its essential geometry. It was the mark she had seen in Clara's journal and in the ledger that recorded Annabelle's name. It was the sigil tied to the Green Healers, the women whose work ran under Brookwood like root and water. It was, in every particular, the same spiral she had seen in the vision back in the bookshop's hidden room. The same hand—or the same lineage of hands—had cut it. Marley felt the recognition strike her in the ribs like a knocking from inside.

She went to her knees. "It's here," she whispered. "Beneath the keeper's room. Not painted. Carved." Her fingers hovered above the groove without touching. The line shone slightly darker than the surrounding wood, less from stain than from the way light caught its depth.

Damien shifted to let her have the angle. He always did that—moved his body without comment to give her the truer view. "Why hide it?" he asked.

"Not hiding," Marley said. "Anchoring. The way you fix a load-bearing column with a plate, so the force routes where you intend. The spiral sets intent into the boards." She met his eyes. "It's not a label. It's a function."

The word landed hard between them. Function. As if the spiral were circuitry.

Marley pulled her notebook and a charcoal pencil. She set the page over the beam and began a rubbing—slow, careful strokes until the circle rose through paper and the spiral walked out of the wood onto the page. When she lifted the sheet, her breath caught. The image was exact and notched at the outer rim—tiny ticks at the thirteen, the seven, and the four o'clock positions. Not decorative. Marks. A code in relief.

She flipped back to earlier pages. There, a sketch she had made months ago in the bookshop's hidden room after the vision: a spiral, same direction, same number of revolutions, same tiny ticks that she had drawn without understanding why. Her scalp prickled. "It matches," she said. "Down to the notches." She didn't look up; she couldn't yet. "Exactly what I saw."

Damien rested his knuckles on the joist and studied the ticks. "Orientation?"

Marley set her compass on the subfloor, watched the needle swing and settle, then aligned the rubbing with the beam. "The long notch at thirteen aligns with true north, not magnetic. That's... unusual."

He nodded slowly. "Which means whoever cut it had a way to correct—a transit or a captain's compass." He gestured to the window and the slice of sea beyond. "Keepers had both."

She reached out at last and pressed two fingers lightly into the groove. The wood was cool, but she felt the idea of warmth—like the ghost of a hand once laid here in the same posture. A memory of heat. She withdrew her touch, not from fear but from respect. "It's not just beneath the room. It's beneath where a keeper slept." She pictured a narrow bed along the east wall, a trunk at its foot, boots tucked beneath. She pictured a hand in the dark, reaching down through a knot-hole to press the spiral the way someone presses a worry stone. "A touch-point."

They lifted a second board to see the continuation on the next beam. The spiral did not repeat; the circle did. At each joist, a circle, and within only a short inward curl, as if the main spiral lived here and the others were satellites— echoes of the original, placed to carry its force across the span. She could not help herself; she smiled. "They understood distribution," she said. "They knew how to make a pattern hold."

Damien looked from the beam to her and back again, and she saw the tilt of his mouth that meant he was letting the evidence move him whether he approved or not. "How old?" he asked.

"Cut after the boards went down," Marley said, running a light across the grain. "But not recently. The edges have worn soft. Decades at least."

"Which means we're not the first to find it."

She swallowed. "Or we're the first to be allowed."

They replaced the boards with care. Damien seated the tongues with the heel of his hand and a folded rag to protect the grain. The seam closed almost true, but the faint crescent remained—the necessary imperfection you accept after lifting what doesn't want to be lifted. He stood and turned a slow circle with his gaze, reading the room as if it might volunteer additional truths. "You'll want to check the keeper's ledger," he said. "Inventory. Repairs. Notes on any 'unusual marks'."

"And the restoration packet," Marley added. "Photographs, if any, before they stripped the paint." She looked down at the rubbing in her hands, the spiral perfect and impossible. "Start cross-referencing this against anything with a margin note," she said, half to him, half to the work itself that had already begun. "If the symbol turns up anywhere, we log it."

Damien took the rubbing and, with his thumb anchored in the lower corner to avoid smudging, held it at arm's length like a blueprint. "I'll start with the older restoration documents," he said. "Schematics. Field notes from the consultants." He offered her a small, pragmatic glance—the kind that had become its own tenderness. "We follow the boring paper first. If the spiral is real, it will show up where people didn't think it mattered."

Marley folded her copy into her notebook. She wanted badly to stay in the quarters until dusk, to sit with her back to the beam and see if the light's pattern changed with a body above the mark. But the day had other work—photocopies, cataloging, the café's kindness of coffee with something inexplicably sweeter than sugar in it. She rose and took a last look around the room. The keeper's chair, the desk, the window. "It waited here," she said softly. "The way people wait with a lamp in a window for someone to come up the path."

"Or like a witness at a bedside," Damien said. He re-seated the final board and stood. "Let's go find your boring paper."

They carried the pry bar, the notebook, and a new nerve out into the fog, closing the door as if closing a storybook you knew you would reopen before night.

THE ARCHIVES in the town office smelled like copier ozone and dust jackets. Damien slid a banker's box onto the broad table and popped the metal stays on a stack of gray folios. Marley stood on the other side with her pencil poised and disciplined. They worked by quiet habit, the rhythm of two people who have learned to share air and evidence without needing to narrate every reach and return.

Photocopies of engineering drawings: plan view, elevation, lantern room section. Consultant field forms from the nineties: "Observed: corrosion to exterior ironwork, cracked glazing; recommend stabilization." Minutes from a grant committee staffed by people with serious handwriting and insufficient money: "Motion to defer lens removal pending funds." A black-and-white photograph: the keeper's quarters taken before the newel post had cracked. In the photo, a small dark circle on the floor, barely there—easy to miss, impossible to ignore once seen. Damien tapped the margin. "There," he said. Marley leaned in. The circle was right where the board seam lived. The photographer had not found it; the camera had.

On a consultant's checklist, a single pencil mark: a ring with a spiral spindle, drawn in the margin beside "interior floor—east." Someone had seen and made the gentlest record a bureaucratic page could bear. No note, no legend, just the small insistence of a hand that could not resist telling the future that the past had left a notch.

Marley copied the mark into her notebook next to her rubbing. She wrote, in neat block capitals: *MATCH* and drew a clean line between them. "Whoever made this mark knew it mattered," she said.

Damien was already flipping to the back to find an initials block. "H.N.," he read. "Harold Nash. Independent consultant from the coast. Retired now or dead. I'll see what else he marked in this packet."

Marley took the photograph to the light and tilted it to see whether any detail rose from the matte. The circle darkened when she shifted the angle—confirmation that the beam had been fresher then. She wrote the photo's accession number and the note *visible pre-paint strip*, then forced herself to stop; if she didn't begin curating this room like a museum, they would drown in paper.

On the third folio, Damien found a stapled memo from the county facilities manager to the restoration committee chair. *Re: keeper's quarters—subfloor irregularity; unknown symbol carved into joist. Concur with consultant's recommendation to leave as-found for study; no funds allocated for further investigation. Recommend documentation only.* He passed it across. "There."

Marley read the words twice. They were exactly the kind of language that hid hot metal under cool water. *Unknown symbol.* She underlined the phrase once and felt something settle—not an answer, but the right question. If the county knew and documented, it lived in more places than this file. She turned another page and found a faded Polaroid with developer lines at its edges, shot crooked by someone crouched over an open floor. The spiral here was unmistakable. The notches showed as lighter ticks where dust had not yet settled. She set the picture beside her rubbing and the two images agreed with a clarity that felt like a vow.

Damien checked the back of the Polaroid for a date. "August 14, 1997," he read. "And—look." The scrawl below the date: *keep.* He exhaled a short almost-laugh. "Whoever wrote that had taste."

"Or orders," Marley said, though she smiled, too. She sat back on her heels and let her gaze go unfocused until the paper blurred and the essence of the thing floated up: a spiral under a bed, a circle repeated down the run of beams, a series of ticks aligned to true north, a mark that said *we were here* and *we are here.* The mark that the vision had planted in her a season ago returned now not as apparition but as wood and dust and administrative record. "Cross-reference the symbol everywhere you can," she said. "Every margin, every stray paper."

Damien nodded and began a list in his narrow print, not looking up: *H.N. field notes; Polaroid; memo; checklist margin; plan photo (keeper's room reference).* He set his phone, face down, on the table, a signal that he would not be drawn from the work by anything less urgent than fire. "I'll check the restoration boxes in storage, too," he said. "The contractor sometimes keeps extras the county never sees."

"Old invoices," Marley said. "They write what they actually did, not what the report says they did."

He raised his brows in agreement. "And they doodle in the margins."

They worked until the fog burned to a white noon and the floorboards in the office warmed enough to make every step sound like a small distant drum. When they left, Marley tucked the memo's language into her pocket—not the paper, which belonged to the town, but the words, which now belonged to her. *Unknown symbol*, she repeated inside her skull until the phrase lost its utility and left only the truth of the thing itself: a known mark, by a known lineage, doing work that someone had decided could sleep so long as no one put weight to it.

Out on the street, the lighthouse held its steady black outline against a bright sky. It looked least guilty in full daylight. Marley felt the rubbing against her notebook's cover the way a person feels a letter sitting in their bag—present, pulling attention to itself whenever thinking wandered. "It's real," she said. "It's recorded." And then, quieter: "It was waiting."

Damien didn't answer. He didn't need to. He matched her stride down to the café, where Evelyn already had the kind of coffee on the counter that meant she had seen them coming through the window and decided they needed saving.

"Two soups," Evelyn said, and then lowered her voice as she set down the bowls. "And mind your steps, loves. The light's remembering." She said it the way one might say *the river's up*—not as omen but as weather report. Marley felt the truth of it settle like a shawl across her shoulders. The light *was* remembering. And the beams beneath the keeper's bed had remembered, too. The spiral was an archive—the kind that refused to live solely on paper.

After lunch, they returned to the shop. Marley taped the rubbing beside her tide charts and below the metronome's hook. The wall began to gather its own order: left—sea and sky data; right—house and symbol data. Between them, the envelope with *Illuminate* lay under its paperweight, a hinge between listening and seeing. She took a breath and allowed herself one line at the bottom of the rubbing: *Not decorative.*

Directive. Then she set the pencil down and said aloud to the empty room, "We see you."

The floorboard under her right heel knocked once. She chose to take it as a coincidence. And also as an answer.

THEY WENT BACK at dusk because that was when the tower told the truth most loudly.

Damien carried a roll of craft paper, blue painter's tape, and a soft graphite stick—the tools of a surveyor who has learned to treat mystery like a wall you can print if you press with the right pressure. Marley carried her notebook, a small square of linen so she wouldn't leave oil from her fingertips on the old wood, and a carpenter's compass she'd borrowed from the antique dealer with the promise that she would return it better oiled than she'd found it.

As the sun sank, the lighthouse grew its taller shadow and laid it over the path like a road they recognized but could never name. Inside the keeper's quarters, the air had cooled, the smell of salt sharper, the sounds of the sea closer —each incoming set folding onto the rocks with a sound like heavy cloth shaken and hung. Marley crouched where they had lifted the board.

"Same joist," she said. "Let's print the whole span."

Damien knelt and set the tape along the board edges, then smoothed the craft paper across the seam. He took the graphite and began to lay it sideways in broad, patient strokes while Marley held the paper steady. The spiral rose again, slower this time, and with more detail: a faint mouth to the groove that had not shown in the small rubbing, knots and saw marks in the surrounding wood, even a nick in the beam outside the circle where someone had missed their place once and corrected without any vanity. When he finished, he blew lightly across the surface and the graphite haze lifted like breath.

They stepped back. The print caught not only the main spiral but also the small satellite circles at the adjacent joists, a constellation of intention hidden beneath the keeper's step. It was lovely. It was also sobering.

"Those ticks," Damien said, pointing with a carpenter's pencil. "Thirteen, seven, four. We know thirteen is true north. Seven... west-southwest, roughly. Four, east-north-east. One inland. Two to sea."

Marley unrolled the coastal survey map she had marked during the last grant season's research for the town committee. She laid the craft paper print over it and rotated until north met north. Then she set her compass point at the spiral's center and walked an arc to match scale from the quarters to the light well. The tick at four o'clock pointed directly toward the headland where the original grove had stood before the road cut its shoulder—where the Green Healers had met, if the ledgers and Clara's journal were to be believed. The tick at seven o'clock matched the angle of the old channel stones near the bridge—the ones that slanted right to catch the river's pull before the new supports were set. The thirteen o'clock tick landed on the lantern room itself. The marks made a triangle, not equilateral but purposeful. "It's a network," Marley said. "Not of places exactly, but of memories that hold each other standing up."

He looked from the print to her, eyes narrowing not in suspicion but in focus. "If the spiral is one node, the lantern is another."

"And the grove a third," she said. "Same spiral in three places. Different scales. Same intent."

Damien set the carpenter's pencil down with unusual

care. "I'm going to say something you deserve to hear from me more often," he said. "You're right."

The admission landed warm in the room. Marley folded the print at its edges as if tucking in a child and slid it into a mailing tube. "We still have to prove it," she said. "A thought is not evidence. But it directs the search."

He nodded. "I started cross-referencing the symbol through the older lighthouse restoration documents at the office." He opened his satchel and pulled a photocopy with a clerk's stamp in the corner: a worksheet H.N. had filled twenty-eight years ago. In the margin, a ring with a spiral and the note *beneath bed—keeper's quarters*. A second copy showed a partial floor plan where the same hand had drawn small circles at each joist on the east run. "There's also a typed index," Damien said, "old, probably scanned from a typewriter ribbon. Five mentions of 'mark—unknown' in the keeper's room. Two in the stairwell. One, disappointingly, in the broom closet." He gave her the smallest smile. "I'll take what I can get."

Marley traced the recorded circles with a fingernail through the paper. "A pattern," she said. "A purposeful repeat. The indexer didn't know what to call it, so they called it nothing. But our eyes know their own." She tapped the two in the stairwell. "We should check those next."

"Tomorrow. In daylight," Damien said. He glanced to the window where dusk was dragging itself down the slope of sky. "Tonight we keep our promise: observe, record, leave." His voice softened, the caution more care than constraint. "No vows."

She smiled without teasing him. "No vows."

They replaced the lifted board and stood, and in doing so the room changed. Not visually—nothing in its arrangement had shifted—but energetically, the way air changes when a congregation stands in unison. The hair on Marley's arms rose. A faint draft, cool and precise, licked across her knuckles as if the building had leaned forward to listen. Then, clear and punctual, the first flash arrived: three quick bursts through the fog-seamed glass, two long. The signal speaking into the room as comfortably as breath.

Marley's hand went to her pocket for the metronome she had begun to carry even when she didn't plan to use it. She set it on the desk and touched the pendulum. Tick. Tick. She recorded the sequence—same intervals as last night, pause shortened by a heartbeat—and then forced herself to lower the pencil. She let the light work without her.

"Does it feel... lower?" she asked, surprising herself with the word.

Damien angled his head. "It does," he said, equally surprised. "As if the beam is routing through the structure instead of across it. Down the iron, through the stair, under us." He pressed his palm to the windowsill. "Resonance."

"The spiral," Marley said, and heard how her own voice had thinned to a thread. "We printed it. We named it out loud. And now the light is using what we woke."

He shifted closer, not to argue but to stand with her inside the realization. "If the lighthouse is a machine for seeing truly—and I am not saying it is—then the spiral is part of its gearing. We found a tooth." He brought his mouth nearer her ear, voice almost apologetic. "That metaphor got away from me."

"I liked it," she said. "It fits."

Another sequence flared. The pause tightened a hair. She wrote *interval shortening again*. Then, in a margin she would resolve later, she printed in small capitals: *S M = SENT / MET? SIGNAL / MEMORY?* She didn't know why the words came in pairs, only that the pattern felt like conversation—call and response, three and two, we and you.

Below them, deep in the stones, a heaviness gathered the way thunderheads gather while you tell yourself it is still only humidity. The bell didn't sound. But its absence had started to feel like an intake of breath.

Damien stepped back and lifted the tube with their print under his arm. He'd begun to hold the day's evidence like a child—a thing you do not drop even to reach for something that glints. "Let's go," he said quietly. "We keep our bargain with the building."

Marley shut the ledger she had not meant to open, pocketed the metronome, and slid her hand along the desk's worn edge as if saying goodnight to a friend who'd taught her something and would teach her more tomorrow. "Thank you," she said to the room, because gratitude is a discipline as much as a response.

On the stair, her hand found the rail where the paint had been rubbed to a dull shine by decades of palms. Two steps down, she stopped. Beneath her palm, beneath paint and rust, the rail was notched. Small. Circular. The same tick. She didn't scrape at it. She didn't need to. She simply said, mostly to herself, "Tomorrow." Damien heard and nodded. They went on down into a night that smelled like iron and brine and the faintest echo of lavender that did not exist and never quite left.

THEY SPREAD the print across the shop table like a chart. Marley weighted the corners with the paperweight and three river stones she had kept in a bowl since the bridge stilled—remnants of one kind of mystery holding steady the study of another. She sketched a cleaner version in her notebook, drawing lines from the ticks to the three locations she and Damien had named: lantern, grove, channel. She sat back and let her eyes blur until the geometry impressed itself past speech.

"Matches the vision," she said finally, and tasted the relief and the danger of saying so out loud. "The same spiral, the same posture."

Damien looked at the wall where her charts had started to form their own grammar. The metronome, the tide tables, the envelope with *Illuminate* anchored under glass. "I began cross-referencing the symbol in the restoration documents today," he said, returning them gently to today's work. "Tomorrow I'll add the building permits and the contractor invoices. If the symbol shows up as a margin note, we'll know where else they found it." He hesitated. "We'll also know where it was removed."

She turned the carpenter's compass in her fingers. "If any were removed, what did that do to the network?"

"Made it noisy," he said without thinking. "Or brittle. Or both."

Marley's mouth went dry with a thought she did not want to dignify and couldn't avoid. "And if someone removed it on purpose?" Her voice dropped to its lowest range. "To change what the lighthouse remembers."

Damien didn't tell her she was borrowing trouble. He had learned what happened when this town's past was pulled into light: it asked for integrity, not expedience. "Then the documents will show the hand," he said. "No one destroys something in a building without leaving a trail—of paperwork, if not repentance."

The shop's clock ticked a patient five minutes. Outside, Brookwood turned off lamps, one by one, in the order of families' habits. Inside, the line of their work had already found its next stones: stair notches to inspect; invoices to read; a grove to stand in with a compass and see if the tick at four o'clock felt like a line you walked as much as drew. The keeper's quarters had given up a secret that felt less like a prize than like an assignment.

Marley lifted the tube and slid the print deeper inside until it sang against the cardboard—a small hollow note like a rung glass. She set it by the door so she would not forget to carry it to the office in the morning. "We closed a circle today," she said.

"We opened a system," Damien corrected softly, and there was no scold in it. Only a kind of quiet awe.

They stood for a while without needing to speak. When they finally parted, he touched his fingers to the tube, a small pragmatic benediction, and she watched the door close on his shoulders and felt equal parts alone and accompanied. Both states, she had learned, were necessary to this work.

On the wall, the metronome sat stilled. She reached and touched the pendulum. Tick. Tick. The rhythm filled the room like breath. Three short. Two long. She smiled despite herself. "We're listening," she said into the quiet, and turned out the light.

THEY FOUND the second mark by accident—because deliberate discoveries are often paid for by the ones you never intended to make.

The next morning, a seaward wind pushed away the fog early. From the cliff path, the ocean threw light back at the sky like a bright refusal. They started in the stairwell, tracing palms over rails and balusters, counting notches with their fingertips the way pianists count scales when they return to an instrument after too long away.

"Here," Damien said, four turns up from the keeper's landing. He had shaved a sliver of old paint with a pocket blade—not enough to wound, just enough to persuade—and there, beneath the white and the iron oxide, a circle with a short inward cut lived exactly where a hand would grip. The wood beneath was dark and sound. He did not score the groove; he only put his thumb in the shallow and felt, as Marley had felt, the ghost of warmth.

"Same hand," Marley said. "Or the same instruction."

"Notches?"

She angled her small flashlight and he angled his body to take the glare. "Thirteen only. North. As if this one's job is to remember direction, not to gather." She avoided the words she wanted—*to instruct*—and took a picture with the little camera she used when she didn't want her phone on a site. She wrote *stairwell—turn four—north tick* in her notebook and drew a circle around the word *turn* as if it mattered. It felt like it did. You honor feelings in the field; you confirm them at the desk.

At the second turn, her fingers found the next—faint, nearly gone under paint, more felt than seen. She didn't push for clarity. She pressed her palm to it as a letter-sealer presses wax and said in the small voice she had learned to keep for these rooms alone, "Seen."

They climbed again to the keeper's quarters and lifted the board once more. Light came cleaner this hour, and the spiral looked less like a symbol and more like a map. Marley set her carpenter's compass on the center and walked its two outer legs in a slow circle over the beam, tracing the distances to each tick and translating them to scale. When she laid the translation over her survey map, the line from the seven o'clock tick struck true toward the river bend by the bridge—the place where the channel stones had once forced the water to behave. She marked it and felt the smallest pain at her breastbone; some grief still lived in the structure of her that the bridge had quieted but not erased. "It connects," she said. "It all connects."

While she worked, Damien sat on the floor with the restoration index and a legal pad. He had begun cross-referencing every mention of *mark—unknown* with page numbers, contractors, dates, and names of attending staff. Patterns showed. H.N. saw more than other consultants. The county clerk in '97 filed more completely than the one in '02. A volunteer named "E. DeWitt" appeared in margins twice in ways that suggested a hand steadier than a casual helper's. He flipped a page and stopped. "Look," he said, passing her a photocopied note—undated, unsigned— clipped to the index. The handwriting was small and compressed. It read: *Mark preserved per request. Leave covered. Purpose per oral history only.* He exhaled a soft incredulous sound. "Per oral history only," he repeated. "Someone told them what it was, and they believed them enough to leave it, but not enough to write it down."

Marley felt the heat of a frustrated flush climb her throat. "Or they wrote it down somewhere else," she said. "Somewhere they thought safer."

"Then we'll find *that* file," he said, not bravely but practically.

She dropped a finger onto the three words *per oral history* and held it there as if she could compel their referent to rise. "Whoever told them," she said, "knew what to keep and what to let go of. They asked for preservation—so it would work for someone later."

"Someone who would look."

"And listen." She glanced down at the rubbing in her notebook. "And see."

They set a small mirror on the floor beside the seam and caught the spiral's reflection intentionally—an indulgence maybe, but it paid a dividend. In the reversed image, the ticks read as outpoints instead of inpoints. The map flipped: lantern, grove, channel. Marley felt the usefulness of seeing something reflected settle into her fingers. She drew the reverse in her notebook and wrote in the margin: *mirror = other half of instruction* and knew that note would sound like mysticism to any clerk. She wrote it anyway. Truth is not obliged to restrict itself to a single category of explanation.

At noon, the antique dealer, Mr. Whitcomb, appeared in the doorway of the quarters as if the tower had smuggled him up the stairs. He carried a small leather case and wore the open, curious face of a man who had found something that wanted a witness.

"Brought this back," he said, flicking the brass latch with the satisfied competence of a person who likes objects that work. Inside lay a carpenter's compass nearly identical to the one Marley had borrowed—older, more used, its points bare of finery. "Came with a chest from an estate sale out on the headland. Inside the lid, initials—A.W." He grinned, unable to help himself. "Thought you'd want to see."

Damien stood slowly, and Marley, who could feel his skepticism and wonder trading the wheel of him back and forth, reached first for gratitude. "We do," she said. She turned the case to the light. The compass's arms had been polished smooth by long hands. She checked the lid and saw the small clean letters: A.W. The name coded itself into her mouth without permission. *Aurelia Ward.* It landed like a stone that makes a circle bigger than its size when it hits the surface. She met Damien's eyes only for a heartbeat—agreement, worry, hope, all the usual chords. Then she breathed out. "Thank you," she said again, and meant it more.

Mr. Whitcomb tapped the desk with two fingers and retreated down the stairs, a man happy to have been the stream that carried a thing to its necessary bank. Marley didn't pick up the compass. She could have. She would, later. For now, she set its case beside the print tube and let it be present in the room without forcing it to perform the function she already guessed it would serve two chapters hence. The outline of their work was clear; the order mattered. She would not sprint ahead of the story the lighthouse was telling them.

They resumed their cross-referencing. Damien built his list, each new line neat as a fence picket: *Stair turn 4—tick north (photograph pending). Stair turn 2—worn; tactile confirmation. Keeper's quarters—primary spiral; satellites; ticks 13/7/4.* He added, *Cross-ref: consultant H.N., memo re: unknown symbol; Polaroid 'keep'.* He was a man for whom lists were a mercy in a storm.

Marley sketched the scene three ways: plan (from above), section (from the side), and perspective (from the floor at knee height, which is how a hand would know it). She labelled the distance between tick and tick with measures that felt waywardly precise—"12.5 in. center to notch"—then translated those to scale for her coastal map. A shape was forming. It didn't claim to be a compass rose or a mandala. It behaved like both and also like neither. It was a *reminder*—the word that kept returning to her whether she invited it or not.

"You're thinking of the vision," Damien said, without lifting his eyes from the list.

"Yes," she admitted, glad the honesty did not require apology. "I am."

"And?"

"It wasn't an omen. It was instruction. This"—she touched the spiral—"is the same. It's not trying to scare us. It's telling us how to see."

He let the sentence be. For a man who would once have fought it on principle, his letting was itself a kind of romance.

In the late afternoon, a squall line approached—one of those clean, narrow bands of weather that crosses a day like handwriting. They replaced the board, closed the window, and gathered their things. On the path down, Marley paused where the cliff offered a full view of the tower and the town beyond. The lighthouse wore the sky's changing like an old coat. She thought of the spiral under the keeper's bed and felt, not fear, but duty.

"Green Healers," she said, low, tasting the lineage for steadiness rather than drama. "They left their mark where the keeper slept. They extended it along the joists. They notched to north, to the grove, to the channel. They didn't hang a sign. They cut a function into the wood."

Damien looked at her with that expression that had become—God help her—part of why she loved him: the mix of admiration, apprehension, and the instinct to put himself between her and anything sharp. "And now we've started the cross-referencing," he said. "We'll follow it where it goes."

"Into boring paper."

"And into the place under the spiral where you're certain there's more." He didn't accuse. He named.

She set the tube more snugly under her arm. "Not yet," she said, honoring the chapter order she had promised herself. "First, we have to prove this isn't just us seeing what we want."

"It isn't," he said, and the sentence held both his doubt and his loyalty like threads woven so close they could pass for one. "But we'll prove it anyway."

They walked back to town as the first drops of rain found the path and darkened it in coins. In the bakery window, Mrs. Bennett was hanging a paper star that would make its own small light when plugged in at dusk. Marley tried not to see omens in everything that offered them. She failed, but forgave herself.

In her apartment, she added three new sheets to the wall. The rubbing. The craft paper print. The stairwell photograph with the arrow she drew and labelled *turn 4 north tick*. She wrote: *Ch. 2 outcomes—discover spiral; match vision from shop hidden room; Damien begins cross-referencing symbol in older restoration documents.* Then, because she had promised herself to follow the outline exactly and she found brief comfort in checking a box that belonged to narrative rather than fate, she put a small, neat check beside each line.

She did not sleep much that night. But when she did, the dream came clean: a bed in a small room, a hand reaching to touch a groove in a beam, a person in the next room noting the weather in a ledger, and the light above not flashing for ships but for people—quiet, stubborn, holding a vigil that outlived anyone who'd ever stood the watch.

And when she woke, she knew the day's work: more boring paper; more beams.

One must hold the light. One must pass it on. The sentence did not belong to this chapter yet. She let it pass through her and out. For now, she had enough: a spiral in wood, a match to vision, and a partner already deep in cross-referencing the mark through the documents other people had been kind enough—or fearful enough—to leave behind.

3

VISITOR WITH A CLAIM

The rumor arrived before she did, the way rumors always do in Brookwood—sliding ahead of the subject with the tide and docking at every counter on Main Street by noon. By the time Marley pushed through the café door, the bell chimed on an inhale of conjecture: *Marwick kin in town,* someone whispered over a plate of scones; *lawyer with her,* someone else added, like weather. Evelyn set a mug on the counter, eyes already soft with the kind of concern that pretends to be curiosity because concern is heavier to carry.

"Don't let them tangle you, dear," Evelyn said, lowering her voice as if the sugar could overhear. "People who travel with papers try to make you forget what you've seen with your own eyes."

"What have I seen?" Marley asked, though they both knew the inventory: a bridge that had learned to speak and then learned to rest, a lighthouse that had chosen a language of flashes—three quick, two long—night after night at dusk, as precise as a clock and as intent as a vow. She had seen a spiral cut into wood beneath a keeper's bed and the same spiral set like a quiet ordinance into the underbones of the stair. She had seen Damien lay paper against old joists and make the marks stand up in graphite like a geography lesson you weren't supposed to pass on. And she had felt, in her palm and in the air itself, that the tower had begun to remember aloud. She had seen enough that new paper could not unsee her. Still, the words *Marwick kin* struck something in her ribs and made it ring.

She didn't have to wait long.

The woman entered alone—no clatter of entourage, no rustle of heavy coats. She wore a long charcoal coat that made the cool morning look curated and gloves of a kind of leather that whispered when she folded them into her purse. Her hair was pinned back, her posture a sentence that said she brought her own chair to any table. The only incongruous detail was the old cedar document case she carried herself instead of handing off: a practical rectangle, brass hinges bright from polish, edges worn smooth by a century of other hands.

"Ms. Taylor?" she asked, as if greeting an appointment she'd set with the day itself.

"Marley," Marley said, not out of familiarity but because the woman had said her last name like a claim. "And you are?"

"Helena Marwick Vale," the woman said, letting each syllable click into place without apology. She did not offer a hand at once. She let the name sit between them first—*Marwick* like a key placed on a table with the teeth pointed your way. Then she lifted her chin toward the corner table by the window, and Marley—who had learned to pick her ground—chose the banquette against the wall.

They sat. The light from the window made a pale coin on the cedar lid. Helena rested her fingertips on the case and spoke like a woman trained to put complicated things into simple sentences for people who would sign but not read. "I'm here for a few days. My family has claim to certain lighthouse artifacts that were deeded in trust at decommission." She tapped the case once, almost absentmindedly. "I've brought the paperwork."

Decommission. The word belonged to 1940-something in Marley's head—the era when the town had decided ships could find their way without a guardian at the headland. She thought of the prologue of the tower's own memory: the lamp removed, the clockwork stilled, watch maintained until spring closure. She kept her face even. "Artifacts?"

"The lens finial," Helena said. "The keeper's ceremonial key. A brass compass kept in the lantern room for inspections. Any personal effects of the founding family stored on site." She spoke like inventory and inheritance shared a border wall.

"Which founding family?" Marley asked, and the question laid itself very neatly between them.

Helena did not flinch. "The Marwicks," she said. "We raised the first scaffolds and paid the first bills. There's a record." Her tone did not invite dispute.

There was a record. There were many records. And some of them were missing pieces. Marley had seen enough slips, margins, and quiet notations to know that the story Brookwood told itself about its beginnings was a quilt that had been mended under dim light. The prologue that had woken in the tower wasn't about a single man and a single check; it was about a web— bridge, grove, lantern; founders plural; a woman erased and a promise threaded through wood. It was about Callum Marwick's family raising the light, yes, but also about the Green Healers' sigil showing up at the base of the tower in ink and hand—the circle and spiral, the mark of guardianship. It was about legacy braided from more than a single surname. It was—Marley could not shake the sense—as much Aurelia Ward as it was Marwick, as much grove as ledger. But you did not say that first to a woman who had traveled with a cedar box and a name that was both passport and weapon. You started with temperature. "What brings you now?"

Helena lifted a small smile that did not travel to her eyes. "The lighthouse has... attracted attention." She did not say *flashing* or *pattern* or *signal*. "This town is very dear to me. I'd like the family's property intact before enthusiasm becomes carelessness." She placed the case between them and turned the brass clasp but did not lift the lid. "I've also brought documents you should see."

"Why me?" Marley asked.

"Because you are the one writing the story the town is starting to believe," Helena said, as if dictating a neutral fact. "And because if there are misunderstandings embedded in Brookwood's official version of events, I prefer to resolve them while we are all at a table rather than months from now in a courtroom."

There it was, stated pleasantly: resolve the story at a table, not at a bench. Marley thought of Damien, of the steadiness of his shoulders when his mind knotted itself up. She thought of the benevolent threat beneath Helena's calm tone. She looked at the case. "May I?" she asked.

Helena's gloved hand rested on the lid a half-second too long, a micro-delay that registered as reluctance. Then she nodded once and drew her hand away. "You may examine them," she said. "But I ask that you not copy or photograph without my consent. These are family papers. I'm extending a courtesy."

Family papers. A courtesy. Marley unlatched the lid and lifted it.

Inside, order. A stack of envelopes sealed in red wax with a crisp M impressed in the center—new wax, but the seal itself was old; its ring had a slightly uneven outer circle the way a tool picks up the scars of its own service. Beneath the envelopes, a shallow tray of older documents tied with cotton tape: brittle ledger pages, a folded deed, a photograph turned so its face lay against the velvet. The cedar smelled faint and clean. Beneath all of it, a second, slimmer packet lay facedown. Helena's hand moved ever so slightly toward it and then withdrew, as if stopping herself from putting a palm over a shirt pocket.

"What am I looking for?" Marley asked, because a person who tells you where to start is also telling you what they hope you won't find.

"Start with the envelopes," Helena said. "Recent transcriptions of older texts. My great-aunt commissioned a historian to make them legible. The originals are... delicate."

Marley smiled because Helena had made *legible* sound like *lawful*. She reached for the first envelope, slid a finger under the wax, and lifted a sheet of thick paper covered in a tidy modern hand that nonetheless did not quite disguise the tilt and peculiarities of something older. It was a letter— Callum Marwick to "the keeper on duty"—asking that the "Marwick instruments be maintained in good order" and specifying the items: a brass compass, a key, a small finial. It also contained a line that caught at Marley's throat like a fishbone: *All this under the original agreement with A.W., whose funds and labors made this light possible, for which our family remains in gratitude, despite later publishings to the contrary.* The letter was dated near the end of the nineteenth century, the ink on the past bleeding into the present through a transcriber's pen.

"A.W.," Marley said aloud, because sometimes you had to give a thing sound to judge how to carry it. "Aurelia Ward." She could feel the name vibrate like a note in a glass. She kept her face impartial and let the word *gratitude* sit on the tabletop like a cup no one would raise yet. The charter fragment naming Ward as co-founder—the Beacon of the Grove—was still in a future chapter, but the outline of the truth had already been sewn into the seams. The woman across from her was offering a sliver of it on her own terms. *A.W.* existed here, inside Marwick handwriting, as a partner acknowledged and then conveniently footnoted later by others. Marley placed a fingertip on the transcription and did not look up. "This contradicts the version of the founding that appears in the Town Day pamphlets."

"It corrects it," Helena said. She let the words be plain and unadorned. "And it situates the Marwick trust where it belongs—at the origin."

"Alongside A.W.," Marley said, keeping her tone gentle and the sentence honest. She set the transcription back in its envelope and lifted another. This one was a 1902 note from a keeper to "Mrs. Ward at the Grove," reporting on repairs to a stair rail and ending with the line, *your circle beneath the bed remains, per request.* There was no wax seal for that letter, no county stamp. There was only the matter-of-fact intimacy of craft and instruction: do this, don't do that, keep this beneath where a body rests. Marley held the page, felt the truth of the spiral she and Damien had rubbed rise under her fingertips in ghost and ink, and then set the page down. "You said artifacts," she reminded herself, because she could feel her center pulling toward the tendon of the story rather than the bones of the claim. "Your family's property."

"Yes," Helena said. "The items named in the agreement. I'm here to arrange for their return to the estate." She let a beat pass and then added, with the smallest of smiles, "Unless the town would prefer to acknowledge their origin and negotiate a loaned exhibit at the lighthouse when it inevitably opens as a heritage site."

Marley pictured the lantern room flooded with visitors on summer afternoons, laughing and lowering their heads to read placards, the gift shop's spinners hung with post-cards of a beacon sold to them as safe nostalgia. She thought of the beam's green-gold memory and the way shadows had cramped and then slid back when the light rose; she thought of the bell deep in the stone and the song it had begun to practice. Heritage. The word did not match the work the tower had set itself to do. But she also knew how towns had to live—in budgets and grants, with plaques and blue ribbons and brochures no one kept past October.

The café's door opened and closed, a draft of salt sliding across their table. Marley felt Helena's gaze follow the breeze to the sea beyond the glass. "You've been up," Helena said. It wasn't a question. "You and Mr. Hawthorne."

Marley didn't grant her the courtesy of surprise that Helena had done her reading. "We've observed," she said.

Helena's attention returned to the case. "Good. Then you won't waste my time with assertions about malfunction. Let's not insult the building." For the first time, her voice also carried something human, a hairline crack in the stone: respect, perhaps, or memory. She touched the lid with three fingers and then folded her hands again. "I'm offering you a look that I have not extended to the council yet. Read what you need. Ask what you need. But I won't leave these papers in your possession."

Marley felt the boundaries land like fence posts in packed ground. She nodded. "Then I'll read," she said, and when Helena inclined her head, Marley began.

Outside, the sea kept its clock. Inside, a different timepiece began to tick: the one that turns when old paper believes it is being seen fairly. Marley held each sheet as if the writing could feel the weight of her attention and then set it down on the cedar in a stack she curated as coolly as she could. She read a "memorandum of understanding" typed in a ribbon's failing ink that tied decommission to reversion of "personal effects" if the lighthouse fell into neglect. She read a note in a woman's hand—*E. DeWitt*—giving "oral history only" about the meaning of certain marks and requesting that they be left undisturbed "for the work to continue." She read a census record that placed a girl with a Marwick surname in a house by the grove and a note, in pencil, that suggested the girl's father owed the grove's apothecary "an old debt." She read—enough, and not enough.

When she lifted her head, Helena had not moved. "Well?" Helena asked, neither impatient nor kind.

"It isn't a simple claim," Marley said. "It's also a correction." She kept her voice steady on the word. "You know that."

Helena's lips parted in the barest suggestion of agreement. "It is what it is," she said. "My job is to keep what belongs to us intact while the truth arranges itself." She rose. The movement loosened the veneer that had made her appear, from across the room, immovable. "You'll come up to the lighthouse this afternoon? My attorney wants to meet with the town."

"I'll be there," Marley said.

"And Mr. Hawthorne?"

"He'll be there," Marley said, because she knew he would, even if he stood half a step behind the table with his arms crossed and his jaw tight to keep the rest of him from saying what needed to be said more measuredly. She watched Helena lift the case, close it, and stand the way a person stands in a courtroom when the judge enters not because they believe in the judge but because they believe in the ceremony that keeps people from burning things down when they disagree.

"Until this afternoon," Helena said, and left the café like a weather change.

Marley sat a long moment with her palms flat on the table as if feeling for aftershock. The café returned to its murmurs, adjusting to the vacancy at the window as water adjusts to a boat pulled from its surface. Evelyn came to the table with a refilled mug and a small plate as if sugar could intervene in destiny. "Well?" Evelyn asked, quiet but unable to be indifferent.

Marley lifted the mug. "A claim," she said. "And something like a confession." She did not add the rest aloud: that the confession was curated; that Helena had let her see enough to implicate the town's official story but not enough to bind the Marwick estate to the reckoning; that the second packet at the bottom of the cedar case was positioned like a heart beneath ribs. She simply drank the coffee and let its heat prove that she was still anchored to the present tense.

Across the street, the sea threw light at the sky. On the headland, the lighthouse held its steady spine. And below, in the stone, something that was not the chapel's bell practiced a single low note the way a singer hums before a hymn begins. The afternoon was waiting.

Visitor with a Claim—arrival and assertion; sealed papers; Marley invited to examine, reluctantly, she wrote later in her notebook, checking boxes she had made for a chapter she had not intended to be writing and was. The outline was a mercy: it told you where to put the weight. The living story would fill itself in.

THEY CHOSE neutral ground for the meeting: the town office conference room with its table too large for the space and its wall of framed photographs of mayors with hair that aged century by century from wild to careful to close-cropped and apologetic. Damien arrived first, with a slim folder and his face arranged into the expression that had made him tolerable to judges and intolerable to people who lied. He stood when Marley came in and the lines at the corners of his mouth softened. "You okay?" he asked under the noise of chairs.

"Paper," she said, and the word made his mouth quirk into what passed for a smile when the day required steady hands.

Helena entered with a man in a navy suit whose shoes were the precise color of his tie, which meant he chose detail with a ruler. He introduced himself as counsel for the Marwick estate and set a neat folder before him as if the folder itself could subpoena them. The council chair, two members with long memories and short patience, and the clerk gathered on the town's side. Marley sat where she always sat—one chair off center, within reach of the notes and out of the way of grandstanding. Damien took the seat beside her without asking whether she'd need his hand; he would give it whether she asked or not.

Helena laid the cedar case on the table but did not open

it. "Thank you for making time," she said, the words brisk and correctly grateful. "We have two matters: the estate's claim to certain artifacts named in the original decommission agreement and the correction of the official narrative for the lighthouse's founding."

"The official narrative?" Damien repeated, as if someone had mispronounced *anthem*.

"Yes," Helena said. "It makes for a clean parade speech. It fails to reflect the documentary record."

Damien did not ask what the documentary record said. He asked, carefully, "Which artifacts?"

Helena named them. The key. The finial. The compass. The clerk confirmed that the key had been logged in the town's holding safe; the finial—if it existed—was still in the lantern room. The compass, according to records, had not been cataloged. Damien made a note and Marley knew, without reading it, that it said: *Compass whereabouts unknown—check lantern logs and restoration boxes.* Damien said the Brookwood Historical Society would review the paperwork. The lawyer slid copies across the table. Helena kept her fingers on the cedar lid.

"And the narrative," Damien said, a touch of fatigue threading his letters the way salt threads into every seam of this town's furniture.

Helena tapped the cedar case once. "The Marwick correspondence acknowledges A.W. as co-founder and as the source of foundational funds and terms," she said. "Your pamphlets and plaques do not." There were no italics in her voice. There did not need to be.

"A.W.," one of the members said softly, because the town itself sometimes knew the truth even when it chose not to say it. He looked at Marley—*what have you found*—and Marley inclined her head a millimeter no one else would notice, a yes that cost nothing and promised nothing.

"We are not here to all-at-once revise banners," Helena went on, "We are here to put paper in the record." She indicated. "To preserve copies where they can be found five years from now by people who did not attend this meeting."

"May we see the documents?" Damien asked, speaking as a neighbor who wanted to die closer to the truth than he had lived.

Helena lifted the lid and kept one hand on the case's rim while the other hand fanned out the top layer—the transcriptions, the typed memo, the Polaroid of the spiral someone had captured in a different decade without asking the building's permission. She did not lift the second packet. She did not let go of the case.

Damien skimmed and nodded in time with his own reluctance to approve anyone else's version of his town and leaned in reading the typed lines as if the typewriter still lived inside them, his face set in the neutrality he cultivated when mapping a blown-out neighborhood of fact and assertion. Marley watched the room rather than the paper. She counted the space between Helena's thumb and the second packet. She watched the lawyer watch Helena, which told her that Helena's hand was decently heavy on the reins. She watched Damien lower his eyes when he reached the line acknowledging A.W. She watched him write *A.W. acknowledged in correspondence; see attached* and felt something in her chest unclench, because writing a line like that in a minute book can be the beginning of a thing not being erased again.

"Ms. Vale," Damien said at last, tapping the typed memorandum with the edge of his knuckle, not rudely. "You understand that the town has an independent duty to authenticate the documents before taking any action."

"Of course," Helena said. "You'll find the originals consistent with the transcriptions."

"And the custody chain?"

"Intact," Helena said. "My family kept these in storage until now. I personally verified the seals last month."

Damien's eyes moved to the wax. "New seals," he observed. "Old seal ring." He did not accuse; he recorded.

Helena smiled without softness. "I preserve what I can," she said, and for once her voice sounded less like a fact and more like an admission that fatigue lives alongside diligence.

Marley turned one of the transcriptions and read again the line about the circle under the bed. In the corner, written in the historian's small hand, someone had added: *per oral history (E.D.), no photographic reproduction requested.* E.D.—E. DeWitt—the volunteer whose tidy initials appeared in the restoration margin notes. The outline in Marley's head flared: council list; restoration notes; a man named Harold Nash who'd drawn a tiny spiral on a checklist because he could not bear to erase what he did not yet understand. This was how the truth had survived in a town that loved its myths: hands in margins, initials in corners, requests honored quietly. She looked up and found Helena watching her.

"You see the sense of it," Helena said softly, as if offering Marley a small kindness in a crowded room. "We correct the record; we safeguard what belongs to us; we allow the town to save face by calling it a shared stewardship. Everyone gets to keep their porch light."

Porch light. Lighthouse. Vigil. It was the same metaphor scaled. Marley felt a wash of heat—annoyance at herself for almost letting the neatness of the phrase flatten the complexity of the day. Then she nodded once. "I see the sense of needing to tell the truth," she said. "The rest will take as long as it takes." She did not say *not on your schedule*; she did not have to.

The meeting ended without drama. That was a kind of drama of its own. Damien said the Brookwood Historical Society would begin the authentication process.

Helena closed the cedar case as if closing the chest of a patient after a surgeon's glance. When she turned toward the door, she hesitated just long enough for Marley to catch the small shift of a decision being made.

"Walk with me," Helena said.

They stepped out into a corridor that smelled faintly of wax and old carpet and then into a day so clean the sun made the ocean look newly minted. The tide had just turned, and the line of wet on the rocks was sharp as a thumbprint on a glass.

"You knew about A.W. before I came," Helena said, as if continuing a conversation they had started in another town in a life neither had lived.

"I knew a letter like the one you showed me had to exist," Marley said. "I didn't know whose attic it would come down from."

Helena's mouth tilted. "Attics are just memory with insulation," she said. She stopped at the bottom of the steps and looked toward the headland. "You think I'm hiding something."

"Yes," Marley said, because the question had been asked like a test you don't pass by pleasing the proctor. "You are."

Helena did not pretend offense. She turned the case in her hands until the sun struck the brass and then watched the bright stripe slide across the catch. "There is a second packet," she said. "It contains family material. It also contains documents that will complicate things for people you care about more than you care about the Marwicks." She lifted her eyes from the brass. "I am not ready to hand you everything and watch you drown trying to carry it alone."

Marley stood still because sudden movement would have made her knees show. "Then why show me anything at all? You don't trust our council," she said and Helena's small noise of amusement was answer enough.

"I trust some of your neighbors," Helena said. "I trust your Mr. Hawthorne even when I dislike him. And I trust the building." She looked toward the headland again. "I don't trust process to keep the edges from being sanded off people who deserve better than monuments."

The wind ran up the street carrying salt and the faint metallic scent of the railings along the cliff path warming. "What do you want from me?" Marley asked.

Helena didn't answer right away. She closed her eyes once, quickly, as if realigning some inner compass. "I want you to keep going," she said. "I want you to read everything you can get your hands on without letting anyone tell you which page matters most. And I want you to hold the town together long enough for it to admit that honesty is not disloyalty." She lifted the case. "And I want my family's property where it belongs, even if it's on loan in a room with a plaque that includes a name it should have included a hundred years ago."

"A.W.," Marley said.

"Aurelia Ward," Helena said back, and for the first time her voice had warmth in it, as if saying the name let her own shoulders settle in a way the coat could not. "Beacon of the Grove. Whether your historical society is ready to put the word *Beacon* on an index card without rolling its eyes remains to be seen."

Marley laughed, because the alternative was to do anything that would make the rest of the day harder than it needed to be. "We'll see," she said.

Helena nodded once and then, before she could make herself less likeable, walked away.

Damien appeared from the conference room and matched Marley's stride without being asked. He did not say *well?* or *what now?* He said, "Let's go up to the tower before dusk. If the finial is still in place, I want eyes on it in case someone decides to be helpful with a wrench."

"Helena," Marley said, "is not a wrench person."

"She is a person who employs wrench people," he said, mildly. "Which is the more effective species."

Marley glanced up Main Street toward the headland. The lighthouse looked taller in clean light, like a person who's slept. "She's also right," Marley said. "Paper needs filing. The truth needs oxygen." She didn't say the rest: that Helena had offered kindness disguised as control and control disguised as kindness; that the second packet—that heart beneath ribs—was not for them yet. She only added, quieter, "She knows more than she is saying."

"So do we," Damien said, without judgement. "That's how negotiations begin."

When they reached the base of the path, he touched her shoulder. "You steady?"

Marley nodded. "Steady."

She wasn't entirely sure it was true. That felt like honesty, too. She let the headland pull her forward, the way big work pulls you regardless of appetite. At the foot of the tower, she placed her palm to the iron door as if saying hello to a patient she'd promised to visit daily. The hinges groaned—good morning, then—and the stair accepted their weight like a structure that had already decided it could carry a little more truth without collapsing.

Visitor produces sealed documents that contradict parts of the official founding story; town begins authentication; Marley reads enough to recognize A.W.; senses a withheld packet, Marley wrote that night on the wall where she kept the outline. She drew a small open box beside *compass whereabouts unknown* and an arrow from *finial still in place?* to *observe before dusk.* She forced herself to write one more sentence in block capitals she could live with later: *HELENA WANTS CONTROL; ALSO WANTS TRUTH—IN THAT ORDER.*

Dusk came down like a curtain pulled by a practiced hand. The wind had shifted—landward, warmer, carrying the smoked sweetness of someone's grill on a back porch and the tidier scent of laundry hung at noon and brought in at four. The lighthouse took the new air and let its own behavior remain precisely itself. Three quick, two long. Pause. Repeat. It held to its rehearsal with the discipline of a dancer keeping time with a piano no one else could hear.

Inside the lantern room, they found the finial: small, fitted atop the lens assembly like a less-than-modest hat, fixed by a bolt that had seized with salt and time. Damien knelt to mark the bolt's position with a grease pencil and then, for his own peace of mind, photographed the mark with the town's camera—no flash—so that if the finial walked off in the night there would be a timestamped record that it had once sat where it belonged. He did not say *in case someone with a cedar case returns with a wrench.* He did not have to.

"The compass," Marley said, scanning the lantern room for the kind of box that had learned to keep its head down.

"Not on record," Damien said, which meant *could still be here where records haven't ruined it.* He checked the shallow drawers where wick trimmers and lens cloths might have lived. Empty. He checked the hollow behind a panel put back slightly wrong fifty years ago. Dust. He checked the space beneath the base where a hand the size of his could slide and find only splinters. Nothing. He looked at the door, thinking of the small closet on the stairs. He turned to Marley and tilted his head—a small ask. She nodded, and they left the lantern room, carried their impatience down two turns, and opened the closet.

Empty shelves. The dust told a different story: something rectangular had sat on the middle shelf long enough to keep that rectangle clean while the rest of the world dirtied around it. Damien measured the ghost with his hands. "Cedar box size," he said. His mouth tilted at the corner but not with humor. "Or something cousin to it."

"Helena said the compass belonged to the estate," Marley said.

"Helena also arrived with an old seal in her pocket and a willingness to use it," Damien said. He set his palms on the shelf, closed his eyes once like a man who can picture a thing in place if he tries hard enough, and then stepped back. "We're not going to win by inventory alone," he said. "We're going to win by sequence."

"By sequence," Marley repeated, because saying the plan aloud pins it to the room so your mind doesn't excuse itself from it later. "Observation, record, comparison. Boring paper first. Flashes later."

"Always boring paper first," he said, smiling with his eyes this time, and for a moment she loved him for being a man who would use bureaucracy as a shield around a lighthouse doing dangerous holy work.

They returned to the lantern room and set the metronome on the iron ring as if testing whether a small ticking thing could persuade a large flashing thing to pick a different tempo. It could not. The light kept its pattern, the pause shortened by the thickness of a breath, and the shadows resisted in their small lizard ways along the circumference before flattening again. Marley watched the beam, watched it encounter the night and find ways of making the night behave that still surprised her. She wrote in her notebook without looking: *Sequence holds. Pause again tighter. Shadows recoil and settle.* She added, smaller: *It wants to be read.*

The bell did not sound tonight. Maybe it had decided to hold its note until people stopped giving speeches in rooms with polished tables. Maybe it had gone below to drink and gossip with the stones. Maybe it had already rung and what she thought was silence was simply her own hearing rearranging itself to accommodate a pitch that was what truth sounds like before it finds a word. She didn't know. She only knew the light had chosen consistency over spectacle, which is a choice any person with an argument to make ought to admire.

They climbed down after the last cycle reached whatever mark it had agreed upon with dusk. At the base of the tower, Helena waited. She had not asked permission to be there because the lighthouse did not belong to any of them in the way that mattered. She held the cedar case, closed. She stood with her back to the sea and her face to the tower like a woman who had waited in a vestibule outside a room where a birth or a death was happening and was ready to be useful rather than important.

"I won't be here tomorrow," she said, before either of them could decide what posture the conversation required. "My attorney will be. He'll manage the paperwork."

"And you'll take the key?" Damien asked.

"When the town finishes its process," Helena said, acknowledging his devotion to sequence with a nod. "Not before."

"The finial stays put," he said, not asking.

"It weighs four pounds and says more than it should," she said. "It can stay for now."

"The compass?" Marley asked.

Helena let her gaze stray to the cliff path and then back. "Not in my possession," she said. "Not yet." She did not elaborate. She did not need to. Marley watched her choose not to say *check your broom closets* or *ask your H.N. where he last saw it.* She simply let the sentence sit, consistent with her habit of letting other people be responsible for the speed at which their own honesty moved.

"You were right this afternoon," Marley said. "About oxygen and accuracy."

Helena's eyebrows lifted a millimeter—a woman saluted in a language she understood. "You'll write fairly," Helena said. It was a prediction, not a request.

"I'll write what's there," Marley said.

Helena nodded as if those two sentences had finally discovered they shared a border. She lifted the cedar case a few inches, a courtesy that pretended to be explanation. "I don't carry this to impress people," she said. "I carry it so my hands remember weight." She looked beyond them at the tower. "The building carries more than it should. We all do. That doesn't make us brave. It makes us necessary."

The phrase surprised Marley with its utility. "Necessary," she repeated. "Not brave."

"Bravery is a performance," Helena said, benignly cynical. "Necessity is weather." She turned to go, then paused, and without changing her voice said, "You are right to distrust me. You are wrong to discard me. Don't confuse the two."

Marley watched her walk into the dusk like someone who had learned to be neither soothed nor hurried by anyone else's cadence. Damien stood beside her and let the silence move through both of them without trying to make it say something nice.

"What do you think is in the second packet?" he asked finally, because curiosity can be a sacrament when used properly.

"Something that confirms what the building will show us anyway," Marley said. "And something that will hurt someone Helena has decided to keep standing until they can sit on their own." She exhaled. "She sees farther than she says."

"Not a sin," he said.

"No," Marley agreed. "But a style."

They walked back toward town with the taste of salt and metal on their tongues and the feel of paper edges still indenting their fingerprints. On the path, a child ran past dragging a stick that made a metronome line in the dirt—tick, tick, tick—before the wind erased it. The houses along Main Street did their evening light trick, windows brightening in succession like a slow Morse none of them had coded but all of them had learned to read. In her apartment, Marley added three new notes to the wall: *Finial marked in place. Closet shelf dust—cedar-box ghost. Council minutes to include A.W. line.* Then, because the outline helped her keep her balance, she wrote beneath *Chapter 3 outcomes* the phrases she had promised herself to deliver: *Visitor with a Claim; sealed documents that contradict parts of the founding story; Marley invited to examine, reluctant consent; senses with-held material.* She put a check beside each in the small modest pleasure of work done at the day's end.

She did not touch the envelope with *Illuminate* tonight. She did not need to. The building had offered its own illumination without paper help. She poured tea she did not drink and stood at the window watching the headland until the first cycle began: three quick, two long. Pause. And in the pause, the town breathed. And in the breath, Marley felt the next chapter sidle up to the house, polite but insistent, the way truth does when it has decided it will be seen whether or not anyone has gone to the trouble of printing programs.

She opened her notebook and wrote four words at the bottom of the page, not to publish but to hold herself together: *We will see clearly.* And then, because she had learned that half of wisdom is knowing when to let sleep be the teacher, she turned out the light.

4

THE CANDLE MAKER'S WARNING

The bell over the metaphysical shop door was tuned too kindly for the news it carried. It chimed a small note—jade-bright, patient—as Marley stepped in from the salt wind. Inside, the air was thick with honey and herb, a low tide of scent settling around her throat and easing her shoulders despite the urgency pulsing in her chest. Shelves lined the narrow space: rolled beeswax tapers bound in twine, pillars swirled with petals, glass jars with hand-lettered labels—rosemary, bay, cedar, lavender. The far wall held a rack of wicks like a harp waiting for weather to play it.

Hazel stood behind the counter pressing a stamp into a cooling puck of wax. Her hair was swept into a careless knot, silver at the temples where the heat did its best to bleach the years out of her. Under the work table, a small dog lifted its head without bothering to test whether the newcomer belonged.

"You're late," Hazel said, then winced and pressed her fingers to the inner corners of her eyes. "Or I'm early, depending on the lighthouse."

Marley paused. "You felt it?"

"Felt it." Hazel kept her hand there a moment longer, as if the gesture itself could move pain along a little faster, then let go and breathed through her nose in that measured way of people who've made a treaty with their own bodies. "It started before dawn. A pressure, like weather with an opinion. Then a jab just over the right eye. My mother would have said, 'Weather's turning; the dead are rearranging their chairs.' She had a way with comfort." Hazel glanced toward the window where Main Street held its breath the way small towns do when they think they aren't watching themselves. "The light's not right," she said, voice dropping without dramatics. "It's remembering something."

It landed in the shop like a fact. This was why Marley had come—to test what she suspected against a person who, when the town tried to make a thing smaller, refused to cut it down. Hazel's migraines rang when the invisible made itself heavier than air. They had rung when the bridge had learned to speak; they rang now.

"What does remembering feel like to you?" Marley asked.

Hazel's mouth tilted. "Like a scent you can't place dragging a picture behind it. Like standing in a doorway while a room you can't quite see arranges itself—chair legs scraping, someone unfolding a blanket, the old clock picking up a beat. You know it's happening because the house tells you with its seams." She set the stamped puck aside and wiped her hands with a linen rag. "And like this." She tapped her brow with two fingers, not gently. "The body's barometer. Captain Pike—my grandfather—said wind leaves his bones talking for three days; this is that, but for light." She studied Marley over the counter, the scrutiny free of suspicion and full of recognition. "You were going to the tower today."

"Yes." Marley set her palms on the glass, cold even through the day's mildness. "I need to sit in the keeper's quarters again. The spiral" —her throat tightened the way it did when a word she cared about made itself smaller to fit into the draught of a sentence— "it's not just decoration. It's... a function."

Hazel nodded once like a person told there's salt in the ocean. "Of course it is."

"You told me once you make blends for vigils." Marley glanced at the display of small tins, each with a strip of paper folded under the lid like a sleeping note. "Do you have one that—"

"—invites ancestral guidance?" Hazel finished without triumph. "I thought you'd come." She reached beneath the counter and brought up a wooden box the size of a hymnbook. Inside lay three small candles, poured into squat creamware cups, the wax pale gold and flecked with something greener near the top. Hazel lifted one and held it under Marley's nose. "Bay for discernment, rosemary for memory, lavender to calm the nerves you don't want making decisions, and cedar for steadiness. Beeswax, always. Salt worked into the pour, a pinch. And a thread of myrrh, because the old things like to know you understand the cost of sweetness."

Marley inhaled. The blend traveled straight to the back of her head and settled. Not a dulling. A clarifying—as if someone had opened a window in a room two rooms away. She thought of the spiral under the keeper's bed, the notches aligned to north, to the grove, to the channel stones; thought of the way the room's air had moved when she printed the pattern on craft paper with Damien's steady graphite strokes. "You got a headache because the lighthouse is remembering," she said slowly, laying the day's shape on the counter to see if it held. "So we help it remember with us instead of at us."

Hazel's laugh lived low. "If you insist on making sense, we'll get along. This is not a spell," she added, the word dry. "It's a way to make your body and the air agree on a pace. You set the candle near the spiral—'near,' not 'on'; don't be rude—and you burn it like a conversation. Open a window. Give what rises somewhere to go. Sit with it. Don't demand. Invite."

Marley glanced at the door, already hearing Damien's voice say *no vows, no names*; already seeing his mouth set at the idea of fire near wood in an old building. "He'll hate this."

Hazel smiled in that wicked aunt way she had with people she liked. "He'll hate it and stay," she said. "Which is the best kind of man when the world starts to do what it was made to do. Tell him his job is to keep time. If he needs purpose, give him the metronome and a pencil."

"He doesn't need purpose," Marley said softly. "He is purpose."

Hazel's eyes softened, migraine or no. "Then he's exactly who you want there when the room gets truer than the pamphlets." She wrapped the box with a strip of muslin and tied it with a knot that looked like it would fall open with a whisper and not before. "One more thing." She added a small glass vial. "Lavender water. Not to drink. To damp your wrists if whatever comes feels like more than today's lungs can manage. It's not a rescue. It's a reminder that human bodies can be warmed and cooled and therefore can choose."

Outside, a gull scolded the roofline and the sea worked

its old arithmetic against the rocks. Marley slid her wallet across the counter. Hazel pushed it back with a look that dared her to make a fuss. "Consider it an advance against all the candles I'm going to sell the day your book comes out and the tourists decide to go home smelling like saints."

Marley set the wallet back in her bag, because arguing against kindness wastes a morning. "What else should I know?"

"Salt's not to keep things out," Hazel said, nimble as she reached for her stamp again. "It's to tell them where the doorway is. Remember that." She hesitated and pressed her fingers to her brow once more, the pain seeing itself out. "And if the bell rings while you're up there, don't talk over it. Let it finish what it started."

"The bell," Marley said, almost to herself. "It hasn't rung in two nights."

"It's listening." Hazel's tone made the sentence a map. "We should try it sometime."

Marley tucked the box into her canvas bag beside the metronome and the small mirror she and Damien had used to watch the spiral reflected. At the door, the bell chimed again, a cleaner note this time, either because her mood had changed or because the shop knew what she carried. On the step, she turned back. "Hazel?"

"Hmm?"

"When you said the light's remembering—do you think it's remembering for us or for itself?"

Hazel didn't blink. "Yes," she said, and bent to pull a wick like a violinist tuning a string that had always known the right sound.

·   ·   ·

Damien met Marley at the bottom of the headland path with a look that told her he'd been in conversation with his better angels all morning and had not allowed them to win by default. He had the metronome in one hand and a metal water bottle in the other, and when she held up the box, he glanced at it the way a man glances at a long letter whose handwriting he recognizes and has not decided to adore or ignore.

"Bay, rosemary, lavender, cedar," Marley said. "Beeswax. A pinch of salt. We'll open a window. We'll keep a sheet pan and water beside it. We'll be careful. It's not a séance. It's an agreement."

"Between?"

"Us and the room."

He considered that. He could have said *rooms are wood and paint*; he could have said *agreement implies agency*; he could have said any number of sentences he had proven to her were not walls so much as handrails. Instead he gestured up the path. "Let's go agree."

They climbed. The day had pulled the fog into ropes and flung them inland, leaving light sharp on the water. Inside the tower, their footsteps sounded less like trespass today and more like repetition—this is how the stairs feel when two people who mean it climb them. In the keeper's quarters, Marley set the muslin-wrapped box on the desk, unwrapped it, and took the time to lay each small object with deliberation: the creamware cup with its pale wax, the glass vial, a short ceramic dish for salt, the metronome on the desk's corner where the pendulum could sway free. She opened the window a measured four inches. The wind put two fingers on her cheek in blessing.

Damien used his pocket knife to shave a patch of raised paint from the sill where it might have caught the curtain if the air shifted. He set the sheet pan on the floor beside the seam where they'd lifted the board days ago. He stowed the water bottle within reach. He looked around like a foreman signing off on a site. "If it gets strange, we stop," he said, making care a sentence instead of a condition.

"We stop," she agreed.

He nodded toward the candle. "Do your... inviting."

She smiled despite herself and knelt near the board seam. The spiral under the joist felt present even under wood. She could picture the groove as clearly as if the floor were made of glass; she could feel its notches—north, grove, channel—like points on a compass she'd come to trust more than headings printed on a map. She set the creamware cup on the floor *near*, not *on*, and sprinkled a small ring of salt that left a gap on the side facing the window. A doorway, not a wall. She touched the wick with her finger, then with the match.

Bay rose first, green and thoughtful. Rosemary followed with its clean insistence. Lavender arrived last like someone meaningful showing up on time without apology. The beeswax warmed and sweetened everything it touched. Marley sat back on her heels and let the blend find the corners of the room, the way soup finds ribs in January. The metronome ticked—sixty beats, the pendulum keeping neutral counsel. Damien leaned a shoulder against the jamb, trying not to look as if he were keeping watch and failing admirably.

"I don't like that my first responsibility here is to the building," he admitted. "It should be to you."

"You're not wrong," Marley said. "But today, they're the same."

He let that be true without pushing on it. The candle burned clean. No sputter. No smoke. Just a steady flame that made the printed spiral in Marley's mind glow as if lit from beneath. She closed her eyes—not to leave the room, but to be in it more completely. The scent lifted, softened, and then began to carry with it something else—not the crash of sea or the distant thud of footfalls on stair; something finer, like the dry slide of paper in a drawer, the whisper of linen sheets, the rasp of a pencil sharpened with a knife like Damien's. A life's small noises, folded and unfolded.

"The light's not right," Hazel had said. "It's remembering something." Marley held the blend on her breath and waited to see what the room would admit.

It started in the soles of their feet—the slightest change in the floorboards, a hush, like wood deciding it could carry an additional story. The candle's flame leaned once and straightened, like a person testing which way the breeze wanted to go. The ring of salt glinted at the doorway gap, perfectly uninterested in theater. Outside, a gull voiced a long metallic complaint that might have been a warning if you were in the habit of hearing warnings everywhere. Inside, the metronome ticked—kind, impartial.

Marley took out the small mirror and set it on the floor beside the seam to catch the spiral in reflection—she'd learned things stood up differently when you watched them backward. The creamware cup sat at the edge of her peripheral, a domestic object doing holy work by pretending to be ordinary. She closed her hand around her pencil just to know where it was.

"Talk to me," Damien said, voice soft, not to interrupt but to anchor. "Tell me what you notice, and I'll write."

She let her eyes stay on the mirror; she let the rest of her listen. "The room's... slower," she said. "Like it's remembering its own breathing and wants us to match it."

Tick. Tick.

"The draft is consistent," Damien reported, practical, and the simple sentence kept them honest amid all the other sentences that were about to get larger. "No cross wind from the window; door closed."

"The scent's changing," Marley said. "Not different—more. The rosemary sits closer to the floor now." She smiled a little, first at herself for saying something that would once have felt precious, then at Damien for not making it so. "Bay's making me behave."

"Noted." His pencil whispered. "Other sensations?"

"Pressure behind the eyes," she said. "Not pain. More like... rooms opening." She angled the mirror to catch the spiral exactly, and though the joist was hidden beneath the floorboard, the reflected pattern lived as surely as if naked to the light. The ticks—thirteen, seven, four—glowed in memory, and as she watched, she realized something she hadn't when they'd printed it: the groove at the center wasn't smooth. It had a slight nick—a maker's mark, maybe, or a correction mid-cut. It made the spiral less pristine and more human. It made her love the room more. "There's a small flaw at the center," she said. "Like somebody's hand shook and then steadied."

Damien's pencil halted. "You're not looking at it," he pointed out gently.

"I am," she said, equally gentle. "Just... through knowing."

He resumed. "Flaw at center—maker's mark or correction."

The candle continued its steady work. The scent drifted, and with it more of the small-room noises arrived, soft as tissue leaving a box. Marley heard—God help her; she heard—a page turning. Not dramatic. Not metaphor. A page. The paper was thick and had been turned thousands of times, so it no longer argued with the hand. Then a scratch, steady—the tip of a nineteenth-century nib writing the date and the weather and the tide and who had come up the path. She didn't see it. She didn't need to. Her body recognized the choreography of a day recorded with attention.

She spoke what she could. "Ledger," she said. "Writing. Someone seated. Not the keeper's careful hand; someone else with their own way of spelling. There's... lavender between the pages. Or near them. Or both."

Damien's eyes flicked to the desk as if expecting something to slide into view. "Smell?"

"Yes," she said, swallowing. "And the sense of it. Pressed between pages long enough to carry a summer into a winter." A wave struck hard below, and the tower shivered. The candle didn't. It held a small circle the way a person holds a baby: without thinking, with everything. On the far wall, a square of sunlight that had made itself at home all morning shifted and made room for something else.

"What else?" Damien asked, voice so even the room used it to keep itself steady.

"Bed," she said. "Sheets. Someone's hand going down through a knot-hole to touch the joist." She let the room show her how to speak with less possession. "A hand. Some-one's hand." Her own fingers hovered above the seam without touching. "It's a waiting posture—like a person at a bedside, except the person is the building."

They breathed together, the way you do in hospitals and watch rooms and churches when the second hand starts to teach you patience. The candle burned; the tick kept; the breeze moved politely. The spiral—unseen and nevertheless central—threaded what wanted to arrive through the simple dignity of wood cut with intention.

"Do you hear that?" Damien asked, and she could tell from his tone that he wasn't sure if he wanted her to.

Marley tilted her head. The room offered a sound just above audibility—a rhythm softer than the metronome, not out of sync with it but older, the movement of breath through a small nose, not yet clogged by winter, from a small chest asleep.

"A child," she said. "Sleeping." It hurt a little to say it because anything you name returns to you with responsibility attached. She made her voice a place you could set a cup. "This is none of my business."

"It is our business because the building has made it our business," Damien said. He was not being mystical. He was being a man who reads what's in front of him and fails to be cruel to it. "What else."

Marley closed her eyes. "Someone humming," she said. "Not a lullaby I know. It's not a song so much as a pressure." The tune walked a narrow range like someone unwilling to wake a house that needed sleep. Her throat tightened, and she steadied herself with the metronome tick—choose a pace, stay with it. "They're staying awake so the child can rest."

Damien's pencil stopped for a heartbeat and started again. He had a daughter. He knew those nights. "Words?"

"No," Marley said. "Just... keep. The sense of *keep*."

Wind pushed a little harder against the window and then backed off, embarrassed to be caught. Marley frowned at the candle, not because it had misbehaved but because something had shifted around it as if the room had taken a step closer. "Damien?" she said.

"I'm here," he answered in the immediate way that proves the sentence true. He moved from the jamb to kneel opposite her, the sheet pan a quiet promise between them. He kept the pencil anyway, as if the act of writing might persuade the building to tell its story in sentences. "If this goes wrong, we stop."

"It isn't wrong," Marley said, surprised at the certainty. "It's... instructive."

"What's it instructing?"

She breathed in the rosemary and the lavender, let them do their differing work, and felt the answer arrive with more humility than explanation. "It's showing us how to hold pressure without breaking. How to carry light, quietly. How not to mistake bravery for necessity."

He looked at the candle then, as if the flame itself might nod. "Hazel speak again?"

"She didn't have to," Marley said, and the smallest laugh escaped because she could feel Hazel's look at that answer even miles away.

The room's older sound began to feather down, the kind of fade that means you were listening to something intended to be temporary. The child slept. The hand on the joist withdrew. The humming ceased like a drawn-out word ending without a period. The metronome kept. The candle guttered once as if to confirm it had a right to behave like flame and then steadied.

"Anything else?" Damien asked, ready to let it end.

Marley had one more sensation to hold—not an image; an imperative: *Remember.* It set itself in the soft place below the bottom rib that aches when you pick up a box you shouldn't and says *carry anyway.* The spiral liked that. It hummed once, not a sound, more a pressure that agreed with both the tick and the flame. She exhaled and felt the day return to its normal size.

"That's enough," she said, conversant with a line she would have crossed six months ago.

He nodded. "We extinguish."

She pinched the wick. No smoke. Just the disappearance of illumination leaving scent behind to make sense do its slower work. She poured a few drops of lavender water on her wrists, not because she needed it but because ritual makes memory easier to carry. The room eased open to ordinary. Wind breathed in and out, dressed like a friend. The desk, the chair, the window—all present tense again.

They sat on the floor across from each other for a minute longer than was convenient. When Damien finally stood, his knees cracked in small admissions. He offered a hand. She took it. Their fingers did the old work of being necessary to each other.

"I hate it," he said mildly, "and I'll stay." Then, aware of what he had just done, he smiled. "That was me agreeing in the wrong tense."

"You stayed," she said, matching his grammar. "Thank you."

"Hazel will call by three to ask if your head hurts," he predicted, which earned the smallest smile from both of them.

Marley wrapped the cooled candle in muslin again and left a small arc of salt at the baseboard like a signature no one else needed to read. She wrote in her notebook without looking at the page: *Burned the blend near the spiral. Invited, didn't demand. Room remembered quietly: ledger/paper; lavender between; humming; hand on joist; child asleep; keep.* She added, smaller: *Flaw at center of spiral—human, precious, functional.* Then: *Damien took time; stayed.*

They closed the window and left the quarters as they'd found them. On the stair, Marley paused at turn four and pressed her palm to the faint circle beneath paint where the north tick lived. The skin on her hand warmed as if the iron had remembered the sun five hours ago and decided to offer it back.

"Tomorrow," she said to the mark, and they went down.

EVELYN INSISTED on tea "to soak your edges," which was her prescription for anybody who had been to the tower and come back looking like themselves but newly thinned. She set a teapot and two cups on the café's corner table and left them unbothered except to add a plate of honey biscuits and say, "Doesn't matter whether you use either; it matters that they know they were invited."

"We're learning to invite correctly today," Marley said, too tired not to tease.

"That why you smell like my soap cupboard?" Evelyn asked over her shoulder, pleased.

Damien sat in the chair that let him see both the door and the window, not because danger was expected but because duty never checks the calendar. He was not a man given to admitting how shaken he was when the world behaved as promised instead of as predicted. But he lingered longer over his first sip than tea required. "Hazel's blend isn't a spell," he said finally, as if needing to hear the sentence in his own voice. "It's a metronome for the body."

"And the room," Marley said.

He conceded with a tilt of his hand. "And that."

They went through the day—not everything (they had learned to stop treating each other like notebooks), but enough. He wrote a brief log entry on his pad: *Candle:*

bay/rosemary/lavender/cedar/beeswax/salt/myrrh. Ventilation: window open 4". Observed: quiet sensory recall; ledger/paper sounds; lavender association; hand on joist; lull; no speech; no vow; no vow. He underlined the last two because caution had become their own oath not to replace what they were dissolving. "What would you call that?" he asked, pen hovering over the term *phenomenon* as if the word might bite.

"Stewardship," Marley said. "The room showed us how to keep. We kept." She pulled the small mirror from her bag and set it on the table between the cups—a habit now, letting reflection share workspace with direct view. "I saw the spiral's flaw without seeing it. I want to confirm it with my eyes tomorrow. But it feels... right. More right than perfection."

"Perfection is for monuments," Damien said. "We're not building monuments."

"What are we building?"

"Room," he said. "For the truth to stand in without tipping."

They sat with that sentence between them until Evelyn pretended to need the sugar bowl and thereby gave them permission to keep using her table without repaying rent in cookies. When they left, the light had shifted lower, a slow gold that makes the town look kinder to its own past.

On the headland path, the air changed. A breath from the sea—cooler, purposeful. The lighthouse's shadow stretched like a long arm and laid a hand on the first white fence. Damien scanned the cliff as if reassurance could be found in the routine of a good railing. Marley carried the muslin-wrapped candle again, not to light it—once was enough for a day—but because its weight had become, unexpectedly, an argument for staying in ordinary time: an object, a thing a person could hand to another person without them needing a glossary.

"Helena leaves tonight," Damien said. "Her attorney will babysit the paperwork. The Historical Society is deferring to the Council and asked for a week to start authentication." He squinted up at the tower. "I don't want anyone touching the finial while we're sorting custody."

"Do you think she'll send someone?" Marley asked.

"I think she'll do exactly what she said," he answered. "Which is keep the edges of her family's story intact while we broaden the canvas." He looked at Marley. "She knows about A.W. She can't un-know it. Now that thread's out, it's not going back in the hem."

"A.W.," Marley repeated, letting the initials move in her mouth like gravel you test with your tongue before you swallow a name. "Hazel would say the room will insist on her whether paper does or doesn't."

"Hazel would be correct," he said, surprising himself with the ease of saying it.

They didn't climb that evening. They stood at the base and watched dusk behave. The first flash rose exactly when it should, three quick, two long, the pause shaved down by the same thin sliver of time Marley had started to feel the way a person feels rain before it appears on skin. Damien took out the metronome and let it tick in his pocket, not to measure, only to prove to himself that he could make and keep a beat even when the world set its own. Marley wrote in her notebook at the margin: *Pattern holds. After candle. After invitation. The light keeps its own counsel and we keep ours. Alignment feels possible, not assumed.*

On the way back toward town, they stopped at Hazel's shop. The bell gave them their note. Hazel looked up from wicking a batch of votives and squinted at them like a woman checking whether two jars had sealed without cracking.

"You're not broken," she diagnosed.

"No," Marley said, amused at how often that sentence needed saying in a place where truth kept showing up with its sleeves rolled. She set the muslin-wrapped candle on the counter like an offering returning from the altar. "We burned it near," she reported. "We opened the window. We invited."

"And?"

"The room told us how to keep," Marley said. "Ledger; lavender; lull. A hand on the joist. A child asleep. No words." Her throat went tight without warning on the last two; she steadied herself with the idea of salt, with the picture of the doorway gap.

Hazel's brow softened. She reached beneath the counter for a small porcelain bowl and slid it toward them. "For the salt," she said. "My grandmother's. It doesn't like being useful without being lovely." Then, slower: "And for what it's worth, when my mother said 'the dead are rearranging their chairs,' she didn't mean haunting. She meant hospitality. They're getting ready to make room for us if we'll sit."

Damien took the bowl as if the thing itself might argue with him for being involved and set it gently back in the muslin. "Thank you," he said, meaning more.

Hazel's migraine had faded to the ghost of itself. She rubbed the back of her neck. "One more caution," she added. "Don't do it two days in a row. The body can attend only so much remembering before it starts making substitutions. Let the room speak tonight. Don't ask it questions until it answers the ones it chose."

Marley felt grateful and tired and peculiar in that clean way you feel when you've done a thing the right way once and don't want to ruin it by proving you can do it again. "We won't," she promised.

Back in her apartment, she added three new cards to the wall—insisting to herself that she continue to behave like her own archivist even when the better line would be to sit with tea and let the day wash her. *Candle Maker's Warning* she wrote at the top of the first: *Migraine; "The light's not right. It's remembering something."* On the second: *Blend— bay/rosemary/lavender/cedar/beeswax/salt/myrrh. Burned near spiral; window open; salt as doorway. Invited, did not demand.* On the third: *Damien unsettled; stayed; kept time. Agreed to no vows; agreed to stay.* She checked the boxes with a small relief stronger than it had any right to be. Chapter structure wasn't a ceremony she performed for someone else. It was ballast.

The room felt normal again, the way normal feels in Brookwood—gently haunted by decency rather than dread. She poured tea and remembered to drink it this time. She stood at the window when the beam made its third sweep, three quick, two long, and watched the town's roofs take the light and give it back in small glints that made even the oldest shingles look new.

The bell did not toll that night. It hummed, once, the way a person hums at a hymn they haven't decided to sing out loud. Marley heard it; or she decided she heard it; or the distinction had become less useful than it used to be. She wrote a last line in her notebook: *Sometimes the work is to invite. Sometimes the work is to witness. Today, it was both.*

When she turned out her lamp, the scent of rosemary and lavender still rode the edges of the hour. She slept without dreams until just before dawn, when a quiet thought walked into the room and put its hand on the bedpost the way the old hand had touched the joist: *Keep.* She woke with it in her chest—a warm weight, not a burden—and knew before she checked her phone that there'd be a message from Damien in the morning that said nothing more than: *Boring paper first.*

She smiled. The work had taught them their roles. The light was remembering. They were learning how to remember with it.

5

———

THE KEEPER'S LOGBOOK

The key to the records room lived on a ring so heavy it could double as a paperweight. Damien signed it out from the clerk with the solemnity of a man borrowing a neighbor's child. The clerk—Mr. Pollard, who had served under three mayors and outlived two—tipped the ring into Damien's palm and said, in the tone of a benediction, "Bring back what you take, and bring back more than you think belongs to us."

It was as close to poetry as the town office allowed.

The basement smelled of cardboard, wintered paint, and the silver-gray tang of old staples. Rows of rolling stacks slept with their cranks folded. Damien set his folder on a metal cart and turned the first handle. Steel ribs parted with the reluctant grace of an old book opening to the middle where a favorite chapter lives. He scanned the stick-on labels—ENGINEERING: 1990–2004; COASTAL PERMITTING: 1972–1989; MARITIME—LIGHTHOUSE: MISC. EPHEMERA.

There. He rolled open a second stack and found, behind a row of photobooks and a string-tied parcel of plans, a low, shallow box with the kind of string no one ties anymore—white cotton, looped carefully, knotted with a bow that assumed the hands that undid it would re-tie it with the same decency. The label was in a hand he recognized from other margins. E. DeWitt. *Keeper's Quarter—notes & smalls.*

He set the box on the cart and breathed out once, the way you do before lifting a stone that might have something living under it. The string slid free with a small sigh. Inside: a folded cotton cloth that had once been white; three Polaroids (keeper's bed corner; stair turn; a close-up of the joist's spiral); a wax-stamped tag reading *do not remove—per oral history only*; and, under the cloth, an oilskin-wrapped ledger half the size of a hymnbook and twice as grave.

The ledger's twine resisted and then yielded like a tight throat. He peeled back the oilskin and did not pretend he wasn't bracing for disappointment. Too often, boxes are just boxes. This one wasn't. He found a book bound in brown leather gone soft with the handling of a hand that believed in writing things down. The front board had separated along the hinge and been repaired with thread so neat it made him blink. Across the flyleaf, in iron gall that had long ago settled into the paper like a tattoo, a keeper's neat, upright hand had written:

Lighthouse—Daily Log. Commenced March 3rd, 1876.

Damien took a breath he would not have taken six months ago. "Thank you," he said, aloud to no one, because gratitude is a discipline as much as a feeling. He pulled a pair of nitrile gloves from the cart drawer—Pollard's idea of modernity—and slipped them on. The pages whispered when he turned them, thick rag stock that had survived storms by minding its own business. Dates lined the left margins; weather rode the right. Between, in an even hand, lived the day.

March 4th: *Fog heavy; bell sounded regular; lamp trimmed; Mrs. Kenner brought bread; children on the cliff walked too near.*

March 7th: *Inspection satisfactory; compass corrected 1° east; keepers instructed to note any "dreamlight patterns" (language not mine) reported by town. Will oblige if something to oblige.* The curl of dry humor wasn't the town's usual; it landed like the wink of a man who knew the sea would outlast everyone's paperwork.

There. *Dreamlight patterns.* He pinched the bridge of his nose, as if the phrase itself pressed a nerve that had been waiting for a name and found one.

He turned another page. March 10th: *No vessels. Sky clear after noon. At dusk, an oddness: light in the glass though lamp unlit—faint, as if a child's breath on a bottle. Marked it here only that memory's tricks be not taken for lies later. Will not alarm Mrs. Kenner, who will spread it like butter.*

He smiled despite himself. And then, as his thumb moved the edge, the room offered him a small scent that did not belong to basements: lavender—pressed-bloom lavender, the kind that survives years between pages and brings a day back when you crack the paper. He angled the book and saw it—a sprig, flattened, more gray than purple, tucked at the top edge so that the stem marked a date like an old woman's finger.

He lifted the page with both hands.

March 18th: *Silent woman again—arrived after last bell, left just after midnight. I have yet to hear her voice with my ears; still she says more than any. She set her palm to the circle beneath the bed and breathed as if remembering what breathing was for. I asked no questions. She placed a small herb in this book "against forgetting." I forget the name—lavender?—but will not forget the meaning. She looked through the lens as a mother looks at a sleeping child—counting breaths, not saints.*

Damien stopped reading only because his throat advised him to. He stood a moment, gloved hands on the cart handle, letting the room have its silence. The phrase *silent woman* felt like a door swinging on a hinge that had been oiled this morning and also twenty-five years ago. It wasn't how men wrote ghosts; it was how keepers wrote people who arrived with authority outside the town ledger.

He turned the page. March 21st: *Dreamlight patterns noted by three fishermen and Mrs. Kenner's boy. Three quick, two long. Same again this night. Lamp unlit. No oil burned. Inspected clockwork—idle. Glass warm to the touch though fire nowhere near. Wrote to Mr. Marwick and to A.W. as agreed.*

He closed his eyes and repeated the new sentence inside his head, letting it land where it would do the most lasting work. *Wrote to Mr. Marwick and to A.W. as agreed.* A.W.— Aurelia Ward—named here without apology or ceremony, a partner placed where partners belong: in the first sentences of the matter at hand. The confidence of it loosened a part of him that had clenched in meetings where people made facts wait outside like bad dogs.

He kept going. March 24th: *A.W. visited with the silent woman, who is not silent with her. They walked the stair without asking permission, then asked my permission to keep what must be kept where it must be. The circle beneath the bed remains. The oath was spoken, which I record here not as a vow but as an instruction should the light falter: If the light falters, the healer's oath must rise.*

The words hit like a bell in the stone.

He set a finger to the margin. The line about the oath was in a different hand—finer, left-leaning, a woman's, perhaps, or simply a man's educated sister learning the slope of a pen. The keeper had added an arrow—polite— pointing to the inserted sentence with a note: *per A.W. &*

E.D. E.D.—he knew the initials now; they had bracketed his day—E. DeWitt, whose margins had carried the town's memory like a mother carries small necessary things in a bag no one else admires.

He glanced toward the stair as if to confirm that the world had not rearranged itself while he read. It had, of course, but it had done so with such a slow diligence that only paper and patience could reveal the change. He turned to April. The entries steadied into weather and ships—*Hayden & Sons, eastbound*—and then, two weeks in, another flicker: *Dreamlight patterns continue; three quick, two long. A.W. says it is not dream but memory. I keep my ledger and my lamp. I am my own business; the light is its.* The keeper's humility made Damien like a man he would never meet.

He checked the back board for loose leaves and found none. He closed the ledger as if closing a child's hand around a coin and re-wrapped it in oilskin that no longer minded its age. He slid the bundle back into the box and placed the Polaroids on top like a few coins on a casket: the token by which the living make themselves feel better about leaving a good thing behind for an hour.

"Pollard?" he called up the stair. "I'll need the scanner room. And a table no one spills coffee on."

The clerk's voice, slow and dry, drifted down. "We haven't had coffee in the scanner room since the flood of '99 took the percolator. But you can have a folding chair with a good back."

Damien allowed himself a small smile. "Perfect." He thumbed his phone to send the one text that would travel faster than weather.

Found something. 1876 keeper's log. Silent woman. Dreamlight patterns. The line you carry in your pocket—written here. Lavender between pages. Can you come quietly?

Marley's reply arrived before he flipped the light in the scanner room. *On my way. Quiet is what I've got.*

He didn't feel the urge to say *hurry.* The book would be here. The town would be here. The past had waited this long. It could wait the time it took a woman with a canvas bag and a metronome to cross Main Street without spilling her coffee.

He set up the cradle and the foam wedges like a man who had done this work under other names in other buildings, because caring for paper becomes a calling the second time you don't do it and regret it for a week. He adjusted the lamps, checked glare, and set the ledger open to March. When he looked up, the door had begun to open.

Marley stepped in with her breath tight and her shoulders set to a pitch that told him she had already guessed what he'd found and was braced to be wrong. He lifted the oilskin and let the scent of lavender do the rest.

LAVENDER ARRIVED before the words did. It braided the air with beeswax and old cotton, and Marley felt the smell travel to that chamber behind the eyes where a good memory nests for winter. For half a breath she was in her aunt's kitchen again—Clara tying bundles of the herb with kitchen string and making the room smell like calm had a sound. She steadied herself with a hand on the edge of the table and let her fingers travel the folded oilskin without touching the leather beneath. "May I?" she asked, because it mattered that she asked him this about a thing he had found.

"You must," Damien said, and stepped aside the way he always did when the better view belonged to her.

She opened the ledger and found not drama but diligence: a narrow, even hand that had practiced its humilities. The entries told the town in weather first and story second, which is how places near water prefer to be told. She read the March lines silently, lips moving the way a person reads prayers not to be overheard by anyone but the god of their choosing. When she reached the first *dreamlight patterns*, her chest pulled once, tight, and let go.

She traced the date with a gloved fingertip. "Three quick, two long," she said, not because she doubted the habit of the light but because affirmation is a kind of reverence for the way the world keeps its own books. "Not a glitch. Not a rumor. 1876," she added, as if saying the year could keep the ledger in the present where her hands could take care of it. "It started then at least. Or that's when they named it." She moved to the next page and felt the pressed sprig before she saw it. She didn't lift the herb; she learned the lesson of its presence instead, the way you learn a person's history by the way they touch the back of your hand.

"Lavender," she said, and looked up because the word required an audience to be true. "Not the kind people throw in soap; the kind that remembers the day it was cut." Her throat tightened, that precise ache that belongs to grief you already metabolized and then are forced to taste again in a better vintage. "Clara used to tuck it between pages so the recipe would be glad to be read."

Damien's hand hovered near the foam wedge and then withdrew. He had learned not to place a palm on a shoulder when paper wanted to be the only thing touching skin. "The line is here," he said, quiet, and angled the book. His pencil had, out of respect, stayed in his pocket. "Not in the keeper's hand. A different slope. 'If the light falters, the healer's oath must rise.'"

The sentence landed like a bell in her bones. She'd seen it in a memo, a margin, a copy of a copy. She had carried it in her pocket on a strip of paper she pretended was a quote and secretly used as a kind of private compass. Here it lived not as rumor but as instruction, placed where men who trimmed wicks would see it and do the dignities it asked.

She looked closer. Beneath the oath, in the same left-leaning hand, the initials: *A.W.* And, smaller, like a signature under a witness mark: *E.D.* Marley's throat tightened in gratitude for unknown women who leave breadcrumbs for other women to find when the men are busy telling their own versions of the same kindness. "Aurelia Ward," she said, a little too quickly, as if the name might escape if she wasn't the first to say it. "And E. DeWitt—who saved us in the margins." She took a breath that one of Clara's blends would have approved of. "This changes... not everything. But the edges. The edges are always where the truth frays first."

Damien gestured to the scanner. "We'll image it all. Low heat. No flash. Pollard will sulk if we forget to put the gloves back in the drawer with the thumbs pointing the right way."

"Pollard can have my firstborn index," she said, and smiled at his small wince on *firstborn*—not because it hurt him but because she loved the proof that words still struck him in places he thought he'd armored. She turned a page.

The *silent woman* rose out of the lines without needing ink. Marley felt the room thin around that phrase—sheets pulled taut, a chair turned, a hand placing a sprig between paper to teach the book how to breathe. She didn't love giving names to people the town had deliberately un-named; she understood why it had worked for as long as it had. But the description made something inside her stand taller. *Silent woman again—arrived after last bell, left just after midnight.* Again. Not apparition. Again. Someone allowed to be necessary without permission from anyone whose voice carries farther than truth on market day.

"Dreamlight patterns," she read aloud, and tasted the town's attempt to call the anomaly something that would not get a letter from the bishop. "Three quick, two long. Same as now." She set the pad of her thumb against the page's edge and felt the roughness where a pen had bitten a little too hard in a hasty hand. She smiled to herself. "The keeper did not want to be the kind of man who wrote the word *dreamlight*," she said, soft, "and became him anyway."

Damien nodded, pleased for reasons he wouldn't pretend he didn't understand. "You see the arrow?" he asked, pointing to the small drawing in the margin. "From the oath to the circle under the bed."

She followed the tiny line, then looked up. "He did not think it ceremony. He thought it wiring."

He grinned, relieved by the metaphor's efficiency. "Function, not flourish," he said, stealing her sentence from two days prior and handing it back with interest.

She reached into her bag for the small mirror and laid it by the ledger the way a carpenter places a square on a workbench because it belongs. She adjusted the lamp to keep glare from the gold leaf and angled the glass to catch the page's reflection. The oath read backward and somehow truer that way, a reminder that instructions are sometimes learned best when they slide into you from a direction your defenses didn't guard. She looked at him through the glass. "I want to bring it to the quarters," she said, surprising herself even as she shaped the sentence. "Not to burn anything. Just to let the page sit where the hand sat when it was written."

Damien didn't say no. He didn't say yes, either. He looked at the ledger the way people look at babies they suspect need sleep more than a parade. "We could carry it up in a case," he said. "No open windows. No candles. No vows. We set it near, not on. We read what we have to. Then we bring it home and scan the rest."

She heard something in his voice she hadn't realized she'd been hoping for: the willingness to let care be a form of courage. "Okay," she said.

They told Pollard. Pollard told them to sign the ledger with the kind of handwriting that would keep their grand-children from being embarrassed. He lent them a shallow archival box that smelled faintly of desiccant and decades. He checked his watch and said, "Back before dusk," as if dusk were a sheriff whose tolerance ran out at the hour when the lighthouse spoke for itself.

On the walk up the headland, Marley carried the box like a sacrament. She did not invoke saints. She invoked hinges. The wind moved in from the water with salt and a rumor of rain. They reached the keeper's quarters without speaking, which was their version of saying a long grace. When the door gave its familiar groan, Marley felt the day align—a ledger where a ledger once sat; a spiral under a bed; a room that knew the difference between spectacle and witness.

She set the box on the desk and lifted the lid. The lavender greeted the quarters like a visitor who remembered exactly where the good chair lived. Damien closed the window because consent matters even when wind is kind. He set the metronome on the desk's corner and did not wind it.

"Which page?" he asked.

"The oath," she said, and opened to the entry with hands that had never forgotten being taught to handle books like bodies.

She read, not aloud the way a person preaches, but aloud the way a person reads a trouble report to a team that knows what a wrench can do and what it can't: "*If the light falters, the healer's oath must rise.*" She didn't add the rest of the sentence that wanted to walk in behind it, the part of her that suspected the oath itself was less event than posture: keep the living; honor the gone; carry the light when others fall asleep; share the burden in a circle; do not let monuments eat people. The room absorbed her restraint like praise.

She set the small mirror on the floor to catch the unseen spiral in reverse and watched the reflection steady the page. Damien stood very still, as if movement might knock something delicate off a high shelf. He kept his hands open, the way men do when nothing needs fixing and a little needs saving.

"Do you smell it?" she asked.

"Lavender," he said.

"And cedar," she added, surprised into a soft laugh. "Hazel's shop followed the book."

"It followed you," he said, and if a sentence can be both tender and practical, his was. "We read two more pages and bring it home." He didn't call the office home often. Today he did. Even courage allows for prudence when paper is involved.

She read the March 21st entry with the note about *wrote to Mr. Marwick and to A.W. as agreed.* The name settled in the plaster without dislodging a thing. Then March 24th, with the arrow and the initials below the oath. She did not read the line about the silent woman arriving after last bell. She let the room have that privacy back.

"We're done," she said, and the part of her that would have stayed to see if the page began to warm like the glass had warmed in 1876 was grateful to be overruled by the part of her that did not confuse impulse with purpose.

Damien nodded once. They closed the ledger, returned it to its case, and paused at the threshold because both of them had learned not to assume their leaving did not matter to rooms. "Thank you," Marley said, and meant it to be heard by paper and spiral both.

On the stairs, she placed her palm at turn four and felt the faint raised circle under paint answer with its own smaller, quieter thanks. At the base, the world was still the world—children on scooters, a dog practicing offense against seagulls, the sea doing math with rocks. She breathed easier not because the work was finished but because they were doing it in the order it asked for.

"Scan," Damien said. "Document. File."

"Then stew," Marley added. "Evelyn's."

"Boring paper first," he said, and they smiled at the joke because it had become a way of praising what saves people from themselves.

THE SCANNER ROOM hummed the way small faithful machines do—content to turn light into files with no need for applause. Pollard had found a taller stool and a softer lamp since noon; he'd also put a sign on the glass door that said *Closed for Preservation*, which sounded like a euphemism and was not. Damien positioned the ledger in the cradle, adjusted the foam supports, and advanced page by page while Marley recorded captions in a hand that would not embarrass anyone.

They read with more attention than appetite. April's entries offered ships and weather. May tucked a line in like a woman slips a note in a pocket: *A.W. says the "dreamlight" is not dream but memory; no need to frighten people with the fact. Let them name it how they can carry it.* June brought a storm that tore a shutter and taught three boys the importance of taking someone seriously the first time they asked. Then, September: *Silent woman again. Pressed her hand to the circle and looked at me with the kind of regard that makes a man stand up straighter. Said nothing I can write without making a liar of the words. Left lavender. Told me to sleep while the building watched.*

Marley leaned back, throat thick. "He trusted the lighthouse," she said. "And the women who told him to."

"Because he had a job and they made it larger, not smaller," Damien said, a little fiercely, surprising himself with the sting in the sentence. It had been a long day of asking men to let women adjust their instruments without taking their hands away.

They closed the book after the last relevant entry out of respect for the rest—no one needs you to read aloud about rope inventories unless rope is your religion. Pollard initialed the chain-of-custody page with his neat P and sent them away with the admonition to drink water. Outside, the air had changed. Cloud rose from the ocean in a bank like a shoulder. The temperature dropped a degree that bodies feel before faces do.

"Storm line," Damien said. "Tomorrow or tonight."

Marley glanced toward the headland. The lighthouse looked taller again, as if wind lengthened stone. She did not flinch. The work, after all, does not ask you to be surprised every time it asks you to show up. "We'll eat," she said. "We'll carry copies to the council for authentication. We'll put the ledger to bed. And we'll not talk to anyone who wants us to tell them how it ends."

"Because it doesn't," Damien said, not to be clever but to be true.

They crossed the street toward the café. The bell over the door rang a note that made Evelyn look up and let her mouth soften without losing any of its authority. She set bowls on the counter. "I had stew ready," she said, as if she ran the weather from the kitchen. "And bread, and a plate of something that should be illegal before a storm."

Marley took the bowls and sank into the corner table she and Damien had worn in with half a year of learning how to keep a town from breaking its own heart. "We found the line," she said. "In a keeper's log."

Evelyn did not ask which line. "Of course you did," she said. "You always find what has decided to be found."

They ate. It tasted of thyme and relief. Damien slid a photocopy of the oath across the table, the ink still faintly warm. Evelyn read it, eyes bright but dry. "My mother said that to me when my father's heart went to sea without him," she said. "Not in those exact words. In the words she had that day."

"We'll file it," Damien said. "Properly. It'll live where it can't be un-lived."

"And the lavender?" Evelyn asked, nose wrinkling like a woman who steadied her own grief with plants she talked to in the afternoon.

"In the ledger," Marley said. "Pressed in 1876."

Evelyn swore quietly, and then said, "Bless them," because in this town the two phrases sometimes share a shelf. "Take tea to Hazel," she added. "Her head will be talking. The wind's turned."

They did. Hazel opened the shop door before they knocked and handed Damien a paper sack without looking into it, because her faith in what people needed had become muscle memory. "For later," she said. "If the bell rings. Keep sugar near. Don't mistake hungry for haunted." She pressed two fingers to her brow and smiled through it. "You found the book."

"We found the book," Marley said, and let herself be held by that plural for a breath longer than grammar strictly requires.

Night carried them back to the headland because habit and responsibility have become twins in them. The first flash arrived at the hour it had arranged with dusk. Three quick, two long. The pause shaved thin again—an old barber liking to show off. Damien checked a watch he didn't need because the building kept better time. Marley set her hand to the iron at the base and felt a hum—not electricity; attention.

"Read it here?" he asked, chin toward the sky.

"Not aloud," she said. "We did enough saying for today." She put the photocopy in her pocket and let the paper warm to her body heat. It felt like a seed.

Above, the lantern room answered a wind they couldn't yet feel on the path. The beam cut the night, found its panes, and swept. Shadows bucked, then flattened, polite. The bell did not toll. Its silence didn't feel like absence; it felt like a long inhale.

"Tomorrow," Damien said, as if speaking to a storm and a book and a council and a woman with a cedar case at once.

"Tomorrow," Marley agreed.

They stood a while longer—two figures watching a tower that had learned to say a small, precise set of things well. When they turned back toward town, the curve of cloud wore a bruise. Thunder practiced somewhere no one could hear. Marley reached for Damien's hand, not for romance or bravery, but for necessity. He took it with the same reasons.

Back in her apartment, she added three new cards to the wall with hands that had been careful all day and were still equal to the task:

Keeper's Logbook—1876.

—"Silent woman" entries (after last bell; lavender left; hand to circle).

—"Dreamlight patterns," three quick / two long; lamp unlit; glass warm.

—"If the light falters, the healer's oath must rise." (A.W., witnessed E.D.)

She taped a smaller scrap beneath—lavender-colored paper she had saved for nothing in particular—and wrote: *He trusted the building; he trusted the women. We can, too.* Then she did the radical thing the day asked of her: she went to bed before midnight and let sleep do some of the keeping.

Out on the headland, the beam found its panes again. Three quick. Two long. It remained stubbornly itself. Inside the stone, the bell decided its note and kept it in its mouth. The wind turned once more, and the town answered in the only liturgy it has ever loved: porch lights, kettle on, a few people sitting in rooms where paper has been touched today by hands that know their job.

Storm tomorrow, the horizon said.

We'll be there, the ledger answered.

And the light, remembering, did not disagree.

6

STORM OVER THE WATER

The storm announced itself in a language the town remembered even when forecasts were wrong: the temperature fell a stitch, the gulls lowered their argument and tucked for shelter, and the horizon put on a bruise the color of old copper. Damien stood on the headland path with his hand up, feeling the wind's first test tap his palm. "We'll go up, latch what can be latched, and come down before it breaks," he said, tone practical—protection disguised as plan.

Marley looked past him to the lighthouse. In the humid lull, the tower seemed to shed a decade of wear—stone tightened, glass darkened to seriousness. "We'll be quick," she said, which was their way of bargaining with a building that kept its own schedule.

They climbed with the efficiency of people who had learned every groan of the stair. Two turns up, the closer weather arrived: a draft as precise as a hand on a forehead, checking for fever. "Pressure's dropping," Damien said, breath steady. At the keeper's landing, he knelt to fit the window brace and test the latch. "We're sealed," he called, and Marley—already lifting the board at the seam—answered, "For now."

They had not come to light a candle or to invite anything. Today required bolts and rainlines and a check of the lantern room's vent. Still, out of habit or reverence, Marley pressed two fingers to the beam beneath the lifted board—the spiral lived there like a heart under a rib. She felt neither heat nor shock, only the insistence of the cut: a groove made by someone who had believed that intention could be laid into wood and hold.

Wind hit the panes with a polite hand the first time. The second time, it did not bother with manners.

Lightning stitched the sky out at the horizon. The air tightened, then loosened too far. "Lantern room," Damien said, already moving. They climbed the last turns together, shoulders nearly touching where the stair narrowed. The door at the top resisted in the new pressure, then yielded, and they stepped into a room becoming storm.

From this height, the sea looked muscled and malevolent—green-gray bands running like a field under invisible fingers. "Vent first," Damien said. He crossed to the louvered opening and set it two notches down—enough to bleed pressure, not enough to invite rain into the gear void. Marley checked the shutters and found one left-of-true; she righted it with the heel of her hand and felt the old stubbornness of iron give to a firmer stubbornness of intent.

Thunder rolled—not overhead yet, but moving like an animal with purpose. The first hard drops struck the panes as if thrown. "We should go," Damien said, but even as he said it the path below vanished in a shiver of water, and the wind snapped thirty degrees without warning, cutting a new line across the cliff. The door at their back shuddered. They turned in the same instant.

The rain did its full-throated work—sheets, then rope, then a continuous fabric that erased distance. The path became a silver ribbon they could not follow. "We aren't going down in that," Damien said, voice bland because panic helps no one. He pulled the door inward and set the inner bolt. "We stay put. Keeper's quarters between waves."

They moved quickly, turning back through the stairwell like people who know the difference between fear and speed. In the quarters, the change in pressure had lifted a small sigh from the old floor; Marley seated the board with her palm, a gesture that felt like apology. They dragged the desk away from the window, not because it would help if the glass failed but because people need to believe in furniture when weather is teaching them humility. Damien tested the lock. Marley folded her coat to make a low nest against the interior wall.

"If we lose the town's grid," he said, "we lose radio. But we've got the lantern." He meant the oil lamp Evelyn had insisted they keep on site after the last wind event—like a grandmother's superstition which had earned the right to be called habit. He lit it, the small, insistent flame steadier than his careful hands.

The first full strike hit out on the water—white sheet, muscle behind it—and an instant later the window shook with the crack. "Close your eyes on the flash," Damien said, and Marley nodded, because your body forgets what your head knows when the sky teaches you scale.

They waited in the intimate radius of lamplight while the storm climbed the headland in long, purposeful strides. The lighthouse around them settled its weight. In that settling, Marley heard the ledger's voice—the even, practical hand that had written weather beside wonder. *Storm. Lamp trimmed. The silent woman after last bell.* She didn't conjure anything. She sat on the floor with her knees up and her back against the interior wall and allowed the building to be the adult in the room.

Lightning walked the ridge behind them. Thunder arrived at once, no pause, dropping a fist onto the tower like a test of faith. The room's small flame flickered, then steadied. Marley bit the inside of her cheek just hard enough to taste iron and did not look at the window.

A gust forced a squeal from the sash that sounded uncomfortably like a living thing scolded past its tolerance. Damien was there in two steps, hand flat to the frame, and the sound ceased. Their breath stayed audible between hits. "We can keep watch in turns," he said, and Marley nodded, though he stayed standing and she stayed sitting because each had adopted a posture that made the other more possible.

One more strike, closer. Another. The next came not as a bolt across the sky but as a spear into the building itself—direct, unambiguous. The tower took it like a ship takes a wave broadside: head down, then up. Ozone punched into the room with a cold fist and a sweet, chemical tang.

"Down," Damien said, hand on Marley's shoulder without thinking and therefore perfectly timed. They crouched. The room's small flame went thin, then straight, then out.

Darkness did not arrive.

It poured.

For a breath, the tower glowed from its bones. Light—green-gold, not lightning-white—ran the seams of stone and iron. The spiral under the floor did not simply remember; it wrote. Through the board above it, words rose as if breathed onto glass—lines and curls, not fire, not paint. Letters older than the room's paint and newer than the ocean's grammar lifted into sight along the path of the carved groove. Marley's mouth opened. She did not make a sound.

Damien's fingers tightened on her shoulder and then eased so his hand would not teach her body the wrong lesson about fear.

The words did not last. They brightened—one phrase, then the next—then permitted the room to be dark again. The oil lamp guttered to life without a match; the flame had kept a coal, apologetic and useful.

"What did you see?" Damien asked, voice almost formal, as if he were taking testimony from someone who would be believed.

Marley closed her eyes and let the afterimage climb from her retina back to sense. "Not letters like ours," she said. "But I know what they meant." She touched the seam —not on, near—and felt heat that was not heat but action. "Keep," she whispered. "Hold. Rise." She opened her eyes. "The oath spoke in the materials."

Thunder rolled away, as if satisfied it had made its point. Rain continued, relentless and impressive without malice. "We're here awhile," Damien said. He sat beside her on the floor, shoulder to shoulder, careful with their weight on the old boards, careful with everything.

The light in the lamp flattened to steadiness. The tower's pulse adjusted to the long work of night.

THEY COULD HAVE SLEPT in turns, but sleep visited only in small mouthfuls and left before anyone could be rude enough to ask for more. Wind went about its industry as if making up for the days it had been asked to behave. Rain found new ways to say the same sentence to the glass.

At some hour that came without a number, the storm shifted from spectacle to insistence—the middle stretch of a long argument when both parties know nothing new will be said and endurance is the only virtue left. Damien stood and counted seconds between the last flash and the next, and Marley listened for the bell that sometimes practiced its note in the stones. It did not ring. She did not want it to. There are nights when silence is protection.

"Tell me again," Damien said, low, warm from sitting. "The words."

"Keep," she said. "Hold. Rise." She didn't try to make a theology out of it. She did not have the appetite and the room did not require it. "It wasn't writing for us," she added. "It was writing as itself."

He nodded, because even a lawyer knows when description has more integrity than explanation. He checked the window again. The glass bowed under pressure and un-bowed on release. In the flex, the white seam where putty met pane appeared and vanished like a pulse.

Another strike, less direct—an ill-tempered cousin. The lamp's flame strained and then held. From the stairwell below came the smallest noise, like a knocked spoon. Marley's head came up. "Do you hear—"

"—something on the landing," Damien finished, already moving toward the door with a steadiness that made panic unnecessary. He opened to the stair's cold, iron smell. A draft moved past his face—the tower inhaling very slowly—and then, below, a faint lucence, as if a banister had learned the trick of old watch dials.

"The tick," Marley said, the word arriving before sense. She came to his shoulder and peered down. The faint ring under the paint at turn four—the north mark—stood out, not bright, not performative; simply present. Not paint. Not heat. The suggestion of a glow the way memory glows when you speak it aloud to someone who will not waste it.

"It's the same as the floor," Damien said.

"No," Marley murmured. "It's different in kind, same in honesty." She didn't know why she said it that way. The stair did not argue.

They closed the door, careful not to silence anything the building still wanted to say. Back in the quarters, Marley set the small mirror on the floor near the seam—not to summon, only to reflect. The spiral did not offer them another phrase. The mirror did something else.

"Look," Damien said.

He meant the mirror's surface, which had carried lamplight and roomlight all evening without fuss. Now, the glass chose to be a pond. Not wet, not warped—simply deeper. In it, the room lay reversed: desk, chair, unmade bench of their coats, window breathing in small incremental argues with the latch. And in the corner where nothing stood in the room itself, a figure.

She stood as if not to startle the room—still, green. Not the lantern's accidental green; not a storm-sick hue. The green of things that remember rain—a dress the color of the grove when rookery shadows lie on fern and moss, a shawl darker at the edges where a woman's hands have habitually gathered its warmth to her throat. Her head was turned, not toward them but toward the desk. A profile: a cheek mapped by life, not by fashion; a crown of hair braided with a competence that had outlived instruction.

Marley did not lower her gaze to check whether the corner held a person. She kept her eyes in the mirror, because some things require the courtesy of meeting them where they choose to stand. "Hello," she said, not breathless, the way you tell a room you're willing to hear it.

The woman did not speak. She moved her hand—slow, as one does around skittish animals—and rested it in air above where the spiral lived under the floor. The mirror caught the gesture and made it usable. Marley felt in her own palm the answer: heat that was not heat; weight that was not pressure; the feeling of a task being acknowledged rather than assigned.

"Do you see her?" she asked, and Damien, still crouched, still himself, said, "Yes."

He saw enough. The mirror gave him the green, the posture, the lowered head that belonged to someone for whom prayer was the same muscle as inventory. No face, no cheap comfort. Just a woman holding the same vigil they were holding, with the conviction of a century's advantage.

"Is she—" he began, then stopped, because *who* is the wrong question when weather is teaching a house to remember.

Marley didn't say *Aurelia.* She didn't say *silent woman.* She didn't throw a name at it and take a step back. "She's working," she said, which was true.

The mirror kept the figure as long as it took the storm to reach a point of its own exhaustion. The pressure rose a hair. The wind, no longer engaged in persuasion, settled for persistence. The woman in green turned—Marley had the impression of eyes brave with their own decisions—and then she was not there.

Not a fade. Not a dissolve.

An end.

Marley's breath left her in a sound that might have embarrassed her in a different room. She smiled at the empty corner the way you smile at the chair of someone who just stepped out, because otherwise you have to talk about absence like crime.

Damien set his hand on the floor near the seam, flat and careful. "We're okay," he said, making the sentence more permission than assessment.

"We are," Marley said, not because she believed in the ease of the world but because believing in the endurance of people felt more useful tonight. She picked up the mirror and set it back on the desk with the reflective side down— less prohibition than gratitude. The lamp flame did its sturdy work.

Rain found an afterlife in drips and seethes. The tower —satisfied with the people inside it and with its own behavior—settled for the hour-to-hour business of refusing the sea's attentions.

They did the same. They ate what they had in their pockets. They wrapped themselves in their coats without apology. They made a plan they knew they wouldn't follow exactly: when the wind shifts, when the path clears, when dawn.

Marley drifted for a minute and found herself awake because a story wanted her attention. *If the light falters, the healer's oath must rise.* The line lived in the ledger, in her pocket, in the wood, and now in the new way light had chosen the groove to speak. She lay with her eyes open to a ceiling that belonged to strangers and felt, not romance, but a deep competence walking the room like a midwife.

When a hard gust rattled the sash, she reached her hand down to the seam, near, not on, and placed her palm above the spiral in that old, new waiting posture.

She kept.

DAWN IN STORMS announces itself in increments, a long negotiation between gray and gray. The rain slackened first, then the wind lost its wrecking appetite and kept only the part of itself that likes to tidy. The window stopped shouldering its frame and resumed sitting in it. The lamp's flame, which had never yet surrendered, now looked unnecessary.

They were stiff and steadier for having been stiff. "We'll wait an hour," Damien said, "and go down on the lull." He opened the window a finger's width and tasted the air like a critic: salt, ozone, the green smell of cliff grass rinsed of dust.

Marley replaced the lifted board and stood, letting blood draw lines back into her feet. She poured a cap of water onto a napkin and wiped the sill where a thin track of silt had collected—the kind of small ordinary kindness houses notice. The room felt relieved without needing to be thanked.

"Before we go," she said.

She set the mirror glass-up again, not to coax anything —if last night had taught her anything, it was that coaxing is a poor substitute for courtesy—but to return the tool to a posture of use. The room returned only what a room offers in morning: reflection of light off walls that had worked, a woman with hair not arranged for anyone but weather, a man checking his pockets for the pencil he had, predictably, put exactly where it always lived. No green. No figure. Simpler honesty.

Marley knelt at the seam. "May I?" she asked, because even after the storm she still liked to practice consent. Damien nodded, and she lifted the board enough to let one eye find the groove. No light ran it now. No script. Only the spiral—cut, intentional, clean, with the small flaw at dead center she had sensed before in reflection and now saw with the eye that counts. She smiled, because imperfection is sometimes the only proof a human got involved in the miracle.

Thunder murmured a polite goodbye out to sea. Far below, a leafed branch—where had it come from, this high? —dripped conscientiously on rock. "We should go," Damien said, not out of anxiety but so that going would belong to them rather than to impulse. He secured the lamp for next time. He opened the door to the stair and listened for the building's answer. It offered a low, agreeable sound he decided was consent.

On turn four, Marley stopped and put her palm to the faint circle beneath the paint. "North," she said. She didn't need the compass. The mark knew what it was for.

They took the last turns carefully. The air in the stair haft smelled like metal that had remembered being ore and was now content to be machine again. At the base, the iron door stuck, thought better of it, and let them out into a morning cleaned to the bone.

The path was scoured, but passable. The cliff edge had been shaved as if the town barber had taken pride in wind. Down on Main Street, a tide of buckets, mops, and neighborly exclamations had already parted and rejoined three times before they reached it. The café door opened before they touched it. Evelyn produced two towels and the old-fashioned kind of breakfast that convinces the body that survival is a habit. She took one look at their faces and nodded once. "You kept," she said, and made it a commendation, not a question.

"Storm took the grid along the bay," someone said in the wave of remarks that always follows crisis. "Phones went down around three." Damien glanced at his; it had died at the strike and now lay dumb in his pocket like a fish that had decided to winter. He didn't need it. The ledger would keep time today.

They sat in the corner with a ledger-sized silence

between them. "I saw her," Damien said after the second cup, which made it an admission rather than a report. "Not as symbol. As person."

Marley didn't reach across to take his hand. She didn't need to. He had done something harder than comfort—he had consented to witness. "A woman in green," she said. "Working."

He nodded. "Not asking to be believed."

"Not needing us," she said. "Choosing us, maybe."

He looked toward the headland, steady. "That will have to be enough."

They walked the town the way people do after a storm— saying the little necessary things that feel like prayers: *you okay; you need help with that; I have extra candles.* The stop at the records office happened because habit steers humans as surely as tide in this town. Pollard met them at the door with a clipboard and a satisfaction he tried to hide under bureaucracy. "The scanner survived," he said. "Bring me the next set when you catch your breath."

"Ledger's safe," Damien said. "And the oath is scanned." He did not say *we saw it write itself in a different alphabet under the bed.* He did not need to formulate everything into the town's ear at once. The town would not stand up to too much honesty before the noon mail.

They took the stone steps behind the office where the sun hits first and sat with their backs warming, letting the cold go the way old pain goes into muscle and out through breath. Marley took the mirror from her bag, looked at their faces in it, and laughed—the rueful, grateful kind. "No green," she said. "Just us."

"Just," Damien said, and made the word large enough to stand in.

When Hazel appeared, her migraine was gone, and her

hands smelled faintly of cedar and smoke. She listened with her face without interrupting, which is as close as Brookwood gets to astonishment. "She shows herself to people doing their jobs," Hazel said finally, as if complimenting the woman in green. "Not to people who ask only to be reassured."

Marley nodded, tired enough to be honest without embroidery. "I was afraid," she said.

"You were allowed," Hazel replied. "The work isn't to be fearless. It's to be faithful." She handed over a tin Marley hadn't asked for. "For the fatigue after the lightning. Rosemary still. But a little lemon peel to remind you that your blood is citrus, not stone."

Afternoon came washed and made, the way a town resets itself just so it can lean into the next weather. By dusk, the headland wore a new shadow where a slab of cliff had let go with the rain—more geometry for the beam to articulate. They went up once more, not to tempt anything or to demand sequel, but to check what required checking before night.

The lantern room felt newly aired, as if a house had thrown all its windows open and then closed them again before supper. Marley touched the frame where lightning had shoved, and the iron—stoic—offered her nothing but itself. The keeper's quarters gave back order without spectacle. The seam lay quiet. The board stayed seated. The mirror reflected what a mirror reflects when no one has asked it to be more than glass: two people who looked like themselves, a room that had done its job.

The beam rose at the hour it had agreed upon with dusk. Three short. Two long. Tonight the pause was the width of a breath that had caught and then continued. Damien set the metronome just to hear the ticks return an ordinary second into the room. Marley stood at the window and watched the light sweep town roofs that had dried enough to be grateful. In the reflection she caught nothing but the sweep and their patience.

"I think she was the one the keeper called the silent woman," Marley said at last. "And I think the dress was the grove's green, not fashion's. But I won't swear to more than that."

"You don't have to," Damien said. "We've got the logbook for the words and the boards for the work." He smiled, small and tired, the way people do after nights that did not kill them. "And boring paper first."

They laughed because that was the only indulgence the room allowed, and because laughter is often the sound of permission to go on.

On the path down, the cliff grass—blown and newly arranged—brushed their legs like small animal backs. The town smelled of insurance and soup. Marley paused where the sea's sound is a little louder and looked back. The lighthouse made no promises. It did not need to. It kept what could be kept. It rose where it had been planted. It remembered in the materials, then in the minds of the people who had decided to keep it company.

When she turned to catch up to Damien, she felt the smallest weight under her palm—phantom, not frightening—the pressure of a hand set above a spiral, acknowledging a task shared rather than given. She didn't speak. She didn't have to. The night answered for her in light.

Three short.

Two long.

And the town, newly washed, lifted its eyelids and watched.

7

THE CHARTER FRAGMENT

The call came from the first Chapel—not the newer hall with its careful HVAC and podium that pretends to be a pulpit, but the salt-stained building the town uses for rummage sales, funerals that expect rain, and elections no one wants to admit matter. Marley stood in the shop arranging the mosaic of her wall—metronome, tide tables, the rubbing of the spiral, the oath copied twice because she could not stop—when the bell on the counter chimed and Evelyn stuck her head in without ceremony.

"They've found a page," Evelyn said, eyes bright and unhelpful. "In the old frame behind the portrait of Mayor Reed's whiskers. Pollard sent me because he knows I know the fastest door to you."

"A page," Marley repeated, not moving yet because words like that are better handled at a near-still. "From?"

"The charter," Evelyn said. She had the decency not to add *I always said.* "Come now, before the helpful people help it into dust."

Marley grabbed her canvas bag, slid her notebook and

the small mirror inside, and ran. Outside, the day after the storm had the scrubbed look of a kitchen you can eat off: clouds stacked clean, air with the new metal scent of mended weather, gulls resuming opinion. She crossed Main Street and took the Chapel steps two at a time, feeling the long building settle around her like an older aunt—comforting, particular, not to be scolded for her habits.

Inside, a cluster of volunteers pressed in a respectful crescent around a six-foot table. Pollard stood at the head with the air of a man guarding a sleeping newborn in a room full of well-meaning cousins. On the table, a warped frame had been opened, its backing pried free to reveal the portrait's reverse: brittle brown paper stamped with a long-ago restorer's optimism. Tucked behind, flattened by forty years of neglect, lay a sheet of laid paper the color of clotted cream, edges deckled, writing in a hand that did not apologize for itself.

Damien arrived as if the building had breathed him in—coat open, jaw already set in the posture that kept people from touching what they shouldn't. He nodded to Pollard, to Evelyn, to Marley last, and the nod to Marley carried an entire case file of shared comprehension: *boring paper first; everything else follows.*

"How long was it behind the frame?" Marley asked.

"Since the bicentennial exhibit," Pollard said. He didn't look at the volunteers when he added, "Which I did not curate, before anyone wonders why I'm wearing such an expression." He indicated the sheet with his chin instead of his hand. "It was slipped in as a stiffener. Perhaps intentionally. Perhaps cowardice got a clever costume that day."

"Let's not malign the dead before we've dated the crime," Damien said gently. He pulled on cotton gloves, and the gesture turned the room from gossip to work. "Everyone give the table three feet. Breath moves paper." The volunteers took two polite steps back and then, recognizing the difference between politeness and usefulness, took a third.

The sheet lay with its face upward. The ink—iron gall gone brown—had traveled obediently with the fiber, not through it. Chain lines ran like ribs; a watermark ghosted low, an anchor and a year inside an oval he could make out if he squinted. The script was both fussy and vigorous—the clerkly hand of a literate person who liked their pen and their influence.

At the top, in splendor that had not tired of itself, the words: *Charter for the Town of Brookwood, adopted in assembly, May 12, 1826.* The next line named what charters everywhere feel compelled to name: obligations to light and harbor, to "the common good and the safety of ships seeking our mercy," to schools, to roads when the river allowed, to a bell to call the living and the lost. And then, lower, in a tidy list with titles assigned like furniture: *Founders and Principal Subscribers: Callum Marwick (Master of Works), Aurelia Ward (Beacon of the Grove), Horace Deacon (Factor), Eliza Boone (Provisions), Isaiah Treadwell (Mason), Reverend Simeon Gray (Chaplain), and such others as affix their names in goodwill.*

Aurelia Ward. The line did not apologize for itself. The title did not blush. Beacon of the Grove. It sat where it belonged—in the first column, not the footnote.

Marley's throat pulled tight and then did its duty. She read the list again, lips moving, until the words ceased feeling like someone else's courage and began feeling like the town's own. "Beacon of the Grove," she said aloud. The phrase moved through the room without snagging on anyone who would scold it for poetry.

"Let's get it flat," Damien said, because some sentences are talismans and others are instructions. He eased a foam board under one half, then the other, and the paper accepted support without resisting the implication that support was needed. He set two unglazed weights at the corners like gentle hands. "Watermark looks like Brackley & Sons," he added. "Portsmouth mill. Twenty-four-pound laid. Right for the year. The clerk's hand is consistent with the rest of our early minutes."

"Our minutes," Pollard confirmed, the possessive making him both prouder and more embarrassed than he cared to show. "And the clerk at the time was one Ruth Emery," he added, which brightened Evelyn's face in a way that had nothing to do with blood and everything to do with stubbornness.

Damien angled the page and ran his eyes along the left margin. Halfway down, a row of small, regular punctures crossed the gutter. He placed a gloved fingertip beside them without touching. "Stitch holes," he said. "The leaf was sewn. Something cut it free."

"Not fell out?" a volunteer ventured, because hope often arrives to meetings late and underdressed.

"Not fell," Damien said, and made the discrepancy between accident and act a mercy rather than an accusation. "The holes are clean. The cut edge is straight—not torn, not brittle until after extraction. And look—" He gestured to the facing board of the frame backing, where a faint ghost of ink remained, reversed. "Offset from the page that once faced it. Our co-founder's name mirrored. The ghost of erasure."

Marley heard only two words at first: *our co-founder.* It tightened something inside that had become too used to proof. She leaned closer, careful to keep her breath behind her lips. The line *Aurelia Ward (Beacon of the Grove)* had a small ink bloom at the downstroke of the *W*—the kind you get if you pause and decide to let the sentence be bolder than paper strictly warrants. She smiled despite herself. "Someone's hand enjoyed writing it," she said. "At least for that instant."

"Or someone's hand trembled and recovered," Pollard said softly, revealing more sentiment than the basement allowed. He cleared his throat and found refuge in clerkly usefulness. "Shall we move to the scanner room, Mr. Hawthorne? Before my nerves begin to act like other people's."

"In a moment," Damien said. He did not look at Marley when he asked, "Do you want to read, before we put it behind glass and make people ask permission to feel something?"

She wanted to; she also wanted not to ruin a thing with wanting. She nodded once, the small vow she uses when larger ones would break her ankle. "Yes."

They read the preamble standing—Pollard because he refuses to sit when history is on its feet, Evelyn because sitting long has never agreed with her, Damien because work stands, Marley because standing is how you watch a page you have begged the world for finally put itself where it cannot be denied. The sentences were as handsome and unwieldy as you'd expect: *We, the undersigned, in tender recognition of the mercy that light affords and the duty owed to the living and the gone, do bind ourselves to keep a beacon at the headland and a bell by the river; to honor the grove which has sheltered our sick and our children; to apportion bread in lean seasons; to instruct our young in letters; and to govern in the manner of neighbors who expect to be buried within sight of each other.* It was both more and less pious than the family pamphlets suggested. It had the tone of a town starting out the way a marriage starts out—romance trimmed to make room for a ledger.

"The grove named," Marley said, not performing surprise. "The headland and the grove in the same breath."

"Beacon of the Grove," Evelyn repeated, lower. "They put it where the parades couldn't."

A volunteer exhaled the sigh of a person happy to have lived long enough to be wrong. "So she was there," the woman said. "And not just in the kitchen."

"She was there," Damien said. He did not make it an argument. He made it a diagnostic.

They moved the page to the scanner room like a procession that had deliberately misplaced its trumpets: no speeches, no tapping of frames. While Pollard fussed his benevolent fuss—humidity, angle, glare—Marley stepped into the hallway and texted Helena Marwick Vale.

We have a fragment. Charter leaf. Your ancestor is named alongside Ward. Beacon of the Grove, in ink. Come if you can behave.

Helena's reply took longer than her usual dispatches. *Behaving is my specialty. Thank you for telling me first.*

"Who'd you tell first?" Damien asked, leaning in the doorway without pretending not to read her face.

"You," she said, because saying so out loud keeps a thing from being weakened by resentment later. Then: "And the person who will try to run the story faster than the truth."

He accepted that line's burden with a small nod. "Let's get the image," he said. "And the chain of custody paperwork that makes adults."

They watched the machine do the work that is never thanked and always essential. The scan revealed more than eyes had. In the watermark—Brackley & Sons—an anchor intersected the oval's year: 1824. Right for an 1826 usage. In the lower right margin, a faint pressed circle showed where a seal had once kissed and been lifted away. A shadow of stitching ran the gutter: the proof the page had been bound. In the left margin's middle, where knife had kissed paper, two small burs rose like gooseflesh.

"It's real," Damien said. No triumph; just verification set neatly where it belongs. "The removal isn't an accident. It's surgery."

The room, which contained four people who had disagreed about the town's origin stories for as long as they'd had the breath for disagreement, did something a Brookwood room rarely does: it went quiet and stayed.

THEY DIDN'T TAKE it to the council first. They took it to the church-that-isn't-a-church, the grove's edge returning to public life after a century of being treated like a pretty superstition. Hazel met them at the path with her hands raw from work that always feels noble and is sometimes only work. She listened without interrupting as Marley read the first paragraph in that respectful reader's voice—the one she has when she is reading for a house instead of herself.

"Beacon of the Grove," Hazel said, and let herself smile in a way that allowed cynicism to keep its seat without ruling the table. "They wrote it down where it couldn't be erased cleanly. That's a kindness and a tactic."

Damien had brought the foam-cradled page in a shallow archival box that looked less important than it deserved to. He set it on the bench beneath the oldest oak and did not take the lid off, because the grove was breathing damp from the storm and paper is insensitive to poetry. "We're not here to feed it to the trees," he said mildly.

"No," Hazel said. "You're here because you know truth likes to be told in the place that lent it its tone." She looked at the box as if it contained a friend's baby. "It's enough for me to stand near it while it's real."

Marley's chest eased. Something about this small stop—this refusal to shove paper directly into politics without letting the place that bore its title witness it—satisfied a fairness she couldn't have explained yesterday without sounding precious. Today it sounded like procedure.

Helena arrived without her attorney and without her coat—the kind of gesture that reads as humility if you're feeling generous and strategy if you aren't. She took in the bench, the box, the unspectacular reverence with which the three others stood and did not say *I told you so.* She said, "May I?"

Damien hesitated the exact length of time it takes decency to remind care that it is not the same as distrust. He lifted the lid. He did not invite her to touch.

Helena leaned. Her eyes held the calm that lives inside anger when anger is useful. She read the line with Aurelia's name twice and then lowered her head in a gesture so small it could have been a leaf shadow. "It's worse and better than I hoped," she said. "Worse, because if it was in our exhibit frame, someone I used to admire put it there. Better, because no one gets to take it out of there now."

Marley watched Helena watch the words: *Aurelia Ward (Beacon of the Grove).* People in this town wear their ancestors like scarves—warm until the wind shifts, then strangling. Helena had always worn hers like a uniform. The softness in her mouth surprised Marley into liking her again.

"My great-grandfather chaired the bicentennial committee," Helena said. "He was a decent man who hated complexity wherever children could hear it. That is not a crime. It is also not an excuse." She looked up, the old steel politely sheathing itself. "You have what you need to change the plaques."

"We have what we need to change the minutes," Pollard corrected, appearing with perfect timing and the air of a man committed to the doctrine that paper is a sacrament. "Plaques are for seasonals. Minutes are for the problems of the living." He turned to Damien. "Shall we do our jobs, Mr. Hawthorne?"

Damien gestured back toward town. "Scanner, then safe," he said. "Then council. In that order."

They walked the fragment back into the world like a small procession returning a relic to its reliquary. In the scanner room, the second pass landed cleaner than the first. In the safe, the page slid into a polyester sleeve as if even old paper enjoys a new soft shirt. Chain-of-custody: signatures and dates and locations and temperature; the clerk's small delight at writing *Brookwood Town Charter—Leaf (Founders)* on a line that had been waiting for years to be filled without anyone noticing it had been waiting.

Then, council.

The afternoon meeting had been called for something else—ditch repair on the south road; a permit for a fence someone would later regret being so tall—and became, in that casual way small governments can surprise themselves with, a reckoning. The chair sat with his hands folded and looked at the archival sleeve as if it might get fingerprints through plastic. Two members leaned forward. One leaned back because leaning forward in public makes him itch. The clerk opened his minutes book as if it were a psalter.

Damien stood, which he dislikes doing, and did the merciful thing: he described. He did not advocate. He placed the page's facts where they could be examined: watermark, chain lines, iron gall, scribe, date; stitch holes;

knife-cut edge; offset; custody. He pointed at nothing. He let the paper teach the room.

"We acknowledge receipt of a fragment of the original 1826 charter," the chair said when words had finally found him. "We acknowledge that it lists Aurelia Ward as co-founder with the title Beacon of the Grove." He swallowed the next sentence, then let it come. "We acknowledge that the fragment was likely removed from the bound document intentionally sometime in the twentieth century." He looked at the clerk. "We will attach a certified image to the charter on file. We will... update public materials." The pause before *public* was a century long.

"May I?" Marley asked, because some sentences behave better when a woman says them. The chair looked relieved and afraid and waved his hand in the direction of common sense.

"This page confirms what many of us already suspected," Marley said. "Aurelia Ward's name belongs in the beginning of our town's story." She kept her tone sheared of romance. "We're not erasing Marwick to make room for Ward. We're correcting the hem so the garment fits." She let the metaphor fall in a room used to buttons. "And for what it's worth: the page was not thrown away. It was put where someone could reasonably find it later if they needed to." She didn't add *and if they were willing to be unpopular.* She didn't need to; half the room had spent years doing the work their neighbors preferred not to applaud.

The chair nodded once, as if acknowledging that soft speech could deliver hard medicine. "We'll form a subcommittee," he said reflexively, then flushed at his own habit. "No. Pollard will file the image and add a note to the charter's record. A plaque will be ordered for the headland memorial." He squinted at Damien. "You write it. You have the hand that offends the fewest."

"Ms. Taylor writes it," Damien said without looking away from Marley.

Marley inclined her head and did not let the smile get past her eyes. "Two names," she said. "One origin."

Helena's attorney cleared his throat in the manner of men whose job is to remind rooms that law exists when feelings begin to believe they predate it. "The Marwick estate has no objection to the correction," he said coolly. "The estate requests that the public record note the estate's cooperation." He didn't look at Helena. He didn't have to. She was looking at the floor the way people look at floors when they prefer not to be caught doing the right thing for complicated reasons.

The vote—because small towns vote even on gravity—was unanimous. The clerk wrote the motion and called the roll and signed his name and let his mouth quirk after the final flourish the way a child's does when a particularly good skip of rope completes a pattern she wasn't sure she had in her.

Outside, the late light had the expensive look of a day that knows it is about to be quoted. The beam at dusk would come; the town would watch. The grove, informed of its promotion to the title block, would not change how it smelled in the hour just after rain. But a seam had shifted. You could feel it even if you couldn't brag about it in a way that satisfied strangers.

When they reached the bottom of the steps, Damien exhaled the kind of breath he keeps for court when the ruling is what it ought to be and therefore harder to live with than the one that flatters your story. "Back to the office," he said. "I want to compare the fragment's stitch holes to the binding of the minutes volume that lost it."

"Lost," Marley echoed, her irony gentle enough not to bruise, and followed.

THE MINUTES BOOK lived where important messy things live: not in a display case but on a shelf that had taught generations to wash their hands before touching it. Pollard brought down Volume One like a priest taking a psalter to a sickbed —you could read the care in his wrists. The binding was a half-leather over boards, repacked twice by someone whose glue had outlived their taste. The first two signatures—gatherings of four sheets each, folded and sewn—sat true. The third carried a limp in its gait.

"Here," Damien said, finger hovering over a place where the thread pattern changed. The kettle stitch at the tail had been resewn—doubled and tied like a seam repaired by a mother who meant for a boy to get one more year out of his shirts. He turned two leaves. The stubs of a leaf remained, knife-cut clean near the fold. Across the gutter, in reverse, an offset ghosted the missing text—ink pressed that day, closed too soon, then forgotten. The impression of a seal ring—just the barest of a circle—bridged gutter to surviving leaf. "The removal happened after binding," he said. "Not before. Someone opened the book, cut the leaf, resewed the signature, and put the book back like the world had not shifted a degree." He looked at Pollard. "It was done with care."

Pollard's jaw worked in a motion that had nothing to do with chewing and everything to do with dignity. "Cowardice," he said again, without heat, which is always more dangerous than heat. "The kind that claims to be protecting children from complication. We have always been harsher to our dead than we think."

Damien didn't argue with or sanctify it. He measured. He placed the fragment's stitch holes over the book's empty space and felt the faint satisfaction you get when a lost screw threads exactly into the hole that has waited with more patience than hardware should endure. "It fits," he said. "Chain lines and hole spacing match. The break lands where the page would have turned at the founders list."

"Who?" Marley asked. Not accusation; inventory. "Who would have done it?"

"A person who loved parades," Evelyn said from the doorway, because in this town evidence often arrives in the hands of people carrying coffee. She set a thermos on the table like an offering and didn't apologize for listening. "A person who thought a complicated story would spoil the pancake breakfast." She smiled without humor. "We can bless them later. Today we fix it."

Damien closed the minutes book and set both hands on the cover, not to claim but to steady. "I'll write a memo with the forensic detail," he said—watermark, chain lines, hole spacing, knife edge, offset, resewn signature. "We'll attach the scan, file the custody log, and publish a notice for the record. The best way to undo an erasure is to make the correction tedious."

"Tedious," Marley repeated, and made it a word she'd like to embroider on a pillow. "Our patron saint."

They walked the memo to the clerk's inbox, because email doesn't make the same sound when it lands. Then Marley and Damien did what they always do when a room has absorbed too much truth in a day—they went to the café and sat near the window not to be seen but to let their bodies understand they were still in the century with spoons and steam.

Hazel came in behind the wind, scarf a leafier green than she usually allows it. She sat without asking and folded her hands around her cup as if it were a small animal that needed warmth. "You did the thing," she said, and didn't need to specify which.

"We did our jobs," Damien said, which is how he says grace when fatigue has made him forget the names of the sacraments.

"Beacon of the Grove," Hazel tested, tasting the line. "That'll look fine in letters a stranger can read."

"In letters our children can read," Evelyn corrected, refilling cups with the right kind of bossiness. "Strangers can buy a magnet."

The day went on being fine. People swept porches. The power company replaced a transformer with a cherry picker that looked too cheerful for the work. The storm's branch pile grew outside the Chapel like a plan for a bonfire no one would allow and everyone would long for. And at dusk, because the world is cruel and kind in steady proportion, the light rose and did what it has done since 1876 and, if anyone has sense, will continue to do after this room's names have been forgotten and the spiral's groove has softened: three short. Two long. Pause.

Marley and Damien climbed, not because the page demanded a vigil but because habit had become a liturgy they trusted. In the lantern room, everything looked the way it looks when a house has chosen to keep you: tidy, opinionated, not new, not ashamed. They stepped into the keeper's quarters and Marley set her palm near the seam, not on, a courtesy that had become a reflex as reliable as breath.

"The page fixes the story," Damien said behind her.

"It fixes the paper," Marley said. "The story will behave when people do." She didn't say *and we will hold them to it.* She didn't have to; he has made a career of fastening the lids of jars other people would leave open.

She lit no candle. The mirror stayed wrapped. The spiral lay quiet, because not every day can be thunder and script; some days need to normalize the behavior of rooms. They stood awhile in the ordinary and let it be the miracle.

On the way down, Marley paused at turn four and pressed her palm to the faint circle under paint—the north tick, the small honest notch. "Beacon," she said softly, as if trying the word on the mark. For a second, either her hand warmed or her body remembered warmth. She smiled at her own susceptibility and decided it didn't matter which.

At the base, the iron door offered a smaller groan than yesterday. They stepped out into the clean-edged evening, and the first sweep reached them: three quick lanes across the water like a signature returned to its owner.

Back in her apartment, Marley added three new cards to the wall because order is how she refuses drift:

Charter Fragment—Founders Leaf (1826)

—Aurelia Ward listed as "Beacon of the Grove."

—Watermark Brackley & Sons (1824), chain lines match, stitch holes indicate bound leaf.

—Leaf removed intentionally; resewn signature; offset ink ghost on facing leaf.

She taped a small copy of the line under it, in her own hand—the long simple title that made itself truer the more she looked at it: *Beacon of the Grove.* Then, because there are days when a person earns the right to be sentimental in private, she bent and pressed a sprig of lavender into the notebook's back page and closed it. Her aunt would have laughed at her for choosing ritual over reason and then handed her a spoon and told her to eat before sleep undid the good.

Damien texted a picture: the archival sleeve inside the safe, the label in Pollard's neat square print. *In custody. Filed. Boring paper first.* She laughed, and the laugh felt less like release and more like readiness.

On the headland, the sweep carried. In the stones, the bell kept its note in its mouth. In the grove, a wind walked the understory the way you walk a room after a meeting that changed less than you hoped and more than you feared.

And on a page that had waited behind a frame, in a room that smelled like floor wax and civic duty, a line sat where it had not sat for a hundred years, doing what lines do when they finally return to their paragraph: making it read the way the day was lived.

8

———

A RIFT IN THE FOG

Fog came in like a deliberation, slow and even, a gray counsel that didn't so much cover the town as invite it to hush. By afternoon, the harbor disappeared into its own breath, and the headland trimmed its silhouette to a single line. Marley stood at the café window with her notebook open and the scan of the charter fragment tucked under the flap, and practiced the sentence she would say to the council in the evening session: *the truth does not require an audience to be true, but it deserves one.*

Damien came in with the weather on his coat and the records room on his face—careful and already tired from being careful. He set down a folder whose weight was administrative rather than moral and gave her the look that meant he had five other looks underneath this one and they all wanted to keep the room from catching fire.

"They want to move slowly," he said, sliding into the chair opposite her. "Add the image to the charter on file, annotate the discrepancy, draft language for the new plaque, run a public comment period. A timeline of weeks. Maybe a month."

"Which is how you keep cows from bolting," Marley said. "Not people."

"It's how you keep a town from burning goodwill on a windy day," he answered, and even in fog the word *windy* drew a line between them. "Donors are already calling. The heritage committee wants to 'curate the announcement.' The chair of the school board wants to 'anticipate classroom questions.' The Marwick attorney wants the correction framed around cooperation, not error. If we push the fragment out tonight, we choose the worst version of our work's arrival."

Marley lifted the scan and set it between them. Even flat and printed, the words kept a temperature of their own: *Aurelia Ward (Beacon of the Grove)*. She remembered Hazel's hands at the grove; Pollard's steadying fuss; Helena looking at the floor because the page had turned on more of her family than she could hold without dropping other pieces. "Or we choose the honest one," Marley said. "No more exhibits with the leaf behind the frame, no more brochures that put a man where a chorus belongs."

Damien glanced toward the fogged window the way a man glances at a jury that hasn't been empaneled yet. "I'm not arguing against honest. I'm arguing for durable. You know how this town works. You put truth on a banner and a third of the room shows up to salute; a third mutters that the font is all wrong; and a third decides to hold a separate parade with pancakes."

"Then let them eat pancakes," she said, too quickly, and saw the flicker in his eyes—how contempt can arrive in a single syllable and take a whole afternoon to evict. She set her palm on the scan, gentled. "I don't mean to sneer. I mean that truth is not a condiment. It's the meal."

Evelyn arrived with the kind of tea people sip between

disagreements and the kind of look people keep for children who are about to climb a fence they've climbed every day of their lives and suddenly decided is too low. "Whatever you're doing," she said, "do it kindly."

"We're negotiating with fog," Damien said, forcing a small smile that didn't manage to be anything but dutiful. "I suppose that's already kind."

Marley ignored the tea until the steam stopped being theatrical and started being practical. "Helena can live with the correction," she said. "Pollard can file it. The council can add it to the minutes. All that's left is to tell the town what the town already knows."

"That last part is a landmine," he said, no heat, just the inventory tone he uses when a street's name changes three blocks from where a person thinks it does. "You want a paragraph in the Brookwood Bulletin that says, 'We erased a co-founder for a hundred years; our bad, here's her name'? You want to watch what happens at the next Town Day when the parade lineup has to put Ward and Marwick on the same banner? You want to listen to councilors who've sold the story their whole careers explain to grand-fathers why they were wrong? Because if you do it tonight —if you put it up on your wall and press publish—it will be you asking them those questions, not the minutes book."

Marley felt the old heat rise at the base of her skull— anger at the way *timing* gets used like a leash. "I don't want to watch anything burn," she said. "I want to stop pretending that keeping people's feelings intact is the same as telling the truth. The fragment exists. The line is clear. The removal was deliberate. We either say that now, in a few honest sentences, or we confirm every suspicion that we prefer to be tasteful rather than accurate." She softened.

"I'm not asking you to hurt anyone. I'm asking you to let the page breathe."

He pushed the folder toward her. Inside: printouts of emails—the heritage committee's desire to "roll this out in alignment with our seasonal programming"; a donor's cool note about "ongoing confidence"; a councilor's worry about "town harmony." He watched her scan them and made himself say the thing that painted him into the corner he was already standing in. "I am charged with keeping this place together," he said. "You know that's not just law—it's budget and grants and fire trucks and fair wages for the crew who puts flags up on the bridge twice a year. If we set this off wrong, I spend six months mopping the floor while you get to write a beautiful column about the stain's shape."

It was not fair; it was also not untrue. She looked up too fast and he flinched, not because she'd hurt him but because he hated how quickly he could make her look at him like that.

"You think I don't mop?" she asked, quiet. "You think telling a story straight doesn't cost?"

"I think our paychecks are signed on different lines," he said. "And I think if the town falls out with the Marwick estate, this building"—he gestured vaguely in the direction of the headland and every room it held—"sits empty an extra winter because the loaned objects stay in someone's climate-controlled closet."

"Then we build another exhibit," she said. "We put the rubbing of the spiral on the wall. We hang the scan. We teach people to love something that isn't behind glass."

He drew a breath and let it out slow, fog making the world look as if it were practicing the same discipline. "Will you wait a week?"

She knew he would ask it the way she knows where the

metronome's weight has to be for the tick to feel like a heartbeat rather than a toy. "No," she said. "We waited a century. I have a line to file—the column is facts with a paragraph of context. Pollard can attach the scan to the minutes today. The council can list the correction. We can announce without fanfare."

He rubbed the bridge of his nose and wondered when the habit had turned from human to cliché. "And if I say hold?"

"I'll print," she said, not a threat; a calibration. "And I'll sleep." Only when she said it did she feel the tremor in her sternum, as if someone had struck a tuning fork there and set all her old loyalties ringing.

He sat back, the creak of the chair loud enough to make Evelyn glance over her shoulder. "You're going to do it anyway."

"I am," she said. "Because the light is remembering and we either rise or we don't." She swallowed the next sentence —*because I saw her*—and kept it for herself. He knew. He had been there. He'd watched the mirror become deeper than glass. None of that mattered in a room where tea cooled and budgets had to balance.

"Then pardon me while I go figure out how not to let your honesty cost my crew their overtime," he said, without cruelty and therefore with more sting. He stood. She stood. They were two people who had kept each other steady in rooms that frightened other people. They looked like adversaries because the moment required the posture.

In the doorway he turned back with the softest possible rebuke. "You tell the town it's a seam," he said. "Not a tear."

"It's a seam," she said, and knew that he was asking her to sew in public without blood.

He left into fog that had grown so complete a person

could get lost between door and curb if they insisted on believing the town would tell them where to go. Marley felt the rift open—not a canyon; not even a crack. A rift in fog: a clarity between them that hurt precisely because she could see his shape so sharply inside it.

She tucked the scan into her bag. She paid for tea. She walked to the headland because the lighthouse, even wrapped in gray, kept the kind of honesty she could hold in her hands, and she needed to touch iron.

DAMIEN DID NOT GO BACK to the records room. He went to the low building behind the garage where the town's equipment sleeps—pickup trucks that do more theology than some sermons, barricades that know the price of parade routes, snow stakes waiting for a season no one is ready to name. He stood amid orange cones and smelled oil and thought of how much of his day is spent convincing stubborn objects to serve humans without complaint.

He loved this job the way a person loves a dog that needs walking at inconvenient hours: fiercely, but with an old anger at how often other people mistake loyalty for availability. He had not planned to be the man who made sure the town's lights worked and its papers kept their spine. But the work had made a habit of him, and habits can be holy if you keep them long enough.

His phone buzzed against the folder. A councilor. Then the chair. Then the heritage committee's chair—who wrote messages as if punctuation were an enemy. He turned the phone face down on the workbench and looked at his hands. He could argue Marley's position better than any of the people who would spend the afternoon asking him to soften a sentence until it became a napkin. He could also argue his own, because practical men grow into practical rooms and then can't tell if the room has grown into them.

He chose the small office off the garage because it had a door that closed and a window that faced nothing but a line of blue recyclables, which made it neutral by design. He sat and wrote the memo he had promised Pollard: *Subject: Founders Leaf—Forensic Summary & Binding Evidence.* He put in the words that strengthened rooms: *watermark, chain lines, stitch holes, resewn signature, offset ink, custody log appended.* He did not add a flourish. He did not need to.

When he finished, he didn't email it. He printed it and carried it across town to the clerk, because paper makes other people sit up straight more reliably than electrons. Pollard nodded through the summary, signed the receipt, and said the kind of sentence that makes Damien forgive the world. "It is a relief to be wrong in the direction of goodness."

"It is," Damien said.

Outside, the fog thickened until the buildings looked like models on a train set someone had forgotten to dust. He walked Main with his hands in his coat and felt the town breathe around him like an old dog. Helena's attorney stepped out of the bank as if waiting for him were part of the man's fee. "Mr. Hawthorne," the attorney said by way of greeting. "When will the council announce the correction? The estate would like to be on hand."

"When we've filed the fragment and drafted language that doesn't make us look like idiots," Damien said. "We're not selecting china patterns. We're acknowledging fact."

"The estate prefers the word *partnership*," the man said.

Damien stared at him until the attorney's smile bled out.

"The estate is welcome to prefer whatever reduces its headache," Damien said. "We will prefer accuracy." He left the man blinking in fog and wondered how many conversations of this type he had left in him before what he loved about the place became the thing that hurt him most.

He cut down to the harbor. Fog turned gulls to rumors and halyards to strings plucked by a tired god. He went to the pier just far enough to smell the tidal rot that keeps a town honest and stood with his hands on the rail until the wet went through his coat and gave him permission to go home.

Home, which is to say the small rented flat over the hardware store with the decent heat and the good morning light and the view of nothing important, received him without questions. He made coffee that had no business being as good as it was and read the letter he'd been not-reading since the storm: his daughter's handwriting, large and careful, asking whether she could come two weekends in a row if the weather held. He said yes out loud to an empty room and laughed at himself for saying it that way. He texted her yes with three exclamation points and then deleted two because he didn't want to embarrass the child into thinking enthusiasm is a disease.

The phone buzzed again. Not his daughter. A man whose name lived on plaques and annual reports. *Slow down,* the donor wrote. *The town needs stability. Tourists need a story they can keep in their heads.* Damien pictured the man's dining room table—wide and oaken—and saw in his mind the neat place cards everyone pretended not to notice. Stability is the word the comfortable use when other people's truths start moving furniture.

He didn't answer. He put the phone face down again like

a parent putting a toy on a shelf because it has become dangerous.

He went out at dusk anyway. Fog thickened toward night until the lighthouse could have been a rumor if you didn't know where to stand. He walked the headland path until the stone underfoot told him he had come far enough, and he watched for the beam he'd spent his adult life telling other people not to romanticize. He had seen the mirror deepen. He had seen the spiral write. He had kept the door shut while lightning tasted iron. If anyone had asked him five years ago what he thought about such things, he would have smiled and gotten on with the ditch permits.

Tonight the light did its pattern—three quick, two long—exact, patient. He felt suddenly and with no warning that he was tired of being patient about other people's fear. He also felt—the thought rose like the fog at his ankles—that he did not know how many more rooms he could stand in where telling the truth cost other people rent money. He had meant the sentence as a line he would never cross; tonight it felt like a line he might have to.

He went home through the gray and slept the wrong kind of sleep—the practical kind that repairs your body and leaves your mind to do its late work alone. Somewhere between two and three he woke with the sense of a hand on his shoulder and the absence of anyone to blame for it. *Cost,* the dark said. He put his forearm over his eyes and waited for morning like a man waiting for a verdict that would be unremarkable and life-altering in equal measure.

MARLEY CLIMBED to the lighthouse the way a person climbs to the only friend who refuses to flatter. The fog made the stairs feel shorter and longer at once. In the keeper's quarters the room held its breath in the way rooms do when the weather convinces them something important is happening and it would be rude to interrupt.

She did not light a candle. She did not open the window. She set the small mirror on the desk face-down because she refused to ask it to be extraordinary three days in a row. She took out her notebook and wrote the column she would file to the Bulletin before midnight—no adjectives, or very few; no speeches; no crusade. *The town has found a missing page from the 1826 charter. The page lists Aurelia Ward as co-founder with the title Beacon of the Grove. The page shows evidence of having been cut from the bound charter. The council has scanned and filed the image to the record.* She added a sentence not perforated with feeling and therefore stronger for it: *It is good for a town to know its own name at the beginning of a paragraph.*

She read it aloud once. Not to dramatic effect—just to see if the room lifted any word and set it back down corrected. It did not. The room agreed with the sentences by refusing to applaud. She sent the text, closed the notebook, and waited for the small tremor in her hands to choose something else to inhabit.

At the stair she met Hazel, who had climbed without rattling because fog allows certain women to arrive without telling anyone what the arrival will cost. "You look like you carried an armful of kindling in from rain and decided to light none of it," Hazel said.

"I filed the column," Marley said.

Hazel studied her face. "And someone you love will be irritated because that is his job."

"He will," Marley said. "I don't love him because he agrees. I love him because he stays."

Hazel touched her own brow briefly, old habit checking on old weather. "He'll stay," she said. "But he'll walk a wider circle around the truth tonight to see if it bites."

"He's allowed," Marley said, because her aunt had taught her that love and permission share more territory than most people want to admit. "I don't have to like it."

They stood shoulder to shoulder for a minute and listened to the fog talk to the glass. It said nothing useful and everything true. "You could take a night off," Hazel said. "Eat soup. Sit by a radiator. Let the light remember without supervision."

"I could," Marley said, and heard in her own voice the way people talk about quitting a job neither money nor common sense will let them abandon. "I'll go home soon."

Hazel squeezed her wrist the way women in this town have taken to touching each other lightly when the town behaves itself and needs no extra ceremony. "I'll walk you down," she said.

At the base, they separated: Hazel further down Main; Marley toward her apartment; the fog toward whatever work fog does when the town sleeps. Her phone ticked with Damien's message before she put the key in the lock.

You filed.

I did, she texted back. She stared at the screen and decided to use punctuation as a peace offering. *I kept it simple.*

He didn't reply right away. She paced the small room, checked her wall, straightened the card that had slipped— *Keeper's Logbook—1876*—and made tea she did not drink. When the phone buzzed she did not pretend she'd been doing anything else.

It's good, he wrote. *It's also going to be loud.*

We can stand loud, she replied. *We've stood lightning.*

Lightning doesn't vote, he wrote, and she laughed despite herself because his worst jokes built scaffolding under her when other people's better ones did not. A minute later another message: *I just need a night.*

She typed *Take two,* then deleted it, because magnanimity is a performance and she didn't want to perform. She wrote, *Take the night. We'll talk in the morning.*

She lay down with the window cracked the way she used to when the town's noises were enough to keep her company and not yet enough to feel like someone else's responsibility. The column went live in five minutes. The comments folder opened in ten like a mouth. She didn't check it. She slept the kind of sleep that comes as a reward for doing the thing you did not want to do and did anyway.

Morning delivered its efficiency: four emails from the council (measured relief/concern), two from donors (cool), one from a teenager (five words: *that name belongs thank you*), and a voicemail from the heritage chair asking whether she might consider the phrase *co-equal stewardship* for the plaque. Marley showered, dressed, ignored her hair, and went to the café.

Damien wasn't there. Evelyn was, handing out coffee like ballast and looking at Marley with the wry mouth of people pleased you did what you were put here to do and sorry for the price of it. "He's at the garage," she said. "Counting sandbags, I expect."

"Do we need sandbags?" Marley asked.

"In this town," Evelyn said, "we always need sandbags. Sometimes they're made of cloth. Sometimes they're called patience." She set a plate down with a slice of something that could forgive most politics. "Eat while you wait or don't wait at all."

Marley took the plate and the door and the fog and

found Damien where Evelyn had said—near the sandbags, near the trucks, near the work that asks for hands and not opinions. He looked at her the way a person looks at a road sign in fog—grateful for the instruction and vaguely irritated that the sign refuses to move closer. "Good column," he said.

"Thank you," she said.

"You made it a seam," he added, and she nodded because sometimes applause is a single accurate critique.

They stood with the smell of wet canvas and oil between them. The rift was still there—a little lane of empty air where something used to live and would again if both of them chose breathing over posture. He kicked a pebble; it made a small sound too definite for fog.

"I'm going to get yelled at tonight," he said without self-pity.

"I know," she said. "I will, too."

"Not by the same people."

"No," she said. "But by relatives."

He laughed, because of course. "I need to say a thing you won't like," he said, bracing.

"Say it," she said, bracing.

"I am not sure," he said, letting each word find its leg, "that we can keep unearthing everything without breaking the floor. There are people whose houses are built on the neat version. There are budgets that will choose between truth and overtime. I am not telling you to stop. I am saying I don't know how far I can go without turning into the kind of man I don't let my daughter see."

It was not the sentence she'd feared. It was worse and better. She felt the reflex rise—*we can do both*—and set it down because she didn't have a plan yet that did not rely on him to absorb the shock. "Then step back when you have to," she said. "I don't need you bruised to prove you care."

He blinked, surprised into relief and irritation. "That's very reasonable," he said, which in his mouth meant *that's very hard.*

She reached, not for his hand, but for the hem of his sleeve the way a person checks the stitch on a seam they sewed last winter and hopes it still holds. "We're not done," she said.

"No," he agreed, looking toward the headland where the lighthouse—only the lower third visible—held its line. "We're just louder."

Fog shifted, flensed by a small wind off the water that had decided to make itself useful. For a breath, the rift between them filled and they were just two people in the same air again. Then it thinned and the shape of each stood out from the other with the precision of a blueprint.

"I have to go," he said, which meant meetings, calls, the tedious construction of a ramp other people would run down and then complain about the angle. "Dinner?"

"Tomorrow," she said.

"Tomorrow," he repeated, which was either a promise or a placeholder; they would decide later.

He walked away with his shoulders making a sentence she had learned to read and not annotate. She stayed a minute longer, listening to the town's small noises discover themselves after a night of comment threads. Then she went to the headland to put her palm near, not on, the seam and tell the lighthouse what she had done.

It offered back the same thing it always offers when people bring it their private dramas: steadiness, without irony. She laughed at herself, at her column, at the way love for a place can trick you into thinking you invented it. Fog thinned, then thickened. The beam, dutiful and untroubled, found its panes: three quick, two long.

She took the stairs down. Halfway to the path she stopped, turned her face toward town, and said out loud to no one in particular, "Truth first," as if reminding fog what shape it had agreed to take.

In the garage, Damien picked up his phone to check a weather advisory and found instead a message from a council member he liked more than he should: *You did fine. It'll be messy a while. Keep your crew close.* He put the phone down and pressed his palms to the workbench until his hands stopped wanting to break something to make order. Across the street a child on a scooter dragged a stick along the curb, drawing a quick line in wet dust that the next car's tire would erase. He watched the mark disappear and did not take it as an omen, only as a report.

He looked toward the headland through the fog, saw nothing, saw everything, and asked the question he had been trying not to hear: *How much of me does this cost?* It did not feel like betrayal. It felt like inventory.

Down the block, Evelyn set out a sign that said SOUP in chalk and drew a little constellation beside it: three quick dots, two long dashes. She didn't know she'd done that. Or she did and had decided that the day could use a joke only the lighthouse would get.

Marley passed the sign and smiled with her whole face and didn't stop to explain to anyone why. She had work to do—the kind that uses both hands—and she'd do it, fog or no fog, with a seam, not a tear, and with patience, even now that patience had turned itself into the thing she would have to ask for and give at the same time.

They were both, in their different rooms, measuring cost and writing receipts in a town that had made them treasurers of a story no longer content to hide. The rift would close when it closed. In the meantime the light kept time like a metronome you can see from anywhere: three short, two long, then a pause that makes room for breath, and in the pause, the quiet knowledge that truth does not behave —it persists.

9

———

A CANDLE FOR SIGHT

The storm's wake had left the town rinsed clean, though in the keeper's quarters the damp clung to the beams with a patience that salt never lost. Marley sat with the small cedar box Hazel had pressed into her hands the morning after—the one with the fresh blend of herbs and tallow poured into wax so pale it looked like winter pressed thin. The scent lifted when she lifted the lid: rosemary for focus, lavender for calm, a thread of cedar to ground, and something sharper she could not name but knew belonged.

She placed the candle near the seam of the floorboards where the spiral lived like a secret heartbeat. The metronome ticked softly on the desk, a courtesy rhythm rather than a command. She struck a match, and the flare startled her with its brightness after the day's long gray. The flame caught, leaned, then steadied, and the room shifted the way rooms do when they accept an invitation.

Damien had not come. Their last conversation still lay between them, a seam held tight with visible stitches. She had not asked him to stand beside her for this—not because she did not want his presence, but because there are some doors a person must open without company. He would have argued the timing, reminded her of the council's evening agenda, but she knew the spiral's patience had limits. It wanted attending, and she could not pretend she hadn't heard it breathe during the storm.

The flame wavered once as if answering the spiral, then flared taller, a tongue reaching toward the ceiling. The scent deepened, weaving with the damp, and Marley's eyes blurred—not with tears but with that particular shift of vision that comes when the line between one reality and another thins.

She leaned forward, hands flat on her knees. "If you're going to speak, speak," she whispered—not defiance, not plea. Simply readiness.

The room folded. Not dark, not gone—folded, as if another skin had slipped over it. Her gaze dropped to the spiral, and what had been carved lines became light: threads of green-gold running the groove like water in a channel. Her body leaned toward it without her permission, eyes fixed.

She did not close them. She let the light climb up her, and when it reached her chest she felt it take the breath she'd meant to draw.

The room dissolved.

She stood on the stairwell of the tower—not the modern stairs with their metal rails, but the older spiral of timber polished by years of feet. She knew because the grain shone as if lit from within, and the air smelled of oil and sea, salt and smoke, as if every lantern trimmed in the century before her still carried its scent forward.

Footsteps pressed above her, lighter than hers. She turned. Aurelia Ward—though Marley knew her name only after her body recognized her—was climbing with steady arms, a child in them. A boy, perhaps no more than three, hair damp from sea air, wrapped in wool. He did not cry. He slept against her shoulder, his face pressed to the green of her shawl.

Aurelia did not look at Marley, though Marley knew she was seen. She climbed, sure-footed, whispering words against the child's hair. Marley strained, and the words fell into her like water down stone.

"He must carry the light forward, no matter the burden."

The sentence struck as firmly as a bell. Marley gripped the rail to steady herself, but her hands found no wood, only light—the stair itself glowing under her touch. She gasped and the vision pulsed brighter, filling her mouth with the taste of salt, her skin with damp as if sea spray had reached her.

Aurelia reached the lantern room door, pressed it open with a shoulder, and vanished into radiance. The child shifted in her arms as if dreaming, but she never broke her step.

The flame on Marley's candle guttered, and the vision bent away like cloth pulled from a table. The tower returned to her body's present: keeper's quarters, desk, seam, spiral, candle. She sat breathless, knees weak, palms wet. She lifted them and stared. They gleamed with moisture though the room had no leak. Salt air lingered on her lips, sharp and bracing, as though she had walked the headland in a gale.

Her breath shook. She reached for the notebook, but her hands trembled enough that the pencil left a jitter in every line. She wrote anyway, pinning the words before they could dissolve into dream. *Aurelia carrying a child. Lantern stairs. Shawl green. Whisper: "He must carry the light forward, no matter the burden." Salt air. Wet skin. Not imagined. Seen.*

She underlined the last two words until the pencil snapped. Then she folded forward, forehead to her knees, and let herself feel the weight of what she had been handed.

The spiral glowed faintly still, as though pleased.

And Marley, breath uneven, knew she had stepped into someone else's memory and come back wearing its salt.

THE CANDLE BURNED STEADY AFTER, as if it had always been meant to light long vigils. Marley sat upright again, forcing her shoulders back, copying the words twice into her notebook in case her hands forgot how to read her own haste. She kept glancing at the seam, half-expecting the glow to return, but the spiral lay quiet, grooves dark again.

Aurelia's whisper repeated in her skull—*He must carry the light forward.* She traced the sentence in the margin with the back of her knuckle, as though the act of writing had etched it deeper into her. Who was *he*? The child? The lineage? The keeper? Damien? Or someone still waiting to be named?

Her heart beat too quickly. She stood and paced, but the room gave her no relief. Every time she drew breath, the tang of salt stung her tongue. She rubbed her palms against her jeans—still damp, still faintly brined. She laughed once, a sound without humor, and whispered, "You weren't subtle, Aurelia."

The lamp on the desk reflected her face, pale and drawn. She thought of Damien and his relentless care for what was durable. He would call this a vision. He would ask if she'd eaten enough, if the candle smoke had played tricks. He would not dismiss her—not after the mirror, not after lightning stitched the spiral—but he would ask for more proof than skin damp with salt. And she had none but the truth of her body.

Still, she had to tell him. She could not let this rest in her alone, not when the spiral had chosen to show her what it had kept hidden for over a century. She closed the notebook, blew out the candle, and gathered both into her bag. The scent clung to her clothes, herbs threaded with sea.

Outside, fog rolled low across the headland. The beam cut through it with patient rhythm, three short, two long, as if reminding her that whatever she had seen was of a piece with the present. She descended the path, heart pounding, and made her way toward the garage where Damien was likely counting something practical enough to resist history's weight.

She found him bent over the sandbags, hands chalked with dust. He looked up, read her face before she spoke, and frowned. "What did you do?"

She didn't waste words. She set the notebook on the bench, opened to the page, and let him read the rushed scrawl. His jaw tightened.

"You burned it again," he said, not a question.

"Yes."

"And you saw—"

"I saw her. Aurelia. Carrying a child up the stairs. She said—" Marley swallowed, her throat dry. "She said, 'He must carry the light forward, no matter the burden.'"

Damien's eyes flickered across her, looking for the proof she couldn't give. His gaze landed on her damp sleeves, the salt crust faintly drying at the edge of her wrist. He reached, touched her palm, and drew back as though the moisture startled him. "You're wet," he said.

"There's no leak in that room."

He closed the notebook slowly, as if afraid of sealing

something inside it. "You're asking me to believe you crossed into her memory."

"I'm not asking," Marley said. "I'm telling you. The spiral showed me. The candle opened it. And now I know there's more here than codes and fragments. There's lineage. There's inheritance."

Damien's brow furrowed. He leaned back against the bench, arms crossed, posture defensive not against her but against what the world kept putting in his hands. "If it's inheritance, then the child matters. Who was he? Where did he go? If he carried the light forward, why did the town erase the one who bore him?"

Marley shivered, the salt drying on her skin tightening. "That's what we have to find out."

He exhaled, long. "And in the meantime, we keep it quiet."

"No." Her voice rose, sharper than she meant, but firm. "Every time we keep it quiet, we repeat what they did. I won't do that."

His eyes narrowed. "Then you'll have to decide if you want to keep me beside you when you do the opposite."

The silence between them held longer than comfort, filled with fog pressing at the door. Marley felt her body still humming with Aurelia's words, with the echo of a child's weight she had not carried, and she thought: some truths are burdens, yes, but they are also torches.

"I'm not letting this go," she said, softer now, but with steel underneath.

"I know," he said. "That's what frightens me."

NIGHT DEEPENED, and Marley returned to her apartment with the candle still unlit in her bag. She set it on the table, staring at the wick, half-tempted to light it again and demand more. But exhaustion wrapped her, and she feared what might answer if she forced the spiral twice in one day. She left it cold.

She changed clothes, but the scent of salt lingered on her skin. She lay on the bed with her notebook beside her, reading the words again and again: *He must carry the light forward, no matter the burden.*

Sleep came in waves, restless. She dreamed of stairs, of shawls green as moss, of small shoulders resting heavy against her own. In the dream she climbed, and each step hummed like the spiral's groove, carrying her higher into light.

When she woke, her throat was dry, her hair damp, and the bedsheets smelled faintly of sea. She touched her lips and tasted salt.

The candle sat where she'd left it. The spiral lay waiting in the tower. The light swept over the town with patient rhythm, three short, two long, as if to say: the burden is real, the burden is yours, the burden is forward.

Marley sat up, reached for her pencil, and wrote one last line before dawn broke the fog: *I carried nothing—but I woke as if I had.*

The page stared back at her, steady as the beam.

And in the quiet, she understood: the spiral had not shown her history. It had handed her an inheritance.

10

———————

THE COUNCIL'S REPROACH

By six, fog had braided itself into the eaves of the Chapel and hung there like a council of elders. The bell-rope in the vestibule breathed a damp, tarry smell, and the floorboards gave their long, civic sighs as shoes found their familiar creaks. Marley arrived with the archival sleeve in a flat gray case Pollard had lent her—the kind of practical object that could pass for a placemat if you weren't paying attention—and a notebook clipped shut with her pencil as if restraint were a tool you should be able to buy.

Damien came in from the side door with the chair of the council and two members Marley could have sketched from posture alone: one who leaned forward when the word *budget* was in the agenda, one who leaned back when the word *change* appeared in any language. He'd shaved, badly, which meant he was nervous. The clerk sat with his minutes book open and a damp press cloth folded on the table for hands as prone to sweat as consciences.

Rows filled with the usual Brookwood cross-section: fishermen who smelled faintly of diesel and good rope;

volunteers in windbreakers bearing logos of events that never required perfect weather to count as success; the heritage committee with their earnest tote bags; three teachers; a pair of teenagers who had come to see whether adulthood was as tedious as rumored. Helena Marwick Vale sat two rows back, hair pinned, expression in that neutral register polished at funerals. Hazel stood by the rear door with a paper cup of something steaming and an expression that would have made most storms correct their posture.

The Mayor, Richard Connelly, rapped his gavel once and dispensed with niceties the way you do when fog and news share a room. "Special session of the Brookwood Town Council," he said. "We are convened to discuss research activities in the lighthouse and the recent publication of a column in the *Brookwood Bulletin*—and to address what some have called disruption of town harmony."

The phrase hit the room like a coat dropped over a chair in a house that had already learned how to wear chill without complaint. Damien's jaw worked. Marley felt heat rise in the back of her throat, that precise salt that means your body recognizes an old word as a new insult. She put her hand on the case, not quite a vow.

"Ms. Taylor," Mayor Connelly said without looking at her. "Mr. Hawthorne. You've been busy."

Pollard cleared his throat as if to remind the room that facts should be placed on the table before opinions set up a card game there. "For the record," he said, one hand on his minutes, "the town received an archival leaf this week—the Founders page from the 1826 charter. It was scanned, logged, and secured. Ms. Taylor reported its existence in the *Bulletin*. Mr. Hawthorne requested a review period for authentication and chain-of-custody."

The mayor nodded. "And yet," he said, turning toward Marley, "you went to print."

"I told the truth," Marley said, no microphone, no apology. "Aurelia Ward is listed as co-founder with the title *Beacon of the Grove*. The page shows it was cut from the bound charter. I wrote exactly that. No adjectives."

A councilor with a tidy beard leaned back, index fingers tented, a posture that usually preceded the kind of sentence that attempts to domesticate trouble. "We've spent a century building consensus around a founding narrative," he said. "Your piece—while no doubt... diligent—has already stirred friction. Donors are concerned. The heritage committee has a calendar."

From the second row, someone snorted softly and failed to say *pancakes*. Hazel didn't move, but her mouth smiled the way a person's mouth smiles when a bishop confuses incense with oxygen.

Marley unclipped her pencil. "Consensus built on omission is not harmony," she said. "It's quiet."

The room did the small intake a town does when a sentence lands in exactly the chair it was placed for. The mayor tapped his gavel once—a courtesy, not a threat. "Let's keep it to procedure."

Damien stepped forward then, a man who has found that if you say *procedure* in the right tone you can get two groups of people who hate each other to agree to pass a salt shaker without poisoning anyone. "We have the fragment," he said. "We have a scan. We have initial forensic consistencies—watermark, chain lines, stitch holes. We have a resewn signature in the minutes book where the page was removed. The proper next step is formal authentication: ink assay, paper dating, comparative script. I'm asking for a week to complete that work and to consult with the state archivist."

He sounded reasonable and therefore, in Brookwood, a little like a traitor to drama.

A woman on the end—teacher, short hair, hands that have passed out more permission slips than are good for anyone—raised a hand halfway to her shoulder and let it fall. "No one needs a week to read a name," she said softly.

"We don't," Damien agreed. "But we need a week to write what happened in a way that can't be un-written the first time someone with a checkbook looks at the ceiling." He didn't look at Helena's attorney; he didn't have to. The man's glare made its own weather.

Another councilor, older, with a tie he had put on crooked and not noticed because the town has never paid an elected person enough to justify a mirror, folded his arms. "And the lighthouse," he said, switching lanes. "This business with candles and... visions? Weren't we told there'd be no ceremony?"

Marley felt the room tilt—the way it does when someone opens a door that would have been safer sealed with tape. "We're not staging rites," she said evenly. "We're listening to the building's history in the materials. We found the keeper's log with references to 'dreamlight patterns' and the 'silent woman.' We documented lightning phenomena in the spiral carving. We have notes, dates, witnesses."

"You lit a candle," the bearded councilor said, as if quoting from a manual on how to reduce complexity to misdemeanor.

"I did," Marley said, because today honesty refused to hide in the pantry. "And I sat while the room remembered. We're caretaking memory. I used to think that job belonged to the library. I was wrong."

A murmur went around the back rows—cautious, not

hostile. The teenagers stopped pretending to be on their phones.

The mayor put both hands on the table. "The phrase 'disrupting town harmony' was not mine," he said, weary without theatrics. "But it has been used. We cannot keep ripping up the boards of our story without considering what happens to the people who live on it."

Marley's pencil clicked against the table once before she put it down. "We're not ripping," she said. "We're lifting a seam and sewing truth back in."

Damien's silence beside her had a temperature she could recognize with her eyes closed. He was doing the math she had mocked in the café—overtime, grants, sandbags, fire trucks, the goodwill banked by a man who keeps things working. He said, very gently: "Give us seven days. Let me do the science and the chain-of-custody and the paperwork so that when we say *Aurelia Ward is co-founder* no one can make it smaller with posture."

Mayor Connelly looked grateful the way people look grateful when someone offers to pay for lunch after you already embarrassed yourself wrestling your wallet. "A week," he said, and rapped his gavel.

From behind Marley's shoulder, a whisper rode the fog in under the door. Or perhaps it was someone in the third row failing to be quiet. Either way, she felt her stomach muscle tighten in recognition of a different kind of weather: warning. She turned her head to see who had breathed it, and met the eyes of Councilwoman Lorraine Gearhart—a woman with soft gray hair and a voice like a coat that has chosen to be warm rather than fashionable. Lorraine's mouth did not move. Her hand did. A paper, folded once, slid along the table edge to rest against Marley's sleeve. No one else noticed. Lorraine's gaze returned to her lap like a pond putting its surface back where it belongs after a breeze.

Marley didn't look. She could feel the temperature of the note through the sleeve of her jacket. The chair moved to the next item. The fog held to the windows. Pollard's pen went about its kind, legal scratching. And in Marley's chest, the echo of a whisper from last night—*He must carry the light forward*—turned itself into posture.

THEY TOOK A RECESS—THE mayor's idea of mercy—so that donors could murmur, the heritage committee could hiss its calendar at the air, and Helena's attorney could practice the kind of smile that fools no one who has ever split the bill. Damien stepped aside with Pollard to discuss scanner settings and heat thresholds the way you discuss coffee when everyone else is scared of the words they mean. Marley slipped the folded paper into her palm, moved three steps toward the vestibule, and read:

The light's been hiding things for a reason.

No signature. No underlining. No explanation. The handwriting was the kind of neat you learn from grade-school notebooks when you were a child in a decade that cared about penmanship. Lorraine Gearhart's, almost certainly—she had labeled bake sale sign-up sheets in that exact square hand for thirty years.

Hiding. Not forgetting. Not losing. Hiding. Marley folded the note back on its crease and slid it into the back of her notebook where good sentences sleep until they know what they weigh.

"Everything all right?" Helena asked, materializing with a gift for timing that would have looked predatory if she weren't so evidently tired of her own family's weather. "You look like someone just told you a riddle with your name at the end."

"Do they all," Marley said, because there are only two ways people like Helena can be managed in public: humor or clips. "We have a week."

Helena's mouth tightened. "You have seven days before people who like their lives neat give themselves permission to find names for you they can say out loud. Use them." She tipped her head toward the front. "He's playing it shrewd," she added, meaning Damien.

"He's buying us time," Marley said. "Which is the same thing." She did not add that time can be both a gift and the place where fear grows legs.

When the gavel called them back, Damien took the center like a reluctant priest. His notes were neat, printed in a hand that would not embarrass a map. "Here's the plan," he said. "We'll verify the fragment with external experts: ink assay at the state lab, paper dating with fiber analysis, comparison of the clerk's hand to other documents in our minutes. We'll examine the bound charter for evidence of removal—thread anomalies, cut edges, signatures resewn. We'll publish the results, attach scans, and file them to the record."

The bearded councilor lifted his brows at the words *publish the results* as if *publish* was a direction only newspapers knew, which explained a lot about this town's tendency to rely on bulletin boards and rumor.

Pollard added dryly, "We'll also correct the display case labels, since it seems we've been wasting a very good frame on a portrait of a beard."

A ripple of laughter loosened the room the way laughter does when it's safe. Mayor Connelly allowed it and then put the lid back on with the gavel, one polite knock. "Any objections?"

"Just the usual," someone muttered. "Change."

The vote to grant the week wasn't formal—Brookwood has the kind of councils where half the decisions are decided by men who know how to read rooms and the other half by the women who mop them—but it carried by posture. The mayor wrote a line. Pollard gave the line a home in the minutes. People stood and stretched, thinking about dinner, television, the weather tomorrow and whether it would remember their errands kindly.

On the way out, Lorraine Gearhart caught Marley's sleeve the way a woman catches a child stepping off a curb into a street she hadn't noticed. "We invited the light for a reason," Lorraine said, not wasting the sentence on anyone but the one it could help. "We hid for one, too."

"Which reason?" Marley asked around the unfamiliar ache in her chest.

"To keep people safe from the wrong kind of weather," Lorraine said. "And to keep the right kind of work from being ruined by the first." She released Marley's sleeve. "You know the difference. Most people don't. Not at speed."

Marley had questions—about the grove, about Aurelia, about that old phrase *silent woman*—but the right number of questions to ask an older woman in a doorway is one fewer than you have. She nodded instead. "Thank you."

Lorraine gave her an expression that belonged on old coins. "Seven days," she said. "That's either a week or a warning."

Outside, fog had gone from foreman to collaborator. It lifted in small lanes without clearing, revealing pockets of brick and lamplight as if the town were learning how to show itself again one wall at a time. Damien was on the steps with the chair, heads inclined, the posture of men negotiating the cost of the right thing. Helena stood at the curb with her attorney and said nothing to him in a way that made her intent clear.

When Damien joined Marley at the bottom of the steps, his shoulders had loosened half an inch, which, for him, counted as yoga. "We have a week," he said, as if the gavel had only just allowed him to say it out loud without consequence.

"I know," she said. "Lorraine Gearhart gave me a note." She passed it. He read, frowned as if trying to see the rest of the sentence on the back, and tucked it back as though it might have a temperature.

"Hiding," he said. "You think she means the town's elders? Or the building?"

"Both," Marley said. "But I don't think she means 'hide it and keep it.' I think she means what Hazel says about salt and doorways. Hiding as in tucking until the weather is right to carry. We're not the first people to choose timing over appetite."

He looked relieved and infuriated by that wisdom, which made her love him and want to push him into the sea in alternating breaths. "You're going to take the note as permission to go faster," he said.

"I'm going to take it as permission to be careful," she returned. "Careful is not slow."

They stood together a moment, a seam in fog closing and opening in front of them like a well-timed breath. The lighthouse beam didn't make it this far down Main, but they could feel its rhythm, a metronome you wear in your chest once you've learned it—not a magic trick, just the body's agreement with an honest second.

"Tomorrow," he said. "State lab. I'll call in a favor."

"I'll go to the grove," she said, because she had already decided that the note's second half—*for a reason*—meant the right place to ask the right question was under trees, not under fluorescents. "Hazel will know which reason applies to today."

He nodded, then didn't move, then nodded again like a man resetting a watch to the time the world is actually keeping. "Don't light anything," he said, and they both smiled at how little either believed in other people's self-restraint.

THEY PARTED—HE toward the office with its humming scanner room, she toward the headland because the notion of going home with the case still in her bag felt like a kind of rudeness to the day. On the path the ocean was hidden in every direction and everywhere at once, the way grief can make a person seem both nearer and far. The keeper's quarters took her in the way a house does when you've kept your appointment with it without scheduling. She set the case on the desk, not to open it—Pollard would have her head—but to let the object feel a room that had borne the first sentence it contained long before glass learned to lie about age.

She did not light the candle. She placed it beside the seam as a courtesy and took out the small mirror to lay facedown, because she could only ask a tool to be brave so many nights in a row without paying for the privilege. She sat, hands on her knees, and listened to the building breathe.

The light's been hiding things for a reason. Whose voice? Lorraine's ink, yes. But farther back, another sentence climbing the stair: *He must carry the light forward, no matter the burden.* She had gone to sleep with the taste of salt on her mouth, had woken with the sentence in her ribs. She felt strangely matter-of-fact about it—like a person told the location of a toolbox in a neighbor's garage and expected to fix a hinge during a storm.

From the stairwell, a small sound: not the bell, not the draft, something like the click a watch makes on a wrist you're still learning to trust. Marley rose, crossed to the door, and put her hand to the iron. It was colder than the room by one true degree. She stood with the door half-open, listening to a darkness that had chosen, for now, to be nobody's enemy.

Below, she heard the echo of a footfall that could have been memory but felt like mercy. Up here, the spiral lived the way a good sentence lives behind your teeth until you need it. She went back to the desk and wrote the week into boxes she could carry without dropping:

Seven Days

— Day 1: Damien—ink assay / paper fiber (state lab); Marley—grove / Hazel—ask why hiding.

— Day 2: Compare stitch holes to bound charter (depth scan); consult regional conservator re: knife marks, resewn signatures.

— Day 3: Keeper's log cross-reference: search for infant/child references, any 'carrying' entries; catalog all mentions of "silent woman."

— Day 4: Oral history: speak with Lorraine Gearhart privately; ask what was hidden to keep whom safe.

— Day 5: Draft public notice; plaque language—two names, one origin; include *Beacon of the Grove*.

— Day 6: Photographs of spiral in raking light; non-invasive UV on carving to check residues; no rituals.

— Day 7: File report; bring biscuits to meeting; prepare for weather, weather being people.

She ran a line through the last item and wrote, lighter, *Remember to eat.* Then she closed the notebook and set her palm near, not on, the seam, a gesture that had become for her what grace used to be when she was young and prayers were recited rather than lived.

"Thank you for the week," she said—addressed to the room, to the council, to the stubbornness in Damien that loved procedure because it believes it can keep people from bleeding when they insist on turning their own knives.

On her way down, at turn four, she touched the faint circle under the paint—the north tick—and felt the smallest warming, or she imagined it and decided the distinction was no longer a helpful god. Outside, fog opened just enough to show the suggestion of sea. Behind her, the tower stood within the weather like a sentence that has been tested and does not need italics to do its work.

Damien's week began before his coffee cooled. He phoned the state lab's archivist—a woman with a steady voice and the kind of enthusiasm you hear only in people who know how to say *no* without apology. "Bring the fragment in the morning," she said. "We'll pull the iron gall kit; fiber microscopy is at your service; I'll throw in two graduate students who think history is a Netflix category."

He laughed for the first time that day and wrote *9 a.m.—state lab* on his legal pad. Then he pulled the charter from the safe, opened to the stitched place, and peered through the loupe at the knife marks near the fold. The cut edge was clean; the resewn thread had been tied with the kind of tight that says *don't come apart on me now*. He documented. He photographed. He wrote in a voice as dry as a judge's mouth. He was good at this; being good at things had kept him safe for most of a life in a town where safety had a high currency and a bad exchange rate.

Helena came by. She didn't sit. "You got your week," she said.

"We did," he answered. If he noticed that they were both using the plural without bravado, he didn't tell his face.

"Make it tedious," she said. "Make it so legal that the men at my family table have to leave the room to shout."

He smiled without showing teeth. "As long as they leave the page alone."

Walking home in thickening dark, Marley reread Lorraine's note at red lights she pretended she hadn't noticed. **The light's been hiding things for a reason.** She let the words find the shape of a story that wasn't a conspiracy but a courtesy: women folding names into books so a time that wanted to smash them wouldn't find them; keepers writing as if the sea might grade their homework; a town that chose the neat version out of fear and now had to learn to live with the one that loved them better.

Her phone vibrated. A text from Hazel: *Come by in the morning. Bring the candle. I have a theory and a headache.* Another from Evenlyn: *Soup pot on at eight. It's democracy-flavored.*

And one from Damien, late enough that its gentleness had no angle: *Thank you for not lighting anything. We're going to need our lungs tomorrow.*

She typed: *I don't promise tomorrow.* Then deleted it and wrote: *See you at nine after the grove.* Then: *Boring paper first.* Then, because tonight had felt like enough bravery for a town that prefers not to clap: *Sleep.*

He replied with a photograph of the loupe over the cut edge, the fiber of old paper bright as hair. *We'll make it hold,* he wrote.

In bed, Marley lay with her palm on her ribs and felt the sentence that had moved into her house—*He must carry the light forward, no matter the burden*—rearrange furniture without asking. If the light had hidden this long for a reason, perhaps the reason had not been to deny, but to prepare. Hiding as seasoning. Hiding as patience.

Fog moved against the window like pages turning. Out on the headland the beam cut its lanes: three short, two long, pause. In the pause, the town inhaled. In the inhalation, a week took shape—long enough to do the work, short enough to make cost plain. And two people who had learned to love each other with their hands full named their chores, set their alarms, and kept the light they could keep: one in paper, one in rooms, both in the stubborn seconds a lighthouse measures without asking who is watching.

11

THE SEA CAPTAIN'S COMPASS

The bell over the bookshop door gave its familiar single-note protest, and Marley glanced up from her notebook, half expecting Damien's shadow or Hazel's scarf. Instead, the antique dealer, Mr. Whitcomb, filled the doorway, his overcoat dripping rain in rivulets and his gloved hands cupped around something small but treated with a reverence most men reserve for chalices or newborns.

"Miss Taylor," he said, his voice warm but tight, as if he had rehearsed being casual and lost conviction halfway through. "I've something that... belongs with you more than with me."

He crossed the shop slowly, his boots leaving small puddles against the polished wood, and set a velvet pouch on the counter between them. Marley's hand twitched at her side, the way it always did when an object's presence arrived before its story.

"What is it?" she asked softly.

"A Compass," he said. His fingers hesitated, then loosened the drawstring and tipped the pouch. The brass disk rolled out with a patient gravity, weighty, weathered, and immediately sure of its own significance. The lid's face bore initials, deep-etched and steady: *A.W.*

Marley inhaled once, sharply. "Aurelia Ward."

Mr. Whitcomb nodded, pulling his gloves tighter at the wrists. "Came into my keeping from an estate lot. Mostly seafaring trinkets—scrimshaw, cracked sextant. But this one..." He tapped the lid lightly. "Belonged to a captain who traded into Brookwood in the 1870s. A man named Elias Ward. He was said to have sailed close with your Ward."

"Ward," Marley echoed, already reaching for her notebook with her free hand. "She traveled with him?"

Mr. Whitcomb shrugged. "Accounts differ. Some say she guided him through storms. Others that he ferried her messages across the coast. The truth is always smaller and larger than rumor. But what matters is inside the lid."

He pressed the latch and opened it with a creak. The needle quivered and steadied north, though the shop had always been a compass-tangled place. Marley leaned close. There, beneath the glass, etched in tiny script no bigger than a signature on a coin: *Guided by light and green flame.*

The words pulled heat into Marley's chest. She mouthed them silently, tracing them with her gaze as though memorizing a prayer.

"Green flame," she whispered. "Always green."

The dealer stepped back, his duty discharged. "It belongs to you now. Or rather, to your work. I'll not sell it to anyone who thinks brass is just brass."

Marley closed the lid gently, as though to spare the words from chill. "Thank you," she said, and meant it with a gravity he seemed to understand. He tipped his hat and left as quietly as he had entered, the rain swallowing his retreat.

Alone, Marley set the compass on the counter and

stared. *A.W.. Guided by light and green flame.* The initials were confirmation, but the inscription—why carve such words into a sailor's tool unless the object was more than orientation? Unless it was covenant?

She ran her thumb across the initials. The shop dimmed around her, or perhaps her mind simply shifted. She pictured Aurelia standing beside a captain, shawl green in lantern glow, pressing the compass into his hand and instructing him to follow not just stars but memory.

A rattle at the door broke her reverie. Damien entered, hair wet, coat collar turned up against the storm. He froze when he saw the object gleaming on the counter.

"What's this?" he asked, stripping off his coat.

Marley gestured. "An arrival. From the dealer. Compass. Initials: *A.W.*"

Damien approached, bent low, his expression narrowing into concentration. He picked it up, turned it, flipped open the lid. The needle quivered again, steadied, as though recognizing the kind of man who handled documents for a living. His gaze snagged on the inscription.

"'Guided by light and green flame,'" he read aloud. His voice carried both skepticism and awe. "Green flame, again." He looked at Marley, eyes darker. "The same phrase from the carvings. From the candle."

"Yes." Her hand touched the spiral sketch pinned on her wall. "And now from the sea itself."

Damien exhaled, sat, and pulled the compass closer to the light. "Elias Ward," he said slowly. "The name's in the logbook. 1876. A ship called *Selene*. Docked twice in Brookwood that year. The keeper noted: 'Ward guided safely by the beacon, accompanied by a woman in green.'"

Marley's pulse leapt. "It's Aurelia. It must be. She wasn't

just co-founder, she was out there—carrying, guiding. The compass is proof."

"Proof of connection," Damien corrected, though his thumb lingered over the initials longer than a mere lawyer's caution allowed. "Not proof of intent. But... enough to keep looking."

Marley leaned forward, the compass between them like a shared heart. "It's not just looking, Damien. It's remembering."

The storm struck the windows harder, and the beam from the lighthouse swept across the shop's panes, three short, two long. The compass needle trembled, then stilled, as though answering.

Neither of them spoke. The silence was not empty—it was charged, waiting, like the moment before a candle's wick decides to take flame.

THE COMPASS TRAVELED with them to the lighthouse that evening, tucked in Marley's bag beside the candle Hazel had blended. The storm had not eased; it pressed rain sideways, lashed their coats, made the climb up the headland path a test of loyalty.

Inside, the keeper's quarters were damp and breathing salt. Marley set the compass on the desk near the spiral seam. The needle quivered instantly, pulling north and yet twitching toward the carving as though iron filings whispered beneath the floorboards.

Damien bent over, his brow furrowed. "It's reacting. Instruments don't do this unless—"

"Unless memory is alive," Marley finished for him. She touched the lid, lifted it again, and let the words glow under the lantern light. *Guided by light and green flame.*

Damien's face softened despite himself. "It could mean navigation. A sailor's metaphor."

"Or it could mean exactly what it says." Marley bent closer, voice almost reverent. "She guided them—with the beacon, with the flame, with whatever green fire the spiral holds. This compass isn't just about north. It's about faith."

He leaned back, rubbing the bridge of his nose. "Faith doesn't hold up in committee."

Marley smiled faintly, though the edge of it trembled. "But it holds up here."

They both looked at the spiral. Rain poured down from above them. The flame of the lantern flickered once, twice, then steadied—as if choosing to echo the compass's words.

Damien shook his head, but when he spoke his voice was quieter, almost resigned. "Elias Ward. I'll pull the ship's manifests. If his name crosses with Aurelia's anywhere else, we'll have a line strong enough to stand in front of the council."

"And when you find it?" Marley asked, brushing her fingers across the brass initials.

He paused. "Then maybe I'll admit this isn't just history."

Marley let the compass rest on the seam. The needle trembled again, not north, not south, but something in between—a direction not on any map. She whispered the words under her breath: *Guided by light and green flame.*

The spiral shimmered faintly, the way it always did when flame touched near.

THEY STAYED LONG PAST MIDNIGHT, the storm refusing to let the town breathe easily. Damien spread papers across the desk, cross-referencing the logbook entry with dates, manifests, and the fragment of the charter. Marley sketched the compass over and over, as if drawing its shape might make its meaning deepen.

At one point, she leaned back, rubbing her eyes. "What if Ward wasn't just a ship captain?" she asked. "What if he was one of them—one of the circle? The guardians? Each in their place: healer, apothecary, keeper, sailor."

Damien's pencil stilled above the page. "And Aurelia?"

"She was the flame. The beacon." Marley's voice dropped. "Maybe she needed him to carry it forward."

Damien tapped the page once, a habit of his when a theory struck too close to dangerous. "If that's true, then legacy isn't just about blood. It's about chosen bearers. Which means..." His eyes flicked toward her, searching, wary. "Which means it doesn't stop with us."

The words hung heavy. Marley thought of his daughter, of the sketch she had made without prompting, spiral and stars etched in a child's hand. She thought of the candle's visions, of Aurelia carrying the child.

The compass needle twitched again, settling toward the spiral.

Marley touched the lid, closed it, and whispered to Damien, "Then we better be ready."

Outside, the storm raged. Inside, the spiral and the compass held their vigil—two instruments, centuries apart, both repeating the same quiet vow: guided by light, guided by flame, guided by the burden that chose them.

12

DAMIEN'S BURIED MEMORY

The lighthouse basement did not so much exist as persist. It carried the damp like a second language and wore the century on its ribs with a kind of square-shouldered modesty: shelves built when men believed in timber that outlasted their opinions, a floor of poured slab that had learned to listen for storms, crates whose rope handles had been gripped by hands that didn't think of themselves as history. The room smelled of salt and iron filings and the small, peppery ghost of creosote that sleeps in old wood.

Damien set the second armful of blueprint tubes on the workbench and breathed through the ache in his forearms with the steadying satisfaction of labor that doesn't argue back. The committee would make more sense after lunch, or never, but paper stayed itself. He liked that. The tubes were a vintage circus of colors—dingy buff, a respectable navy, two that had once been white and refused to be reminded. Pollard had produced them from a steel cabinet with the air of a mage whose magic runs on catalog numbers. *"The old sets,"* he'd said. *"Keeper's alterations, tower inspections, lens platform refits—'76, '92, and that terrible decade when someone thought plywood is a philosophy."*

Damien slit a tube with a bone folder rather than a knife —a superstition gained from losing one too many edges— then rolled the first sheet flat under weights from the harmonium he'd salvaged at the church-that-isn't-a-church. The paper sighed the way paper does when it is grateful. *Plan—Headland Beacon: Lower Service Rooms & Cistern.* The scale crouched polite at the corner; the draftsman's small, tidy pride lived in a faint flourish on the "R" of *Rooms.* He smiled despite himself. Men who draw lines for a living all have one letter that betrays them.

The next tube yielded a detail of the spiral stair with notes on tread wear and a stern marginal warning about "shoes with exposed nails," underlined three times by a hand that knew the value of underlining to keep certain boys alive. The third revealed a map of the service shaft and the drainage channel that, if the drawing could be believed, threaded along the inner foundation wall like a quiet idea. Damien placed the pages side by side and felt the click he lives for, the one that happens when separate things realize they belong to the same sentence.

A drop fell—somewhere behind him, near the cistern. He checked the clock because he likes to catch leaks in the act with a timestamp and because his brain prefers a little theater to carry it through the damp. 10:17. The sound came again: not a leak; a tick—then a small, precise drip into water. He followed it with a lamp through the low arch where the foundation thickened and found the little stone trough the blueprint had promised, carrying a thin, disciplined line of seepage toward a covered drain. He stooped, adjusted the lamp, and saw it: the faintest curve scratched into the stone rim, a spiral no larger than his palm. Not cut, not formal—no keeper had spent a day here with a chisel to make a future archivist's heart quicken—but traced, as if a hand, waiting on a wet night, had idly used a nail to draw what it knew to be true under whatever floorboards or vows lived upstairs.

He crouched until his knees made their familiar complaint. The spiral's curve was clumsy and perfect in the way children's drawings are perfect—confident in shape, careless with audience. His right hand hovered, then found the stone without touching the mark itself, the way he has learned to handle what may be older than the budget that allows him to study it. He felt the chill before his skin ever found the cold. Not air—the old cabin scent of water that has minded its business for a long time. And beneath that, a sound, so small it might have been his pulse—a susurrus, as if water moved in circles under the slab.

He closed his eyes against habit because sometimes removing sight gives other senses permission to send their reports without being edited. The room's smell reorganized itself: iron, linen, rope, salt—and something sweeter, unhelpfully kind. He saw nothing. He saw everything. The low ceiling above him, the swing of a lamp, the oil in it steady as a held breath. His hands were smaller, the world wider because it was taller. Light poured down from some-where that in his grown life is above his head but here was both above and beside—flicker, shadow, a shoulder moving between him and brightness.

A voice—low, not speaking to be heard beyond a room: *"I've got you."*

A sleeve the color of kelp, or a boiled-wool jacket that knew rain and took it without ceremony. A palm on his ster-num, the pressure that says *stay* without shame. He swal-lowed seawater and coughed it back into the world and watched it flick in the lamplight in a bright little arc that, if he'd been older, would have embarrassed him. He wasn't older. He was small and furious at air and then grateful for it with animal sincerity.

He opened his eyes with his adult body's discipline and found the dumb present waiting with its blessed ordinariness: lamp, stone, blueprint weights like squat little saints, the trough's faint trickle. His knees ached now in the honest way that feels like proof you haven't lied to yourself about what decade you're in. He sat back onto the cold floor before his thighs told him in a louder voice to do so.

The basement didn't change shape. He had. He sat very still. The first thing he did was check his hand for shaking. It wasn't. The second was to put his fingertips flat to the slab, not on the spiral, near it—because consent belongs to stone as surely as to people. The third was to say out loud, to the damp and the blueprint and whatever in his life had decided to hide its most necessary truths in rooms that smelled of iron: "Huh."

Not prayer, not curse, not triumph. Inventory.

He stood slow and went back to the bench. The blueprint for the service rooms made a little more sense now; the line of the drainage channel rested in the margin like a confession. He opened another tube. The paper inside had been rolled with care that had survived ownership. He coaxed it flat and frowned. The title block was half torn, a mouse's century-old appetite having edited the draftsman's pride. What remained: —*neth the* —*ame*. Beneath the title, a detail drawing of the area under the lantern pedestal not as it exists on his maintenance rounds, but as a thought: a cavity, a void, a space between weight and foundation. He circled the line with the pencil he'd just sharpened out of habit, then set the sheet aside, refusing the pleasure of that particular speculation because it did not belong to today's list.

He returned to the service drawing because it had been kind enough to deliver something without drama. He leaned—just enough to put weight on the bench, not enough to ask it to hold a confession. He kept his eyes on the measured lines because abandoning measurement when the world slips even an inch is how some men lose the floor for good. He breathed. The smell of rope rose and fell. The aftertaste of salt reached up through memory like a joke you suddenly get five minutes into the next conversation.

He did not intend to say *Marley* out loud. He did. The room did not answer back. He let himself say one more thing: "I think I was pulled out of the water here." He didn't add *once* or *before* or *when I was small.* The sentence held enough.

A drop fell in the trough behind him, as if the room had nodded.

He took his phone from his pocket and, because a person can choose to ask the kind of help that comes with questions, he texted: *Blueprints in the basement. Found a spiral scratched by the cistern. Something else—memory? Can you come down? Bring the mirror?* He added a second message before his better judgment could have its say: *Please.*

He stayed standing, for dignity, or to be taller than the past for one more minute, until he heard her boots on the service stair. He exhaled and the room did not grow larger, but he had the sense it stopped holding his posture against him.

.   .   .

MARLEY ARRIVED with the mirror wrapped in a cloth the color of old tea and her breath still warm from running. She took in his face first because she has learned this year that paper can be triage and people feel better when you start with them. She put the mirror on the bench but didn't unwrap it yet. "What did the room say," she asked, and somehow made the question secular and reverent at once.

He gestured toward the trough with the lamp. "There," he said. "A mark. Spiral, small. I knelt to look. Then—" He stopped, not for effect, but because he had learned to be careful with the moment when a memory realizes it has acquired an audience. "Then I remembered something I didn't know I had to forget."

She followed him into the nook and squatted without complaining about the cold. She bent, lamp angled, and saw the spiral he had seen. "Children's hand," she said. "Or a man trying to remember one." She didn't touch it. She put her fingers to the stone next to it, the same courtesy he had practiced, and closed her eyes. He watched her from the side and thought, selfishly, that her face has learned how to belong in rooms he spends his life pretending require only paperwork.

"What did it give you?" she asked, eyes still shut.

"Not give," he said. "Take back." He told it—his voice becoming something too even to be called steady. The cold stone, the lamplight, the sleeve the color of kelp, the hand on his chest, the cough, the arc of water, the sentence: *I've got you.* He told it without embroidery and without shame, because shame is what men are taught to use when saying what hurt them, and he hadn't the appetite for it now.

When he finished, Marley opened her eyes and didn't reach for him. Bless her and curse her for that good boundary. She nodded. "You were little," she said, testing the size of the past in his mouth. "Who pulled you?"

"I don't know," he said. "Green garment. Woman's voice. The steadiness of it felt like the opposite of a rescue, if that makes sense—like we were finishing a job someone had started rather than saving a life going wrong."

"It makes sense," she said softly. "Some people pull you back into your story rather than away from an accident." She leaned her shoulder to the cool wall and looked at the scratched spiral as if it were a child's face. "You didn't know this was here."

"I didn't know I was," he said, surprising himself with the accuracy of the grammar. "I've built my life around this place—its budgets, its special protections, its stupid locks. I thought I came to it because I believe in duty." He huffed once, without humor. "Which is true, and not all the truth."

"You came because something in you recognized where you'd been carried," Marley said, no pity in it, only the kind of kindness that makes grown men want to throw chairs until their bodies give up. "And then you sealed it up because sealing is how you keep going when you're ten and no one in your family has the money or the words for what to do with a boy who goes green at the sight of waves."

He looked sideways at her. "I don't go green."

"You flinch," she said gently. "I've seen you choose the inland side of a sidewalk three times in a row. And when the bell bites the stone on a wind change, you taste the metal in your mouth and pretend it's coffee."

He could have argued. He didn't. "Why now?" he asked, keeping the anger out of it by not using all his breath. "Why does it come now, in a basement that has not changed, with pipes I've checked, with the same leak and the same trough?"

"Because the building is remembering," she said simply. "And because you gave it permission when you stayed during the storm." She added, after a beat, "And because we've been moving the story toward you like a tide. Trauma is smart. It likes to hide when there's no one around to lift the heavy end."

He rolled the bone folder from one palm to the other and found it ridiculous and satisfying to have an object in his hand. "You think trauma did the hiding."

"I think your nervous system did the job of keeping you alive," she said. "And when bodies keep you alive, they're not picky about which rooms they lock from the inside. It blocked the memory. It might have blocked other things, too —pieces of how you feel when you hear the light click over. The part of you that trusts being held."

He made a small face that she could not have seen in the gloom but did, because she has chosen to be good at seeing what people hope their friends can't read. "Held," he repeated, as if the word were an unfamiliar implement he might cut himself on if he used it wrong.

She unwrapped the mirror and set it on the floor where the trough made its small right angle into the drain. "May I?" she asked, because consent belongs here the way it belongs in upstairs rooms.

He nodded. The mirror lay like a small still pool. In it, the ceiling beams, the lip of stone, his shoulder, her hair escaping the tie because the day had been unkind to discipline. Nothing ghostly. Nothing green. Just the basement reversed, which felt honest enough to proceed.

"Touch where you would have put your hand, then," she said. "Not on the spiral—near. And say the piece you remember out loud once, with me hearing you."

He obeyed and found that obedience, in small, practical

things, can be cleaner than courage. He placed his palm flat to stone that gave nothing except its own plain cold. "I was under," he said, and heard a boy's throat in his adult mouth. "A hand pressed here. I coughed. She said, 'I've got you.' And then I slept somewhere warm."

He closed his eyes. In the mirror, nothing altered except the fact of his lashes on his cheeks. Marley's hand hovered near his forearm and did not land. "You don't have to know who she was yet," she said. "We can let the building do that part of the remembering. We can ask other things first."

He opened his eyes. "Like what?"

"What being pulled out of water felt like." She smiled without teeth. "Besides wet."

He laughed once, short, grateful for the excuse. "Like shame, for a second, and then like fury that the air wanted so much of me. And then—" He paused, found it. "Like— warmth without conditions." He looked at her, and because he loves saying precise things, he made the sentence exact: "I am not practiced at that."

She nodded. "I know." Then: "That's a part trauma locks, too. The part that believes being kept is an economy that belongs to you." She blew hair out of her eye and glanced at the blueprint, because she also knows when to turn a heat down before it boils the room. "You found something else."

He gestured with his chin toward the bench. "Title chewed off. Reads like *Beneath the*—" He stopped himself, a little superstitious about saying the last word in a stone room that likes to echo. "It's a detail of the pedestal. A void." He shrugged. "Probably nothing. Probably just the draftsman leaving space for how the lantern weight distributes."

Marley didn't smile because she doesn't like to be caught being right about a thing before it wants to be true. "We're not in that chapter yet," she said. "We can leave that sheet rolled."

He made a sound between a snort and a sigh. "You've learned to narrate me."

"I've learned to narrate the way you keep yourself safe," she corrected. "There's a difference."

He looked again at the little scratched spiral and felt the wild urge to smooth it out with his thumb, which he of course did not do. "I never remembered this," he said, and there was fury in it now, at himself, at the boring inevitability of being a man whose body did the reasonable thing and then demanded a day like this as the interest payment. "All these years."

"You remembered enough to choose your job," she said, not letting him hand her the whip for free. "You remembered enough to stay in rooms that scared you without waking up the part of you that had to be small to fit. That's a miracle, not a failure. But I won't pretend it isn't also work you shouldn't have had to do alone."

He swallowed. A drop fell in the trough like a period at the end of someone else's sentence. He looked at the mirror. It held the basement, reversed, no extra guest. He was grateful for the absence. He wasn't ready to be watched by another century when he could barely stand his own attention.

"I want to know if it was here," he said. "If I was dragged in through that door and laid there and told not to die in the stupid loud way children like to try doing things."

"We'll ask your father," she said gently, a sentence you don't say to a man in his forties unless you've earned it. "Or someone who remembers your shirts. And we'll ask Hazel, Evelyn, and even Mrs. Bennett." She wrapped the mirror again. "And we'll ask the logbook. Not for you. But for the day. Sometimes men write their days in a way that acciden-tally catches children who almost invented ghosts."

He stood, and his knees agreed. "I'm not sure what I am to this place," he said, voice too level to fool anyone, least of all her. "Custodian, yes. Lawyer. The man who keeps other men from putting plywood where history belongs. But today... I'm something else, and I don't have time, Marley, I don't have time to be something else."

She slid the mirror into her bag and answered with the one kind of mercy she will not soften: "You don't have time not to be." She saw him flinch and added, kindly, nearly light, "We'll make it boring. If it helps, we'll schedule it. Tuesdays and alternating Thursdays: being the boy who was saved."

He laughed, and the laugh found the old crack in him and chose not to widen it. "Fine," he said. "Put it on the council agenda between ditch repair and parade routes."

They both looked at the little spiral again. It did not glow. It did not speak. It lay like a sketch a child made while waiting for a man to decide whether the weather deserved a swear.

THEY TOOK the blueprints upstairs because Damien could not bear leaving the "Beneath the—" sheet in a room that had taken more of him than he had planned to give before lunch. In the keeper's quarters, the air felt immediately less like a hand on a sternum and more like a hand on a shoulder—still, weight, a kind of occupancy that expects you to rise without telling you your name. Marley set the mirror on the desk the way other people set down bread, and Damien laid the service room sheet beside the rubbing of the upstairs spiral as if the two might start a courteous conversation about gravity.

The compass sat where they had left it the night before. It noticed them, or he projected and let himself believe it had, because his body liked feeling seen by objects that had not learned to hurt him. The needle flicked toward north and then made a smaller, more intimate motion in the direction of the seam in the floorboards.

Marley didn't reach for the candle. She set it near the seam unlit, a sign that attention can be an offering without spectacle. "Tell me the other part," she said. "The one you didn't put words to in the basement because the stone was too close to your face for you to hear the sentence."

He stared at the metronome until the tick-tick disentangled from his pulse. "I think someone carried me up," he said finally. "Not far. Not like a parade. But up. Out of the wet. I think I slept here." He gestured toward the bench under the window—the one he has moved twice to check for rot and once to hide from a councilor who believes in sitting while disagreeing, as if posture makes principle gentler. "I think a woman in green put a blanket on me that smelled like smoke and rosemary and something else I don't have a word for."

"Relief," Marley said. "Your own."

He swallowed. "I don't like that you're good at this."

"I'm only good at hearing you," she said. "It's a cheap trick. Your mouth is better than your self-protection at telling the truth."

He put both hands flat on the desk, like a man pleading guilty to a well-meaning charge. "If I was pulled out of water by someone in green in this building, the older men in my family would have said a thousand practical things about it and then laughed me out of my own memory for trying to assign meaning to survival. And then they would have died, and I would have kept the job and not the story."

"Let's not give them all that power," she said, not with disdain—never with disdain—but with the refusal that has saved her from becoming a professional mourner for other people's choices. She flipped open her notebook as if the act could make oxygen easier to metabolize. "Do you want me to write the first sentence for you?"

He looked at the seam. The board sat exactly where it should. He didn't lift it. His hand hovered over the place where he has learned to place it and did. Near, not on. "Write this," he said. "*I was a small boy and I drowned a little and I didn't die and I forgot until today because forgetting was cheaper than duct tape and because no one told me that the building would remember for me until I was ready to tribute the difference.*"

She did, pencil moving, breathing. She read it back to him, unglamorous and perfect, and he nodded, once, in the manner of men who know when they have managed to be both accurate and alive.

"Now the question," she said gently. "If the building is remembering with you... what else did it put behind the door with the memory? You don't have to open it today. Naming the door is enough."

He didn't answer at first because he is stingy with names when they can't yet be subpoenaed. He looked at the compass. The needle had relaxed into obedience. He looked at the rubbing of the upstairs spiral, at the pressed sprig of lavender in the logbook page now protected in a sleeve that made him feel better about oxygen. He looked at the chair, at the window, at the small crack in the plaster he would always mean to patch and never patch because a small crack in a lighthouse is a sentence you learn to love rather than fix. "Trust," he said finally. "And grief. And how to be held when I'm not carrying a tool or a rule."

"Good," she said, and the word did not flatter. "We can carry those together. They weigh less when somebody counts."

He opened his hands, not emptying them of anything, just making them available. "What if I don't want to be... chosen by this place," he asked, and made the question as honest as he could without throwing it out the window.

"Then you aren't," she said, immediately. "Chosen isn't a kidnapping. It's an invitation. And we can RSVP late. Or send regrets. And still keep the light on and the locks oiled."

He sat on the bench without making the motion dramatic. He looked like a man who had let a room see him breathe and discovered that oxygen did not, in fact, run on other people's permission. "I need to ask my father," he said with the same tone he uses for line items and hazard mitigation. "He took me to the headland when I was small. Once. I remember the rope on his wrist and his laugh and how he always smelled like cedar shavings and work. I don't remember him being afraid. But I remember... after he fell ill, he didn't like the sea. He said it rattled his teeth." He rubbed his jaw as if the sentence lived there still. "Maybe he was there. Maybe he watched somebody with a green jacket put me on a bench and told me to lie about it for no reason except his own terror."

Marley closed the notebook. "You'll call him."

"I will," he said. "And I will hate the conversation and I will love the man and both things will be the same size and I will survive that arithmetic."

"Good," she echoed, and then—because she knows when to change the subject by one degree, not ten—she said, "Help me move the desk. I want to see the seam in raking light. Hazel says sometimes old cuts show a shine when they're in the mood to be dramatic."

They moved the desk together, not talking, not pretending the old piece of furniture didn't deserve a "thank you" when it slid without protest. The seam caught the angled lamp. The spiral under the floor did not show—no glow, no script, no hint of theater. But in the very line where two boards met, a tiny grain shift made a notched crescent —cheap, accidental, easy to call nothing unless your body had become a magnet for certain shapes.

Damien leaned. "It's everywhere," he said, half exasperated, half ready to be charmed to death. "Once you see it."

Marley smiled. "It's a language. It doesn't need to shout." She set her palm near once more, a practiced grace. "You know, Lorraine's note said the light's been hiding things for a reason. Maybe this is the reason. Not to keep you from yourself. To keep you for yourself until you could ask."

He laughed softly, a sound he would not have permitted in a meeting but which rooms like this one earned. "You're turning town gossip into pastoral care."

"I'm turning a basement into a chapel without asking it to believe in anything," she said. "Also, Hazel says you should eat after you let a room do this to you, or you'll get the wrong kind of lightheaded and attribute it to ghosts when really it's blood sugar."

He stood. The normal world arranged itself obligingly around his height. "Evelyn's?"

"Democracy-flavored soup," Marley said. "According to her sign. Which is either a joke only the lighthouse gets or exactly what we need."

They put the desk back with the kind of care that makes furniture feel seen. Damien lifted the compass, considered pocketing it, and set it down again with a small nod to brass and the past. He took one last look at the seam like a man making sure a door is latched even when he knows it is. Marley wrapped the mirror. They left the room better than they found it, because that is a vow they made without saying it the first day they both had keys.

At the stair, he paused at turn four and set his palm to the faint circle under the paint. North. His skin was warm again, and the paint, cool, learned the difference. He felt nothing and then, not nothing: the certainty that a hand had been here before his, and that hands will be here after, and that the value of his life might not be in refusing to add his palm to the ledger but in doing so when it costs him the most dignity.

Outside, the day had decided to be undecided. Fog in lanes. Wind practicing. The beam, when it rose, would find its panes and do its duty with the cheerful stubbornness of a metronome. At the bottom of the path, Marley matched him step for step and did not take his hand because she had learned that sometimes love is the part where you walk alongside a man who is trying very hard not to drown on dry land.

In the café, Evelyn spooned stew as if votes depended on it and saw something in Damien's face that made her press an extra piece of bread into his hand without the dignity of a plate. "You kept," she said simply, which appears to be the only commendation the town is willing to give without forming a subcommittee.

He ate. He stopped tasting metal. The laugh he had been withholding found him again near the bottom of the bowl, and when it did, it didn't break anything fragile. Marley, across from him, made a small note on an index card she didn't need to share: *Basement—spiral, trough. Memory: pulled from water. Green sleeve. "I've got you." Check with father. Ask*

Hazel re: local rescues in 1986–1992? She stuck the card to the wall in her mind where she keeps promises she will not let herself forget for other people's comfort.

When they stepped back into the afternoon, the lighthouse did not look any taller than it had in the morning. It didn't have to. It had added a ledger entry. The boy who had drowned a little had placed his palm to stone and to wood and said yes to being kept by a building that had learned its manners from women who put lavender between pages. The man who was learning how to narrate that boy without apologizing for how long it took would now go to the state lab in the morning and ask iron gall to confess what ink it loved first. He would keep schedules and minutes and blueprints and sandbags in a town that mistakes stability for kindness. He would do all of it with wet in the seam of his palm that would take until evening to dry because the body does not hurry when it has decided to return from a lock it built for its own good.

Above them, the light prepared itself. Three short. Two long. Not a miracle. A metronome, turned toward the sea. He could do metronomes. He had, all his life. Now he knew what they were counting.

13

THE NIGHT WATCH

Marley did not plan courage; she packed for it. A thermos the color of pewter. Two sharpened pencils and a third in her braid for luck. Her metronome—the small brass kind that ticks without apology. The watch log she had designed like a ship's ledger with columns that steadied her even before ink touched them:

Time — Weather — Wind/Sea — Pattern — Anomaly — Notes

She left the candle at home on purpose. Tonight was not for beckoning; it was for sitting still and watching the way a room breathes when no one asks it to sing.

By twilight the headland had set its jaw against a light onshore wind. The lighthouse accepted the closing day like a professional—no theatrics, just the familiar steps. At the keeper's landing, Marley braced the window, then checked the latch a second time because the habit calmed that small, needless clatter inside her chest. In the lantern room the glass looked newly washed, though she hadn't touched it since the storm; prisms waited in composure. Down in the quarters, she laid her things out with the calm choreography of someone who has survived both hunger and plenty:

thermos on the desk; metronome beside the spiral seam; logbook open on a wooden clipboard; compass (the captain's compass) closed, initials *A.W.* catching the very last of the day. The small mirror she set face-down; respect, not superstition.

"Objective," she wrote on the first line, because a sentence that begins as if it is a lab report often behaves better: *Observe pattern through the night; document any deviations; no rituals; no provocations; witness only.* She printed the hour suite down the margin: **8:00 p.m., 9:00, 10:00,** all the way through **4:00 a.m.,** then left a generous blank beneath **3:00–3:30**because even sensible women allow folklore its chair in the corner. At the top she wrote the beacon's current gait—**3 short / 2 long / pause**—and drew five small boxes to tick each time the pattern completed a flawless cycle.

Damien had not argued with the plan. He had, in his way, tried to smooth its edges—*Text me on the hour; if anything electrical goes sideways, shut everything down, leave it; no heroics; I will be awake at 2.*—and she had kissed the air between them the way you do when both heads are already full of other things and said, "Boring paper first." He had smiled despite himself and then had looked at her as if the room had turned its head and he wasn't sure he liked being noticed by architecture. "Lock the lower door," he'd said. "Twice." "Twice," she'd promised.

By nine the beam was in good humor—clear air, dry pane, no sea-birds testing their luck. Three short sweeps in clean succession, two long thrown farther outward, a pause that let the town remember it was allowed to breathe. She listened to the metronome and then moved it half a hair until tick and light agreed on second, not just mood. She noted small honest things: **9:12**—wind SSW, steady 8; **9:41**—

faint halo visible on inner pane; wiped with lint-free cloth; **10:05**—pattern true; no hesitations; three pleats of light clean on fog bank offshore; **10:27**—compass needle trembles during long sweep; settles.

She walked the stair twice in one hour because the body must be reminded of its perimeter when the mind decides to pitch a tent and read all night. At turn four she touched the faint circle under paint—the north tick—and felt nothing except the correct cool of iron, the way a door that has done its work all day feels under a grateful hand. She did not lift the board above the spiral. She set her palm near, not on, and said *stay* in a tone that was both prayer and instruction to herself.

At midnight she poured coffee; it tasted like a sensible choice rather than a sacrament. The town's noises thinned until even the gulls' gossip sounded like someone else's dream. She checked her phone and found nothing dramatic —Damien's last text at 12:02, *Awake*, and Evelyn's at 8:48, *Soup tomorrow. Don't forget to be human.* She turned the screen face-down. The watch log's line under **12:00** she filled with careful words: **Clear sky; Orion low over river; humidity rising; lens warm to touch (back rail), safe.** She took a temperature reading at the pedestal and wrote it down because numbers make good anchors when you intend to spend hours floating.

Between one and two the ocean settled into the soft talk that comes after a day of opinions. She heard rope speak on a boat she could not see. She watched fog think about forming and then decide against it. She wrote **1:37**—glint on prism #4 (inner facet) resolved by shift in vent. She drank water like a responsible adult and simultaneously like a person trying to keep her body too busy to invent omens.

She set the metronome again; the tick had migrated; she refused to take it personally.

At **2:19** she felt the shift she would later learn to call the room's inhale. The beam did nothing odd; the pane did not tremble; no candle flared because no candle had been lit. The only change was the way the darkness seemed to concentrate rather than spread, like ink when you draw the brush back through it. She did not write it down. There are some notes you make with your posture because pencils can't carry them without blushing. She stood and moved to the lantern room and counted twelve breath cycles with her hands in her pockets, then came back down and made one square of the metronome's face with her thumbnail, a private square.

Just before three she took inventory. Thermos half-full. Pencils two and a quarter. A warmth on her palms not explained by coffee or friction. She flexed her fingers and realized her hands felt the way they do after kneading bread —tired in the good way, ready to be useful again. "We're here," she told the lens, which is an absurd sentence until you've spent enough evenings with glass that knows the tide tables by smell. The beam answered with its exactness. Three beats. Two. Pause.

She checked the time: **3:13**. She wrote it. She underlined the dash to the **3:30** block and sat straighter than she had at any point all night. There is a portion of the world between three and four when even sensible women are willing to admit that a town's oldest room might have something to say that didn't fit on signs. She capped her pen. She opened her mouth, then shut it. Witness, not conductor. She put her hands palm-down on her knees. The metronome ticked. The beam rotated. The building breathed.

The watch log's line for **3:17** remained blank, not because she hadn't the will to fill it, but because the world briefly forgot how ink worked.

IT BEGAN with a tremor too quick for thought and too slow for pure electricity—a shiver that ran the length of the lantern pedestal and into the bones of the room the way a plucked string decides to teach the table about pitch. Marley felt it in her ankles first, then in the small of her back, then in the soft spot at the base of her skull where old stories enter when you aren't guarding the door.

The beacon's rhythm quickened. Not by much—no calamity, no obvious failure—but enough that the three shorts found a staccato impatience, each sweep clapping the far water like a hand urging a child to hurry. One-two-three —then two long that were not long at all, a pair of longer blinks pressed by something that wanted a third. The metronome refused to follow. It ticked at its chosen speed and became, for the first time that night, an instrument of arrogance rather than comfort.

Marley stood without meaning to. She put her hand on the cool rail of the lantern room and exhaled like a swimmer. 3:17 impression itself into the watch on her wrist. The second hand stepped onto the twelve and waited there, then—didn't. The beam's cage hummed low; the motor whispered its agreeable, lifelong hum; the world continued—in fact. And yet the sweep stopped mid-turn.

Not a failure. Not a blackout. Mid-sweep, the great glass eye looked straight through its own shoulder into the seam where sea and sky exchange secrets, and held. The light itself—caught—burned without motion: a straight, unwavering ribbon that cut the fogless night into a true and a false. Down in town, windows received a longer attention than anyone had paid them in years.

Marley's breath hitched and realized it was unnecessary—some other set of lungs had taken the room's oxygen rhythms for a moment and were doing it better. The air chilled—or she changed temperature relative to it. The smell altered first: mineral oil, whale if you'd read too much history and liked to test your nose; salt sharper, as if concentrated by tin; a sweetness not of lavender but of something more workmanlike—tallow, perhaps, or beeswax carried up in some keeper's coat. The panes around her were the panes; they were not the panes. Someone had replaced time with a familiarity so persuasive she didn't think to object.

The woman stood a body-length away. Not apparition, not transparency. Present, layered in like a page of vellum over a map. Bare-headed; hair braided in a line practical enough to be beautiful; the dress a work gown, not green this time but a brown so deep it took the light and gave it back warmed. Her shawl—green—was tossed over the pedestal rail as if a moment's heat had required sudden discarding. Her hands were empty. No match, no striker, no taper. Just hands: palms nicked with the small history of work; fingers quick with the memory of a hundred thousand knotted tasks.

She did not look up. She did not look at Marley. She cut the wick with her thumb and forefinger the way a midwife trims a truth and then, astonishingly, put her right hand over the burner as if to cover a child's eyes. Marley's body recoiled—a modern reflex learning respect too late—and then stopped, because the room had already decided. The woman's hand closed, opened, and flame stood where there had been none.

It was not theatrically green. It was not any color a fairytale might shout about. It was flame: ordinary, excellent, courageous because it belonged to this world. And yet—its core did throw a shade that made Marley's bones think of moss in heavy light. The lens took it hungrily, not like a beast but like a covenant—light offered, light multiplied, light shaped into lanes. The prisms sang. There is no better word. A chord too low for human ears taught her skin what sound can do to water.

The woman spoke one word, not loudly, not for anyone but the flame. "Illuminate," she said, and the syllables struck the room the way a bell strikes stone—not bruising, convincing. It was not an order. It was the only instruction that has ever mattered in rooms that keep people alive: *Do your work.*

Time, which had paused on its own polite hinge, resumed. The second hand leapt. The beam, caught mid-sweep, completed it with a composure that made Marley feel both like laughing and like crying at the same time. The metronome—insensitive as a good heart valve—clicked on, refusing to apologize for having doubted.

Marley saw the woman's hands again—palms up now, held briefly at chest height as if thanking were a muscle. Scar at the base of the thumb. Ink stain on the middle finger of the left hand, smudged in the place clerks get it when the day's work refuses to be contained. She saw the shawl's edge —a tear neatly mended, the repair as honest as a song. She saw the way the woman placed two fingers to the iron of the pedestal for exactly the span of one breath. She saw all this in a single compression of perception and memory that she knew would later unpack itself across three pages of her notebook and still not feel like enough.

The room normaled. Not like after a trick, when the stage is a wound. Like after a delivery, when everyone in the room knows a thing that the hallway will never understand. Marley's knees remembered their century and quivered. She set one hand on the rail and the other on the warm lip of glass and waited for nausea that did not come. Her palms felt hot, not burned; the heat wore the same moral weight as the woman's voice—imperative, kind.

She looked at her wrist. **3:17** had become **3:18** without condescension. She looked at the log. The line under **3:17** would have to carry more truth than any pencil had ever asked to hold.

She wrote, on a single breath: *3:17 a.m.—Rapid flicker, then freeze mid-sweep. Smell shift (oil/tallow). Time-slip: woman present at lens; lit wick with bare hand—no match. Whispered word: "Illuminate." Flame normal color with green core (brief). Beam resumed. Palms warm; no injury.* She underlined *Illuminate* because to do otherwise felt like gossiping about a saint.

Above, the lens hummed the way a kept promise hums when you lean too close to hear whether it is still good. Outside, the beam laid its lanes over water that did not know and did not need to know what had been asked and answered in a room ninety feet above its patience.

Marley put the pencil down. She closed her eyes and spoke what she knew she would forget if she did not say it to the air and the iron at once. "You can light a thing with your hands if you've promised it your life," she said, and then laughed at herself because that's not science and she has made a religion of science for years. She poured water—not coffee—and drank long, until her mouth belonged to this hour and not to a century that liked whale oil and truth more than comfort.

She stood there a long time looking at nothing, which is one of the correct ways to look at a lens after it has done something you cannot explain. The beam ticked. The metronome obeyed. The town slept. The one word—*Illuminate*—kept doing its work under all the rooms' doors.

AFTER, the night felt simpler rather than stranger. The way a difficult piece of music sounds easy right after a musician nails the hard passage; the way a storm-renamed street makes sense because your feet remember where you've turned all your life. Marley's body arranged itself around the idea that something had happened and would happen again and did not require her rescue.

She reopened the lid of the captain's compass. The needle trembled, swung north, then did a small, unmistakable curtsey toward the lantern room above, as if some metal in its bones had heard the low chord and liked it. Inside the lid the tiny engraving—*Guided by light and green flame*—looked, for the first time, less like an inscription and more like a request. She touched the initials *A.W.* with the back of a fingernail and felt only brass; the warmth in her palms had settled to a persuasion rather than a heat.

She wrote an addendum in the log, careful, factual, generous to skepticism without selling experience for cheap: *No observed electrical failure. Motor constant; bearing sound. Freeze did not produce stall/power loss. Beam resumed smoothly. No smoke. Room temperature drop ~2°F (estimate) during anomaly; return to baseline within 60 seconds. Olfactory notes: whale/mineral oil; tallow/beeswax; absent post-event.*

Then the part she would defend in any room, even one full of men who liked words like *anecdote* and *hysteria* when women talk about seeing: *Vision consistent in affect with previous spiral events; unlike spiral events, no carved light; instead: direct intervention at lens. Bare-hand ignition may be metaphorical recollection by site memory OR actual phenomenon within time-slip. Primary data: warmth to witness palms; smell shift; freeze/resume; word "Illuminate."*

She set the pencil down before it turned into a wand; even practical women get tempted around 3:30. She texted Damien three sentences exactly as agreed. *3:17 anomaly. Flicker > freeze > resume. Will brief at dawn.* She did not include the word. Not yet. The gift of a week buys the gift of measured speech.

Her hands wanted to touch the seam over the spiral. She let them. Near, not on. The old groove gave back nothing but the confidence of wood that has said yes to storms that have forgotten their manners. "Illuminate," she whispered to it anyway, and felt the slightest pressure against her palm from the inside—nothing anyone else in any courtroom would call a thing; everything she would stake her next hour's oxygen on.

She took the mirror in both hands. For a long second she considered turning it face-up and asking to be watched. She did not. The mirror remained belly-down, and the restraint made the room exhale in relief. Not every truth wants to be looked at twice in one hour.

The clock drifted toward four. She walked the stair, slow, careful, not reverent, exactly—competent. At turn four she touched the north tick and spoke the word like a layperson learning liturgy. "Illuminate." It felt foolish and then it felt like washing your hands in a certain sink at a hospital without thinking about infection rates because your bones remember what happens if you don't.

In the lantern room she checked the vents, noted the absence of condensation, ran the back of her hand along the iron guard and felt the usual cold argue with the stored warmth of busy metal. She let her breath fog the glass on purpose and wrote her name in it, then wiped it away because love for a building must outgrow adolescence eventually.

Back below, she added a sketch to the log: the woman's hands over the burner, the posture of them—the exact angle of the wrist, the way the index finger on the left hand bent slightly more than the right, the healed cut at the base of the thumb. The shawl tossed over the rail; the mended tear. Underneath she wrote, because she could not stop herself, *If the flame dies, she must rise—only blood can rekindle the path.* The burned page from the lens base had said as much. Tonight's word didn't contradict; it focused. Not *rise* as sacrifice. *Illumine* as labor. Legacy, not martyrdom. Or both, the old voice in the back of the head said, and she told it to take a number and sit down.

She poured the last of the coffee and didn't drink it. Dawn would come tender and then indecently fast. She wanted to meet it with a mouth that belonged to this century. She cleaned up—metronome back to its box, compass in the pouch, pencils capped, log page dated and clipped. She folded into the chair and set her hands on her knees again and thought of the boy Damien said he might have been, the one who coughed back into a room and learned that sometimes being told "I've got you" is a kind of ignition a child can carry for decades without remembering the word.

She heard a gull before she saw any color to the window. Then she saw the color—not pink but a gray that had changed its mind into pearl. She stood. She did her small liturgy—hand near seam; palm to rail; tick of metronome against her wrist to remind her body what belongs to what. The beam's last pre-dawn sweep stretched thinner, then seemed to take a bow; the lens eased into day with the tidy, almost comical humility of a master at the end of a shift. She whispered *thank you* to glass, iron, oil, wood, and to whatever in the room had been willing to carry memory across years and lay it in her open hands with the grace of someone placing a sleeping child where the light will wake him gently.

Outside, the path held dew with a newborn's carelessness. She locked the lower door—twice—because promises matter more after wonder. Halfway down the headland she stopped and turned around and looked up. The lamp was an ordinary lantern now, a machine at rest. She put her hands into her coat sleeves to keep them warm and found— grease, faint, at the base of her thumbs, a smell that did not belong to pencils or thermoses. She lifted them to her nose and breathed mineral oil and something sweeter, and laughed once, out loud, like a woman who has accepted that evidence does not always come with an invoice.

At the café Evelyn was pinning up the sign: SOUP, the chalk star beside it—three quick dots, two long dashes— habit or joke or prophecy, who could say. Marley raised her hand in greeting, kept moving. She wanted her wall before she wanted broth. In the shop she taped a new card under **Chapter Notes—Solstice:**

— *3:17 event: "Illuminate."*

— *Hands > flame (no taper).*

— *Not green fire; ordinary flame with green heart (brief).*

— *Legacy instruction? Not martyrdom. Not only.*

— *Compass bowed when lens lit.*

— *Tie to burned line ("If the flame dies... she must rise").*

— *Hazel: ask re: bare-hand lighting rituals / folk practice (if any).*

— *Damien: deliver clean version; no adjectives; say the time twice.*

She texted him anyway, already breaking her own rules. *She put her hand over the wick and lit it. Word: Illuminate. I'm okay. Palms warm, not burned.* The dots pulsed. Then his reply, dry even in relief: *Of course you didn't light anything. The room did. I'm on my way. Don't touch your face.*

She smiled, because even now, the man's first instinct was to set a barrier between wonder and infection. "Boring paper first," she said to the empty room, and turned to the ledger to make the column straight. In the space where you write *Anomaly* she wrote **Night Watch—Confirmed** and felt her heart take the word into itself and repeat it without hurry.

On the headland, the beam's work handed the horizon to day. In the keeper's quarters, the faintest warmth lingered where a woman's palms had been. And in Marley's chest, the imperative lived the way a metronome lives under a musician's skin long after the case is shut: *Illuminate.*

14

PRINT SHOP BLUEPRINTS

Damien had always found the archives too warm, the kind of warmth made not by fire but by ink— the chemical tang of drying agents, the faint musk of paper left too long in stacks that remembered a damp corner of a ship's hold. It was a room where the past slept rolled, shelved, or bundled with string, but never willingly discarded.

He came not for newsprint this time but for the archives Pollard insisted on storing here: copies of charters, plats, engineering drafts, and blueprints that had been loaned out from county record vaults in an era when duplication meant a chemical bath rather than a digital scan. Pollard had waved a hand toward a drawer as if introducing a parishioner: *"Restoration records, 1860s to 1930s. Anything you find, copy it before you sneeze. The ink is temperamental."*

Damien pulled the drawer. Inside lay a flat file of drawings, each sheet wide enough to cover his dining table, paper blued by chemical wash, the lines stark and white, precise as an oath. He lifted them one by one, the smell of ammonia still faint in the fibers despite the century.

There: *Headland Beacon—Elevation and Section, 1873.* Another: *Lens Pedestal—Modification 1891.* Then: *Drainage and Foundation, 1876.* He spread them across the long oak worktable, weighting the corners with ink bottles, the room's presses quiet now, as if pausing to respect the shape of memory.

His eye snagged on a sheet darker than the rest. The title block, faint with age: *Lantern Tower—Detail, 1874 (Proposed).* He bent close, lamp steady. And there it was, unmistakable: a rectangle drawn directly beneath the pedestal base, hatched to indicate a void. Across it, in careful hand-lettered capitals: **BENEATH THE FLAME.**

His pulse tightened, the way it did in courtrooms when the right word appeared in the right deposition. He traced the lines with a forefinger. The space was no larger than twelve by eight, a chamber not marked in any of the later blueprints he had memorized through years of repair work. No door was drawn; no stair, no hatch, nothing to suggest ingress. Just the void, boxed by lines, labeled with intention.

He adjusted his glasses and leaned in farther. The margin bore a faint annotation in a different hand, diagonal, almost furtive, as though added by a draftsman when no one else was watching. Ink brown now, not the same crisp black: *Healer's threshold – sealed but not lost.*

The words stopped him. He sat back, chair creaking, as if the blueprint itself had struck him. *Healer's threshold.* Not keeper's, not captain's, not clerk's. Healer's. The spiral, the candle, the carved sigil beneath the boards—they leapt together, pieces that had waited years for a hand steady enough to connect them.

Sealed but not lost.

He pressed his palms to the table, steadying himself. This was not rumor or anecdote. This was a physical plan, an architect's hand. There had been a chamber. Intentionally made. And later—intentionally hidden.

He rubbed the bridge of his nose. His training rose reflexively: weigh evidence, authenticate, test for forgery. But his body carried another kind of certainty, the kind that knew when a piece of history did not lie. He folded the page back into its sleeve, careful, then refolded it as if to reassure himself the lines were still there.

Behind him, a loud tick once, perhaps a settling of metal. He looked over his shoulder, half-expecting to see Marley, though she was miles away in the shop, no doubt still re-reading her notes from the Night Watch. He would have to show her. She would see instantly what the words implied. She would say what he already feared to think: *The spiral is the threshold. The chamber is waiting.*

He closed his eyes and saw it already: a secret room beneath the flame, sealed, not lost.

HE CARRIED the blueprint to the lighthouse, rolled tight, case slung over his shoulder like contraband. Marley was already there, her watch log open on the desk, her handwriting tight and spare from the long vigil. She looked up at his face and read the gravity there before he spoke.

"What?" she asked.

He unrolled the sheet across the desk, flattening it with palms, and pointed. "Here. Lantern Tower. 1874."

Her breath caught. She leaned closer, hair falling forward, eyes wide. "Beneath the Flame." She said it aloud like scripture.

"Yes." He tapped the margin. "And this."

She bent, squinting at the faint script. "'Healer's threshold – sealed but not lost.'" She looked up at him, face pale and alive all at once. "Damien. This isn't metaphor. This is architectural."

He nodded grimly. "But no door. No access. Later plans erase it entirely."

Marley's hand drifted to the floorboards over the spiral, her palm hovering. "It's here. Underneath. That's why the carving matters. It's not just symbol—it's a lock."

He exhaled, rubbing his jaw. "Or a warning. Or both."

They studied the sheet together. The chamber's dimensions were clear, its walls outlined with double lines that indicated masonry. A void deliberately constructed. Not a mistake. Not empty space. A room.

"What would they keep there?" she asked softly.

He looked at her, his lawyer's face unwilling to give the answer but his heart already knowing. "Something they couldn't let burn. Or something they couldn't let loose."

She touched the margin again, tracing the faint words. "Healer's threshold. Damien, that's the spiral. I've seen it in the visions. Aurelia walked it. The candle opened it. This blueprint proves it exists physically, not just in memory."

He closed the compass lid with a click, needing the sound. "If there's a chamber, it's sealed. We don't even know where the seam is. And if we did—"

She cut him off, voice sharp with conviction. "Then we would have to choose. Whether to open it. Whether to carry what's inside. 'Sealed but not lost'—that means it's waiting. Waiting for us."

His throat tightened. He remembered the child he had once been, pulled from water by a green sleeve, the words *I've got you.* He remembered forgetting, the long years of sealing his own memory away. He understood too well what it meant to lock something inside for safety.

"Marley," he said quietly. "What if it's sealed for a reason? What if breaking it undoes more than it reveals?"

Her hand remained steady over the boards. "And what if keeping it hidden is why the light falters now? What if the prophecy depends on us finding it?"

The blueprint lay between them, the lines stark and undeniable. It was not legend. It was architecture.

THEY STAYED LONG into the night, blueprint spread, logbooks stacked, the storm rising again beyond the headland. Marley sketched the spiral again and again, overlaying it onto the blueprint, tracing how the lines aligned with the chamber marked beneath the pedestal. Each time she drew it, her conviction grew.

"It's a map," she whispered. "The spiral leads down, not just in vision, but in stone. This room—'Beneath the Flame'—it's behind the threshold. It's real."

Damien leaned back, eyes shadowed, weary from the weight of responsibility. "Real or not, we have no idea how to open it. No hatch, no stair, no key."

"Unless the key isn't a key," Marley said. She held up the compass, the initials A.W. glinting in the lamplight. "'Guided by light and green flame.' What if the flame itself is the key? The candle, the green heart of the fire I saw, the word Aurelia whispered—'Illuminate.' What if the light is what unseals it?"

He pressed his hands to his face, then lowered them, his eyes bleak but unwilling to deny her. "If you're right, then opening it might cost more than we're ready to pay."

She nodded, not with doubt but with acknowledgment of the weight. "Then we prepare. We study every log, every margin note. We find out why they sealed it. Because if it is 'not lost,' then sooner or later it will be found. And I'd rather it be us than someone who doesn't understand the burden."

The lamp guttered with the storm's breath. The spiral on the floorboard seemed to shimmer faintly, as if listening.

Damien gathered the blueprint carefully, slid it back into its case. His hands were steady, but his voice carried the tremor of a man who knows he has just accepted a task larger than his own story.

"Beneath the Flame," he murmured. "Healer's threshold—sealed but not lost. Marley... we may have just found the heart of the prophecy."

Her eyes held his. "Not found. Remembered."

The storm struck the lighthouse then, a gust that rattled the panes and hummed down the stair like a choir of ghosts. The light swept, steady, over sea and town alike. Beneath its patient flame, two keepers of a new generation stood on the edge of a choice older than the town itself.

And under the floorboards, the spiral waited—doorway, threshold, promise.

15

DAMIEN'S DAUGHTER AND THE FLAME

Saturday put a quiet shine on Main Street—shop windows wiped of storm salt, gulls resuming their sophistry over the river, the bell at the chapel testing a single polite note to make sure it still belonged to the town. Damien parked in front of the hardware store and took the stairs two at a time to the flat above, the way he always did when a different kind of duty waited on the other side of his door.

His daughter sat at the kitchen table with her backpack exploded into a still life—colored pencils in a small drift, a notebook opened to a fresh page, the compass of childhood mess pointing in every direction and somehow managing to be north.

"Sophie," he said, and the word did what it always did— made the room better arranged.

She looked up, grinned, and went back to drawing as if the pencil's tip would cool if she let it. "Hi, Dad."

"You started without me," he said. He meant breakfast, but she heard drawing.

"It was in my head," she said, as if the sentence excused everything it ever needed to excuse.

He came around the table and stopped. The spiral lay on the page—a clean, sure line nested five times, the outermost ring opening at the bottom into a small notch. Above it, floating, a cluster of five stars sketched as points with small rays, arranged in a triangle with two more tucked along one side as if someone had gently nudged them there. The pencil marks weren't tentative; they belonged to the hand of a person copying something they'd studied, not inventing it.

"That's the pattern from the lighthouse," he said carefully. "The one under the floor."

She nodded, shading the inner ring with the side of her pencil. "I dreamed it. Not like a nightmare. Like... when a song gets stuck in your head, but it's not a song." She tapped the inner circle. "There's light inside it."

Damien's mouth went dry in the way it had in court on the day his own voice had tried to leave him before the verdict. "Inside," he repeated.

"Uh-huh." She pointed to the stars. "And these were above it. Here." She put her finger over the paper in the air, holding a map he couldn't see. "Like a kite, but not a kite. Three really bright ones and two not as bright." She glanced up at him then with a hesitation he recognized as the early muscle of caution, the one children grow when they begin to realize adults can be frightened. "Is that... weird?"

He pulled a chair and sat, forcing his hands to fold on the table to keep them from reaching for her too fast. "It's not weird," he said, aiming for truth that wouldn't make the world too loud. "It's... familiar."

She tilted her head. "From when you were little?"

He swallowed. "Maybe. From when I didn't know how to

say things about the lighthouse out loud." After a beat: "Tell me the dream."

Sophie considered him, weighing the room the way her father does with a witness. "I was in the tower. Not the new stairs, the old ones. I could tell because the steps made my feet feel like I was walking on someone else's shoes. A woman was there." She frowned, trying on memory to see if it fit better if she described it sideways. "Not scary. Strong. She held out her hand over a candle and it lit." She seemed to realize the strangeness of the claim and rushed to make it smaller. "Maybe my brain made that up."

"Maybe," he said, and decided that this was the day he would allow generosity to outrun self-protection. "And maybe the brain remembers things we haven't told it yet."

She went back to the drawing and added a small mark near the outer ring. "There's a little bite here, like a clock. Is that real?"

His throat tightened. The north tick under the paint at turn four had exactly that slight crescent. "It is," he said, more to himself than to her.

The bell on the downstairs door chimed once and Marley's voice floated up the stairwell. "Permission to enter the tiny kingdom of pencils?"

"In here," Damien called.

Marley stepped inside, the shop's morning air coming with her as if she were its escort. Her hair was up with the third pencil; the other two were on the table. She saw Sophie first, then the page, and her hands found the back of the chair the way a person's hands find a rail on the third turn of a spiral they've walked so often their body arrives before their mind.

"That's beautiful," Marley said. "May I look?"

Sophie slid the notebook a little toward her, proud

without the garnish of bragging. "It was in my dream. The light was inside. Not like a lightbulb. Like... a heartbeat."

Marley met Damien's eyes briefly, and in that one glance they made a complicated decision together: they would not lie to the child about the world and they would not hand her its hardest weather in a teacup. "I've dreamed it, too," Marley said softly. "And I've seen it when I wasn't asleep." She touched the edge of the page with the careful finger of a person taught to handle paper as if it has nerves. "What about these?" She tapped the stars.

"They were above it," Sophie said. "Like they were listening." She peered at Marley. "Is that possible?"

"It is," Marley said, with that solid warmth she uses when truth needs to be built like a porch. "Sometimes a place and a sky have an old agreement."

Sophie nodded as if she had suspected adults had been keeping that from her for years.

Damien made coffee, not because he needed it but because the ritual kept his hands useful. From the kitchen he watched them—Marley asking without prying, Sophie narrating without preening—and felt an old latch in his chest lift with a click he couldn't have produced by will. There it was again: that double feeling the lighthouse kept teaching him—the kind of fear that measured how much you loved things and the kind of courage that reached out its hand anyway.

When he set a mug beside Marley, she didn't look away from the page. "Did you see a word?" she asked Sophie. "Sometimes I hear one when the light does its... remembering."

Sophie hesitated. Children learn the cadence of being believed long before they can quote the text. "I heard 'turn,'" she said finally. "But not like 'turn around.' More like... 'it's your turn.'"

Damien gripped the back of a chair. The blueprint from the print shop had said *Healer's threshold – sealed but not lost.* The night watch had offered *Illuminate.* The beam itself had insisted that time was not just sequence but invitation. He reached for humor because he needed to put his feet under him. "We're not putting you on a rotating schedule, kiddo."

Sophie smirked. "I'm eleven. I can only work weekends."

Marley laughed—real, grateful. "Union rules." Then, more seriously, to Damien: "We need to consider that she might be seeing what we see. And that the lighthouse... might be seeing her."

He nodded, carefully, the way you nod when the ground agrees to carry your weight for one more minute. "We consider. And we protect." He looked back to Sophie. "Deal?"

"Deal," she said, sliding the notebook closer to herself again and adding a tiny arrow pointing from the star cluster toward the spiral as if annotating an old map. "Can we go up there later?" she asked. "I won't touch anything."

Marley's hand twitched—yes. Damien's heart argued. The world does not get to make a habit of asking eleven-year-olds to stand inside prophecies. But the other truth, sharp and kind, was already on its feet: children stand inside prophecies every time adults make choices about what to hide and what to name.

"Daylight only," he said. "And you stay between us. And if anything feels wrong, you say so and we come down."

Sophie nodded solemnly. "And we bring snacks."

"Union rules," Marley repeated.

•　•　•

THEY CLIMBED the tower in the calm blue of late afternoon, the sea trimmed and respectful as if it had been reminded of its manners by a morning sermon. Damien led, not because he needed to but because the habit comforted him; Marley walked behind Sophie with the infinite attention of a person spotting a child learning a new balance beam. At turn four Sophie slowed, reached a tentative hand toward the faint crescent under the paint, and glanced back for permission.

"Near, not on," Marley said softly, and Sophie nodded and did just that—palm hovering an inch from the mark, eyes half-closed as if listening with skin.

"What do you hear?" Damien asked, keeping his voice casual, as if he were inquiring about a song from the radio and not the architecture of their lives.

Sophie wrinkled her nose. "Like when you put a shell to your ear, but it's a whisper and it's saying... not words. A feeling. Like 'soon.'"

They reached the keeper's quarters. Marley left the candle unlit on the desk, a declaration of restraint. The compass lay beside it; when Sophie approached, the needle made its small, friendly tremor toward the seam.

"Can I draw here?" Sophie asked.

Marley fetched a board and a piece of soft graphite and showed her where to sit so the light from the window made the page honest. Sophie set to work without ceremony, re-sketching the spiral, then adding the star cluster above it with the same quiet accuracy as at the kitchen table. This time she shaded the inner ring more heavily, a small dark heart.

"What's that?" Damien asked, pointing to the stars.

Sophie chewed her lip, then shrugged. "I don't know their names. I just know where they go." She put a dot off to one side, then erased it. "Not that one."

Marley crouched beside her. "May I?" She took a pencil and drew an imaginary horizon line with her finger over the page. "If you were standing on the headland and you were looking up at midnight in June, would this one be here?" She tapped the top star of the triangle.

Sophie frowned at the window as if June might step through it to help. "Higher. And the bottom two would line up with the path."

"The Summer Triangle," Marley murmured, almost to herself. "Vega, Deneb, Altair."

"Bless you," Damien said automatically, and she smirked at him without looking up.

Sophie added two fainter stars along one side of the triangle, as if pinning the shape to the world. "These were there too," she said. "But dim, like they weren't sure if it was their turn."

He saw the word land and sting and lighten. He crouched at her other side, his hands empty and allowed to be empty. "You didn't do anything wrong," he said. "Dreams are a way rooms practice talking."

"Adults are weird," Sophie said, but she was smiling.

They stayed that way for some time—Sophie drawing without the drama of genius, Marley making notes in her watcher's ledger, Damien doing the small work of telling his body that nothing bad was approaching from the stair. The light made its late-day compromise with the glass. A gull laughed at them, badly, from the weather vane.

When Sophie finished, she slid the drawing toward her father with a little lift of chin like a craftsman presenting an honest piece. The spiral was steady; the star figure hovered above it like a seal placed near a vow. The small shaded heart glowed simply because graphite knows how to promise a dark.

"It's good," Damien said. He meant the lines. He meant the fact of the child drawing in a room that had tried to frighten his younger self into being smaller than the shape of his life. "We'll keep it safe."

Marley pulled a clear sleeve from the cabinet and slipped the page inside before the air could get ideas about touching it. "No fire near this," she said lightly, and then winced. "Sorry. Bad joke."

"It's fine," Sophie said, with the generosity children have for adults trying to keep up.

On their way down, Sophie paused at the stair again and touched air near the north tick. "It feels less... hungry," she said. "Than in my dream."

"Hunger isn't always danger," Marley said. "Sometimes it's a sign that what's coming belongs."

"And sometimes it's a sign to pack snacks," Sophie said, which was how she'd learned to carry the world—lightly when possible, accurately when necessary.

Back at the flat, Sophie taped her drawing to the wall over the desk where Damien keeps his unpaid bills, and both of them laughed because it was the correct place to keep a prophecy from getting cocky. She went to wash her hands and came back smelling faintly of lavender from the soap Mrs. Bennett insists on selling him at a discount he doesn't deserve.

"Does this mean I'm... special?" Sophie asked, picking at a piece of tape.

Damien shot a look at Marley like a man on a high wire who knows he needs a net woven of a better material than law. Marley took the opening with care. "It means you're attentive," she said. "And the world is talking back. That can be wonderful. It can be noisy. We'll help you turn the volume down when you need to. And you get to choose what you keep."

Sophie nodded as if the rules of the best game had just been explained. "Do I have to tell Mom?"

"If you want to," Damien said, and didn't flinch at how honest that was. "We don't keep secrets in a way that makes anyone lonely. But we also don't try to explain things before we have the words."

Sophie considered that, found it fair, and went to rifle the pantry for crackers, which is how you close a conversation about inheritance at eleven.

When she'd retreated to the couch with a book, Damien leaned against the sink and let his forehead touch the cabinets for a second. "I don't want this to cost her," he said quietly.

"It already costs her to be alive," Marley replied. "The best we can do is teach her the exchange rate."

He huffed a small laugh that wasn't quite laughter. "You're going to put that on a mug."

"Union rules," she said, and he let himself be held upright by the ordinary until he could do it without the furniture.

By nine Sophie was asleep, sprawled in the uncompromising geometry of children who trust mattresses. Damien stood in the doorway longer than he meant to, just looking—at the hair spilled over the pillow, at the drawing propped on the dresser, at the way the world can be briefly simple when a small person's breathing sets the room's metronome. He closed the door soft and found Marley at the kitchen table with the compass open, the initials *A.W.* catching lamplight, and a cheap circular star chart she'd pulled from a dusty drawer he hadn't opened in a decade.

"I knew you'd have one," she said. "You have a drawer for everything."

"Some drawers are for hiding from the future," he said. "Some are for being an adult with batteries. Which category is that?"

"Both." She spun the star wheel until **June** slid under **midnight**. The printed constellations drifted into their places, the names in tiny uncompromising type. "Summer Triangle," she said, turning the dial until Vega sat where Sophie had insisted it belonged—higher, tipped. "Look." She set the wheel atop the drawing. The three bright stars fell neatly over the triangle Sophie had sketched; the two faint ones along the side kissed the line of Cygnus's wing.

Damien let out a breath that had been waiting all day at the base of his spine. "She didn't guess."

"No," Marley said. "She remembered."

He traced the edge of the wheel with one finger, then tapped the date. "Solstice," he said. "It puts those stars right over the headland, midnight to three."

"Three-seventeen," she said without meaning to, and he closed his eyes for a second because the hour had made a home in his chest without asking permission.

They sat with the chart and the drawing and the compass between them—the table a small altar, stubborn and secular. Outside, the river shouldered its way toward the sea in the same unromantic, holy motion it has used since the trees learned to be trees. The lighthouse turned its patient gearwork.

"What do we do?" Damien asked, not as a bureaucrat

but as a father who knows the line between refusing a calling and misnaming it is narrow and steep.

"We learn," Marley said. "We make a plan that's kinder than prophecy and safer than denial. If she's dreaming the shape of the sky over the spiral at solstice, it's an invitation to witness, not to perform. We don't bring her into anything we can't explain while she's awake. We tell her that listening is not the same as agreeing."

He let the words settle. "The blueprint's line—'Healer's threshold – sealed but not lost'—feels like instructions for us, not just for stone."

"It is," Marley said. "It's how to keep her whole while we figure out what the room wants. Thresholds are for pausing. For asking consent."

He turned the compass in his hand, the needle making its small, companionable dance. "She said the stars looked like they were listening."

"They are," Marley said. "Or we are, through them. Folklore is a long conversation between place and sky, conducted with people as translators who keep changing languages."

He smiled, finally. "Put that on a mug."

She grew serious again and touched the drawing's small shaded heart. "This... this worries me." She chose the word on purpose. "Not because it's dark. Because it's heavy. The light inside the spiral might be asking for a promise. We don't ask an eleven-year-old to sign anything that can't be amended later."

"Amended," he repeated, test-driving the mercy of it. "I can live with that." After a beat: "Can the lighthouse?"

"It has so far," Marley said. "It's been amending us."

He nodded, ran a hand through his hair, and looked toward the closed bedroom door. "I keep thinking about what I forgot," he said. "How my body decided the best way to keep me was to lock a room and throw away the key. I won't let that be her story. If she learns to put her hand near the seam and not on it until it's time, that will be enough for now."

Marley folded the star wheel over the drawing and slid both into a sleeve. "Solstice is in three weeks," she said. "Between now and then, we watch the light. We read. We ask Hazel what the constellation means to the grove. We ask Lorraine what the elders hid, and why. We teach Sophie how to name her yes and her no." She hesitated, then added, because a promise can sometimes anchor a parent better than any map: "And we will not, under any circumstance, let the building borrow her without a signed permission slip from all three of us."

He laughed, startled and grateful. "Union rules," he said again, and the refrain felt like a spell this time.

They cleaned the table the way people do when the conversation has done the real work and the rest is hands. He walked Marley to the door and the hallway where the light from the shop downstairs climbs in polite increments. She touched his shoulder, briefly, the exact weight of confidence and reluctance. "You're doing it," she said. "The hard part—loving without pretending it's easy."

He nodded and didn't try to make the moment larger than it was. "Text me when you get home," he said, because practicalities make a better benediction than most benedictions do.

"Boring paper first," she replied, and left.

In the quiet, he checked Sophie again. Asleep still, the way only children and certain saints manage. He stood in the doorway and whispered because the house taught him to. "You get to choose," he said. "Always."

Back at the table, the compass needle had settled. He closed the lid and brushed a thumb over the initials. *A.W.* The engraving inside—*Guided by light and green flame*—felt less like instruction tonight and more like permission to wait. He set the compass beside the star wheel and Sophie's drawing and turned off the lamp.

On the headland, the beacon made its rounds with the patience of an instrument that has outlived every petty argument ever held beneath its glow. Somewhere in the river a fish turned in its sleep. Somewhere in the grove a wind chose a path that did not frighten anyone. And above it— above them—the triangle kept its post, summer's quiet geometry waiting for the night when the town would look up all at once and hear, perhaps in their own throats, a word that asked nothing impossible of them except this: to see.

16

THE LIGHTHOUSE KEEPER'S LETTER

The chest was an afterthought, which is how important things prefer to be found. Pollard had called to say the storage room behind the municipal staging area needed a once-over before the county inspector named forty new reasons to buy shelves. Marley brought gloves and a thermos, expecting mouse nests and mildewed receipts. Instead she found the cedar box under a tarp of respectable dust, iron-strapped, rope-handled, with a faded stencil on the side that made her skin go quiet: **LIGHTHOUSE—PRIVATE MATERIALS** and, in a hand later and shakier, a brush-painted year: **1892**.

She knelt. The rope handles left grit on her palms. When she pulled, the box resisted like an old dog deciding whether the walk was worth the trouble; then it came. The lid creaked open on brass pins with the discreet dignity of a door into a room that still expects the right company to know how to behave.

Inside: folded linens gone brittle with good intentions, a small tin of lamp black snuggled in a cloth that had once been white, two coil-bound ledgers with rat-chewed corners, and a stack of envelopes bound by twine that remembered clever knots. The top envelope bore a hand that had practiced straightness against the will of ink: **To My Wife, E.** In the corner, a keeper's habit—tiny ledger marks: **Posted? No.** Then a single word like a blessing withheld or postponed: **Keep.**

Marley looked over her shoulder, though the storage room was empty. She put on the thin cotton gloves she uses for objects that want to be trusted. The twine came away with the satisfied sigh of a knot released after holding a duty longer than anyone could fairly ask. She lifted the top envelope; the paper was heavier than modern stationery, rag-content honest, edges soft from being handled by hands that had not yet learned to scroll. The seal—a pressed circle of brown wax—had been cut years ago. The flap lifted willingly, as if grateful that the letter had waited this long and might yet reach its intended reader, or someone who could hold the hearing rightly.

She slid the sheet free. The ink had browned toward sepia, but the strokes were firm, the hand of a man who sharpened a nib daily and preferred his words tied down to the line.

March 3, 1892

My dearest Eliza,

If I were a better husband I would leave you only accounts of weather and wages, the whaleboat fetched, the keeper's kit in order, the panes kept. But it would be a poor marriage if the sea was the only subject, and besides, the sea is not the only subject that keeps me.

I have dreamed again. I have had the voices again. And though I am less ashamed of it than a Christian ought to be, I confess it here because I cannot confess it to the log.

Last night—in the third watch—the light burned true, the wind sou'west, the bell due to chime. I slept not quite sleeping in the chair by the stair because Jim was down with the grip and I would not leave him to hear the glass sing alone. I heard then a voice as plain as if you had set a kettle on the hob and told me to mind it. It said only a word—**Illuminate**—and if I had had sense I would have put it down at once to fancy. But I could not, for directly I heard it, I looked up and saw a woman in a shawl as green as a spring hedge put her hand to the burner, as if to cover a child's eyes for a rougher sight, and the wick took to her as honest as a lamb to the ewe.

I am not about to turn Papist on you, Eliza, nor do I pretend to have seen a saint. She was no saint. She was a person doing the work. She did not look at me. She said— this is my shame to write, for I do not wish to frighten you— "Protect the boy."

Now, my heart, you will say *what boy*, and that is my trouble. There is no boy here—for we are two men only, and the clerk's nephew did not return after Christmas, and the chair that broke in October would not bear a child if we had him. And yet I tell you true, the word laid itself on me like a hand on the chest of a man who is getting above himself and means to run.

I am a keeper of ships, Eliza. But this place keeps more than ships. I have heard voices at the stair that are not the sea's. I have seen writing on the boards in the lightning that was not the storm's. There is a mark beneath the floor, an old curl that the old men call the healer's sign. I would not trouble you with this if I thought it idle. But I think it is charge.

If the town sends you to me here (as God send they do not, for this is a lonely place), bring the boy if they ask it of you. I cannot say why. I can only tell you the words as they were given.

Your Thomas

Marley read it once, then again, then lowered the sheet to the open chest as if her hands could not be trusted to keep the page aloft without trembling. She breathed, counted, then read a second letter farther down the stack, same hand, dated *June 14*:

June 14, 1892

Dearest E.,

There is a boy now. Do not take fright; he is not ours but he is ours to mind. He came half-dead out of a skiff that wandered in on the tide like a thought that lost its way and liked where it ended up. The woman in green was with him in the dream and then she was with him in the room, for when I took him from the door he had sea salt in his hair and a smell on him that was not the river's, and I have never seen anyone sleep so hard for having been so nearly drowned.

I do not know who sent him. I do not ask in the log, for the log is a public book and this is a private mercy. I put him on the bench where the sun comes in the morning and I told Jim to say he broke the lamp chimney so the clerk would scold him and not count the stores too carefully. The woman came in the night watch and said only, "Keep." She had ink on her fingers and a tear in her shawl neatly mended. I confess to you, E., that I wanted to ask her name, but it seemed wrong to make her talk when she was doing the light's work.

If anyone asks you, say only that the glass sings true.

Ever, T.

Marley's throat closed on a sound that might have been a laugh if it hadn't been trying to be a cry first. **Protect the**

boy. Keep. The phrases rang against the words they had been living with for weeks—**He must carry the light forward; Healer's threshold—sealed but not lost; Illuminate.** She touched the edge of the page, the way you test whether a thing is real when your history has not often been kind enough to present itself with postage.

She pulled her phone and took the kind of photo a person takes when they know a document will be proof and mercy both. Then she did the not-modern thing, because He had taught her how to be a decent citizen: she slid the letter back into its envelope and wrote, with Pollard's care in her bones, *Removed for copying—M.T., date and time* on a slip she folded into the stack.

Before she closed the chest, she looked under the linens and found two small sachets, each tied with string, filled with dried lavender and something woody—cedar shavings, likely, the friend of moths and men who hate them. She held one to her face and smelled kitchens she had never cooked in and voice-warmed rooms she had never sat in and a kind of housekeeping that made the word sound like liturgy.

She replaced everything as it had been. She closed the lid. She rested both palms on the iron straps and gave herself the simple permission to say a sentence without feeling foolish.

"Thank you for the letter," she said to no one and to Thomas and to the woman and to the boy and to the building that had decided to speak in ink when flames could not be trusted to write legibly.

Then she lifted the chest's rope handles and did a thing her chiropractor would scold. The box was not as heavy as she had built it to be with fear. She could carry it. She did, into the dryer light of afternoon, up the headland, toward the keeper's quarters where the spiral and the metronome and her friend's steadiness had taught her how to file charges of wonder without turning them into spectacle.

DAMIEN LISTENED the way men listen when they want to give the right weight to a story and are not sure yet which shelf in their body will hold it. He stood while she read, because sitting felt impious, because his knees were talking to him again, because part of him was already downstairs in the basement by the trough, a small boy and a green sleeve and a hand on his chest.

When Marley finished the second letter his face had gone oddly calm, which with him is a more dangerous weather than temper. He reached for the page with his gloved hand, then stopped, then took it—because consent had already been given in 1892 when a man addressed his wife and the town stole the letter and now someone had to be decent about it. He read the words that had asked him to be born into a building he had thought he simply worked for.

"'Protect the boy,'" he repeated, steady and not at all steady. "'This place keeps more than ships.'"

Pollard hovered in the doorway like a deacon who has been allowed to stay for the good part of a service, his minutes book tucked under his arm as if the sight of old ink might cause his present ink to misbehave if not supervised. "Chain-of-custody," he said automatically, then, softer, almost apologetic, "—and the rest."

Marley gave him a copy. "Photographed," she said. "Slip left. I'll draft a custody log for the chest." She turned to Damien. "He saw her. He heard the word you heard. And he kept a boy who wasn't his and made it the town's business by making it no one's business."

Damien folded the letter carefully, once, twice, clean corners, and set it down on the desk as if it had bones. "We've been cataloging the wrong kind of safety," he said, and it sounded like a confession. "We brag about how many ships the light has spared and forget to count the souls gathered where ships cannot go. Sanctuary is not just a harbor word."

"Sanctuary is a house word," Marley said. "A hand word." She put her palm near the spiral; the board knew the difference between near and on. "If the keeper sheltered a child, if the woman instructed it, if the light listened to her and met the boy halfway—" She stopped because the sentence was making itself too large for a single room to hold. She set it down gently. "It changes what this place owes and what it's for."

Damien nodded. "If it's sanctuary, it has rules." He reached for the ledger, paging to 1892. The keeper's official entries for March were dry—wind directions, lamp trimmed, inspection of ventilators satisfactory, one note about a broken chimney with a margin mark that must have been Jim's. In June, the handwriting was tighter, as if the writer kept remembering something else he had to leave out. "No mention of a child," Damien said. "Of course no mention. The log is a witness you invite only when you want the room to be crowded."

He looked up. "The boy in the letter—"

"I know," Marley said, and neither of them had to say *you*. "But he's not the only one."

Pollard cleared his throat in a way that meant an idea had asked for his attention and refused to leave. "There was a briefer's note," he said, opening his minutes book to an older insert he kept against the back cover for luck. "Handed down to me when I took this job. 'When you do not know what to write, write: weather, wind, wages, lamps. When you do not know what to say, say: keep.' It was attributed to a keeper in the 1890s. I thought it was only craft." He looked at the letter, at them. "Perhaps it was also code."

"Keep," Marley echoed. "As instruction and as noun."

Damien's jaw worked. "And 'Protect the boy'—written as if it were a sentence others would recognize. Not 'this boy,' not 'a boy.' The boy." He was a lawyer again, but a softened one, the kind who speaks as if the child in the case can hear him through the door. "A title, almost."

Marley lifted the compass lid and the needle quivered toward the seam. "We keep thinking legacy is a thing we dig up and hand like a plaque. It might be a person we shelter until he can carry the light without being burned by it." She paused. "Or until he can carry the light because he has been burned by it and learned what heat is for."

Damien rubbed his thumb and forefinger together, an old, unkind habit that usually meant he was counting money he'd rather not think about. "If the lighthouse keeps more than ships," he said, "then the town's laws need to remember how to do that without a line item." He looked at the letter again. "The keeper hid the boy in plain sight— under wages and lamp chimneys and 'weather.' He lied to the log in order to tell the truth to a life."

Marley smiled despite the ache behind her eyes. "You want to write a policy," she teased gently, which in their language means *I love you for being the person who wants to make rooms safer by adding clauses while I stand here lighting candles and arguing with ghosts.*

He shot her a look that was half a grin and half a plea. "I

want to write a policy," he admitted. "Copy: 'When sanctuary is required, count it as lamp maintenance and do not invoice the child.'"

Pollard, who will die with a pen in his hand and a sandwich untouched on his desk, nodded solemnly and wrote, *Lamp maintenance (child),* in a margin he will never be brave enough to show anyone and will keep forever like a joke only the lighthouse gets.

Marley turned the letter over. On the back, in pencil, a small rubbed circle—almost erased as if someone had used the sheet under another piece of paper when making a tracing. The circle bore a notch at the bottom—north tick. She looked at Damien. "He drew the spiral without wanting to mark the letter," she said. "He used it as backing."

"Or," Damien said quietly, "the spiral bled through."

They stood without moving. Rooms become chapels without sacraments if enough people breathe together with a purpose they don't know how to name yet.

Finally, because they are not a religion but a pair of people, they did what they are built for: they made a plan.

"Scan the letter," Marley said. "Two copies. One for town record, one for our wall. We keep the original in a sleeve. We ask Hazel for context—who in 1892 would have been 'the boy' to protect. We ask Helena whether the Marwick account books show extra bread going out the lighthouse door that summer. We ask Lorraine Gearhart what 'keep' means when the elders say it with a certain face."

"And I go back to the archives," Damien said. "There may be more blueprints labeled with the language of thresholds. If they hid a room, they learned to hide other things too. In margins."

He looked past Marley to the seam. "And we do not open anything."

"Not yet," Marley agreed. "We ask first."

He nodded, relieved by that discipline. "If this building once took in a child like a ship, it did it with rules. We owe it the courtesy of learning them before we sail."

Marley slid the letter into a sleeve, then into a box that felt cheery calling itself archival when all it wanted to be was a safer pocket. She labeled the tab in the tidy print she reserves for pain she can't fix and therefore must organize: **1892—Keeper (Thomas) to E.—"Protect the boy"**. She breathed, accidentally and deliberately, for what felt like the first time since the lid of the chest had lifted.

"Sanctuary," she said, testing the taste of the word against tea, dust, and oil. "A hand word."

"And a line item," Damien said, because love and law have decided to be married in this town whether or not anyone throws them rice.

DUSK DECIDED to be blue instead of gray, which in Brookwood is the same as a benediction. They left the chest with Pollard for cataloging, with a threat disguised as a promise that if anyone called it "ephemera," Pollard would personally remember the names of their grandmothers. Then they walked the headland with the letter's words folded into their pockets and into the muscles of their legs, as if language can be metabolized by motion and turned into stronger lungs.

On the path, Hazel waited with her scarf like a standard, the kind of color you can spot even in forgetful weather. She didn't ask; Marley held up the sleeve and Hazel set two fingers to the plastic like a nun greeting a relic made of braver matter than bone.

"Read it to me later," Hazel said. "For now, say the

sentence that you will pretend is about the past and which is actually about Damien."

Marley looked at him without moving her head. "Sanctuary," she said.

Hazel nodded once. "And the boy?"

"Ink on the fingers of the woman," Marley said, as if that explained everything and also nothing. "A mended tear. A bench near a morning sun."

Hazel's eyes, old with the right kind of age, softened. "Every house in this town was meant to be a school for who we intend to become," she said. "The lighthouse has the hardest class. It was never going to get away with just glass and oil."

They climbed. At turn four, Hazel pressed her thumb near the faint north tick and made a small sound in her throat reserved for lit stoves and steady babies. In the keeper's quarters, Marley laid the sleeve on the desk. Damien stood with his hands behind his back the way he does when he is about to let a room make him honest.

"Read it aloud," Hazel said. "He wrote it for a woman. Let the room hear a woman carry it."

Marley did. She read Thomas's confession of dreams and voices, the instruction to protect the boy, the June letter that turned confession into maintenance, *Keep*. When she said the word **Illuminate**, the lantern—quiet, patient, off-duty in daylight—did not answer. The room did. Not with light, not with script, but with the feeling of iron holding its breath in approval. It is a thing you must live with glass awhile to learn, that glass likes to be thanked in good sentences.

When Marley finished, Damien spoke into the hush because it felt rude not to fill the polite silence after a story with a sentence of your own. "I thought my job was ships," he said. "I thought my job was budgets. I thought my job was keeping the glass singing. My job is also hiding children in plain sight until they can name themselves."

Hazel made a small hum that meant *and* rather than *but*. "Your job is also asking for help when you haven't any hands left that aren't already holding this place up," she said gently. "Sanctuary is communal. Otherwise it's just one man with a broom."

He laughed at his own expense, which is the right way to clean a room before somebody else has to, then sobered. "I have to tell Sophie something. Not this—" He tapped the sleeve. "Not yet. But that she isn't imagining the light when it talks. That listening is a job and not everyone is hired. That she can say no."

Marley nodded. "And that when it says 'turn,' she can pass and the light will not punish her for waiting her turn later."

"Union rules," Hazel said with a smile that had lost none of its sorrow to all the jokes made on its behalf.

They sat at the desk and mapped the week like people planning a harvest. **Tomorrow**—Pollard scans, Marley transcribes, Damien returns to the print shop for any blueprint with margins gone strangely literary. **Wednesday**—Lorraine Gearhart, kitchen table, biscuits, questions about 1892 phrased in the grammars the elders permit. **Thursday**—Helena, who owes them less than she pays but sometimes tips with truth when she's tired enough of being careful. **Friday**—Hazel in the grove, asking whether folk memory recalls the boy as person or role. **Saturday**—no one touches a candle; everyone goes to the jazz rehearsal to listen for a waltz that once lived in a music box and now rattles chains in saxophones. **Sunday**—rest, they wrote dutifully, and then wrote smaller in the margin, *as if.*

"Say it," Hazel told Marley once the map was drawn. "The thing you're not saying because you don't want to sound like the kind of woman who hears prophecy in laundry."

Marley touched the seam with one finger, near, always near. "The chamber labeled **BENEATH THE FLAME**," she said. "The blueprint called the spiral a threshold. The letter called the boy a charge. If there is a room under the pedestal —and if it is sealed but not lost—and if that seal is held by the healer's sign—then opening isn't vandalism. It's midwifery."

Damien's stomach did a small, brave turn. "You want to break floorboards based on a letter."

"I want to learn what breaking means in a town whose elders used the word 'keep' the way sailors use rope," she said. "And I am not breaking. I am asking the building to tell us where it hid its mercy."

Hazel put a palm flat on the desk with the authority of a woman who has been aunts to more people than she is related to by blood. "You will not move a board until we have three kinds of yes," she said. "The building's, the town's, and the child's."

"The child?" Damien asked, and it came out hoarser than he meant.

"The boy is a role," Hazel said. "Not a possession. If the chamber belongs to the charge, then the charge gets a say in whether it is opened. Maybe not the present child. Maybe the lineage of it. But consent is not a modern fad; it is an old rule that spiritual people broke for centuries and are only now learning to obey. We will not make the light go backward."

Marley took that like a ledger entry and wrote it down where she keeps her vows. Damien exhaled, long, and felt his shoulders admit to the room how much they had been hauling and for how many years they had been doing it without telling him.

Night came in unevenly—first downriver, then up, then all at once on the headland when the wind decided to carry out its part of the plan. They stood in the lantern room and watched the first sweep, three short, two long, pause. The beam ran its lanes over the water like a schoolteacher patting the heads of children about to be dismissed into darkness. Damien laid two fingers on the guard just long enough to learn what temperature iron holds when it has decided to do the right thing again.

"Sanctuary," he said, because it seemed improper to let the light go off to work without its new name written into the shift report.

"Sanctuary," Marley echoed. "Sanctuary," Hazel said, and the third repetition made it a chord and not a slogan.

Back down in the quarters, Marley set the letter where the morning sun would find it and warm the ink the way Thomas had warmed the boy. Damien locked the lower door—twice—because superstition that keeps you alive is called practice. They walked the path toward town without speaking, the kind of silence you can only have with people who will not fill it to punish you.

At the café, Evelyn looked up from the tray of rolls and made the face you make when people come in from a shift you cannot name but recognize. "Soup," she said. "No questions and no seconds unless you ask nicely."

Damien, who had been taught not to take seconds, asked nicely. Marley, who had been taught to make do, took seconds anyway and said *thank you* with her mouth full in a way that offered the town the only apology it deserves for being praised: a clean bowl returned to the counter.

When they came back onto Main, the light gave them each a sweep that did not belong to them but did not mind being seen. Damien thought of Sophie asleep under a triangle of stars she had drawn without learning their names and of a bench in 1892 where a boy had been kept warm by a sentence a woman spoke to a man who wrote it down for his wife. He did not think of law. He thought of bread and bodies and doors opened in time.

"Tomorrow," Marley said soft enough to make the word equal to a prayer and a list.

"Tomorrow," Damien said, and heard in the word the old sentence Thomas had written in his letter without knowing that a century later a man with the same job would stand in the same room and receive the same charge, in language that does not wear out if you let it be used properly: **Keep.**

17

THE APOTHECARY'S DISAPPEARANCE

The clipping fell out of a book with a thud far too loud for something the size and weight of a wafer. Marley had been mending a cracked spine on a county almanac when the paste brush lifted and the back board sighed, and a sliver of history released itself from the glue line, fluttered, and landed face-down on the work table like a small, fainting bird.

She turned it over with two fingers. Old newsprint is a puzzle: brittle at the edges, stubborn in the center, smelling faintly of coal smoke and cloves, as if it had sat for a winter in someone's pocket with a handful of whole spice to trick the hungry. The masthead fragment left just enough to identify the source—**Brookwood Gazette,** the year line cut in half. A lower corner carried the number **1889** in a clerk's blotted pencil. Above it, the headline in unabashed Victorian bluntness:

APOTHECARY MISSING

M.C. LAST SEEN AT DUSK—TOWARD THE HEADLAND

Marley's thumb pressed the clipping to the mat as if to

hold it steady while the room resized itself around the words. Beneath, in tight columns:

*Miss M—— C——, of the apothecary shop on Main Street, was last observed by Mr. S. Baird at the foot of the headland path shortly before the eighth bell this Wednesday last. She was attired in her customary dark dress and carried a parcel.

Several parties were formed to search the path and the beacon, but neither the keeper nor assistant observed her arrival. Her shop was found in good order. Ledger and accounts balanced, mortar and pestle left clean.

Miss C—— is known for her skill with herbs and for a charitable habit toward the poor who cannot pay for draughts and infusions. She is of middling height, with eyes described as green in certain lights, and hair the color of chestnut. Those with knowledge of her whereabouts are urged to communicate to the council. It is feared she has met with misadventure.

The bottom edge had been cut, and with it whatever small cruelties or reassurances the column might have ended with. Marley read it twice, then a third time for the sentence that didn't know it had been written for her: **carried a parcel.** She felt the room lean toward that word. Parcel. As if the body were not burden enough, some things insist on traveling with their keepers.

She looked up toward the shop window. Morning river light measured itself neatly across the counter; gulls litigated weather a block away; a customer coughed on the sidewalk in that way adults use when they want to be noticed only a little. She set the clipping aside, slid her notebook out from beneath the paste pot, and wrote what she knew and what she suspected: *Apothecary. 1889. Initials M.C. Last seen walking to lighthouse at dusk. Ledger balanced. Parcel.*

— *Circle of Seven? M.C. matches.* She underlined *M.C.* and felt the line land on a name that had introduced itself months ago in chalk dust in the hidden room at the back of the shop—a list of initials carved into the plaster behind a shelf when they had moved it to clean, seven letters, seven marks, none polite enough to explain themselves. **A.W.** she had since learned. **M.C.**—she had not.

She took a breath to steady herself against the quick, unhelpful anger old stories can wake in the living—anger at a century that allowed certain women to disappear elegantly and then told itself it had done everything it could because it had printed a paragraph and sent men with lanterns to walk the obvious path. She ran her nail along the almanac's hinge to knock loose the last of the old paste and let herself think the thought she had been circling for days without naming: *Each woman was posted.* Aurelia at the grove. Another at the lighthouse. Another at the apothecary. Another at the print shop, perhaps—the one who wrote margins. Another at the school where the children's recitations were tidy and the teacher's hands were always ink-stained. Seven, not because seven is magic, but because seven is enough to cover a town without requiring any one body to be everywhere at once.

She set the clipping on blotting paper, slid it into a sleeve, and wrote across the top with her small, courthouse print: **BROOKWOOD GAZETTE, 1889—APOTHECARY MISSING—M.C. (Circle of Seven?)** Then she snapped a photograph and sent it to Damien with no commentary, because when she sent him adjectives he read them; and when she sent him nouns, he moved mountains.

The phone buzzed almost immediately. *Where did you find it?* he wrote. She sent back a photograph of the almanac's spine and the mat knife, and he sent a row of ellipses that in their own severe way meant *I'm already in the truck.*

He arrived at the door out of breath, carrying the case with the 1874 blueprint inside, the way some men carry a child—too carefully to be casual, too accustomed to be ceremony. She passed him the sleeve, watched his eyes narrow, watched him begin to sort the world again into the piles he trusts: Now, Later, Denial, Debt.

"M.C.," he said, and his researcher's engine kicked into its low caution. "Circle of Seven."

Marley nodded. "The initials were chalked into the wall under the shelf. A.W., H.G., R.A., L.S., one that look like E—, one I couldn't read, and M.C. Nobody writes themselves into a room they don't plan to inhabit."

He took the sleeve out into the shop's light and read aloud the half-vowels and dashed names with the kind of affectionate contempt reserved for old newspapers and new bylaws. "'Eyes described as green in certain lights.' Is that meant to be helpful?" Then, softer: "Parcel." He touched the word as if it might answer under his finger. "What did she carry?"

"A room," Marley said without smiling, because sometimes you have to answer devotion with a metaphor. "Or the piece of a room that the lighthouse could not admit in its log. If she's the M.C. of the circle, the apothecary is her post. She vanishes toward the headland in 1889. The keeper writes three years later of a boy who appears out of the tide and a woman in green who tells him to keep. It's not a straight line, but the thread is the right color."

He laid the clipping on the counter with reverence inappropriate for a penny sheet and glanced toward the shelf where the chalk initials remained hidden behind a row of books about boats too handsome to have ever done real work. "Marley," he said quietly. "What if each station carried the same charge? To protect. To hold. To 'keep.' And when one station could not—when a woman vanished—the burden shifted to another. From apothecary to lighthouse. From grove to... wherever the next one stood watch."

She nodded. She had already drawn the map in her head: the grove, the headland, the apothecary's old storefront on Main, the chapel, the print shop, the school, and—she had not worked out the seventh. The river lock? The bell foundry long since repurposed as a coffee shop? The dock office where men with clipboards pretend to control tides?

"Stations," she said. "Posted. Not saints. Workers. If M.C. vanished, she didn't leave a vacancy. She handed off the watch."

"Or," Damien said, treachery of care in his voice, "she went where the work went."

They both looked toward the headland then, though the lighthouse was not in view from the bookshop. The day came in tidy. The beam slept. The clipping smelled like the ghost of anise and horse.

"Let's go to Moon & Morrow, the old apothecary," Marley said. "We should see where her hands were."

"Lunch first," Damien said, because the new religion of Brookwood insists on bread before revelations. When he returned with two paper cups and a sandwich contrived by a woman determined to save the town with tuna, he set one cup beside the sleeve and the other in his own hand and said, with that quietness that had at last learned it is not the same thing as weakness, "If the lighthouse kept ships and children, the apothecary kept... what?"

"Bodies," Marley said. "And recipes. And the names of who could not pay and who pretended they could not pay so they could pretend not to owe. She would have had a ledger of debts she turned into herbs and a ledger of herbs she turned into debts. She would have carried both to the light."

He nodded. "Bring the clipping," he said. "And your notebook. I'll bring the blueprint. The town should never have let the past go for a walk without a chaperone."

"You say that like we're the chaperones."

"We are," he said. "Union rules."

EVERYONE IN TOWN knows Hazel's metaphysical shop, *Moon & Morrow* is the old apothecary. The building had been three things since an apothecary in 1889: a hat shop, a travel agency that took pride in brochures for places no one in Brookwood had money to go, and now a place that sold unique fragrance candles, hopes of good fortunes, and crystals for every protective truths. The transom still held its etched glass—*APOTHECARY* in letters so elegant even gulls would hesitate to soil them. Inside, the counter ran along the north wall where it always had, and if you leaned your hip in the right spot, you could feel, under the modern wainscot, the oak heart of the original, which had been scratched and polished by so many elbows the grain had chosen to be a story.

Marley didn't have to ask Hazel's permission before getting her approval.

"Have at it," the Hazel said cheerfully. "Just don't move the sourdough starter. It's angrier than me."

They walked the perimeter like animals reacquainting themselves with a former den. Marley ran her hand along the edge of a built-in case and felt the faintest groove: a narrow, shallow carving, no deeper than a thumbnail's thickness, curled once and again and once more—a poor man's spiral, hidden under paint, patient as a held breath. She knelt and used the light on her phone at an angle. There it was, clear enough when you knew how to look: the healer's sign, scratched into the beadboard where a person's hand would fall if they reached for a bottle of lavender or a jar of pennyroyal and needed the room to steady them before they asked the remedy to try.

"Here," she said.

Damien crouched beside her, shoulders touching hers like truce flags. He traced the groove without touching it and made the small humming sound he makes when an answer clicks into place in his body before it reaches his mouth. "Stations," he said. Then, because he will always check his facts even when his bones have cosigned the sentence: "We should ask to pull the baseboard."

"What will we tell Hazel?" Marley asked.

"The truth," he said. "Which is another way of asking to borrow a pry bar."

They didn't pry. Not yet. They rounded the counter and looked behind it and found a ghost they had not expected to recognize: a narrow shelf running waist-high along the wall, shallow enough for small bottles and slips of paper. Between two nails that remembered having once been hooks, a rectangle of wood had been set into the panel and then carefully painted over. The lines were clean in that too-clean way that says *someone cut me out with such concentration that it was almost a prayer*.

"Door," Marley whispered. "Not the kind you walk through. The kind you reach through."

Marley pressed her palm near—not on—the panel, and felt the faintest cool draft slip through a seam no one else would notice. Behind her the sourdough starter burped, offended by how long the oven was taking to get to proper temper. The room smelled of yeast and the dry sweetness of star anise and something medicinal that lived in the wood itself, as if old tinctures had taught pine how to taste like alcohol for an hour a day and the wood had never entirely sobered up.

When they stepped back into the street, the day had sharpened its light. River traffic stitched the same seam it always did; in the window of the print shop a stack of broadsheets waited to be folded with human hands because machines cannot do certain chores without getting depressed. They crossed to Pollard's domain. He met them with the expression of a man capable of keeping three secrets and refusing the fourth on principle.

"I know that face," he said to Damien. "It says *I brought homework with feelings.*"

Damien put the clipping on the counter and the blueprint beside it. Pollard's eyebrows did a small, agile dance. "Ah," he said. "The town's bad habits." He flipped the roll— **BENEATH THE FLAME**—then looked at the newsprint. His finger tapped the date-line fragment. "Eighth bell," he said. "If that's summer, that's just before nine."

"Dusk," Marley said. "She walked up with a parcel."

Pollard made a thoughtful hum and reached behind him for a bound volume with more dust than malice. "Gazette, bound, 1887–1890." He opened to the index, ran his finger down a column, and landed on a number. He flipped, turned, found the date, and drew a breath. The clipping in Marley's sleeve had been cut from the original paper exactly where bound volumes hate to be cut. Still, enough remained above and below to add two sentences:

*Witness Baird reports Miss C—— to have paused at the headland path to touch the stone with her hand as if in prayer. He attests a second figure behind her, not clearly seen.

Women of the charity circle will attend to the apothecary shop until such time as Miss C—— returns or other determination is made.

"Second figure," Damien said. "Not seen."

"Seen," Marley corrected. "But not permitted to be named in a newspaper that worries about being accused of writing poems."

Pollard looked from blueprint to clipping to Marley and then back to Damien. "You're going to tell me this 'M.C.' is one of your seven," he said. "And I'm going to ask whether you have anything that looks like proof."

Damien lifted the blueprint. "The proof I have is timber and ink and the fact that this town treats the truth like a quilt—patches on top of patches, all of it warm, none of it flat." He turned to Marley. "You think each woman's station held a piece of the threshold—sigils scratched into wood, rituals practiced at dusk, parcels carried toward the headland when other men were counting their change."

"Yes," she said. "And I think what M.C. carried that night was either a remedy the light needed or a debt it had to take from her using the language she knew." She glanced at the added sentence—*Women of the charity circle will attend...* "Charity circle. That's how you rename a coven when you need the town to send casseroles."

Pollard coughed into his hand so that the town wouldn't mistake his laughter for disrespect. "Ask Lorraine," he said. "Her grandmother ran that circle. She will pretend she doesn't know what you're talking about. Then she will feed you and tell you which drawer the minutes are in."

They found Lorraine at her kitchen table where all weather is made and repaired. Marley slid the clipping across wood that had heard more useful secrets than the town hall. Lorraine read without the obligation to impress anyone with how quickly she could. She sipped. She stared out the window. She set the paper down and put one finger over the initials.

"Mirabel Colvin," she said quietly. "M.C. She'd have hated the 'Miss.' Widowed at twenty-five, more backbone than vinegar, and that is saying something. She taught the rest of us the proper ratios for sorrow."

"You knew her," Damien said, surprised by his own quick grief.

"I knew the women who kept knowing her after she walked," Lorraine said. "They never once called it 'disappearance.' Not among themselves. They said 'sent.' And yes, that is the language of people who lose their minds a little when the sea takes what they love, but sometimes the sea delivers a letter back."

"Where was her station?" Marley asked, although she already knew.

Lorraine smiled in a way that pierced and blessed at once. "Where do you think? She had glass bottles to talk to and a scale that measured more than ounces. We posted ourselves where we belonged. I say 'we' as if I had a post. Some of us were born late for that particular grammar." She reached for Marley's hand across the table. "Or right on time for the one that followed."

"Did she carry a parcel," Marley asked, "when she went toward the headland?"

"She always did," Lorraine said. "Bread. Salt. A packet wrapped in a green handkerchief. I never learned what was in it. The older women wouldn't tell us because we were sloppy with wonder and they didn't trust us not to anthropologize a thing that only stays alive if it's loved in the native tongue." She turned to Damien. "You're making a face that says *policy*. Say your sentence anyway."

"If the lighthouse is sanctuary," he said, "and the apothecary was station, then the circle redistributed the weight of the town's keeping across seven points. It's a good plan, lenient toward failure, generous toward exhaustion. But if one of those points is removed..."

"You post someone else," Lorraine said. "Or you take turns." She glanced at Marley. "Or you ask the light to hold the weight for a spell and promise to bring back what you took with interest."

"And what did they bring back?" Marley asked.

"Children," Lorraine said simply. "The kept and the keeping. Sometimes the same person, just a different decade."

Marley looked at the clipping, at the careful omission of names, at the single sentence about a hand touching stone. "She touched the headland before she began," she said softly. "The way we touch turn four."

"Because thresholds are jealous of being ignored," Lorraine said. "They are not offended if you step over them. They are offended if you forget to nod."

Damien rubbed his jaw and then set both palms on the table to keep from calling a meeting. "I want to say we should leave all of it alone," he said finally. "And I want to say we should open the floor tomorrow. Both desires feel like bad weather in different hats."

"Then don't do either," Lorraine said. "Ask the right person the right question at the right hour. And if you don't know who that person is, begin at the place with the cleanest floor. Which in this town is always the apothecary."

Marley laughed, because grief had been given a chair and it was time to move it a little so it didn't block the door.

"We'll start there," she said. "With whatever remains behind its shelves."

"Bring a screwdriver," Lorraine said. "And biscuits."

THEY RETURNED TO *MOON & Morrow* at day's end with biscuits and the kind of humility that carries its own broom.

Marley knelt at the painted panel and slid the blade into the hairline seam. The paint cracked softly, not in anger but in that particular relief of a thing that has been waiting, and the rectangle freed with the gentle reluctance of a book you've already read twice. Behind, a shelf no deeper than her palm held a single glass bottle the size of a thumb, cork dark with age, and a folded scrap of rag that had once been green enough to tell pine what green meant. Beneath the bottle, secured with two pins like a butterfly, lay a card written in even, uncompromising hand:

When the light falters, carry this to the headland.

Leave it at the fourth turn.

Do not call a name.

Do not bargain.

Do not look behind.

—M.C.

"We're not at the looking-behind part," Marley whispered, not as disobedience, but as a woman reminding herself why her hands were steady. She did not touch the bottle. She did not touch the rag. She slid the panel closed again, ran her thumb along the seam to smooth the paint back into its old lie, and stood. Her knees objected in the polite way knees do when it is not their fault you have asked too much of them.

Damien looked like a man arguing with two good angels and one trustworthy devil. "Do we take it?" he asked, and the legal pronoun was deliberate. *We*. Not *you*. Not *I*. "The instruction is clear enough for the last century. Is it still our job? Are we the kind of people who can carry a bottle to turn four without inventing a ceremony around it and calling that obedience?"

"We won't take it tonight," Marley said. "We will tell the room we know where it lives. We will bow to the instruction and not perform it. We are not in the business of picking locks because we believe the furniture is bored."

He exhaled, grateful and still hungry. "Tomorrow we ask Hazel," he said. "And Lorraine. And Helena, because she knows money and money knows how legacy gets miscounted."

"And Evelyn," Marley said. "Because soup is a sacrament."

They left the shop with a promise—quiet, unpretty, the kind that lives longer than guilt. On the sidewalk, men were heaving a piano up the steps of the chapel, huffing and grinning with the stubborn cheer required to keep joy from falling on its face. "Jazz rehearsal," one called, and Marley felt, with a start, the thin thread of a waltz line in the air, the one that would arrive in its own chapter and make the room remember a melody older than anyone had intended to carry.

Down at the river, the evening set its colors to ordinaries: pewter, green, brick, smoke. They took the long way to the headland because sometimes the shortest path is rude. When they reached the stair, Marley laid her hand near— not on—the fourth turn, and felt the faintest cool greet. She did not bring the bottle. She did not say the name that wasn't hers to say. She did not look behind. She and Damien stood there a long minute, doing nothing with such fidelity it became a kind of craft.

"Stations," she said finally, and the word came out a breath and a plan. "Apothecary. Grove. Lighthouse. Print. School. Chapel. A seventh we haven't placed yet."

"Dock office," Damien offered. "Or bellfoundry. Or the little river lock no one thinks about until it sticks and then all of us are late to whatever we weren't brave enough to cancel."

"Seven," Marley said, not as magic, but as arithmetic. "Each with a drawer, a mark, a duty. Each able to hand the burden to another when needed. Each posted." She looked toward the lantern room, where glass sat in patient geometry. "And the lighthouse in the middle, holding more than ships. Holding the kept."

He put two fingers to the rail, just long enough for iron to memorize his temperature for later. "If M.C. walked up with a parcel in 1889 and the town printed her absence as misadventure, and if three years later Thomas wrote 'protect the boy,' we are missing the middle sentence."

"We'll find it," Marley said. "In a ledger, in a drawer, in a song. In the blueprint's margins. In the way the room changes temperature when it is about to speak."

They went back down the path like people who have learned a choreography from watching older dancers and now practice it on sidewalks where the young can see and forgive them. As they crossed Main, she touched his sleeve. "Sophie," she said. "We keep her out of all of it until solstice. Or longer. The light can ask. It doesn't get to demand."

He nodded. "We'll teach her the word 'no' as a key." Then, because he needed a sentence he could carry home that would not set his own father's ghost on fire, he added, "We will not be Mirabel's newspaper. We will not call sent disappearance. We will not call duty misadventure."

She smiled, which in their language means *amen*. The

beam turned its first sweep into the dark, three short, two long, pause. A gull changed its mind about the Chapel roof. Somewhere a trumpet licked a phrase and backed off, the rehearsal deciding whether a town can be taught a waltz it already knows.

In the keeper's quarters, later, Marley slid the clipping into the wall of cards on her desk. Under it she wrote three lines:

— *M.C. = Mirabel Colvin (Lorraine).*

— *Parcel; drawer behind apothecary panel; bottle + green rag; instructions for turn four.*

— *Stations posted: seven. The light is the hinge.*

She capped the pen. She put her hand near the seam. She listened until the building breathed and let the day step into its ledger. And somewhere in the long, generous arithmetic of Brookwood, a sentence they had not yet earned turned itself toward them and tried a shape in the dark: *Keep.*

18

THE JAZZ MELODY RETURNS

The Chapel always smelled faintly of lemon oil and stubbornness. Polished pews, old hymn numbers still slotted at the front like a town that refuses to forget its fractions, and a scuffed maple floor now pressed into service for cymbal stands and folding chairs. Evelyn presided from the kitchen pass like a benevolent stationmaster—paper cups, sliced oranges, the sign taped up with direct democracy: **Midsummer Jazz Rehearsal—Be Kind, Be In Time.**

Marley slid into the back pew with her notebook and the cheap pencil that seemed to be everywhere lately, as if graphite had become the town's shared nerve. Bass warmed the air in test pulses, piano found its vowels, drums brushed triplets on a snare; the room adjusted its shoulders and agreed to be a club for an afternoon. The saxophone player —mid-twenties, hair like a storm reconsidered, long fingers —stood a little apart from the tangle of microphone cables, reeds soaking in a small cup like a ritual too practical to be occult. He was new to town; she'd seen him once at Moon & Morrow buying crystals with cash, the honest way.

"Count us," the pianist called. "Let's set the opener and then give the waltz a shot."

Marley lifted her head. "What waltz?" she whispered to no one, and the room pretended not to answer.

They started with a blues; the Chapel forgave the key. She scribbled a few notes about tempos and arrangements because she can't help herself—documentation is how a heart like hers sits still. On the break the sax player turned his back to the band, worked his mouthpiece, tongued a scale that sounded like a street too slick to walk, and then, on an exhale that reseated the room around a different axis, began.

Three. Not four. The waltz arrived as if it had always owned her lungs.

It wasn't the kind of waltz childhoods learn at weddings, all cake and obligation. It was slow enough to walk to without getting anywhere, a left-hand circle with right-hand ache. The melody came simple—an arpeggio that refused to climb all the way to the top, the third flattened into a confession, the minor not theatrical but implacably true. First phrase: two bars rising, one falling like a breath you didn't realize you were holding. Second phrase: the same, slower, a hesitation and then a yes. In Marley's chest a chord resolved that had been waiting since three seventeen.

She was already standing before she knew why. The aisle was empty; she moved three steps forward and set her palm on the varnished back of the last pew as if steadying a child taking his first stairs. The saxophone line reached the place where, in her memory, the music box had sprung its little heart open—the three-note turn she had learned by touch before she learned it by ear—and there it was, in reed and breath: not a quote but a remembering. She tasted salt; she smelled oil; the lantern room came clean and complete into the back of her vision, not as a vision, exactly, but as a room that had recently loaned her oxygen.

She breathed his phrases the way she breathes the beam's sweep: three short, two long, a pause packed so full with patience it counted as a sentence. The drummer figured it out early, brushes feathering one-two-three like a hand soothing a fever; the bass found the root and refused to apologize for simplicity; the piano kept its left hand close, its right hand out like a door held quietly open. The melody circled, then tilted once into the sunlight and showed its true color: the green not of paint but of living flame, that heat at the center you only see when you stop trying to be seen.

When he ended—no flourish, just a last note held until it found its own weight—the room exhaled audibly. Even Evelyn didn't talk first.

The bandleader blinked, whistled low, and said, "You didn't bring that to the first rehearsal why?"

The sax player shrugged, suddenly younger. "It came last night," he said. "I tried to not bring it. It followed me."

"Name?" the drummer asked, which is how jazz musicians ask if a tune intends to stay.

He shrugged again, embarrassed. "I walked the lighthouse trail at dusk," he said, almost apologizing to the town for using it without paying. "I got to the turn where people touch the wall—" here he made the gesture, palm hovering a breath above the air "—and there was this... I don't know... chord in the stones. I went home and slept and woke up with this in my mouth." He lifted the sax a fraction as if to indicate which mouth he meant. "I don't... normally write in three. Or write."

Marley couldn't help it. She said, "What did you dream?"

He looked past her like a person checking whether it's

raining before admitting he forgot an umbrella. "A woman with a shawl. Not old, not young. She put her hand over a candle and it lit. It didn't burn her." He flushed at how foolish the sentence is in daylight, added quickly, "I know that makes no sense."

"It makes more sense than most policy," Evelyn muttered from the kitchen, pretending to stir as if stirring could keep the town decently silent.

"Do you have a title?" the bandleader prodded.

The sax player considered. "I wrote 'Headland Waltz' on the chart," he said, and then, not liking the way it sounded —too pretty—amended, "Maybe 'Illuminate.'"

The word landed in Marley's chest on the exact shelf where she keeps things that will be needed later in court. "May I see the chart?" she asked.

He blinked. "You read?"

"Enough to talk to a ghost without making a mess," she said lightly, and he laughed and handed it over.

Four staves, pencil neat, the kind of hand that knows its own shyness. She traced the opening motif—the step up to the minor third, the fall to the second, the turn. The tempo marking read *largo* crossed out, then *andante* as if he had argued with himself about how much to ask of people.

Damien slid in beside her as if he had been there all along, which is one of his newer tricks—arrive at the hour when the room chooses to show its hand. He didn't need to see her face to know; he looked at the chart, looked at the sax, looked at the aisle where everything important always walks, then said in that very quiet voice the town has learned to respect, "Play it again."

They did. On the second pass Damien closed his eyes and counted. Marley heard him under his breath—one-two-three, one-two-three—like the old metronome in human throat. The bandleader leaned back and let the room hold the downbeat; the sax leaned into the second phrase and let the line ride the air farther than it had any right to. When they stopped, Damien nodded once, the way he nods when a clause fits without force.

"It's the box," he said to Marley. "Slower. Almost bar for bar."

She was already unwrapping it in her head: the music box in the hidden room behind her shop, the brass cylinder with its stubborn pins and the little dancer who refused to dance unless you wound her without hurried hands. The tune she and Damien had both heard that first winter when the town insisted on being haunted one polite thing at a time—three notes rising, a catch, and the descent that sounded like mercy.

"We'll need the box," she said.

"We'll need permission," he said reflexively, and the reflex made both of them smile.

THEY SET the music box on the Chapel piano as if it were a communion vessel. The band drifted close without pretending it wasn't ceremony. The sax player—"Call me Rick," he said, a name shy about being Richard—stepped back, hands clasped, reed drying on his tongue like a stubborn weather forecast.

Marley wound the key. The mechanism clicked and then took hold with that satisfying small confidence a good tool has when it recognizes a human who knows not to overdo it. The cylinder turned, pins lifted, the comb plucked its way into the air. There it was: the same waltz, bones exposed. The music box's tempo sat higher—closer to a clock's patience than a heart's—but the melody matched like handwriting that doesn't realize it's forged its own younger self.

Damien pulled out his phone and set it on the piano, voice memos blooming on the screen like tin medals. "Box first," he said, and they all listened to the metal sing. "Now Rick," and Rick, with a breath, laid his line over the box's tune without stepping on it, sax carrying comb as if the instrument were a child on a parent's shoes.

The Chapel changed temperature by a single, notable degree. No gust, no theatrical flicker, just the kind of shift that signals the room has added a person to its guest list and expects you to guess who. Marley scribbled, drew little ladders between the notes she recognized and the ones the box insisted upon. "Slower by a factor of almost two," she murmured. "Same intervals. He keeps the minor third. The turn is intact. And there—" she pointed at measure thirteen "—the hesitation the box made when the spring was stiff? He wrote it as a fermata."

Rick looked a little stricken. "I don't know what that is."

"You wrote how you breathe," Damien said, not unkind. "That's usually the right notation."

Pollard, who had slipped in under the pretense of returning hymnals to a closet, now leaned against the jamb taking notes in his head. "Are we documenting this for the program notes," he asked dryly, "or for the archives?"

"Yes," Marley and Damien said together.

Hazel arrived mid-phrase, the door conceding without a creak. She took in the scene—box, sax, band, the town's two most sincere bureaucrats pretending not to cry—and said, "At last," in the tone of a woman who has been standing in the vestibule of a century and is pleased to see the ushers have learned how to seat people properly.

Marley wound again. Royce played again. This time the

drums did something new—on the second beat of each bar, a brush lifted just a hair and set back down, a heartbeat reaching for itself. The bass slid into the relative major and back again like a thought trying to forgive someone. The piano added a left-hand drone so soft it was almost furniture.

When they stopped, the room held its inaudible chord for a count long enough to be polite. Then Hazel said, "It's slower because it's for the living." She touched the music box, then Rick's elbow with equal propriety. "The box was a promise for the trapped. This is a direction for bodies. We will need both."

"The solstice," Damien said. "Light. Song. Memory."

"The stations," Marley added. "Seven points. One melody."

Pollard cleared his throat to hide emotion and produced two envelopes. "I took the liberty," he said, "of drafting letters of agreement. One for performing the piece, one for the use of the music box as accompaniment. We have to keep the insurance people from developing ideologies."

Marley signed without rolling her eyes. Royce blinked at the word **agreement** and then, perhaps for the first time in a long while, looked relieved that grown-ups had paperwork. He wrote his name carefully where Pollard pointed.

"Where did you say you walked?" Marley asked him gently, because asking twice is a courtesy when someone says a true thing that embarrassed them.

"Up the headland," he said. "The fourth turn. I didn't know... anything about it. I saw the marks—like a little bite?—and put my hand near. It felt... not like a tingle. Like when you put your ear on a railroad track and you can tell if a train is coming even if it isn't on the timetable."

"You don't do that," Damien said, father in his voice. "We do not teach the children to put their ears on rails."

"I didn't," Royce said earnestly. "I just—in my head. The feeling. Then I went back to town. I didn't sleep. Then I slept and the tune was there. It wanted to be slower than my hands wanted to play."

"Because bodies," Hazel said again, with that infuriating, trustworthy calm, "must carry it, not just recognize it."

Marley touched the page where Royce had written *largo* and then crossed it out. "The box belongs to the room," she said softly. "The waltz belongs to the people."

Evelyn ladled into cups unasked, practical hospitality that doubles as punctuation. "We're not making a temple out of the Chapel," she told the air. "We are making rehearsal soup."

They ran it twice more. By the second time the horn had found a thread in the upper register that lifted at the end of the second eight and landed on a held note that laced the room to the thing Marley had seen: a woman with a shawl placing her bare hand over flame without fear and the glass singing yes in harmonics no one can teach.

After the third pass, Royce put his sax on the stand as if returning a borrowed bird, and said, quieter than the room needed, "I dreamed the word 'Illuminate,' too. It's... arrogant to borrow a town's word. I can call it something else."

"It's our word," Hazel said briskly, "because the room lent it. You may use it. You will forget to thank it in a way it appreciates. That is fine. We have tomorrow to remember our manners."

Marley gathered the box, the chart, the voice memos. On impulse she asked Rick, "Will you come up tonight? Not to play. To listen."

He looked at his shoes and then at the window where

the headland gave nothing away except scale. "Yes," he said, and the yes had the shape of a person giving consent to be surprised.

EVENING DID its best impression of calm. The river unrolled; the smell of cut grass lifted off the lower park; the band's laughter thinned into the kind of fatigue artists pretend is athleticism when really it is just gratitude that someone else took the last solo. Marley, Damien, Hazel, and Royce walked the headland path without talking, the metronome of their feet finding the tempo the waltz had asked for. At the fourth turn Royce paused, his hand hovering without being told the rule.

"Near, not on," Damien said, less as instruction than as the mantra it had become.

Rick nodded and held his palm in the air for a breath, like a person trying to remember a name he knows he knows. "There," he said. "That hum. I don't know words for it."

"You have a horn," Marley said. "That's your vocabulary."

They didn't light a candle. They didn't bargain. They didn't call names. They let the beam lift out of the lantern room into its work and answer their restraint with attention: three short sweeps, two long, pause. At the pause Royce shivered once, not from cold. "That bar," he said. "The one where I hold the note. It's here."

They climbed to the keeper's quarters. Evelyn, who appears everywhere under the jurisdiction of soup, had left a basket on the bench: bread, a dark jar of something that turned out to be a kind of jam that apologized for itself by being excellent, and a note that read simply, **Play it, but**

don't play it. —E. Marley put the basket aside and set the box on the desk. She did not wind it. She set her hand near the seam, as she always did, and said the word as a courtesy rather than a command.

"Illuminate."

The room answered with the smallest warmth—a sigh that found her palms and rehearsed itself for a later performance. Royce stood at the window looking out over the flight of stairs that look, at night, like pages laid open to be read by the tide. He didn't touch his horn. He didn't hum. He put one finger against the glass and watched the beam pass through it, a straight line drawn by a patient god.

"What if we don't perform it?" Damien asked quietly, betraying his heart's two parties and making a coalition out of their disagreement by simply letting it be said. "What if we let it be a rehearsal for rooms and not an event for people?"

Marley considered. "Then those who need it will never have permission to bring their bodies to it," she said. "Songs are not complete until they find lungs they didn't originate in."

"Also," Hazel said from the doorway, and no one jumped because no one jumps anymore when the town decides a door has hallway privileges, "if you don't play it, someone with less sense will. And they'll sell t-shirts."

"Union rules," Damien muttered, and Royce laughed softly, the sound a minor third that wished it could resolve and didn't need to.

They didn't test the box against glass; they didn't try tricks. They sat, three people and a room that had taken on the shape of a century's worth of agreements. Royce held his sax the way a person holds an instrument when they're deciding whether to be owned by it. "I'm not from here," he said. "I can go if—"

"You're from anywhere you show up with your hands empty and your ears open," Hazel said. "That's the rule that predates all the other rules."

Damien took his daughter's star wheel out of his bag—habit now, talisman—and spun it to **June**, **Midnight**. The triangle arranged itself obediently over the paper horizon. "On solstice," he said, "at midnight, those stars stand like a crown over the headland. Sophie drew them. The waltz sits under them like a promise waiting for a sentence."

Rick looked at the chart and then through the wall, imaging the sky he had not yet earned. "Then I'll play at midnight," he said, as if asking for a shift. "Not for a crowd. For the room."

"For the people," Marley corrected gently. "There is a difference."

He nodded, accepting the kind of correction that makes men safer. "For the people."

They descended at dusk, careful with their feet, careful with their breath. At the fourth turn Royce stopped again, set his hand in the air, and said, under his breath, not to be heard but to be true, "It's your turn." The wall, being wall, said nothing. The air, being air, agreed.

Down on Main the band had spilled out onto the steps of the Chapel with ice cream in paper cups, the drummer practicing the brush pattern against his knee with a spoon, the pianist playing chords on the railing as if it were impervious to harmony. Ms. Hart waved from her porch with a book in her lap and the look of someone who had arranged the furniture of her day to face exactly this part of the street. Pollard stood under the angrier of the two lampposts talking to a councilor about insurance; he signed something without reading it and then read it anyway and then signed again just to be sure.

In the shop later, Marley wound the box once for herself and once for the wall of cards where she keeps everything that hasn't decided what shape to be yet: **Beneath the Flame, Healer's threshold, Protect the boy, Stations, Mirabel Colvin—parcel**, and now **Waltz— Royce —Slower**. She wrote, underlining the last word as if it were a secret the town could be trusted with: *The melody is nearly identical to the music box. The tempo is the difference between being mourned and being carried.*

She closed the lid on the box, knowing it would hum anyway in its sleep. She texted Damien: *We have the song.* He replied, *We have the hour.* She added, *We have the hand.* He sent a single word back that, for once, didn't scare her by being grand: *Together.*

On the headland the beam made its rounds like a story that refuses to be shortened. In a second-floor walk-up, Royce put his horn on the chair, wrote *Illuminate* across the top of his chart, crossed it out, then wrote it again. He turned off the lamp and lay on his back and counted one-two-three into the ceiling, not to sleep but to make sure the room remembered that music is what happens when breath refuses to be only oxygen.

And in the Chapel, under the placard that used to read **Be Still** and now reads **Be Kind, Be In Time**, the air held a note that wasn't a note, a preparation and a promise, a fermata over a century, waiting for a downbeat no one could hear yet and everyone had already felt.

19

THE BURNED PAGE

The discovery came by accident, which in Brookwood often means the room had finally decided they were ready to see what it had been hiding. Damien was in the lantern room alone, cataloguing the condition of the lens brackets for the council's restoration report. It was a task he approached with the usual rigor —clipboard steady, pencil sharpened to severity, each note written as if an audit might descend from heaven unannounced.

He knelt near the base, feeling for cracks along the iron rim where the lens assembly met its platform. His hand caught against a ridge not meant to be there—a slight bulge where the paneling had warped. Frowning, he ran his fingers along the seam. Something was lodged, brittle against the iron.

He pulled a small tool from his pocket—an archivist's blade he'd taken to carrying as naturally as other men carry keys—and coaxed the object free. What slid out was not stone, not insect, not detritus from a century of storms. It was a scrap of paper, charred at the edges, its surface warped but legible enough to hold words.

Damien's pulse jolted. He stood, brought it closer to the lantern's light, and read.

If the flame dies, she must rise—only blood can rekindle the path.

The words blackened toward the margins, but the sentence was whole.

For a long moment he did not breathe. The keeper's logbook had warned of a "healer's oath." The compass lid bore the phrase "Guided by light and green flame." The charter fragment had named Aurelia Ward *Beacon of the Grove.* And now this: a declaration, a contingency plan, an instruction disguised as prophecy.

He set the scrap carefully on the desk, anchoring it with the compass so the sea-breath that sneaks in through every seam wouldn't take it. His lawyer's instinct catalogued: *condition: poor; authenticity: likely; provenance: lighthouse base.* But his chest catalogued something else—dread, certainty, and a trace of grief too quick to name.

By the time Marley climbed the spiral stair, the paper was waiting like a witness on trial. She stopped in the doorway at the sight of Damien's posture—rigid, jaw set, as if he were reading a verdict he did not intend to announce.

"What is it?" she asked, her voice quieter than the storm-muted glass.

He gestured. "It was inside the base. Burned, but not lost."

She came close, bent, and read. The sentence moved through her like a cold wave. She pressed her hand to her mouth and whispered it aloud as if saying it would soften its edge.

"If the flame dies, she must rise—only blood can rekindle the path."

The silence after was not empty—it was a bell still ringing.

"Blood," she said finally, her voice breaking on the word. "Damien—this is sacrifice. It's saying if the light fails, a woman must give herself. Rise, not just stand. Blood, not memory. This is what they built the spiral to hide."

He reached to steady the page before her breath could shift it. "Or it's metaphor. *Blood* as in lineage. Legacy. Only the bloodline can rekindle. If Aurelia kept a child, if the keeper protected a boy, if every station carried part of the charge, then *blood* is responsibility, not slaughter."

She shook her head, fear too familiar in her eyes. "You always want the law to interpret. But prophecy doesn't bend to precedent. Words like these are never casual. 'If the flame dies'—that's more than metaphor. That's failure. That's catastrophe. And 'she must rise'—" Her voice faltered. "What if it means me?"

The weight of her question rooted between them. Damien looked at her, really looked, and saw the exhaustion that had been following her since the Night Watch, the tremor in her hands that came not from cold but from carrying too much of the town's forgotten grammar.

He reached across the desk, covered her hand with his. "It doesn't mean you. Not alone. Not singular. *She* can mean the station, the circle, the line of keepers. Not a martyrdom. A role."

"But roles bleed too," she whispered.

The page blackened at its corners, fragile but stubborn. Neither of them moved it. The lantern above threw its steady beam: three short, two long, the pause heavy with things not yet decided.

"We'll test it," Damien said finally. "Not with blood. With ceremony. With light and song and memory. We'll prepare at solstice. If the prophecy is instruction, we'll follow its form without conceding its cruelty."

Marley closed her eyes and let his certainty hold her upright. But the words lingered anyway, coiling in her chest like smoke that refuses to leave: *She must rise.*

THE BURNED page lived on the desk in a protective sleeve Pollard provided within the hour. Marley insisted on the sleeve, Damien insisted on chain-of-custody notes, and between them the scrap of prophecy was catalogued like a witness neither trusted nor dismissed.

At night they sat in the keeper's quarters with the logbook open to 1876, the compass lid reflecting lamplight, the clipping of Mirabel Colvin's disappearance beside the bottle hidden in the former apothecary's panel, and now this new page joining the chorus.

Marley paced as she read it again, her voice taut. "*If the flame dies, she must rise—only blood can rekindle the path.* It's always about fire, always about women, always about inheritance. What if Aurelia's circle knew the light would falter— that it *had* to falter—and they left these instructions to bind us into repeating it?"

Damien rubbed his temple. "Or what if they knew the town would forget, and they wanted a safeguard? A ritual, not a tragedy."

"But rituals often *are* tragedies," Marley pressed. "Burning. Binding. Sacrifice. Every line we find leans toward blood."

He tapped the sleeve. "Or toward lineage. *Blood* doesn't only mean sacrifice. It means descent, responsibility, kinship. You said yourself—Sophie sketched the spiral without ever seeing it. She dreamed the stars over it. That's blood as memory, not blood as offering."

Marley stopped pacing. The mention of his daughter softened the fury but not the fear. "And if it means both? If legacy demands sacrifice?"

The question cracked something in him. He stood, restless, moved to the window where the beam cut sea from sky. "Then we decide otherwise. We interpret. That's what survival is—choosing the meaning that lets us go on."

She watched him, the stubborn line of his shoulders, the lawyer who wanted clauses where prophecy offered riddles. "You can't litigate with fire," she said quietly.

"No," he admitted. "But you can prepare. And that's what we'll do."

They planned because planning was the only antidote to despair. Damien took notes with his relentless neatness; Marley walked the room, tracing spirals in the air.

"Light," he said. "The flame. If it dies, we ensure it doesn't. Lantern, candle, compass reflection. Every form of light we've gathered."

"Song," she added. "The waltz Royce dreamed. The music box melody. The hymn hidden in the jazz. Sound is memory's twin. If the flame falters, we sing it steady."

"Memory," he concluded. "The documents. The letters. The clippings. Each artifact is a vessel. We bring them together at solstice, not hidden in drawers but exposed to the beam."

She stopped pacing. "A ceremony," she said. "To prove that blood can mean legacy. That rising can mean remembrance. That prophecy can be answered without repeating its violence."

He looked at her, his face shadowed by exhaustion but

lit by determination. "Exactly. We refuse the cruel interpretation. We build a new one."

The burned page rested between them, the words stubborn but not omnipotent. Above, the lantern swept another arc over the dark water. For a moment Marley imagined Aurelia herself in the green shawl, watching, waiting to see how this generation would interpret what hers had left behind.

"Solstice," Marley said. "We give it back to the light. All of it. Together."

THEY SPENT the next days gathering. Hazel blended new candles with herbs tied to lineage—lavender for memory, rosemary for keeping, cedar for endurance. Pollard combed the archives for corroboration, producing receipts, margin notes, even a draft sermon from 1890 that warned against "bloodletting in matters of light." Lorraine Gearhart brought bread and reminded them that circles survive by feeding, not fasting.

And Royce —awkward, earnest Royce —stood in the Chapel playing the waltz again and again until it became less a melody and more a tide, a current carrying breath where words could not.

Still, the burned page hovered in their minds.

One evening, Marley sat alone with it in the keeper's quarters. The lantern above turned steadily, but she lit a candle at the spiral anyway. The flame trembled, green at its heart, as if acknowledging its kinship with the inscription. She whispered the words aloud, her voice unsteady:

"*If the flame dies, she must rise—only blood can rekindle the path.*"

The candle wavered. The spiral shimmered faintly, not

with menace but with invitation. And in that moment, Marley understood what frightened her most: not that the prophecy required her sacrifice, but that she might be willing to give it if the town demanded.

She blew the candle out sharply, unwilling to let the thought linger. Smoke curled, the scent of herbs clinging to her hands.

When Damien found her later, she confessed the thought. He set his hands on her shoulders and spoke with a steadiness she envied.

"No," he said. "That's not the bargain. That's not what it means. You're not here to bleed for them, Marley. You're here to remember. To *carry*."

"But what if carrying costs—"

He cut her off gently. "Then we all carry. Together. Blood as kinship. Not sacrifice."

The conviction in his voice steadied her more than the candle ever could.

By week's end they had a plan: On solstice night, they would gather at the headland. The music box and the waltz, the compass and the charter fragment, the letter and the candle, all brought together under the beam. Light, song, memory—woven into a ceremony strong enough to redefine the prophecy.

They did not speak aloud the possibility of failure. They did not admit how fragile burned paper is, or how insistent old words can be. They only wrote the time in their notebooks, each in their own hand: *Solstice—midnight.*

The burned page lay sleeved on the desk, waiting, a sentence charred but not silenced. And above it the lantern turned, steady for now, but one day destined to falter—unless their ceremony could convince prophecy to mean survival rather than sacrifice.

20

A SECRET SHARED

They had been making lists until the ink gave up on them—who would carry the box, who would steady the candle, who would set the compass where the beam's edge might catch the lid and throw the initials into a soft shine. The table in the keeper's quarters looked like a votive altar made by a clerk: cards, sleeves, the burned page in its careful plastic, the waltz chart folded into thirds, Hazel's taper resting in a dish of coarse salt. Outside, the sea had stopped arguing and settled into a judgment that felt, for once, like permission.

Marley capped her pen and felt the room tilt toward ordinary. "That's enough bureaucracy for one night," she said, more tenderness than mockery in it. "We'll forget something anyway. The town will bring it unasked."

Damien nodded, but he didn't stand. He sat very straight, as if waiting for a verdict that belonged to no courtroom he'd ever argued in. Behind him, the lantern made its patient round—three short, two long, the pause full of a patience he had lately learned to envy.

"Stay a minute," he said. He didn't look at her. He was

looking at the beam, studying the pause the way you study a person who has just told you the thing you'd secretly hoped not to be told. "There's something I should have said earlier. Something I should have said... years ago."

Marley leaned an elbow on the table and did not fold her arms. Whatever was about to cross the room would need space to land. "All right," she said, and let the quiet teach him that she would hold the weight.

He traced the edge of the compass lid with his thumb the way a man might trace the rim of a glass he's not drinking from. "Jackie," he said—"She used to walk up here at dusk. Not often. Not dramatically. She'd come to the last turn and stand with her hand just... near." He smiled without softness. "Before we had language for that. Before we decided a wall could be a listening instrument instead of just a wall."

Marley said nothing, but she let her gaze rest where his had—a little to the left of the door, where the spiral beneath the floorboard casts its restraint on everything placed above it.

"She called it a pull," he went on. "I remember the day she chose that word because it annoyed me. Lawyers like pushes. We like cause and effect. Pulls sound like poetry. She didn't insist. She didn't perform it. She just... told me. 'I feel called to the lighthouse,' she said one night in the kitchen. Sophie was little and asleep. I had work spread everywhere. I had a brief due that might save a business from entropy and a family from ruin. I kissed her cheek and said, 'We live in a town shaped like a story; everyone feels called to the lighthouse.'"

He breathed out once, a sound with grit in it. "I was being kind, in my head. I was lightening it. What I was actually doing was... not hearing her."

Marley's hand moved, then stopped, then moved anyway. She placed it on the table between them, palm up, offering the clean, quiet surface a hand becomes when it's not trying to fix anything. He did not take it. He wasn't refusing. He was not ready to be steadied by something he hadn't earned.

"The night Sophie was born," he said, "Jackie had been up at the headland the evening before. She told me she needed the sea's braid under her feet. She said it that way— 'braid'—as if the river and the ocean and the wind had been taught to plait each other's hair and she wanted to watch the work. She came back flushed and quiet and said, 'I think the light knows me.'"

He swallowed. The beam passed over the glass in a slow, domestic benediction. "And then she died. Years later, not then. Nothing neat. No romance. I don't know why I'm telling you that part except to make sure the room hears me say: there was no bargain. No melodrama. A medical event with an ugly name, a terrible night, a hospital that did its job and couldn't do the miracle, a child asleep at a neighbor's house, a man with papers in his hand good for absolutely nothing. She had never told me more about what 'called' meant. I decided—because deciding is how I win arguments I never needed to start—that it had been a mood. A phase. I folded the word 'called' and put it in a drawer like a sweater that would keep without air."

Marley felt her throat answer with the kind of sound you make when a truth that has been kept too long finally learns daylight. "You were surviving," she said.

"I was surviving," he agreed. "But I was also... diminishing her. It's only these last months—Aurelia, the spiral, the letter from Thomas, Mirabel Colvin, Rick's waltz—that I hear her sentence the way it wanted to be heard. It had the same grammar as all of this. It had that hour's breath in it—three short, two long, pause."

He set the compass lid down and finally reached for Marley's hand. His palm was colder than the iron guard upstairs. "I see her in you," he said. "Not the way people say that when they want to make grief easier by turning the living into haunted furniture. Not like that. I see her steadiness. The way you test a room with your body before you ask it to sing. The way you categorize even the mysteries because you know precision is a form of care. I see her, and I am ashamed that when she offered me that version of herself I chose a joke over a chair."

The lantern hummed faintly—mechanics, not omen. Marley squeezed his hand once and let go, because sometimes you prove you heard someone by not holding on too hard.

"What did she do up here?" she asked, which is to say: tell me the shape of her devotion without me taking it from her.

"Nothing," he said. "And everything. She walked. She put her hand near. She stood. She breathed in time with the beam. If there's a ledger for that, I hope someone kept it on paper that won't catch fire."

"She told you she was called." Marley's voice was low, steady. "That's the whole entry."

He nodded, the movement carefully small, as if the air had become a liquid and he was learning to swim in it. "That's the whole entry. And I filed it under 'Not actionable.'"

He looked up finally. "I am telling you because the burned page—'If the flame dies, she must rise—only blood can rekindle the path'—has been speaking to me in a voice that is not language. It isn't asking me to bleed. It's asking me to keep the thing I was handed and didn't know how to hold. Her sense of being called. Her... portion of this. I can't give it back to her. I can give it forward."

Marley nodded. The metronome of the building took one breath in. "All right," she said. "Let's talk about what that looks like."

THEY LEFT the desk because desks make confessions sound like minutes and both of them were tired of behaving as though sorrow requires a clerk. In the lantern room the glass waited like an elder with good posture. Damien rested two fingers on the iron guard, then took them away, obeying the house rule before Marley even had to think it: near, not on. The world outside had gone to ink; the beam wrote in it without scolding.

"After Jackie died," he said, watching his hand not touch, "I took the word 'called' and replaced it with tasks. Budget lines. Brackets. Bearings. It worked. The light kept. The town kept. I kept. I also trained myself to flinch whenever anyone—including you—used any sentence that wasn't prosecutable."

"I noticed," Marley said, not unkindly.

He laughed—a brief, late admission of the obvious. "I know you did. When you said 'Illuminate' after the Night Watch, I wanted to put it in a chain of custody sleeve. Clip it to a report. Ask the town to initial here and here."

"In triplicate," she said.

"Union rules."

They stood side by side, the way colleagues do when they agree there's too much between them for opposite chairs. He reached into his jacket pocket and drew out a small paper, folded into fourths, then eighths, the corners softened by years of wallet and habit. He unfolded it with the care you give to a thin thing you have decided to stop punishing. In the center, in Jackie's looping hand, was a spiral—not exactly the healer's sigil, but kin to it—five turns, the outermost opening into a notch. At the top she had written two words: **Keep faith.**

"I found this after she died," he said. "It was in a book she'd left by the bed, the kind you read with one eye after the good eye has gone to sleep. I thought—" he made a small face at his younger self "—that it was a religious thing. A reminder. It may have been. But I'm also allowing that she meant the word literally. Keep. Faith." He tapped the spiral. "She walked it with a pencil because we hadn't yet learned to walk it on the floor without waking the house."

Marley reached without touching, the way you step toward a baby animal in the brush and wait for the decision to be made by something older than etiquette. "She had the mark," she said. "She had the grammar. She did not need permission. But she asked anyway. And you didn't know how to answer."

"I gave her a joke," he said. "Because it is easier to be charming than to admit you don't understand the language your family is trying to live in."

They watched the beam pass. The prism sang its invisibles. Damien breathed in sync with it without deciding to.

"She isn't a ghost in this room," Marley said. "She's a blueprint." She glanced at him to make sure metaphor didn't feel like theft. "If the light keeps more than ships, and the stations are posted, and Mirabel's bottle sits behind the panel with instructions that assume we will know how to walk when called—then Jackie was one of the people who made sure the path did not close. You're not seeing her in me because you want to replace her. You're seeing her because the building is reminding you that the work goes on regardless of who's breathing."

He nodded, a muscle working in his jaw that had nothing to do with anger and everything to do with thawing. "I am afraid," he said, voice smaller, honest in a new way, "that I dismissed her and now I am... overcorrecting. That I am making a church out of this because I neglected a prayer. That I'm seeing her where she shouldn't be."

Marley let the words sit between them, not blocking the beam, not in its way. "You're seeing her because she was here," she said simply. "And because you loved her. Love is a calibration device. It tunes rooms. If the tuning shows you echoes of her in me, the thing to do is not to undazzle yourself. It's to make sure you're not mistaking an echo for an assignment."

He absorbed that the way a body absorbs broth after a day on its feet. "And if there is an assignment?"

"Then it will arrive without asking that you throw yourself into anything that burns you. The burned page is a relic; it is not a god. We have already decided how to read it. 'Only blood can rekindle the path' means lineage, obligation, table-setting. It doesn't mean a leap."

He looked down at the paper again. **Keep faith.** He caught on the verb. "Keep," he repeated.

Marley smiled slightly. "The town's password."

He slid the paper back into his pocket and felt the oddest relief—as if his wife had been returned to him not as a shrine but as a task list with better verbs. "I want to tell Sophie," he said. "Not the whole of it. Not the parts that would let fear think it had an office here. But that her mother stood at the fourth turn and breathed in time with the beam. That if she dreams the spiral and the stars again, she's not the first in our kitchen to do so. That 'called' is not a demand. It's an invitation. Declining is allowed."

"Good," Marley said. "And tell her the union rule about snacks."

He huffed a real laugh this time. The beam took it and did nothing dramatic with it except let it be a man's breath in a room that has carried too many unsaid sentences. He turned to Marley, and because the floor had been built by people who understood balance, he felt something inside him find the level.

"Every time you stand in this room," he said, "I see the way I failed to stand with Jackie. It's... hard."

"I know," she said. "And every time you make a list and insist we follow it, I see the way I would have burned myself down in this room if you weren't here to insist on boring paper. We're trading inheritances."

"The good kind," he said. "The ones that don't make Thanksgiving impossible."

He went quiet then in that purposeful way he does when choosing a sentence that could easily go wrong. "I see echoes of her in you," he said again, steady now, "and I'm learning to let them be echoes. Not replacements. Not demands. Just... music the room remembers, played on a different instrument."

Marley did not flinch at the compliment. She took it for what it was: a man laying his guilt down and picking up his share. "Then we play in tune," she said. "And when one of us slips, the other adjusts."

"Be kind," he said.

"Be in time," she answered, and it felt like both an inside joke and a rubric.

· · ·

Back at the table, they let the artifacts be less sacred and more useful. Marley slid the burned page into the stack of items for the solstice ceremony: compass, letter, charter fragment, music box, Rick's chart, Mirabel's instructions copied out clean in Hazel's upright hand. She added a card at the end that read in her tidy print: **Jackie—Keep faith (spiral).** A memory is allowed to take a seat next to a map.

"Tell me what you're afraid of now," she said—not the earlier fear, the larger one, but the one that can be written on a line and handed to the room without it becoming an autobiography.

He didn't answer at once. He looked at his hands. He has good hands—workman's hands disguised as a lawyer's, the kind that remember a wrench as easily as a pen. "That I will ask too much of Sophie," he said finally. "That I will hear 'blood' and say 'legacy' in the way fathers do when they need to make their own childhoods make sense. That I will bring her up here on solstice and make her an instrument before she knows which notes she's willing to play."

Marley nodded, relief sneaking in with sorrow—he was naming the right monster. "So we write a counter-spell," she said. "It is one sentence long and we can both memorize it. 'You may say no, and in this house no is holy.'"

He breathed. "Yes." Then, because he has been trained by life to make things safely official: "We write it. We put it on the inside of the door. We make the building read it before it starts any more grammar lessons."

She smiled. "You're going to make me a sign."

"I am," he said. "With good type. Pollard will weep."

She sobered then, not to scold the joke, but to place her words where they could do the most good. "Damien," she said. "Maybe it's not just about what you missed. Maybe it's about what you're meant to carry now."

He closed his eyes. When he opened them the room had done the small kindness it can do on command: it had stayed. "Say it again," he asked quietly, not because he hadn't heard, but because he wanted the sentence to lay track through him on a second pass.

"Maybe it's not just about what you missed," she repeated, slower this time so that the beam's rhythm could seat it where decisions live, "Maybe it's about what you're meant to carry now."

He nodded, once, and with that nod the future shifted its weight from one foot to the other and decided not to leave. "All right," he said. "I will carry the boring paper. I will carry the 'no' sign. I will carry the way Jackie stood at turn four. I will carry the fact that this room cannot be trusted without us and cannot be trusted if it has only us. I will carry the duty of not letting the word 'blood' get lazy."

"And I'll carry the candle," Marley said. "And the box. And the ridiculous courage to say a word to a room and expect it to answer with something kinder than spectacle."

"The waltz," he added. "We'll carry that together."

They looked at the schedule Pollard had written on a card with ink that made even the steady laugh: **Solstice—Midnight. Light. Song. Memory.** Beneath it, in a different hand—Hazel's—someone had written, **Union rules: feed everyone.** Evelyn had already drawn a star and written **soup** next to it in tiny capitals shaped like generosity.

Damien took out his phone, considered, then put it away. "No texts tonight," he said. "I'll tell Sophie in the morning. In daylight. With pancakes. Seven is a magic number because it is how many pancakes it takes to absorb terror into carbohydrates."

"Peer-reviewed," Marley said.

"That reminds me," he said. "I'm going to the print shop

at dawn to pull any blueprint that dares to have a margin. Join me?"

"I'll come after I stop by Moon & Morrow," she said. "Mirabel's panel is still a seam. We'll ask the room for permission to borrow her bottle for one night. We'll leave more than we take."

He nodded. "Consent," he said, half to himself. "The old rule we've just remembered."

They cleaned up together, the way people do when their hands have to learn the same liturgy or else the words they just said will fall through the floorboards. Compass closed. Sleeve straightened. Box set back in its place. Candle snuffed—Marley let the smoke rise and did not interpret it into a parade.

On the stair, at the fourth turn, they stopped. He reached toward the wall; she put her hand near. They stood like that, two people at a threshold that had become as familiar as a kitchen sink and as unforgiving as a judge. He said softly, to the stone and to Jackie and to the boy in 1892 and to every woman who had been posted at stations in this town—grove, apothecary, print, school, Chapel, docks, and the one they still hadn't found—"We keep."

Marley added, because some sentences ask for their companion to complete them, "We keep faith."

Down on Main, the Café door clicked as Evelyn locked up later than she should. In the window of the print shop a lamp still burned and Pollard refusing to be told what hour counts as decent for an archivist. On a second-floor walk-up a child turned in her sleep and dreamed of five stars that hold a triangle over a spiral and of a word that sounds like light learning to be kind.

21

THE HIDDEN CELLAR DOOR

The solstice sky had settled into its patient geometry, the stars arranging themselves as if on cue. Damien held the star wheel Sophie had left on the kitchen table—her careful lines and constellations, the same she had sketched from dream. The triangle crowned the lighthouse headland just as she'd drawn it: Vega, Altair, Deneb. Above, the lantern beam swept in its usual rhythm, but the pause between its arcs seemed longer tonight, weighted.

Marley knelt on the keeper's floor with the blueprint stretched out before her. Candlelight warmed the edges of the paper, making the faded ink sharper, as if it wanted to be read in firelight, not daylight. Her finger traced the marginal note: *Beneath the Flame—Healer's threshold, sealed but not lost.*

"Here," she murmured, pointing to the spiral carved into the floorboards. The blueprint's lines converged exactly there, as though the architect had drawn a doorway disguised as a symbol. "The solstice stars mark the angle. That's the key."

Damien crouched beside her, lamp in hand. "You're saying the spiral isn't just decoration. It's... instructions."

"Not just instructions," Marley corrected, brushing her palm lightly over the grooves. "It's a map."

The spiral's curves gleamed faintly, as if the wood remembered every hand that had pressed against it. Damien reached for the crowbar he'd brought up under the pretense of checking floor stability. He wedged it into the board's seam. At first nothing yielded. Then—softly, like breath withheld for a century—the boards shifted.

A hollow thud answered. Marley's heart jolted. Damien pried again. The spiral's center lifted, revealing an iron ring flush against stone. He looked at her once before pulling. Together, they raised a concealed trapdoor, the wood groaning in protest, and a waft of air drifted upward—cool, mineral, tinged with wax long burned to memory.

Beneath: a narrow stone stair, descending into shadow.

Marley lit a fresh taper from Hazel's candle, passing it to Damien. He set it inside the opening. The flame didn't flicker as it should have; it steadied, then leaned downward as though called.

"After you," Damien said softly.

Marley swallowed the tremor in her throat and stepped onto the first stone tread. The spiral carving hovered behind them like a guardian seal. She descended slowly, candlelight revealing walls etched with faint symbols—spirals repeating in variations, crescents and full moons scratched shallow but deliberate. Dust lay heavy, yet there was a strange order to it, like a room that had been waiting, not abandoned.

At the bottom, her foot touched level ground. She held the taper higher. A stone chamber opened around her, circular, its ceiling low, the walls lined with shallow shelves. Remnants of candles stood in clusters—melted stubs fused together, wax puddled in shapes like frozen rivers. The air was dense with the faint perfume of beeswax, lavender, and smoke.

Damien joined her, his lantern casting a steadier glow. They moved slowly, reverently, along the wall. Every few feet another spiral was carved into the stone—seven in total, aligned with phases of the moon scratched beside them. Wax drippings clung beneath as though each carving had once been an altar.

"This was no storage cellar," Marley whispered. "It was ritual space."

At the far side, a recess in the wall caught the light. An alcove, sealed by fitted stone. Upon its face, etched into the lintel, was a sun-moon glyph, perfectly balanced: one half golden rays, the other silver crescents. At its center, faint but clear, two initials entwined: **A.W.**

Marley's breath hitched. "Aurelia Ward."

Damien pressed his palm near—not on—the seal. "The alcove is intact. Not broken into. Whoever closed it meant it to stay closed."

"And yet," Marley said, her voice steady despite the quiver of awe, "they left a door."

His lawyer's caution flared. "Do we open it?"

She looked at the spiral carvings surrounding them, the wax remnants, the phases of the moon aligned with the chamber's circumference. Every symbol pointed here. Every remnant led to this alcove.

"Yes," Marley whispered. "We were meant to."

The glyph glimmered faintly under the lantern, as though the solstice sky above and the spiral path below had conspired to bring them to this moment.

· · ·

THE ALCOVE RESISTED, as though stone had learned loyalty. Damien ran his hand along the seams, searching for a hinge, a weakness. Marley placed the taper in a wax puddle on the nearest shelf and crouched, studying the glyph.

"The sun and moon," she murmured. "Balance of opposites. The Circle always worked in pairs—Aurelia in the grove, Mirabel in the apothecary, the keeper at the headland. Each post was partnered. The glyph says the chest inside belongs not just to her, but to the union she stood for."

Damien pressed lightly, and the stone gave the faintest echo of hollowness. "There's space beyond," he said. "We'll need leverage."

From his satchel he drew a mason's chisel and mallet. He set the edge carefully, glancing once at Marley as though asking permission from both her and the room. She nodded.

He struck once. The sound carried, low and resonant, like a bell buried under rock. The alcove seam cracked. He struck again. Stone shifted, dust whispering down.

Together they pried the slab loose and slid it forward. Behind it, dark and narrow, the alcove revealed its secret.

There, set into the recess, rested a wooden chest. Its surface was dark with age but intact, bound with iron straps. On its lid, Aurelia's initials were burned deep: **A.W.** Beneath them, carved into the wood itself, the same sun-moon glyph glowed faintly in the lantern light.

Marley reached, then drew her hand back before touching. Reverence steadied her. "She sealed it herself," she said. "This is no council record. This is Circle."

Damien crouched, ran his hand near the lock. The iron was ornate, not rusted through. A keyhole shaped like a crescent moon yawned, waiting.

"No key," he muttered.

Marley's eyes flicked to the shelf of candle remnants, then to the spiral carvings. "Maybe the lock isn't only mechanical." She took up the taper, held it over the chest. For a moment nothing happened. Then the flame steadied —unnaturally, without flicker, as though arrested in time. A faint line of green shimmered across the lock.

Damien drew a sharp breath. "The flame answers."

She set the taper down. "Not yet," she said. "Not here, not rushed. If the Circle sealed this chest with ritual, then it should be opened with ritual. At solstice, under the beam."

He hesitated, then nodded. "We'll carry it up. Carefully."

Between them, they lifted the chest from the alcove. It was heavier than its size warranted, as if time itself weighed inside. The wood groaned softly, but the straps held. They set it onto the chamber's floor, the glyph glinting faintly in the light.

The spiral carvings on the walls seemed to watch.

Damien wiped stone dust from his hands. "This room was their sanctuary," he said. "Shelves for candles, symbols to track the moon, space to gather. And when the Circle dissolved, they sealed what remained. A record, a tool, maybe both."

Marley studied the spirals, tracing one shallow groove with her fingertip. "They didn't dissolve," she whispered. "They went underground. They left this for us. Not just to find—but to finish."

THEY CARRIED the chest up the stair slowly, each step echoing with the weight of secrecy unveiled. The trapdoor closed above them with a final groan, the spiral carving once more a lid over what lay beneath.

In the keeper's quarters, they set the chest upon the desk where the logbook, compass, and burned page already rested. The Circle's archive was assembling itself piece by piece, an inheritance that demanded stewardship.

Marley brushed her fingers lightly across the lid, tracing Aurelia's initials. "She marked it for us. For those who would come after. Justice and memory. Sun and moon."

Damien set his lantern beside it, his voice steady. "We'll wait for the solstice. The flame, the song, the memory—all together. That's when it should be opened."

Marley nodded, though impatience coiled inside her. She could feel the chest hum faintly under her palm, as if alive with something preserved. "Do you hear it?" she asked.

Damien listened. The lantern ticked, the sea breathed, but beneath it—something else. A low, rhythmic thrum, like a heart behind wood.

"Yes," he said quietly. "I hear it."

They exchanged no further words. The beam swept over the windows, steady and insistent. The chest waited, glyph faintly glimmering, Aurelia's name a promise pressed into wood.

For the first time since uncovering the Circle's traces, Marley felt less like an intruder and more like an heir. And with that realization came the weight of responsibility: to open, to understand, to carry.

At the solstice, they would lift the lid. And whatever waited inside—ritual, relic, or revelation—would turn the prophecy toward its next chapter.

22

THE GREEN FLAME

Midnight gathered like a held note. Outside the lantern room, the solstice sky wore the Summer Triangle as if it had been stitched there by a careful hand—Vega high and bright, Deneb and Altair making their steady argument toward the river. Inside, the beam made its measured rounds: three short, two long, a pause weighted enough to feel like a door waiting on its hinge. The trapdoor we'd found beneath the keeper's spiral had been resealed for now—respect, not retreat. The chest sat on the table in the keeper's quarters, haloed by the candle Marley had kindled from Hazel's tapers. The sun–moon glyph on the lid—half rays, half crescent—seemed to breathe with the flame.

Damien set a palm near the lock, not on it. "If there's a key," he said, "the Circle kept it in a language, not a drawer."

Marley nodded, steadying the wick with two fingers to coax the flame upright without touching it. "Light, song, memory," she said. "Open with what it was sealed with."

He took a breath, and the room answered with its small, private shift in temperature—the way iron inhales when it's about to agree. From the piano bench by the window, he placed his phone face-down and set the old music box beside it. "One pass," he said, almost apologizing to the century, and wound the key. The comb's first plucked notes unfurled into the air—Rick's waltz, slowed and skeletonized, three to the bar like a heartbeat that has learned patience. Marley hummed the line under her breath, neither performance nor prayer, only remembering out loud. On the desk, the compass needle quivered toward the seam as if iron, too, can learn a ritual when it's loved long enough.

When the first strain reached the little held turn—the note Royce writes as a fermata because breath deserves a moment—the candle's heart flashed green. Not a flare, not a trick of wax. Green: unmistakable as sea glass. The lock answered with a quiet click that felt indecently soft for something that had been holding its breath for a hundred and thirty years.

Damien looked at her. She looked back. She didn't say *now*. She didn't have to.

He lifted the hasp. The straps did not protest. The lid opened on oiled hinges with the genteel sigh of an old door forgiving new hands.

Inside, the air smelled of cedar rubbed with lavender and the faint metallic tang of time. The first object sat in a carved niche as if the box itself had grown around it: a small glass vial stoppered with dark wax, no larger than a thumb. It glowed as though remembering light rather than emitting it—an inner radiance shivering from green to greener, like the heart of a flame seen through the back of a leaf. Its label had been written in a hand that knew both patience and ceremony:

Aequitas et Lux.

Marley exhaled too fast and laughed at herself for doing it. "It's... alive."

Damien's college brain still knew Latin even when his body was doing church. "*Aequitas et Lux*," he read, quiet. "Justice and Light." He touched nothing. He only leaned closer, eyes narrowed as if scholarship might save him from awe. "Not *justitia*. *Aequitas*. Equity. The law when it remembers its heart."

"That's what the Circle asked the light to be," Marley said, wonder expanding behind her sternum until it made a new room. "Not merely bright. Fair." She felt the words line up behind others: the charter fragment naming Aurelia Ward *Beacon of the Grove*; the keeper's letter, *Protect the boy*; the burned page that had scared her—*only blood can rekindle the path*—now leaning toward legacy, not knives.

Beneath the vial lay a shallow bowl wrapped in a square of cloth. Damien lifted the cloth by its corners and set the bowl on the table. It was ceramic, not precious in the way museums like—the kind of useful vessel a healer would have trusted, glazed a quiet cream with a ring of green at the lip. The cloth itself had weight. When Marley unfolded it, the breath caught in her throat as distinctly as if someone had tapped a glass.

Seven initials had been embroidered in a circle with thread the color of new leaves:

A.W. • M.C. • L.S. • R.A. • J.N. • H.G. • E.M.

She touched each letter with the softness of a fingertip deciding where it belongs. "Aurelia Ward," she whispered. "Mirabel Colvin." She looked across the cloth at Damien. "H.G.—Lorraine's grandmother's name was Hannah Gearhart." She lifted her eyes, startled. "R.A.—that chalked initial I never placed, L.S., J.N. And E.M. We thought the circle's list would only be initials. Here are seven, sewn with a needle, like signatures."

"They bound themselves together in thread," Damien said, throat rough. "So the town couldn't unbind them in ink." He set the bowl gently on the cloth—as if placing a word back into its etymology—and looked into the chest again.

A packet lay under the niche, sealed with wax pressed into the sun–moon glyph. Damien glanced at Marley. When she nodded, he loosened the cord and opened it. Inside was a single page, thick rag paper edged with age, ink browned toward the same steady sepia as Thomas's letters.

At the top, in careful script:

THE LIGHTHOUSE RITE

Marley reached for it and stopped, her hands changing their minds in midair—they wanted to handle and be handled at once. Damien offered it across the desk as if passing a child.

She read. Not everything. Enough to let the architecture of the thing reveal itself like a map under clean water.

At solstice when the crown is set (Vega, Deneb, Altair) and the beam keeps the sea's breath,

Light seven tapers in a circle, each walked by her post (grove, apothecary, headland, school, print, Chapel, docks),

and place the heart of the flame at the center to marry green to gold.

Let the bowl hold memory: salt, herb, bread; let each name be said and not erased;

and if the light falters, then equity shall lift it, not blood alone.

She could not help it; her eyes leapt to the bottom margin where a later hand had penciled a sparer line, almost a correction: *One must hold the light. One must pass it on.*

Damien saw the way the words landed inside her. He lifted his gaze from the page, past her, to the window's dark. "The rite is a ceremony of distribution," he said softly. "Not a sacrifice. Seven posts. A bowl that receives and returns. A vial that binds."

"And the crown is the Triangle above us," Marley said. "We're standing in the right hour. The box wanted solstice. The lock answered to the song." She looked back into the chest, expecting now what the Circle had taught her to expect: clarity braided with withholding. Beneath the packet lay a small bundle of matches hand-tied with green thread, their heads waxed. A thin length of ribbon. A sprig of lavender so desiccated it had become fragrance without mass.

Damien's jaw worked as he read the page again and again, lawyer and husband and keeper aligned in an awkward grace. "It reads like directions and like a will."

"Or like an apology," Marley said. "For what they couldn't finish."

He frowned. "What makes you think they didn't?"

She laid her palm—not touching—over the embroidered initials. "Because there are names we have, and others we don't. Because Mirabel walked to the headland and did not come back to keep her post. Because the keeper's letter about the boy came three years after her clipping. The sequence... sags. Something in the arc of their work fell; they bound what they could and hid the rest."

He looked at the vial again—its green alive as nicked mint—and then at the bowl and the cloth. "Then this is the residue of an unfinished rite."

"Or the start of its completion," Marley said. "They left us more than memory. They left us tools."

The beam passed, counting itself out on the desk's edge.

"Justice and Light," Damien murmured. "If we pour it. If we dare."

Marley held his gaze. "We *don't* pour it yet." She set the page gently down. "We read it properly. We ask the stations. We place what goes in the bowl. We bring the women's names. We make sure we don't perform what we don't understand."

Damien nodded, relief and resolve braided tight. "Agreed. Private. Careful. With witnesses who know how not to clap."

The vial pulsed once, faint as a sleeping pulse. Marley and Damien stood with the chest open between them, solstice crowned over the roof, a page titled *The Lighthouse Rite* on the table like a covenant that had waited for paper to mature into instruction.

"We finish what they began," Marley said, but not to hurry—only to promise.

By the time the waltz's echo had faded from the plank floor and the lantern's pause had moved one inch toward morning, the desk had become a tidy altar to logistics. Damien laid out the cloth so the initials formed a compass rose—A.W. at true north because Aurelia had been the axis of their inheritance whether or not she intended to be. M.C. at the apothecary's quarter. L.S. where the Chapel would sit if you drew town atop the table. R.A., J.N., H.G., E.M.—they would find those posts in the days ahead and nail them to memories that had dared to survive without registrars.

Marley took up a pencil and, on a yellow card Pollard would have found satisfying, transcribed the Rite's bones in her own plain hand:

- **Crown set:** Vega, Deneb, Altair visible.
- **Seven tapers:** one for each station: grove, apothecary, headland, school, print, Chapel, docks.
- **Center:** bowl with *salt, herb, bread.*
- **Vial:** Aequitas et Lux—"marry green to gold."
- **Speak names. Do not erase.**

She read the last line again—not one of Aurelia's sentences, but the penciled note at the bottom: *One must hold the light. One must pass it on.* She thought of Jackie at turn four, breathing in time with glass; of Sophie, eleven and grave, drawing the star crown with her pencil and calling it a dream; of victims of the light, if that was what Mirabel had become, and of the keepers who made sure victim was not the only name the room could pin to a woman who walked toward it.

Damien bent over the bowl. "Salt, herb, bread," he repeated. "Not oil and ash. Not blood." He glanced at her, apology and argument at rest between them. "If the burned page in the base wanted to frighten us into sacrifice, this one counters it with sustenance."

"It reframes," Marley said. "Blood as kin. Equity as flame. Mercy as fuel."

He checked the matches, the thread, the ribbon: practical redundancies disguised as talismans. "We'll need a circle we trust," he said. "No gawkers. No councilors who want to convert the encounter into a proclamation before we've finished breathing."

"Hazel," Marley said. "Lorraine. Evelyn, Tessa, Mrs. Bennett—because bread is not a metaphor in her hands. And Helena, because she knows what money does to stories and can bar the door from commerce."

"And Sophie?" Damien asked, carefully, the way you ask a child's name in a room that hears every thought spoken about children as policy.

"Not for the first lighting," Marley said. "She's part of the posterity we're protecting. She'll walk the spiral with the rest of the town when it's time. But the trial must be with those who can carry panic and not call it truth."

He nodded, relief honest enough to bow.

They turned the vial together in the lantern light without lifting it. The green moved like intention, not like liquid, as if the glass contained a verb. The label remained legible, the Latin frank. Aequitas et Lux. Marley felt a private astonishment that when the Circle wanted to name their heart they had not reached for a hex or a hush—they had chosen an ethic and an element and married them with a conjunction.

"Who made it?" she asked, half to Damien, half to the names stitched into the cloth. "Mirabel? Aurelia? The old apothecary's shelf kept a bottle marked for turn four, but not this." She thought of the alcove's seal, of the sun–moon glyph glinting through dust as if dust were simply a veil and the real work was fidelity.

"The page says 'marry green to gold,'" Damien said. "Perhaps the vial is only part—green as equity, gold as the beam. Candle as officiant."

Marley smiled at that, because it was the sort of sentence she could imagine the Circle sewing into a hem where a certain kind of historian would never think to look. "Then we'll bring the candle and the lens," she said, head bowed over the bowl like a congregant who has finally found a liturgy blunt enough to live with.

She lifted the cloth, bracing its edges over the table, and pressed the pad of her thumb against each stitched set of initials. The thread was slightly raised, a tactile rosary. She resisted the urge to read each name out loud; the Rite forbade erasure and demanded speaking, but it was not yet the hour. Words obtrude when they are rushed—this she had learned from both ghosts and courts.

The lantern made its long swing again. Down in town, the Chapel would be dark; even Mrs. Bennett sleeps sometimes. The river shouldered moonlight, making it look as if someone had poured thin brass along the surface. The beam separated sea from sky and, just beyond the horizon, re-braided them. Marley, hand hovering over the vial, felt unexpectedly simple. Not brave; not wise; just present.

"Do you still hear her?" Damien asked, voice careful. "Jackie?"

"Yes," Marley said, without the apology women are taught to staple to sentences like that. "But it's not an instruction. More like... bench space. The feel of someone having warmed the spot you're about to sit in."

He nodded, his eyes on the green. "I'll tell Sophie in the morning that her mother kept faith by standing still. Not by staging miracles. By not turning away."

"Union rules," Marley said, and the joke did what it always did: kept them from drowning in meaning by teaching the meaning to sit and heel.

They read *The Lighthouse Rite* one more time and put it back into its packet. Marley folded the cloth and tucked it with the bowl. Damien closed the lid of the chest but did not latch it. Some doors, once opened, deserve a nap rather than a lock.

"Tomorrow," he said, "we ask the posts."

"Tomorrow," she agreed, and let the word stand like a candle whose wick has not yet learned the taste of fire.

They walked back toward town with their steps unconsciously landing one-two-three, one-two-three, the waltz folding itself into their ankles. At the bottom of the headland, Damien stopped and looked up at the lantern as if the building had asked his attention and he had decided to give it freely.

At the shop door, Marley paused with the key. "On solstice," she said, "when the beam pauses, we'll stand in it. Not because we deserve to. Because we learned how to listen."

"And because we brought soup," he said.

"Union rules."

He grinned, and when he did, the town felt marginally more possible. Above them the light swung its patient instrument across the water, three short, two long, the pause saying in a grammar older than prophecy and newer than grief: keep. Illuminate. Carry.

Morning changed everything and nothing. The solstice crown still sat in the sky, only bluer and farther; the river changed outfits and went to work; the lighthouse did what it always does—turn fog into a job it can perform. Marley and Damien distributed invitations by hand like contraband: quiet, plain sentences written on linen index cards in Marley's careful print:

Keeper's quarters, midnight. Private preparation. Bring what belongs to your post. No spectators. No speeches.

Hazel's reply arrived in the form of a jar of herb-and-wax candles and a note that said, *I have seven pairs of hands if the room requires borrowing.* Evelyn sent a thermos of coffee and paper cups, enough for everyone. Lorraine sent biscuits and her name written in a card with a small envelope as if names are fragile, which they are. Tessa, brought a little pewter scoop of salt that had belonged to her mother, the kind of woman who taught a whole generation of boys to pronounce the words "there's enough" without swagger. Mrs. Bennett simply filled a basket and harrumphed, which meant *yes* twice. Helena offered an empty ledger and the promise it would remain empty. Royce came with his horn swaddled and a look that asked if the room might consent to music as witness, not as guest of honor.

In the hours it took Brookwood to live its day, Marley and Damien shaped the evening like bread. They cleaned the keeper's quarters until the dust had nowhere left to hide except in the story where dust always belongs. They carried the bowl to the window to learn how it liked light. They set the compass where the beam might choose to play off its lid and wrote, in Tessa's smallest fountain pen, the names they would speak:

Aurelia Ward. Mirabel Colvin. Hannah Gearhart. Lydia Sparrow. Joan Nye. Ruth Averill. Eliza Merrick.

"Where did you get the last three?" Damien asked softly.

Marley touched the cloth. The initials had been thread. The names had been coaxed—some from Lorraine's memory of who used to sit where at the charity circle's long table, some from the Moon & Morrow's old ledger that recorded credit in code only women would read, some from a penciled note in the margin of a sermon Pollard had found and pretended not to find: *Bless J. Nye for the tincture that spared us.* Tessa had required only that Marley ask the print shop to tell her who paid for paper when the minutes got long and hands needed folding. Not everything the town forgot wished to stay missing.

They placed salt in the bowl—scooped from Tessa's little spoon, not tabled—then a sprig of rosemary Hazel had tied with plain string, then bread, one heel broken from Mrs. Bennett's newest miraculous loaf and set with the plainness of consent. The objects sat together without arguing, as if reminded they come from the same agricultural grammar.

At eleven-thirty, the post keepers climbed the stair. Hazel came last, because she likes to close doors that the young open without meaning to. They arranged themselves without choreographing: seven people around the desk, two keepers at its edges, a horn by the window, a ledger on a chair because some books need to sit alone.

Marley set the cloth first, the initials outward. Damien placed the bowl in the center. Hazel lit seven tapers, pausing between each the way a person pauses between sentences when they've learned that breath is not an interruption of thought but its author.

"Speak the names," she said, not theatrically.

Marley began. "Aurelia Ward." Hazel: "Mirabel Colvin." Lorraine: "Hannah Gearhart." Helena, surprising herself with the gentleness of her own voice: "Eliza Merrick," Evelyn—who had never met a century—said "Joan Nye," simple as if asking a neighbor to pass the salt. Tessa, who put her faith in ink because she once learned to apologize for feeling, said "Ruth Averill" without apology. Mrs. Bennett, who knows more midwives' names than anyone, said "Lydia Sparrow." and the room made a sound that was not a sound, a slow settling like a large animal deciding to lie where it's always lain.

Damien reached for the chest, lifted the vial without tilting. It was lighter than it had a right to be, like a decision finally made. He held it over the bowl. The green within did not slosh. It adjusted. It brightened when the seven flames leaned inward.

"Marry green to gold," Marley said; then, remembering

the Rite's second sentence—*let each name be said and not erased*—she spoke again, steadier: "We remember you. We do not erase you." She nodded to Damien and he loosened the wax with the heat of a taper. The seal gave with a hushed sound, not a crack. The scent that lifted surprised them—rosemary, cedar, something mineral the color of river stones, and a brightness like wind after thunder.

He did not pour.

"Not yet," he said, and the room relieved itself of a nearly made error. "We finish the instructions." He looked not at the page but at the woman who had taught him to know when the law needs a witness. "Bowl holds memory. Names said. Crown set. Beam steady." He glanced at the window where the lantern's pause waited like a consent form. "When the pause arrives—on that count."

They waited. The waltz was nowhere in the room and everywhere in their pulses. Three. Two. One—the beam slowed over the glass like a hand placed over a child's eyes before a surprise too bright for first seeing.

"Now," Marley said.

He tipped the vial. A single drop, no more, fell into the bowl. It did not splash. It sighed as if remembering rain. The green inside the glass kissed the salt and went gold; it found the herb and went greener; it met the bread and turned clear. The tapers' flames leaned toward one another and then steadied. For a heartbeat nothing spectacular happened, which is how most holy things prefer it.

Marley waited to see if fear would arrive wearing its usual outfits. It didn't. What came instead was a sense she'd felt once as a child when she'd wandered into a church on a weekday and found the sanctuary empty: the room had not become larger; she had become the right size.

"The Rite is not incomplete," she said softly, understanding snapping into place like a hinge being remembered. "We were. The rest was waiting on us to carry it." She looked across the candlelit desk at Damien. "We've turned the burned page sideways. *Only blood can rekindle the path—only kinship. Only care. Equity first, then light.*"

Hazel's mouth curved, a private amendment accepted. Lorraine pressed her fingers to the cloth over Hannah's initials and did not weep because it would have been a show and grief hates being asked to perform. Rick's hand hovered over his horn, then fell; he understood without being told that sometimes the music is finished when the room says it is.

Damien held the vial upright again. The remaining green shivered as if satisfied with modesty. "We seal it," he said. "We keep it for the mirror of another night." He stoppered the mouth with the softened wax and held it over a taper to coax it back into honesty. The label—*Aequitas et Lux*—shone briefly then went humble.

The seven tapers burned without drama. The beam resumed its rounds. The bowl sat with bread and herb and salt and a single secret married into it, doing nothing urgent except be present.

Marley placed her palm near the edge of the spiral beneath the boards, an old habit rewarded with the faintest cool. "We'll put this away," she said, meaning the vial and meaning something else. "Not to forget. To prove we can."

Damien nodded. "And tomorrow, we'll begin explaining in the smallest possible sentences to the largest possible room."

"Union rules," Evelyn said, and blew out one taper, then another, not in order, leaving three and two and then the pause burning, because ritual has a memory for jokes if you teach it gently.

They cleaned the table as if cleaning were a sacrament, which, in town, it often is. Hazel took the cloth to fold; Lorraine brushed salt back into the bowl; Royce carried the horn downstairs as tenderly as a child at last falling asleep.

When the last guest had gone and the lock had acknowledged itself without spoken orders, Damien rested both hands on the desk and looked at Marley. "We finish what they began," he said again, less as resolve than as inventory. "We will walk this into the council without demanding applause. We will publish what can be published and keep what requires keeping. We will not sell it to fund a gazebo."

"We will teach the town to stand quietly," Marley answered, "and to call names without erasing anyone else's."

He lifted the vial one more time to the lamplight—the green quiet now, the glass ordinary. "Justice and Light," he murmured. "At last in the same sentence."

"Solstice gave us the opening," she said. "The rest is our day shift."

Outside, the triangle kept watch. The lantern's pause, having been honored, returned to duty with an ease that felt like a smile in the machinery. The spiral under their feet did not glow; it did not need to. It knew who was on watch and that the bowl had been fed.

They shut the chest without locking it, which in their grammar counted as trust. And as a new hour took its place where midnight had been, the green at the center of the dark learned to be patient again—held, not hidden.

23

THE LANTERN RITUAL

They sent everyone home.

Hazel had stayed in the doorway long enough to argue that a rite is most itself when witnessed by those who can keep their mouths shut; Mrs. Bennett had left biscuits as if starch could steady a room; Eveyln had muttered something about soup finding its own altar and refused to take back the ladle. Royce had hovered, horn in hand, until Marley touched the bell and said, "Not tonight," which is how you tell a musician that silence is part of the score.

When the stair was empty and the door below had admitted it without sulking, Marley and Damien climbed the last turn with the chest, the bowl, the cloth, and the vial between them. The lantern room waited like a held breath. Below, the keeper's quarters still smelled faintly of rosemary and warm bread. Above, glass regarded them without favor.

"It should be here," Marley said, voice low against all that iron. "The Rite names the beam."

Damien nodded, relief and caution tied together. "Private," he said, agreeing not to scare himself with the word *alone.* He set the bowl on the little service table beneath the lens and placed the compass where the beam's edge could decide whether to play with it.

Through the panes the solstice crown held steady. Deneb, Altair, Vega—there was the triangle Sophie had drawn from her dream, correct and indifferent. The beam did what it always does: three short sweeps, two long, pause. The pause felt different, but then everything did now that they had a page with instructions and a vial labeled in a language that had decided to keep its heart.

Marley unfurled the cloth so that the initials ringed the bowl like posts around a green. **A.W.** • **M.C.** • **H.G.** • **R.A.** • **J.N.** • **L.S.** • **E.M.** She placed salt in the bowl, then broke the heel of bread and set it beside rosemary Hazel had tied with plain string. Practical, not precious. The kind of ingredients that know how to work without applause.

"Seven tapers," Damien said, remembering the Rite aloud to keep from sprinting ahead of it. He set them around the lens pedestal at intervals that mirrored the shallow moon phases carved into the cellar's stone: new, crescent, first quarter, gibbous, full, waning, gone. He didn't measure; his hands knew the room's arithmetic. Each beeswax taper sat in an old brass cup he had polished until it forgave his father's fingerprints.

They stood on the far side of the beam for a minute, breathing into the task until their lungs agreed to the new rhythm. Marley felt the vial in her pocket—a careful pulse against the cloth—then drew it out and held it toward the lantern's light. The green moved as if it had a spine.

"The Rite says 'marry green to gold,'" she said. "No pouring. No spectacle. The way a promise marries a day."

Damien took the vial into his hand the way you take a

word someone trusted you with. "We say the names," he said.

They did. Not for a crowd. For the room. "Aurelia Ward," Marley said first. "Mirabel Colvin," Damien said, and the former apothecary's drawer slid open in his memory—the instruction pinned there with two pins like a butterfly. Marley: "Hannah Gearhart." Damien: "Lydia Sparrow." Marley: "Joan Nye." Damien: "Ruth Averill." Marley: "Eliza Merrick." After each name, the bowl did not change, which is how you hope your life behaves when you add truth to it.

"All right," Marley said softly, steadying her hands over the match. "The circle."

She struck the first match and lit the first taper—new moon. Then the next—crescent—then first quarter, and so on, around the pedestal, the glow low and human against the great machine's indifferent star-work. The seven flames trembled toward one another and steadied—a silent choir that had learned its place in the bar.

"Now," Damien said, handing her the vial.

She uncorked it by softening the wax with the edge of a taper. The scent rose—rosemary, cedar, a brightness she'd tasted once in the grove after a storm. She tipped the vial until a single green bead gathered at the lip, fat with decision.

"For Aurelia," she said, and let the drop fall onto the wick at north. It kissed the flame. Green flared and braided itself to gold, not overtaking it but making the hearth deeper.

"For Mirabel," she said, moving clockwise, and the second flame took the green like a memory finally put where it belongs. For Hannah. For Lydia. For Joan. For Ruth.

Six flames now: each with a green heart braided to its gold, the color not theatrical but persuasive. The lantern's beam swept; on the pause, the little circle seemed to gather itself, a collar of light warm enough to imagine wearing.

Damien watched and—nothing. Glass. Fire. Breath. The green was green; his eyes reported it; his heart did not. He did not panic. He did not invent something to make her feel less alone. He adjusted a cup so the brass didn't scorch a seam.

"Last," Marley said. "Eliza Merrick." She glanced up at him, that half-smile she uses when she trusts a room to behave. "You do this one."

He swallowed. He'd thought to stand back and carry the boring part—notes, safety, the part of ritual that turns it from show into vow. He took the vial. It was lighter now; it warmed his fingers. He held it over the seventh flame and waited for the beam's pause, because some lessons arrive once and want to be used. The lantern drew its breath. The world made room for a count of no numbers.

"Now," Marley said, and he tipped.

The bead fell. Green married gold. The circle closed.

MARLEY FELT them before she saw them: the tiny shift in pressure a room makes when it admits more bodies than it has chairs, the way iron changes temperature when someone it remembers steps over a threshold. Then the air by each taper thickened and lifted, as if flame were an invitation to take on shape, and they were there—the Circle, not as ghosts you could photograph but as presence you could steady your spine against.

Aurelia stood at north, shawl green, fingers bare. The light welcomed her hand the way glass welcomes a steady cleaner. Mirabel's apron was tied too tight because women often forget to leave room for their own breath; her eyes were rainwashed green; she carried a small parcel she did not yet set down. Hannah Gearhart held her chin at the angle of the unrepentant kind. Lydia Sparrow's hair was an argument with the weather; Joan Nye's wrists were inked with the faint stains of herbs; Ruth Averill had the square shoulders of a teacher who turns twelve children into a quorum; Eliza Merrick had a bell's humor—the kind that rings to call and then rings to dismiss.

Each woman held a flame in her palms. It did not burn them. It was the kind of heat you get from telling the truth carefully. They stepped inward until their ring of bodies matched the ring of the tapers, green braided into gold, the light not separate from the hands that carried it.

The lantern paused again. The beam seemed to lean down to listen.

"Look," Marley whispered, and then stopped because naming is sometimes a way of closing a door. She breathed instead.

The vision shone without demanding attention. She saw Aurelia tilt her head toward the bowl as if to ask—have you fed it rightly?—and Marley nodded before remembering that nodding is not translation. Mirabel touched the sprig of rosemary with two fingers and an old grief crossed her face —quick, private, not demanding anyone make it better. Hannah's mouth crooked as if saying *finally*. Lydia's eyes shone; she cut a look—affectionate, disciplining—at Marley's hands to make sure the vial did not get ideas about abundance. Joan set her flame slightly down and adjusted a brass cup that had skewed; she was the tidy one, the one who writes the rules after everyone has broken them kindly. Ruth looked out the panes to the triangle and took attendance among the stars. Eliza Merrick—oh, Eliza—she looked straight at Damien, laughed without sound, and lifted her flame higher like a cook who knows the difference between simmer and boil.

Marley had the sudden, ridiculous thought that she should offer them chairs and then the deeper realization that they did not sit for this work. They held their posts. They had come to stand.

The waltz—no, not played, nothing blown, nothing struck—threaded the room anyway, the way a tune your grandmother hummed will haunt your wrist while you knead bread. Three. Two. One. The green hearts in each candle answered the phrasing, pulsing softly at the exact place where Royce holds his breath, the room turning into time.

Damien saw nothing. He had prepared himself not to be punished for it. He focused on the safety of things: the distance between brass and wood, the glass's mood, the wick length, the fact that the breeze from the vent needed a quarter turn or the seventh flame would gutter. He put one finger to the vent's lever and the flame steadied, and he thought with sudden gratitude that not seeing is not the same as not keeping.

"Do you—" Marley began, then stopped. He shook his head once, not apologizing. He didn't want her to shrink her seeing to match his night.

She stood within the ring of women and felt a cool hand at her back. Not push, not pull. Placement. As if someone put a palm between her shoulder blades to remind her that bodies are meant to line up with their work, not posture against it.

"Illuminate," she heard. Not from the room, not from the lantern, not from a pipe's hum. From the circle. From mouths she would never rinse out for being too reverent.

Aurelia lifted her flame. The others lifted theirs. The

green in the wicks leapt, just once, high enough to touch the lens pedestal's rim. The beam passed and caught the lift and braided it—impossible, but she saw it—into the sweep, so that for a single arc the light that had spent a century guiding ships wore, along its gold, a stitch of green.

Damien blinked hard. In the moment his lids covered the room—no more than the space of a heartbeat—she appeared in the place where his skepticism had been keeping watch. A woman at north. Green shawl. Bare hand. She placed that hand, firm and maternal, on Marley's shoulder.

He opened his eyes, throat lodging on a curse and a prayer both. For a second he thought he'd fainted; he had not. The room held. The beam swung. The circle stood. And the woman he had not allowed himself to want let the weight of her hand rest on the person he had learned to love without comparison.

"Aurelia?" he said before he knew he was saying it.

The name did not leave his mouth. It stayed in his teeth like a word you rehearse before it walks into the air where it could hurt someone. The woman turned her head—not toward him; toward the flame—and nodded, once, the way you nod at a baby choosing the right stair by accident.

Marley felt the hand lift and set itself again. The second touch wasn't emphasis. It was permission. She heard a phrase—not English, not Latin—like a chord held by seven throats. Not a warning. A coda.

And then, because rooms try to embarrass only those who arrive late and necessary, the ordinary came back—the squeak of metal as the lens train adjusted, the soft tick of heat on brass, the river settling its agreements with the tide. The circle didn't disappear; it stopped asking her to look directly. She could see if she wanted; she chose not to.

Choosing not to look, she had learned, is a way of proving you believe a thing exists without it performing for you.

Damien stepped back from the pedestal and put his hand on the iron guard—near, not on, muscle memory catching him mid-instinct. He looked at Marley with eyes that had the same shape they always did and an expression he'd never worn in this room: relieved grief.

"I saw," he said, honestly.

"I know," she said, as if they were discussing a shared client, as if some part of her had been in his body when the lids came down and let the room show him the thing it had been holding out like a hat nobody would try on.

THEY DID NOT HURRY. The Rite does not like haste. Marley moved clockwise, pinching each wick down a fraction with one practiced swallow of breath, listening more than acting. The green in the hearts did not go out; it dimmed politely, as if agreeing to be stored for later. She corked the vial and warmed the wax smooth with her thumb. The label—**Aequitas et Lux**—had taken on the hard-earned humility of a sentence used correctly.

Damien stood where he could catch her if the room decided to play tricks with gravity. It didn't. The beam paused. They did nothing. The beam swept. They did nothing. Doing nothing became the craft the Circle had meant to leave them: *keep* as a verb, not an emotion.

"The line in the Rite," Marley said when speech was safe again, "—'and if the light falters, then equity shall lift it, not blood alone'—it wasn't theory. We watched it."

"We did," he said, voice quiet enough to be believed when carried outside this room. He looked at the seventh cup where his drop had fallen. A dot of dried green clung at the rim like a memory that refuses to be sanded out. "I saw her hand. On you."

Marley put two fingers on the place where the touch had been. "It felt like instruction," she said. "Not possession. The way your aunt sits you in front of the bowl and says, 'Here is how you turn dough gently'."

"I think," he offered carefully, because a man in his position learns to make observations rather than sermons, "that the Circle wanted the lighthouse to keep more than ships and less than people. They wanted it to keep the practice. The hand on the shoulder is a practice. It keeps you from leaning too far forward or pretending to be shorter than your work."

She smiled, the private kind that never quite figures out what to do with its own joy. "And the green in the beam?"

"Equity remembered itself," he said. "It will go back to being invisible until someone needs it to show. That's part of its dignity."

They lowered the tapers one by one, but not in order. She let the seventh burn longer because she is sentimental; he let the third burn longer because he trusts counting more than favorite children. The last flame went out and left the smell of warmed brass and honey in the air.

"Thank you," Marley said to the empty space where a ring of women had happily refused to sit. "For finishing with us."

They replaced the cloth. The initials faced inward, as if resting. The bowl, now heavier in some way that logic cannot weigh, held what it had been told to hold. Damien took the ladder and adjusted a vent that would keep the room from forming new bad habits out of good heat. Neither of them touched the lens.

"Tomorrow," he said, "I walk the council through it: the

page, the vial, the Rite. No spectacle. No quaver in the voice. They'll deny it in public and write me notes in private ordering tickets to the next miracle."

"And we'll charge them in bread," Marley said. "Union rules."

He laughed without apology. The lantern took it and tucked it somewhere safe, to use later when someone needed a joke more than a ghost.

They carried the chest back down the stairs and set it behind the desk where the trapdoor's seam is content to be a seam again. Marley laid the vial in its niche. It did not pulse like earlier; it rested, and rest is a proof of life as good as any. She closed the lid halfway—neither locked nor bragging.

On the stairs, they paused at the fourth turn because you do when you love a room and it has just allowed you to use it properly. Damien reached his hand toward the stone —near, not on. Marley mirrored him. The air there is always a fraction cooler, a hidden spring in the wall. He said a sentence that had no verbs and yet did work anyway: "Aurelia, thank you." And because he is learning to be less formal with dead women who respected plain speech, he added, "We'll carry. We won't bleed."

"Legacy, not sacrifice," Marley said. She heard, very faintly, seven voices answer: *Yes.*

They stepped into the keeper's quarters and the room did that small kindness again: it sat. Marley gathered the cloth and stroked the raised letters with two fingers. "Soon," she said to the names. "Public. Carefully." She imagined the council's faces—the polite denial, the quiet gratitude. She imagined the Mirror Room the blueprint had hinted at, the glass fragments that had been arranged not to show faces but years. She imagined Damien bracing himself against spectacle and being granted a vision anyway at the last candle, the way the town has started rewarding his decency with mercies that do not humiliate him.

Down on Main, a truck shifted in its sleep. In the Chapel, the "BE KIND, BE IN TIME" placard caught a draft and rattled without alarm. Far upriver, a train sounded the barest, kindest note—its own three-to-the-bar.

"We'll sleep," Damien said, and then, because he is honest enough now to admit what he wants, "—or we'll try. I'll tell Sophie in the morning that I touched her mother's hour and it answered me without making a fool of me. I'll tell her that saying 'no' is still holy. I'll tell her the union rule about pancakes."

Marley set the waltz chart on top of the chest, where it would be the first thing her hand found if she forgot what the room sounds like when it sings. "And I'll tell Hazel we didn't ruin anything," she said. "Which is almost the same as saying we did something right."

He looked at her then—the long look that means a man has decided not to miss his own life while cataloguing other people's. "You carried it," he said. "You didn't let it carry you."

"We carried it," she said, adjusting his grammar as if it were a cup too near a ledge.

They turned out the lamp and let the lantern have the last say. Three short, two long, pause. Somewhere in the beam's arc, for just a heartbeat, a stitch of green threaded the gold. No one saw it but the room. That counted.

On the walk down the headland path, they did not talk. At turn four they didn't put their hands out; the wall already knew their measure. At the bottom, Mrs. Bennett had left a basket as if she couldn't help herself. Inside: bread, apples, a note with three words: **Keep. Eat. Sleep.**

"Union rules," Damien said again, weary and young.

"Union rules," Marley agreed, and they laughed, which is the body's way of letting the beam do its job without interference.

Behind them, the lighthouse made itself ordinary again, which is the highest compliment a holy place can pay the living. The Rite had been recreated, not as reenactment but as work. The Circle had stood, flames in hand, and a modern woman with a pencil behind her ear had found herself permitted to see. A modern man who loves lists more than visions had been given one anyway at exactly the hour he promised not to perform.

In the morning there would be council. Then the Mirror Room and its fragments. Then legibility and its tedious necessary cousins. But for now the only instruction on the page was the one Aurelia had written without ink on the skin between Marley's neck and shoulder: a hand placed there, not to possess, but to place.

Keep. Illuminate. Carry.

24

COUNCIL CONFRONTATION

The council chamber was built for utility and purpose - varnished dais, a clutch of chairs set in dutiful rows, and fluorescents hummed overhead; someone had set out a carafe of water next to a plate of store-bought cookies that pretended not to know they'd been invited to a hearing. The bulletin board hung on the far wall with the town's values—**COURTESY • WORK • HARBOR • HOME**— as if waiting for an addendum the room hadn't yet earned.

Marley stood when her name was called. She had brought a banker's box, the least romantic vessel for the most tender cargo. Damien stood beside her with a flat portfolio and the unglamorous confidence of a man who knows where the originals are and what happens to towns that lose their originals. Pollard sat four rows back, hands folded over a legal pad he had sworn not to use. Lorraine and Hazel occupied the aisle seats like benevolent sentries. Evelyn had threatened to bring soup; mercifully, she brought silence instead.

"Ms. Taylor," said Mayor Richard Connelly, whose

posture suggested decades of lifting a town with his shoulders. "You requested time to present material relating to the lighthouse and the town's founding."

"Yes," Marley said, voice steady, pencil tucked behind her ear as if she might be asked to diagram a sentence at any moment. She set the banker's box on the table and lifted, in order, the things that had turned their days into liturgy. "I'm submitting for the record copies of the following: a fragment of the original charter naming Aurelia Ward as co-founder, titled *Beacon of the Grove.* A lighthouse keeper's logbook, 1876, with entries referencing a 'silent woman,' 'dreamlight patterns,' and a line we have corroborated elsewhere—*If the light falters, the healer's oath must rise.* A burned page recovered from the lens base reading *If the flame dies, she must rise—only blood can rekindle the path.* And a document titled *The Lighthouse Rite,* sealed within a chest marked with A.W. and a sun-moon glyph, describing a solstice ceremony of seven stations—grove, apothecary, headland, school, print, Chapel, docks—meant to bind equity to light."

The room did the thing rooms do when they understand they're being asked to learn: it made itself quieter than a hundred throats could manage on their own.

Marley laid the copies in a neat fan, each in a clear sleeve, originals secured in Damien's portfolio and in Pollard's chain-of-custody ledger by affidavit. "We also submit testimony," she said, "from living keepers of memory." She nodded toward Lorraine, toward Hazel. "And from the building itself. The keeper's quarters contained a concealed trapdoor beneath the spiral. A cellar chamber with seven carved spirals and moon phases. A sealed alcove with the chest. We opened it at the solstice. We followed the Rite—light, song, and memory—and we watched the lantern take on what the document names *Aequitas et Lux.* Justice and Light."

Mayor Connelly adjusted his glasses with the care of a man who hasn't yet decided whether what he's seeing belongs in a museum or a sermon. "You are saying," he said carefully, "that ritual was performed."

"I am saying that stewardship was resumed," Marley answered. "What the town forgot to keep, we kept."

Damien stepped forward, easing a paperclip from the portfolio as if it were a safety on a temper. "Mr. Mayor," he said, "councilors. We've authenticated what can be authenticated. The charter fragment's pulp and ink are period-correct; the logbook's hand matches other entries by Keeper Thomas Colvin; the cellar is in the lighthouse, not in our imaginations; the chest is real. The only parts of this that beggar the formal record are the parts we usually reserve for witnesses. So I'm giving you witnesses. Ms. Gearhart. Ms. Vale. And I'm asking you to treat the lighthouse like you treat the river: necessary. Sometimes unpredictable. And worth keeping whole."

He slid forward a single page with seven names written in Marley's even hand. "These are the women of the Circle as we can presently name them: Aurelia Ward. Mirabel Colvin. Hannah Gearhart. Lydia Sparrow. Joan Nye. Ruth Averill. Eliza Merrick. Their initials are stitched into a cloth found with the Rite. Their work appears in ledgers, margin notes, and in the gaps your predecessors politely papered over."

A murmur ran along the folding chairs—there is a particular sound people make when they hear their dead called by name in a public place and are not prepared to forgive the room for letting it happen. Evelyn pressed her lips together and looked down; Pollard watched his own hands as if they might volunteer the correct reaction for the crowd and he could simply copy it.

Councilor Whitaker, a man whose neckties looked like they'd been ironed at home by duty, cleared his throat. "This is all very... evocative," he said, choosing a word that behaves like an umbrella and a shrug at once. "But Brookwood is committed to history, not folklore. We have process. We cannot allow mysticism to revise the founding story every time someone finds a family legend written on the back of a hymn."

Marley smiled. It was not unkind. "We brought you ledgers, Councilor. We brought you a charter fragment with the town seal faint in the pulp. We brought you a keeper's testimony. If we had only a story, we'd have stayed home."

He color-blotched, but only a little. "The charter names a woman whose contributions we've long... appreciated," he conceded, as if appreciation were a currency the room could spend. "But that is not the same as... ritual. The town's beacon guides ships; it is not a sanctuary for... other obligations."

Hazel, who had promised Marley to remain silent unless the council asked her a direct question, managed to communicate three sentences with one eyebrow. Councilor Lorraine Gearheart took out a handkerchief with the kind of finesse that says both *I am moved* and *you will not see me moved twice.*

Mayor Connelly held up a pacifying hand. "Ms. Taylor," he said, softening his tone. "Please continue."

Marley did not offer theatrics. She simply told them what had happened, and because she is incapable of lying in rooms that long to be lied to, she told it the way a person tells a child how a drawer works.

"On solstice," she said, "we lit seven tapers for the posts

the Rite names. We said the women's names aloud, because erasure is also a ritual and we wanted to interrupt it. We dropped a single bead from a vial labeled *Aequitas et Lux* into a bowl with salt, herb, and bread. The flames took on a green heart braided to gold. At the lantern's pause, the beam wore that green for a single sweep—no spectacle, no trick. We witnessed what the Rite describes: equity married to light."

Whitaker inhaled to object. Mayor Connelly gestured him down with the smallest possible movement. "And the prophecy?" he asked.

Marley kept her hands flat on the table to keep them from volunteering to hold his caution. "We brought you the burned page from the lens base," she said. "*—If the flame dies, she must rise—only blood can rekindle the path.* We feared what it might require. We chose an interpretation that favors legacy over sacrifice. The Rite itself supports it: *if the light falters, then equity shall lift it, not blood alone.* We are not asking the town to bleed. We are asking the town to keep."

Behind her, a chair creaked. Councilor Miriam Merrick —quiet always, practical to a fault, a woman who wore her hair in a way that said mornings were for doing, not arranging—held Marley with a gaze that had learned how to read letters in lamplight. "Eliza Merrick," she said, voice barely above the hum. "My grandmother."

Marley nodded once. "Yes, Councilor."

Miriam's eyes went glassy and did not apologize. "Thank you," she whispered. "For bringing her name back into the light."

The sentence landed in the room like a kind of permission. It did not sway Whitaker, whose arguments prefer their opposite numbers sober and unadorned. It steadied everyone else—the mayor, whose neutrality had begun to feel like a policy; Councilor Alvarez, who takes minutes in her head; two shopkeepers in the back who had come because they always come; a teenager on summer break who had been told to "see how government works" and had found something older and less predictable instead.

"Let the record reflect," the mayor said carefully, "Councilor Merrick's statement."

Damien slid the portfolio slightly forward, a gesture that reads like aggression only to people accustomed to avoiding adjectives. "And let the record consider," he said, "the liability of remaining wrong. If the town declines to acknowledge the Circle's contributions, history remains a lie. Lies have costs. They rot foundations. They teach children to mispronounce their inheritance. The council has a chance to keep the truth. To do equity in public."

Whitaker bristled. "We cannot adopt unproven rites into policy."

"Don't," Damien said, without heat. "Adopt facts. A charter fragment. A keeper's log. A chest sealed within your lighthouse under a floor your own maintenance crews wax. Publish what is verifiable and stop pretending the rest doesn't smell like beeswax and lavender."

The room's hum rose and fell like a bar of the waltz. The mayor tapped his pen twice—one-two—and the chamber stilled, chastened and curious.

QUESTIONS ARRIVED the way summer rain does in Brookwood—sudden, then honest. Councilor Alvarez asked for dates; Marley gave them. Councilor Pierce asked how the cellar had been missed; Damien gave him the blueprint margin—*Beneath the Flame*—*Healer's threshold, sealed but not lost*—and the explanation every archivist knows: when a town chooses not to look, it calls the hidden "structural."

Whitaker tried another angle. "Even if we agree to... the significance of Mrs. Ward, we cannot endorse the idea that a town has been protected by... secret practitioners."

Evelyn, from the aisle, pressed her lips together hard enough to turn them white. Hazel's eyebrow contributed a rebuttal that would have been struck from the record if anyone had the courage to transcribe it. Marley ignored the bait; she had learned not to argue definitions in rooms that prefer their dictionaries thin.

"We're not asking you to endorse secrecy," she said. "We're asking you to acknowledge that labor was performed. By women. In plain sight. Under different names." She looked down at her list. "Charity circles. Ledgers no man thought to audit. A teacher who 'just happened' to walk children in a spiral before exams. A printer who 'just happened' to comp paper when minutes ran long. A baker who 'just happened' to bring soup on the nights grief meant no one could cook. Posts. Stations. Kept."

Councilor Merrick's hand moved—half-raise, half-promise of a raise to come. "My grandmother kept a ledger," she said, steady now. "We've argued in my family for years about what it recorded. I'd like to bring it to Mr. Hawthorne and Mr. Pollard for preservation."

Whitaker seized on the name like a man grabbing a railing during a sudden swell. "Mr. Hawthorne's... enthusiasm for preservation is well known," he said with a smile that mistook civility for argument. "But the council must consider perception. If we attach the lighthouse to... rites, we risk tourism, sensationalism, misuse. The harbor master already complains about kayaks."

It was a fair point twisted toward dullness. Damien picked it up and untwisted it. "We will not stage a pageant," he said. "We will not profit from a Rite that isn't a show. We will not let the beam become a brand. You have my word. Publish the documents. Mount a modest exhibit. Teach."

Mayor Connelly glanced at the copies again, eyes lingering on the burned page as if it might singe his fingertips through plastic. "What of that sentence," he asked, nodding at the line that had kept Marley awake, "*—only blood can rekindle the path*? You've interpreted it one way. Others may... read it with less... kindness."

Marley did not look at Damien. She didn't need to; he was already meeting the room where it had chosen to be afraid. "We brought you the counter-text," she said. "*If the light falters, then equity shall lift it, not blood alone.* We brought you the Rite: salt, herb, bread—nourishment; names spoken —restoration; a vial named Justice and Light—ethics, not appetite. If you publish the burned page without the Rite, you make fear the only grammar. If you publish the Rite with the page, you tell the story the way the town's matriarchs meant it: keep the light by keeping each other."

A man in a ball cap in the back—Harbor Master Doyle, utterly without guile in all things except fish—lifted a hand halfway as if hailing a taxi. "My crew sees the beam for a living," he said. "It swept green the other night. We all saw it. Nobody ran aground. If you can make the light keep like that without cutting anyone, I'll dock for the parade."

Laughter softened the floorboards. Even Whitaker let it move his shoulders—the human body will betray the sternest ideals if fed properly. Mrs. Bennett allowed herself one audible *hm* of satisfaction.

Mayor Connelly leaned back, the chair complaining as if asked to stretch beyond its design. "I will entertain," he said slowly, "a motion to receive Ms. Taylor's submissions into the archive and to empanel a small committee to draft an acknowledgment of the Circle's contributions to Brookwood's founding and ongoing welfare, to be read at midsummer."

Whitaker's hand lifted, palm already readying its amendments. "With due respect," he said, "such a statement risks politicizing... grief. I propose we... accept the documents into the archive pending further authentication, and defer any public proclamation. We mustn't alarm donors— or the state—by appearing to endorse... occult narratives."

It was an old move—dress fear in fiduciary clothing and ask it to chair the board. Damien did not scoff. He has learned that scoffing ruins minutes. "Deferral is a decision," he said, the kind of sentence law schools love and towns remember. "It teaches the living to wait for the dead to be palatable. We can guard against spectacle without strangling truth."

Councilor Gearhart raised a finger. "Compromise," she offered. "Two actions. One: accept and archive, with Mr. Hawthorn and his team to secure preservation and digitization. Two: instruct the historical society to draft a public history of Brookwood that includes the Circle by name, with footnotes, sources, and the phrase *provisional* if you need it to sleep. And schedule a listening session before midsummer to gather community testimony."

Miriam Merrick nodded, relief uncoiling in her shoulders like a string finally allowed to lie flat. Whitaker frowned, calculating risk. The mayor looked at the room the way a carpenter looks at a plank—checking for knots that will split later.

Damien Hawthorne sensed the vote tilting into the territory where good intentions go to be negotiated into furniture. He stepped back to the table and placed one hand near —not on—the stack of pages. "Let me be plain," he said. "If we do not acknowledge the Circle's contributions, history remains a lie. And lies metabolize. They become ordinances. Traditions. Budgets. They decide which children qualify for inheritance and which do not. This is not about mysticism. It's about whether you want to keep teaching Brookwood to forget the hands that held its light."

Silence. Then Pollard, from the fourth row, where archivists sit when they want to obey decorum and still be heard, cleared his throat. "As the person who will have to use the word 'provisional' in a footnote," he said dryly, "I would appreciate the council's permission to spell out every name Ms. Taylor has submitted and to file them under **Founding Labor—Circle of Seven**. We can litigate adjectives later."

Whitaker actually smiled. "Mr. Pollard," he said, "you will be the death of my inbox."

"Union rules," Mrs. Bennett murmured, and the back row laughed again, which is how towns accept small revolutions without getting hives.

THEY VOTED. Government rarely looks like thunder; it looks like hands raised, hesitations measured, a chair's voice performing arithmetic with more grace than algebra should allow. The motion, as Councilor Gearhart had drafted it, carried: archive and digitize; draft a public history naming the Circle; schedule a listening session. Whitaker's *nay* landed like a necessary punctuation—a reminder that unanimity can be a form of laziness. Miriam

Merrick's *aye* shook once as it lifted, a tremor of generational weight finding a place to set itself down.

"Carried," Mayor Connelly said. He sounded like a man who'd just decided to let new air into a room with old walls. "Ms. Taylor, Mr. Hawthorne—thank you."

Marley let out a breath she hadn't planned to hold. She collected the sleeves with the same care she uses on bodies —books, jars, rooms—and slid them back into the box. Damien slid the portfolio shut but did not clip it; it felt wrong to fasten a thing the town had decided to open, even provisionally.

Then, because towns put their truth where no one thinks to look, Councilor Whitaker stood and demonstrated what it means to lose a vote with dignity. "For the record," he said, "my objection is to haste, not to facts. If Ms. Taylor's *facts* hold, I will gladly eat cookies at a midsummer proclamation."

Marley, who has never learned to despise her own impulse to be gentle with men who are trying, gave him the smallest nod. "I'll bake," she said. "They won't be from a box."

A murmur moved through the chamber—satisfaction, amusement, relief. People began to stand, the way they always do when the official part is over even if the important part is still happening quietly at the edges.

Miriam Merrick approached the table. Up close she looked less like a councilor and more like a granddaughter calling a thing by its proper name for the first time. She touched the edge of the sleeve that held the cloth with the embroidered initials but did not lift it. "In my grandmother's kitchen," she said, "there was a drawer no one opened unless she said to. I thought she was hiding candy. I understand now." Her throat worked. "Thank you for bringing her name back into the light."

The sentence, spoken for the second time, did work the first could not. It sealed. It made room for the next. It gave Damien permission to say the thing he needed to leave behind in the minutes.

"If we don't acknowledge them," he said to Miriam and to the chair and to Whitaker and to the empty hymn board with its patient nails, "we keep living under a story that asked the wrong people to be invisible. It makes cowards of archivists and liars of fathers. I won't have it."

No one accused him of grandstanding. The room had learned, these last months, that when Damien's voice moves down into the register that barely carries, he is not trying to be heard by more people—he is trying to be heard by the right ones.

The mayor nodded. "Duly noted," he said, which is parliamentary for *you have the floor whether or not the agenda says so.*

They adjourned. People shook hands in that awkward way small towns do when they realize their grandfather's story has just gained a grandmother. Royce clapped Damien on the shoulder hard enough to be a vote of confidence. Pollard murmured something about proper humidity for cloth. Lorraine pressed a folded scrap into Marley's palm— *Hannah Gearhart's apron pin,* written in pencil—and walked away before it could turn into a scene. Hazel's eyebrow resumed its resting skepticism. Evelyn pointed at the door with her chin: **eat.**

On the steps outside, the air tasted like the moment after a storm where you inventory your roof and your courage and decide both can be mended. The lighthouse stood where it always stands. The beam took its time being obvious.

Marley sat on the railing, letting her skirt find its own compromise with fresh paint. Damien rested his elbows beside her, far enough that it wasn't an assumption, near enough that it wasn't a joke.

"You were right to warn them," she said.

"It's my least favorite verb," he admitted. "But I don't know any other word for telling a room it has misfiled its soul."

"You were kinder than you think," she said. "You gave them lanes."

He smiled, the slanting kind reserved for her. "You gave them names."

A gull shouted something profane about the sanctity of public proceedings. Down the block, the print shop's door banged; Pollard had gone back to his humidity. In the Chapel window, the placard—**BE KIND, BE IN TIME**—caught a draft and tapped the glass in time with a beat neither of them announced aloud.

"Next," Marley said, "we prepare for the listening session. We give people a way to speak their grandmother's sentences without being mocked."

"And we write the smallest possible proclamation," Damien said, "so the town can say it and mean it, and the Circle can ignore it and keep working."

She reached into her pocket and took out a linen index card, already written in her careful hand—the sentence she had intended to read if the vote went badly, the sentence she realized the town deserved to hear even in victory. She read it to him in the twilight like a promise and a warning both.

"*May all who bear witness find truth in the light.*"

He closed his eyes for a heartbeat—the exact length of

the lantern's pause—and opened them easier. "We'll put it on the hymn board," he said. "Under **HOME**."

She laughed. "Pollard will die."

"Union rules," he said.

They started toward the square, box and portfolio between them like a third person. At the corner, a child on a bicycle looked up at the headland and said to no one in particular, "It was green last night." No one corrected her. No one needed to. A truth can be a child's sentence and still stand in the record.

At the bottom of the steps, Miriam Merrick caught Marley's sleeve. "One more thing," she said, voice level again. "If anyone asks whether we are 'endorsing the occult,' I will say: *We are acknowledging women who fed us.*"

Marley nodded. "You're going to be very good at this."

Miriam shrugged. "I had a good grandmother." Then she took a breath, and wiped at one eye with the motion of a woman who has a meeting in five minutes and refuses to show up as grief. "Keep going."

They did. Past the shop windows, past the Chapel where Royce would rehearse a waltz that now belonged to people with names, past the coffee place that used to be a bell foundry and still smelled, on damp mornings, like iron and hymnals. Up on the headland, the beam cut its three-two-one and, for one sweep only, wore a thread of green so fine it could have been a rumor if you didn't know how to keep your eyes open at the right place in the bar.

"History," Damien said, almost to himself, as if tasting a word he had previously only argued with.

"Kept," Marley answered, and the verb felt exactly right in her mouth.

They turned toward home—his to pancakes and a morning where a daughter would be told her mother's hour honestly; hers to a table that had learned to hold bowls and pages and the kinds of names that make rooms choose their size. Behind them, the council chamber emptied. Above them, the lighthouse continued its one job, untroubled by minutes and votes, stubbornly certain that nothing stays saved unless someone stands up in a public room and says why.

25

____

THE MIRROR ROOM

They did not tell anyone they were going back down.

No note on the shop door. No text to Hazel, who would have approved and then found a way to be waiting on the last stair just in case the room wrote a foot-note. No message to Pollard, who would have arrived with an instrument designed to measure something no one else had remembered to name. Even Mrs. Bennett was spared the errand of a basket. This hour belonged to the two people who had opened the chest and read the Rite without asking the room to make a spectacle of their competence.

Damien slid the spiral's center board aside; the iron ring lifted easy as a hinged sentence. The trapdoor sighed the way wood sighs when it has decided to trust you twice. The air that rose was cool, salted, faintly sweet—beeswax and rosemary and the chalky breath of stone. Marley lowered her taper until the first curve of stair admitted its light, and then they went down the narrow, spiral throat.

The chamber met them as before: circular, low, ringed with shallow shelves and seven carved spirals beneath paired moon phases. The alcove gaped open where the chest had rested; its lintel glyph, sun married to moon, caught and held the taper's little fire. The bowl they had used the previous night waited on a flat of stone, bread crumb dried to a memory, rosemary stem now only a scent remembering its shape. The place was not abandoned. It had the tidy look of a kitchen that expects its cooks to return after a short nap.

"We missed something," Marley said softly. Not accusation. Not regret. Just the field note of a woman who trusts the way rooms pace themselves.

"Look for what we didn't have language for yesterday," Damien said. He raised his lantern; the flame leaned toward the far wall. That is how they saw the circle.

At first it read as a decoration: a round, waist-high arrangement of glass—shards and fragments—set into the stone like a mosaic the mason had been allowed to finish in his own time. Triangles, half-moons, long slivers blackened at their edges, a few arcs the size of a hand, one that suggested it had once been a perfect oval before heat turned it into a question. They had not looked long enough before because the eye, trained by stories to choose either beauty or utility, had filed it under *old lens pieces: interesting, later.* But lantern-light answered from the glass as if the fragments had been waiting to be identified by their use instead of their origin.

Damien stepped nearer—near, not on—and lifted the lantern shoulder height so its flame would sit even with the ring's center. The glass did not throw back their faces in the usual way. It gathered the light and thinned it until you could see not through it, not into the stone behind it, but along the skin of time itself—a sheen like breath on a window that has decided to become script.

Marley set her taper in a wax puddle at a carved notch. "Seven," she said. She moved clockwise, setting candles where the wall offered its old little altars: crescent, quarter, gibbous, full, waning, gone, new. One by one, the flames found their composure. One by one, the shards surrendered their dullness.

"What is it?" Damien asked, though the part of him that understands the law of rooms already knew the answer.

"Not a mirror," Marley said. "A witness." She read the faintest line etched above the circle, a sentence worn by breath more than by chisel. "*Memoria, non umbra.*"

"Memory, not shadow," he translated. He swallowed; translation went down hard sometimes.

She stood opposite him so the ring of glass had their two lights at perfect offset. For a breath the fragments held only amber. Then one shard—narrow, finger-long—took on a green seam, and another—curve of a lens—found a gold that came from no candle in that room. The circle did what circles do when they learn they are whole: it steadied. The shards did what shards do when they find the geometry they were cut for: they worked together.

"Near," Marley reminded herself under her breath, out of habit, out of love, and because the difference between keeping and possession is often only the width of a hand.

The first image did not pounce. It thickened. Light became a surface that could be read. The slivers' edges softened like silk under steam and, in their angle, a small, complete scene arrived not as theater but as information: a hand setting a taper into a brass cup; a second hand hovering over the flame until its heart flickered green; seven cups answering like a chord built on bodies.

Marley went very still. Damien lowered the lantern an inch, then raised it, testing the room's appetite for light. The scene adjusted but did not vanish. He breathed. The circle breathed with him. Memory, not shadow. Not the absence of light. Its discipline.

"Look," Marley whispered, not as instruction but as reverence, and the fragments obeyed: they looked, and let themselves be looked through.

THE NEXT SCENE lived in the shallow arc at the circle's left—a crescent of glass blackened along one lip, as if it had spent a century learning what fire steals and what it leaves alone. A shawl moved through it, green as rosemary oil poured thin. The hand holding the shawl had a callus at the base of the thumb, the kind you get from lifting wet baskets, heavy paper, babies. Marley's throat closed. She had known this hand since the first time she read the charter fragment and pictured its author with more shoulders than history permits women to keep.

"Aurelia," she said, and the name found its own chair in the room.

Aurelia did not pose. The glass would not have allowed it. She tied the shawl's knot with hands that had learned to tie knots when tying meant shelter, not costume. In a neighboring shard, a lens curve held her face at an angle no portrait would have chosen—the three-quarter turn of someone listening for a child in a room that isn't supposed to contain children. Marley's chest stumbled on a sudden, unreasoned affection. If you guessed at Aurelia's beauty, you guessed wrong. She was not decorative. She was accurate.

"Watch the way the room remembers her," Damien murmured. "Not as a saint. As a person whose wrists got tired."

The glass agreed. It offered another memory, the scale

humbler: Aurelia's knuckles red from cold water, pressing lavender into cloth; a child laughing off-screen; the quick, almost irritated tenderness of someone who loves and needs to finish what she started. Marley's mouth tilted at the corner. Not so different from her aunt.

Her aunt arrived before she completed the thought, as if the circle had learned to hear her through inference. In a long shard toward the bottom—ground glass that could not be polished back into clarity—Marley's aunt moved through the back room of Moon & Morrow with the same economy Aurelia had, a jar in each hand, a song near her mouth. The little bell over the front door did not ring in the memory— no customers, no pretense—only the careful way she tested wicks by running her fingers under the flame. Marley resisted the reach of her own hand—a reflex to touch what you've already lost. Near, not on. The room granted her the decency of not making it a test.

Her aunt looked up in the shard. She did not see Marley exactly. Vision is not glass and glass is not a door. But she paused in that precise, human way you pause when someone you love enters a room she isn't supposed to be in and you decide quickly to forgive the architecture. A half-smile. A little shake of the head at the wick. Back to work. The mercy of ordinary.

"Do you see?" Marley breathed. "It doesn't perform grief. It refuses to posture. It lets them work."

She moved her taper a fraction. The color in each fragment answered. Between Aurelia's shawl and her aunt's jars another face surfaced—not in full, not staring, but caught in the action of lighting: Marley herself, last night, a hand steadying a match, a mouth saying a name with more care than pronouncing warrants. She startled. Not from vanity— from sudden, clean recognition. In the memory she had what memory always gives you only when it's finished with you: composure.

"Don't look away," Damien said softly, eyes on the glass, not on her. "You earned seeing yourself without editorial."

She didn't. She let the scene hold. She watched herself set the vial above the bowl, the bead of green gather itself like a sentence spoken once and for all, and then she watched the scene let go before it became a loop. The circle refused to let her watch herself too long. Vanity is a kind of erasure. The glass would not risk it.

Another piece brightened: a slender triangle that made light look like it had decided to whisper. Lydia Sparrow—young, hair down, candle smoke smudging the knuckles where she had once burned herself and learned something she refuses to teach with words. A scrap of paper, rolled, slipped into a seam in the lighthouse base—Lydia looking over her shoulder, not from fear, from policy. Marley grinned. Of course. Some rules are older than law.

The memories did not line up like a slideshow. They arrived like tides do—ripples and returns, a current you feel in your ankles before you see it lift a whole river's skin. In one shard, Mirabel Colvin walked toward the headland at dusk, the parcel in her hands wrapped plain. The circle wouldn't show more; it is skilled at refusing to let pain dress itself up as information. In another, Hannah Gearhart wrote a name in a ledger with a pen whose nib had a kink from being gripped too hard. In another, Eliza Merrick rang a handbell once and then laughed at herself for being sincere in public.

Marley listened to all of it. Not as a voyeur. As the person who had been asked to keep. The circle accepted her acceptance as its price of admission.

"Try your light," she said, stepping back a half-pace so the lantern could carry without her taper drowning it.

Damien lifted the lantern as evenly as a man carrying a baptism; the flame steadied; the circle changed temperature again.

In the far-right segment—two curved pieces meeting at a dull corner—the image gathered in such plain domesticity it hurt more than spectacle ever could: a kitchen drainboard. A towel. A cup turned upside down to dry. A hand—Jackie's hand—flicking water from her fingers with that quick, efficient motion she had when her mind was already out the door. Marley felt her own eyes sting and did nothing to manage it. Damien went very still.

The shard held. It did not leap. It did not leap because what came next belonged not to the whole town. It belonged to a man who had learned, at last, to let rooms decide how much of him they could afford to carry.

"Let it," Marley said, the smallest push a friend can give without shoving.

HIS FIRST THOUGHT, when the circle decided to show him, was that the room had made a mistake. The infant on Jackie's shoulder could not be Sophie. They had not moved to Brookwood yet. The checked cloth on Jackie's back was one he remembered from their apartment in a different town. The shawl at the edge of the frame was not Jackie's; he had never seen it in their house. The lens behind her—there, in a curved shard about the size of his palm—was the Brookwood lens, unmistakable even in memory: the old brass guard, the very slope of the prisms he had catalogued so carefully. He ran the calculus in an instant—time, place, the impossible arithmetic of grief—and then, because the room would not reward algebra, he stopped trying to fit the scene inside a compare-and-contrast he could win.

Jackie stood in the lantern room. The beam was not lit. Daylight made the prisms look like a stack of seas thawing. She held the baby the way you hold a new human when it is still astonishing to both of you that anything so loud can be that small. The infant's hair was ridiculous—dark and upright as a grievance—and her mouth was the mouth he kissed goodnight now, only smaller and still learning the shape of yes.

"How," he said, not to Marley, not to the room, to nobody, because why is not a question the circle answers.

Jackie laughed at something off to the left—someone making a face, perhaps; a woman offering a shawl; a hand he could not see taking the diaper bag from her shoulder. She looked tired, in that glamorous way women refuse to call glamorous, the kind of tired men write poems about when they are ready to be mistaken. She swung the baby once, barely—comfort without orchestration. The infant yawned, eyes rolling up, and then—this was the part that bent him—she opened them again when the beam's place in the room would have passed if the beam had been lit. A pause where light would be. A child's body knowing a grammar that hadn't been introduced yet.

"Jackie," he said, not to summon, not to claim. To acknowledge.

The scene shifted minutely. In a neighboring shard, a hand entered—ringless, slender, unafraid—and placed a palm against Jackie's shoulder blade. Not the way you push a person forward. The way you steady a person not to tip a cup. Familiar and not his. Tender and utterly impersonal: the benediction of a station hand on someone whose work temporarily overlaps your work. Jackie didn't startle. She adjusted her weight and accepted the hand without diminishing her own stance.

"You brought her here," Damien said, as if reporting the fact to a clerk. "Before I knew what I was refusing to know."

The glass refused him more past tense than was healthy. It offered him present, the only verb the Circle trusts. Jackie kissed the infant's ear and said, as clearly as if the shard had been fitted with an excellent microphone, "Keep faith." Not an appeal. An instruction. Then she laughed again—someone off-screen had made a smart remark she would tease them for later—and the shard let the image thin until it surrendered to stone.

He did not reach out. He did not touch. He held the lantern steady until his hands learned the new weight of what he had just been given: not a wound, not an apology, a fact. A day he hadn't witnessed that had nonetheless belonged to his life the entire time.

Marley barely breathed. She had watched men be destroyed by rooms, and she had watched men be repaired; she could tell which one she was watching now by the way his shoulder blades lowered by a half-inch and stayed there. He did not weep; he refused to be brave. He just let his face agree with itself for once.

"She came," he said, the word so modest it should have been incapable of carrying the amount of light it carried. "With Sophie. Before we moved. She brought her here."

"Maybe she recognized a room she'd already dreamed," Marley said. "Maybe the room recognized her. Maybe the Circle was doing what it always did—keeping the living who hadn't learned the address yet."

He nodded. He did not demand a theory. He did not write one out of fear. "I never asked why she liked lighthouses," he said, then corrected himself immediately, not from shame but from accuracy: "I asked. I made jokes when I didn't understand the answer. Then I stopped asking."

"Now you can ask the person who remembers," Marley said, meaning Sophie.

"Yes." He swallowed. "And I can answer the part that belongs to me."

They let the lantern lower. The circle dimmed without withdrawing its consent to be looked at again. One shard— thin, nearly clear—held the faintest afterimage of Jackie's sleeve. He did not look away from it. He looked at it until it ceased to be a trick and became, again, glass.

He set the lantern on a shelf. The flame steadied itself into a practical height. He turned, and because the room meant to be kind, he found Marley already beside him, not touching his arm, not performing compassion, simply present the way a wall is present when you lean—not as furniture, as architecture.

"Thank you," he said, which could have been aimed at her, the circle, Jackie, Sophie's ridiculous hair. It landed in all the necessary places.

"What did you see before that?" she asked after a respectful piece of silence, because sometimes it helps to build a small bridge from the floodplain into the hour ahead.

He told her—the towel, the cup, the drainboard—and watched her smile. "The Circle refuses to let us make altars out of anything that doesn't feed someone," she said. "Domesticity is part of the spell."

He laughed once, and the laugh did the trick of getting the rest of his breath past the place where his chest had been holding it like a law school footnote. "We'll bring Sophie," he said, and then shook his head. "No. We'll ask her. We'll tell her what you tell rooms when they're new to the work: 'You may say no, and in this house no is holy.'"

"Union rules," Marley said, because the rule had become a form of piety.

They stood a minute longer and were greedy enough to ask for one more thing. The circle obliged without being called names. In a small piece near the top—a sliver thin as a fingernail—it offered them a brief, unglamorous view: Lydia Sparrow older, hair gone to its stubborn gray, placing a glass fragment into the ring with pliers and muttering to herself about men who don't carry their weight. She set the shard, wiped her forehead with the back of her wrist, and left a little crescent of wax on the stone. She didn't clean it. She had other rooms to keep. The shard caught a stitch of her laugh and gave it back.

"That's enough," Marley said. She pinched one taper, then another; she did not follow the moon's order; she followed breath. The green in the hearts went shy. The circle accepted darkness the way a faithful animal accepts its leash—not as punishment, as permission to rest.

Damien replaced the trapdoor with the care you give to a lid that has, at last, decided to bear your family name without sarcasm. The spiral lay clean under his hands. He didn't trace it. He had learned not to touch policies with fingers meant for people.

In the keeper's quarters, they sat without doing the thing towns do—summarize. Marley took out a linen card and wrote two sentences, neither of which she read aloud: *Memoria, non umbra. Show only what feeds.* She tucked the card under the chest lid so the room could study its own best advice later.

Damien put his palm near the desk—not on it—and said the words he had dreaded and desired in equal measure. "When I tell Sophie, I'll say her mother kept faith by bringing her to the light before anyone had given her permission to want it. I'll tell her that the room remembered what I forgot to ask. And that memory is not a shadow. It is the part of light that knows how to stay."

Marley nodded. "And we'll write that on the hymn board," she said. "Under **HOME.**"

He smiled the way you smile when the world has just made itself larger in the precise measure of the thing you thought would make it smaller. "Pollard will die," he said.

"Union rules," she answered, which is to say: *we'll feed him first.*

They rose. On the stair, at the fourth turn, they did nothing grand. Near, not on. Breath, not proclamation. At the bottom, the lighthouse lifted its patient head over the town as if amused at the idea that men could refuse to be kept. On Main, a child in a purple raincoat hopped a hopscotch chalked by someone who still makes their 7 backward. The beam took its three-two-one like a song that has discovered it is not finished after all. And somewhere under the floor, the circle of shards rested, ready to refuse spectacle at every opportunity and ready, when asked with discipline, to show the kind of mercy that looks like a kitchen towel and an impossible day finally given back to the person it belongs to.

26

DAMIEN'S VISION

The house kept its own small watch. Pipes settled; the fridge muttered; outside, the river traded confidences with the tide in the alley the way it always did when people were supposed to be sleeping. Sophie had gone under quickly—a book face-down on her chest, pencil fallen into the duvet like a twig on snow. He'd told her, in the calmest father voice he owned, that he had seen a memory of her mother in the light and that it had been a gift, not a punishment. He'd told her she could ask anything. She'd asked for pancakes in the morning and a promise that he wouldn't make her go up the headland if her stomach felt wrong. He'd said yes to both, because "no is holy" only works if "yes" is honest.

The star wheel sat on the nightstand, a tiny paper sky watching his breath. He tried to read—polling briefs, the kind of cleanly written boredom that usually sanded his mind down to sleep—but the letters shrugged off duty. Sometime after midnight, he set the book aside and let the room dim. The last thing he saw before sleep took its place was the circle he'd carried all day inside his sternum: seven posts, seven flames, the bowl holding bread and herb and salt while the vial's green made its one small vow.

The dream gathered without permission or grammar. He walked the headland and did not feel the climb. He opened the lighthouse door and did not hear its hinge. He took the stair and the stair took him as if the building had joined his muscles to its own. When he stepped into the lantern room, the beam wasn't turning. Dawn barely lived yet in the glass.

They were already there.

He understood it was dream by the economy of the scene—no drafts to check, no cups to polish, no rope burn in his hands from giving himself the kind of work that proves a man necessary. Just the circle: seven women set around a cradle not of wood but of light, a low nest of reflections at the room's center where the pedestal would otherwise insist on working alone. The faces were not theatrically clear and the edges did not glow. Each woman wore the kind of expression work gives a body when purpose has replaced narrative. Aurelia stood north, shawl green, hand bare. Mirabel Colvin held a small parcel she did not open. Hannah Gearhart's mouth waited in its permanent almost-laugh, the kind that means you've learned to live with other people's seriousness without letting it steal your appetite. Lydia Sparrow's hair refused domesticity; Joan Nye's wrists were stained by useful plants; Ruth Averill's shoulders kept their square on behalf of children; Eliza Merrick balanced humor and propriety like a tray set neatly for tea and tinctures both.

In the nest of light lay a baby.

No one told him whose. He understood in an ordinary, unarguable way that the baby was whoever needed keeping at the hour a town decides to try and forget itself. A boy in

1876, perhaps. A child carried by a woman who walked to the apothecary with answers in a jar and came home with less breath. A girl with a star wheel and a father who had learned to put his hand near, not on. If the dream wanted to be coy, it didn't. The face was any infant's. The fists were the stubborn poetry of the species.

They were chanting. Not loud, not seductive. Practical music. The kind of rhythm that organizes hands.

One—two—three. One—two.

Three short. Two long. The beacon's pulse repurposed into speech.

"Keep. Illuminate. Carry," the circle sang, not with sopranos and altos but with a range of lives. The words braided with others—Latin not drawn for the sake of fancy but because a tool made long ago still fits the human mouth: "Aequitas. Lux." Equity and light. Then a list that turned posts into a prayer: "Grove. Apothecary. Headland. School. Print. Chapel. Docks."

They did not look at him. Of course they didn't. He wasn't the point. He stood where a man who's learning stands: one step back, as if he's the usher who makes sure doors don't shut on the hems of women doing the parts of history that won't wait for the minutes to catch up.

Aurelia bent her head toward the infant, not with ownership, with intention; her lips moved on a sentence whose shape he somehow understood before he could hear it. "Keep faith," she said, which doubled itself into Jackie's voice for the length of one heartbeat and then did the kindness of returning to its source. Mirabel touched a tiny heel with two fingers as if counting pulse, then set her parcel beside the light and withdrew, the way you take your hands away from an instrument you trust to play the rest of the measure on its own. Hannah nodded toward the bowl, and bread appeared there (no trick, no miracle, only the certainty that a town that eats together keeps together); Lydia adjusted a wick without scolding; Joan added a sprig of rosemary; Ruth tipped a scoop of salt that did not clump; Eliza smiled at the baby the way old women smile when they know a baby is not a project.

The chant held its uncomplicated rhythm.

One—two—three. One—two.

At the edge of the circle, he felt himself counted—not as a keeper yet, maybe not ever as they were, but as a post that had learned its verb. He opened his mouth to tell them he was sorry—sorry for the joke he made in the kitchen when Jackie said "called"; sorry for the months he spent arguing with a building instead of learning how to be in a room—but the dream withdrew mercy from performance. No apologies. Work only. He closed his mouth and listened.

The beam, unlit, nonetheless lent its pause to the rhythm, the way a metronome can still rule a room after the piano is shut. At that silent high mark, the women lifted their flames a fraction. The baby, impossible and ordinary, opened its eyes. Not to look at anyone. To understand the tempo.

He recognized the feeling with something like relief that hurt: this is what it is to be in the presence of a practice older than you. Not a pageant. A procedure. Not a goddess. A job. The light never belonged only to ships. It had been built to carry people through weather men do not boast about surviving because survival doesn't look good on a plaque. He felt the sentence seat itself in his ribs where his skins are stubborn: *The beam is a pledge, not a spotlight.*

The chant altered, just once, adding a fourth word that landed quietly and would not leave later: "Mend."

Keep. Illuminate. Carry. Mend.

Enactment, not theory. Bread, not metaphor. Salt, not romance. He understood something the way you understand a law when you see the harm it prevents, not just the text on the page. The Circle wasn't protecting innocence or chastity or any virtue that looks good on a Sunday. They were protecting continuance. The right to remain, with one another, here.

Aurelia lifted her hand, palm steady. The green found the gold in a line so thin it could have been mistaken for a rumor by anyone with less patience. He heard the town's whole body say yes—unseen, unfancy—a collective exhale he'd never noticed before because he was always listening for claims, not breath.

He wanted to promise something big. He wanted to give a speech. The dream pulled him like a tide toward the door, reminder and blessing both. The circle did not vanish. It did not need his belief to exist. It kept. It would keep. But now he knew which part of the keeping belonged to him: stop pretending the beam is an ornament; stop downgrading women's work to folklore; stop hiding your belief behind decent paperwork. Carry.

He woke with his hand halfway raised to a room that did not require it.

The clock said 3:17. Of course it did.

He lay there and listened to the house a full minute to be sure he had brought his breath back into the hour. Sophie turned once in the next room and, in turning, murmured a word that would have scared him two months ago and now sounded like a direction from someone who had read the map aloud: "Illuminate." He did not move to her. Consent is the first rule of ritual and of waking children. He watched the ceiling lose one shade of dark. He said the four words under his breath as if fitting a tool back into a drawer: "Keep. Illuminate. Carry. Mend."

On the nightstand, the star wheel made its own small sense. He rotated the disk to **June** and **Dawn**; the Triangle shifted; the crown lowered closer to the river. He pictured the circle's flames as stars inside the room, each one an answer to a station that had loaned the town its vertebrae for a century. He could feel the pull toward the lighthouse like a cord that had learned politeness—no demand, still real.

He gave himself ten minutes. In that ten minutes he took inventory the way a father who is also a keeper learns to do: phone in pocket, yes; keys, yes; notebook, yes; guilt, no; grief, yes, but not the kind that takes you hostage. He wrote three lines in his notebook in a print legible even if the room tried to shake his hands: *The light is a promise to the living. Equity is its fuel. Stop being surprised it works.*

The street kept a sane hour. A truck whispered past. The headland, from this distance, had the posture of a sleeping animal that knows its duty isn't finished just because a clock ran out of courage. He went outside barefoot and stood on the stoop the way he had the night he told Jackie he'd found a house he could imagine growing old in. The same air. New job.

He didn't go up the headland. He didn't need pilgrimage to make the dream true. He stood in a square of quiet town and let the beam do the one trick it has never forgotten: it showed him where the water stops being the water and starts being dark. It was enough.

Back inside he made coffee badly and forgave himself without ceremony. He stared at Sophie's star wheel again and thought of the baby in the dream, everyone's and no one's, lifted by a ring of flames. He thought of his own child's infant weight on his shoulder the night the hospital finally let them go home, how he had stood in the kitchen at three in the morning and told the sink and the stove and the window and the neighbors' gutters that he would not ruin her, as if making vows to appliances made them binding.

He understood why the town had been built this way— lighthouse at the point, Chapel shoulder to the wind, school set back just so, the print shop not far, the apothecary within a grown woman's stride of anything that might want mending. Not a superstition, a layout. The Circle had drawn the map and then walked it until the pavement learned the steps.

By the time the kettle had achieved something like a boil, he knew the difference between doubt and humility. Doubt had been keeping him safe from a room that didn't want safety. Humility could keep him where he belonged: nearby, no speeches. The beam had not asked to turn him into a convert; it had asked him to finally admit what work requires when it is honest: witnesses.

He woke Sophie gently for school. "I dreamed about the headland," she told him when her eyes were truly open. "We were on a boat made out of windows." He said, "Put that one in your pocket." She nodded, Siri-like, and did. He made pancakes imperfectly and let the burnt ones be the ones he ate. He sent a text to Marley: *I need to come by early if you have an hour. I finally have my verbs in the right order.* She responded with a thumb-up and, because she is incapable of leaving a joke unmarried, *Bring your star wheel. Union rules.*

He showered, put on the jacket that made him look like a person a council might still trust, and checked the portfolio even though there was nothing inside he needed to prove anything. He hesitated at the door to Sophie's room. "I saw a baby in the light last night," he said—to the crown of his daughter's head, not to his own fear. "Many babies. You, maybe. Others. They sang. It was ordinary and I think that's why I'm going to be okay."

She listened with that mild, ferocious attention children give when they know a parent is trying to hand them something that used to be too heavy. "Okay," she said. "Save me one of the pancakes that looks like Florida."

He did, and the ordinary, again, mended things that would have broken if he'd tried to be impressive. He cleaned the pan. He checked the clock. He picked up the notebook with the three lines.

On the walk to Moon & Morrow the town put its same old face on: the bell in the Chapel had the good manners to be quiet, the print shop was open too early, Mrs. Bennett's blinds were mostly down but you could see the corner of a loaf cooling on the sill. A young man on a bench picked out a guitar line that wanted to be a waltz but didn't want to be sentimental about it. The river forgot to pretend to be mysterious and just went about the work of being moved.

He turned the corner and saw Marley through the shopfront window at her worktable with the chest lid propped at an angle that looked exactly like trust. She looked up, saw his face, and did not make him pretend to be fine. She unlocked the door and didn't say any greeting words that would make him spend what he had brought.

"Come on," she said. "Tell it once so you don't have to carry it twice."

HE TOLD it in three breaths, not because he was dramatic but because the room gave the story back as soon as he put it down. He described the circle the way a court asks you to describe a scene—no embellishments, only what your eyes and ears told you. He said "baby" without specifying because he knew how to let a word stay plural when a town needs it to be. He spoke the chant and let the rhythm determine the volume: "Keep. Illuminate. Carry. Mend." He told her it had not felt like a miracle and he watched her nod at that honest relief. He told her he'd wanted to apologize and the dream had declined with good manners. He told her, finally, that he woke at 3:17 and that he was done requiring the light to justify itself as a municipal utility.

Marley listened the way rooms prefer: with a pencil she never used, her body leaned toward him, her impulse to interpret leashed to her discipline. When he finished, she set the pencil down and did not touch his sleeve. "All right," she said. "Say the sentence you called me here to say."

He exhaled like a man stepping out of bad boots at the end of a day. "I don't doubt it anymore," he said. "Not any of it. The Rite. The Circle. The way the building keeps people, not only ships. I believe in what we're uncovering. Not as a story I like, but as a thing I now owe."

"That was two sentences," she said, because a joke is a way to make belief wearable.

He smiled, unoffended. "I intend to make many procedural errors today." He tapped his notebook. "I want to say them in daylight so I can hear whether my mouth still makes them sound stupid. One: The lighthouse is a beacon of ancestral protection. Two: Equity is not charity; it's the fuel the beam was designed to run on. Three: Legacy is the blood the burned page means. Four: The union rule about 'no' remains in effect even if I'm excited."

She leaned back, satisfied.

He looked at the chest, the cloth with the seven initials,

the bowl without theatrics now holding a dry crumb and a stem that had given everything it had been asked to give. "I want to bring Sophie," he said, "—to the Mirror Room, someday soon. But I want to ask her. And I want to teach her the rule. 'Near, not on.' 'No is holy.' 'Keep faith' is something you can do from the doorway."

Marley nodded. "We'll ask the room first," she said. "Then we'll ask her. Then we'll ask the room again, because sometimes consent on Tuesday calls in sick on Thursday."

He laughed, and it changed the temperature in the shop by one degree. He looked at her, at this woman around whom rooms refused to perform and therefore chose to be truer. "When we're in council rooms," he said, "I'll still be the person who asks for footnotes and humidity control. I won't make you do that dance. But I will no longer be the person who's waiting for something to embarrass itself before he admits he loves it."

"Good," she said simply. "Because the town is going to want to borrow your steadiness. And because I was going to tell you to stop anyway."

He told her the fourth word. "Mend," he said. "It arrived like an amendment. I think it belongs in how we talk about the Rite. Not as penance. As repair."

She wrote it on a linen card and slid it under the chest lid with the other sentences that had learned how to live here. "Keep, illuminate, carry, mend," she read, and added, "eat," because Evelyn had walked past the window just then and pointed to the basket on the step like a general sending a runner to the front with soup.

He told her about Jackie's hand on Marley's shoulder in the lantern room and then, clumsily because it was the only honest route, about the dream's baby and the way his body had recognized the beam's pause as part of his own breathing. She let a long silence be the agreement it was.

"Now you know," she said at last, "what you were meant to carry."

He nodded. "And that it's lighter when I don't insist on making it sacred. When I let it be a job."

"Jobs are sacred," she said, unbothered by the contradiction she had just cancelled. "But yes. We will teach the town to stand quietly. To call names without demanding spectacle. To fund Pollard when he tells them linen costs more than lies."

"Union rules," he said automatically, and both of them felt the house laugh.

He told her the plan as his mind had laid it out between coffee and bicycles: the listening session the council had agreed to; the draft for the acknowledgement text no longer provisional in his chest; the line from Aurelia's journal—*One must hold the light. One must pass it on.*—slotted in at the end not as a quotation tossed like a flower but as instruction posted like a fire exit diagram.

"We'll write it now," Marley said. "While you still have dream in your voice. Short. Clean. Bread words. No velvet."

He dictated, and she wrote, and together they produced a paragraph that managed the rare trick of telling the truth without, as he put it, "scaring donors or children." It named the Seven. It located the posts. It named equity as the beam's grammar. It promised no pageants. It invited memory. It ended, quietly, with the four words the dream had set in him like a metronome and the line they had borrowed from the century behind them:

We keep, we illuminate, we carry, we mend. One must hold the light. One must pass it on.

Marley slid the page into the portfolio and closed it with care. Not a lock. A lid.

"You'll still get people who don't believe," she said, not as warning, just as weather.

He nodded. "They don't have to. I just don't get to hide behind them anymore." He picked up the star wheel from his pocket and looked at its paper crown. "Sophie's bringing hers to the listening session. She told me she's going to ask whether it's rude to draw during public comment."

"It is not," Marley said. "It's the only way to keep the minutes accurate."

They ate a heel of bread with jam while the shop filled with the scintillating fragrance of candles cooling into dignity. He told her about the guitar player and the almost-waltz. She told him about Hazel leaving wax crescents on stone on purpose because rooms need the signature of the living. The door bell chimed and nobody came in; sometimes buildings rehearse their hospitality.

When he stood to go, he reached without thinking and then checked himself and left his hand hovering mid-air. "Near, not on," he said, and she reached too and did the same. The almost-touch looked ridiculous and was, therefore, true.

On the step, Evelyn pointed at the basket again—biscuits this time, and a note: **Mend means feed. —E.** He lifted the basket for Marley, then carried it down to the square because a man who has finally obeyed a dream is a man who should deliver breakfast without waiting to be thanked.

The lighthouse kept its schedule. Three short. Two long. Pause. In the pause a stitch of green threaded the gold so modestly he would have missed it last month, last year, last life. He didn't miss it now. He didn't turn it into a sermon. He let it sew its seam, quietly, through the morning.

Later, when Sophie bounced down the Chapel steps after the listening session with a page of stars she called "the crown," he would say yes without correcting her constellation. Later, when Whitaker made another decent fuss about adjectives, he would translate crankiness into care. Later, when the town asked for a path it could walk without falling into worship or cynicism, he would give them the four words from the dream and a map drawn at human speed.

For now, he walked back toward his child and the day and the work that would add itself to the other work. He didn't look back at the headland. You don't check on a lighthouse when it's doing its job. You check on the people who can be kept by it.

He knew, in a way that would not embarrass him later, that he believed. Not because someone had proven anything to him. Because his life had just become easier to tell the truth about. And because somewhere between midnight and three-seventeen a room had decided to lend him its breath long enough for him to learn how to carry his own.

27

A LONG-LOST MEDICAL JOURNAL

They chose an unromantic hour for romance with paper. Mid-morning—sun square in the shop window, kettle's second boil, the town learning its tempo again after the listening session. Marley had stacked the lighthouse cartons Pollard delivered the night before into a disorder that only an archivist would call a system: ledger boxes from three decades, a shallow tray of glass plates, a hatbox that had no business pretending to be storage, and a salt-stiff canvas roll bound with twine and patience. Damien, sleeves rolled, managed the dull glory—labeling, inventory numbers, humidity notes—while Sophie, deputized with a soft brush, licked a finger and stopped herself, because children can learn preservation faster than adults learn reverence.

"Canvas first," Marley said. The roll had that tactile promise you feel on a gift handed down two full generations: something soft inside, something that remembered being carried. She worried at the twine, resisted the urge to cut it, and unrolled the canvas onto the table.

Inside: cloth, oil, and a rectangle too confident to be

merely a notebook. The leather cover had been rubbed by hands that knew work; its edges curved the way objects do when the body forgives their corners. A strap still held; a brass stud kept its post like a soldier waiting to be relieved. On the front, pressed without flourish: **A. W.**

Marley's throat hit a small speed bump. The initials meant so many women across so much time, and yet here they narrowed without diminishing: Aurelia Ward. Healer. Co-founder. The person who had named Marley without using her name since before the shop had smelled like wax.

Damien offered a clean handkerchief. "You're allowed to touch it," he said, not as permission—she needed none—but as an invitation to trust her hands.

She slid the strap, lifted the cover, and knew at once this was not a commonplace book. The first page wore a lattice of symbols that made the eye blink and recalibrate: circles quartered into moon phases; little botanical glyphs—sprigs, thorns, the suggestion of a root; lines and dots in sequences that felt like music rearranged for optics. Along the top margin, a neat hand had written in common script: **Pharmacopeia & Keeping**. Then, in the same hand, a sentence in Latin, not ornament, instruction: **"Memoria manet ubi manus laborant."** Memory remains where hands work.

"It's ciphered," Marley breathed. Not a schoolgirl's substitution; not a coy diary. A system. "Botanical runes keyed to phases. The dots—counts. The lines—breath or steps."

Sophie angled in, reverent and nosy. "Like the star wheel," she said. "Only with plants."

Marley smiled without turning. "Exactly like the star wheel."

Damien set the shop's magnifier into its weighted base, unsentimental as a surgeon laying out a beloved instrument.

"Method," he said, which is how a lawyer says *I'm excited* without alarming the room. "Nocturnal key: moon phase. Diurnal variable: tide up or tide out. Tertiary: plant initial? A for Achillea—yarrow. R for Rosmarinus—rosemary. W—Salix—willow by the older spelling... this might be older still."

Marley was already translating with her body before her mind caught up: the left-hand column a table of winds; the right a litany of aches and fevers; the center—her pulse ticked—recipes that refused to be only recipes. She copied one carefully on a linen card in her own precise hand:

For fever & agitation:

Salix bark (waning), mint (first quarter), a pinch of white salt. Boil three breaths after first steam. Let cool in moonlight, not windowsill. Speak the name of the one to be steadied, not as plea, as table-setting. Feed with bread.

—*A.W.*

"Farmhouse medicine," Damien said, and then, softer, not to demote it: "Law for bodies."

"It's more," Marley said, tracing a line of dots that ran from the recipe into a small spiral that wasn't merely decorative. "Energy work through breath and pattern. The Rite in miniature. The way you say a name to invite equity to the table instead of loss."

Sophie leaned her cheek into her palm. "Does it have any... curses?" she asked, the way a child asks about tigers when she knows very well the zoo is closed.

"If it does," Marley said, delighted by the practical impertinence, "it will call them by better names. Unbinding. Repair. Correctives." She turned the page. The leather murmured. A sketch of the headland revealed itself, not cartographic but anatomical—the lighthouse spined like a fish, the keeper's quarters a heart, the stair a rib, the lens an iris. Along the margin, in that same disciplined hand: **"The beam is a promise. Do not negotiate with it."**

They breathed.

Marley turned more pages. Remedies made in kitchens with ingredients that remembered the grove; poultices annotated with the moon's temper in the corners like weather; tiny rituals interleaving the practical with the structural: *Walk the circle with children before they're tested, to teach the body a grammar the mind will need. Lay rosemary at the Chapel threshold on nights grief will be speaking. If the harbor master swears, let him; the river answers to salt, not decorum.* A voice emerged—not a dowser's, not a bishop's—a woman's: specific, unromantic, exacting in her care.

Halfway through, Marley's knuckles tightened. In the gutter a scrap of green thread—faded to brown—had been caught accidentally under stitch. It matched the green used to embroider the seven initials on the cloth of the Rite. The Circle had stitched their signatures into everything they meant to survive them.

"Pollard is going to need to sit down," Damien said, and then added, because humor is a brace: "We'll feed him first."

"Union rules," Sophie said, and they laughed, and the book became—blessedly—more possible to carry.

Near the back, a different hand intruded for a page— less tidy, more urgent. A keeper's note: **"June 17, 1876. The silent woman stood at the fourth turn. I could not hear what she asked. The pattern held."** Marley felt the old logbook in her pocket and did not take it out; she knew the sentence by muscle memory now, the way you know a newborn's cries on the second night.

She reached the final folio, a thicker sheet glued down at the inner edge. She lifted its corner as if doing so could bruise someone, and the page gave, revealing one last entry written in the clean, unhurried script she had been learning to recognize across ledger margins and bottle labels. No cipher this time. Aurelia wanted this read quickly and by anyone with decent eyes and an honest mouth.

One must hold the light. One must pass it on.

Marley did not cry. She nodded once, the way you nod when someone has given you a sentence you plan to use until it goes threadbare in the best possible way.

Sophie breathed it out as if it had been waiting at the edge of her teeth. Damien stood motionless, giving the line the legal weight of a precedent and the domestic weight of an instruction taped to a refrigerator door.

"We will keep this," he said, quiet and plain. "Not in a drawer. Not as a secret. As a town's book."

THEY DID NOT LET excitement become haste. Marley washed her hands again and set the journal on blocks—the little foam rests Pollard swears by—so the spine didn't have to carry the whole century by itself. Damien called the print shop and, in his litigation voice used exclusively for emergencies that involve linen and glue, informed Pollard that humidity would be obeyed.

"He's already on his way," Marley said after she hung up. "He told the linotype to guard the door and promised it a biscuit."

They returned to the first page and began to read in the only cadence the book deserved: out loud, softly, with pauses long enough for the ink to become speech. The cipher yielded the moment they treated it like language instead of mystery. You didn't so much crack it as learn it, the way a child learns where doors are by walking into them a few times.

Aurelia's entries braided three kinds of care without apology. Remedies—ratios, measures, times: *Yarrow, for bleeding and stubborn men; willow, for ribs that refuse to forget waves; lavender, for breath that has forgotten its count; nettle, for stubborn children who need iron more than instructions.* Energetic rituals—breath counts keyed to phase: *On waning, exhale twice as long; on waxing, name what you're adding; on full, do not bargain with sleep.* And structures—what to do with buildings: *If the Chapel is to keep people, sweep it in spirals; if the school is to make brave readers, let them read under windows without curtains; if the lighthouse is to remember equity, salt its steps and say names when you do.*

Marley copied like a scribe and like a granddaughter. The table grew handsome: cards, clips, weights; the journal itself like a hearth around which implements go to become obedient. Sophie, patient as a child can be when she knows the work is more than homework, traced the moon quarter icons into her own sketchbook, then drew a diagram of "the breath that belongs to gibbous" with little arrows and the annotation **NO HURRY**.

They found a page that made Marley's mouth go dry and then sweeten with relief. A recipe in the same tidy cipher, labeled with a corner flourish of care:

For marrying green to gold:

Rosmarinus (crescent) infused in spring water; a pinch of salt that remembers the river's mouth; a breath held at the beam's pause, then released into the flame's belly. Keep in glass; seal with beeswax; label with the grammar you intend to teach it. **—Aequitas et Lux.**

"The vial," Damien said.

"The grammar," Marley corrected, smiling. "This is why the light wore green without throwing itself a parade."

A margin note stood beside the recipe, stitched into the

page with a dot pattern that had begun to feel like family: **"Never alone. Seven or three. Two and one if you must."** He pointed at it, brows lifting. "Seven stations; three steps—keep, illuminate, carry—now mend; two and one—the pair and the witness."

"It's a working constitution," Marley said, and he didn't flinch at the improvisation.

Another entry read like a ledger until it asked something harder: *If the flame dies, read the boy's name, then the mother's, then the keeper's, then the one who will carry next. Names spoken in sequence mend paths better than knives do.* Marley put her hand near the page and let those names be plural in her mind—she had none to add and many to honor.

Midway through, a paragraph in Aurelia's venomous neatness addressed misuse:

If a man asks for a potion to make him loved, give him rosemary for his memory and a list of chores; love that is not invited is a theft. If a council asks for a secret recipe to sell to visitors, give them soup. If a town asks for its history, read them this.

Marley laughed out loud—grateful, from belly to brow. Damien shook his head slowly, the way you do when your elders scold you from a century away and you deserve it.

At the back, before the final charge, lay one more section, written in a cipher that pulled different organs into the work—figures that danced the way waltz meter does on paper. *A chant for the beam when storm's grammar insists on running the meeting.* The dots ran three-two, three-two, with a tiny breath mark at the pause. Text beside it: *Keep. Illuminate. Carry. Mend.* Underlined once. No Latin necessary; the line had learned English since the last time it needed to travel.

Sophie set her star wheel atop the open page, crown aligned with the header as if she'd always known where it belonged. "It matches," she said. "Three stars, two stars. And the blank." She tapped the pause place. "The place where you don't play a note because that's where the music lives."

Pollard arrived then with a humidity meter and a granola bar, greeted the journal like a parishioner greeting a relic, and did not faint, to his own surprise. "We'll build the box," he said after a long, reverent silence. "Unbleached linen. Lignin-free tissue. Two types of foam. The *good* magnets." He pulled a pencil from behind his ear and wrote, upside down so Marley could read it, a small policy on the blotter: **No flash / Gloves optional if clean / No lipstick near the pages.**

Damien, whose love language is procedure, placed a hand near the policy and nodded solemnly. "We'll draft an access protocol," he said. "Community first. Students next. Scholars with manners. No one gets to monetize while the ink is still being introduced to air."

"And a digital surrogate," Pollard added, his voice softening where it gets most righteous. "So the town can keep the words even if someone leaves a window open."

"Union rules," Sophie murmured, and the men agreed —because at this table the twelve-year-old often has the best phrasing.

Only then did Marley lift the last page again and let the final line occupy the room. She read it out loud without vibrato, the way you read a line you mean to use:

"One must hold the light. One must pass it on."

She did not look at Damien. She didn't need to; she could feel the way the sentence found his bones.

THE ARGUMENT about heirlooms didn't even dignify itself

with volume. It walked into the shop, removed its hat, and sat down as if invited.

"We could keep it here," Hazel said at noon, after she'd returned from a delivery with flour on her chin and the news that three people had stopped her to ask if the light had been *really* green or only the color of rumor. "Under your counter. Close to the spiral. Safe under hands that already know its verbs."

Marley kept her fingers flat on the blotter, listening, because she had been a shopkeeper long enough to know that even good advice comes in with dust from other rooms. "We could," she said. "And we can for now. But the book isn't a charm; it's a constitution."

"It's also an heirloom," Hazel said. "And heirlooms belong to people, not boards."

Damien, who had let the women speak before adding his defense, cleared his throat, which is what men raised in good kitchens do when they are about to disagree. "This one," he said, "belongs to people by belonging to a board." He held Hazel's gaze so she could see he wasn't flipping the table. "Aurelia wrote an *us*, not a *mine*. She stitched the Circle into its cloth—seven initials—then put it with a Rite that requires the town to show up in pairs and triads and circles. The book wants a room. With hours. And humidity. And a lock that is a promise, not a secret."

Hazel's eyebrow twitched. "You want to build a shrine."

"I want to build a reading room," he said. "No velvet ropes. Bread on Thursdays. The only exhibit snot we tolerate will be on the faces of people who remembered their grandmothers out loud."

Pollard, who had been calibrating his humidity meter as if it were a barometer for moral pressure, looked up. "He's right," he said, and Hazel rolled her eyes at the pleasure of hearing him admit it in front of other humans. "I want high-resolution scans so your nephew can read the fever recipe on his phone at two in the morning without texting you. I want a facsimile so the original can sleep part of the day. I want sign-up sheets Sophie is allowed to illustrate. I want the book to be a town thing because the alternative is that it becomes an heirloom thing and we have already seen what heirlooms do when they get stubborn: they end up in basements next to bowling trophies."

Hazel let the corner of her mouth betray her. "Fine," she said. "But the reading room gets a kettle. And a sign with the rules in words regular people read."

Sophie had already drawn a draft, of course—**BE KIND, BE IN TIME, BE NEAR (NOT ON), SAY NO IF YOU NEED TO.** She added a flourish under the last line: **KEEP FAITH.**

They walked the journal over to the Chapel that evening, not as a parade, just the way you deliver a casserole—between two people with a third carrying the door. Miriam Merrick met them at the steps with a ring of keys and a reticent face that could barely keep from softening. "We cleared the east room," she said. "Pollard lost the argument about ficus plants." She unlocked. The space smelled like pine soap and patience; the table had been moved toward the window; a fan hummed as if it had taken a vow of non-disruptive service.

"Before we set it down," Damien said, "we should tell the room what we're doing. You know. Consent." He was half-joking, which is how the best new liturgies begin.

Marley placed her palm near the table—not on it—and said the sentence that had become Brookwood's quiet pledge: "We keep. We illuminate. We carry. We mend." She nodded to Pollard. "And we log."

He brought his ledger—paper heavy enough to press a

temper into good behavior—and wrote: **Aurelia Ward, *Pharmacopeia & Keeping*, deposited by Moon & Morrow on behalf of the town.** He paused, then added, uncharacteristically, **Thank you.** The archivist's version of a hosanna.

They set the journal on its blocks. Damien read aloud a short statement he'd drafted between coffee and panic attacks:

This book is ours and not ours. It was written by hands that expected to be argued with kindly. You may read it if you read it like a neighbor. You may copy it if you copy it like a recipe and not a secret. You may carry its sentences into kitchens, boats, classrooms, and council chambers. You may not sell it, brand it, or pretend it loves you more than it loves the person who comes in after you. One must hold the light. One must pass it on.

Miriam Merrick, who had brought a vase and then put the vase back in the closet because flowers would have felt like a performance, stood with her hands behind her back the way people do when they mean to keep them from asking for more than they need. "My grandmother's ledger is in my purse," she said. "I would like to leave it here on loan. I would like to sit in that chair every Tuesday and read a page of this out loud to whoever is there. And I would like," she added, surprising herself with the audacity that grief, when fed, can afford, "to ask that we put a small plaque under the window that says **HOME** and nothing else."

Hazel nodded vigorously. Pollard wrote **HOME** in enormous block letters on his blotter as if fearing the word might wander. Sophie held up her sign. Miriam laughed and cried at once and wiped her face like a woman who understood that dignity and tears share a locker.

Back at the shop, as twilight argued warmly with the

river about who owned which shade of blue, Marley returned to her own ledger and wrote down the last thing Aurelia's book had taught her today that had nothing to do with tinctures or tides: *Remedies are only half for bodies. The other half is for rooms.*

She closed the ledger and leaned her head against the cool of the counter. Damien reached out—near, not on—and then did, at last, lay his hand lightly over hers because some touches are how you file gratitude. "Thank you for finding it," he said.

"I didn't find it," she answered. "We got ready, and it let itself be found."

"Same difference," he said, and she let the imprecision be a gift.

On the headland, the lamp spun its three, then two, then offered the pause that belongs to everyone and no one. In the Chapel, the journal settled into its box as if sleep were a form of being read. In the print shop window, Pollard taped up Sophie's rules and stood back, hands on hips, to admire the brave dignity of paper. In kitchens, someone boiled willow and someone salted a doorstep and someone taught a child to say a name without erasing anyone else's.

And in the little space between sentences, where books breathe and towns decide their verbs, the final line kept its shape without becoming an emblem:

One must hold the light. One must pass it on.

28

LIGHTHOUSE LEGACY

The request came in the quiet way Brookwood did important things: no proclamation, no fanfare, only a gathering of elders at the Chapel table, the sort of circle where bread sat in the middle as a reminder that conversations stay honest when food is nearby. Miriam Merrick had summoned Marley, and when she arrived Damien was already waiting by the door, jacket folded over his arm, notebook in hand, the look of someone both ready to defend and willing to listen.

The council's elders were not all elected figures—some were simply the oldest steady hands the town trusted. Miriam sat at the head, her ledger balanced neatly before her. Beside her was Whitaker with his careful spectacles, and three others whose memories stretched far deeper than their resumes: Ruth Caldwell, who had run the school library for forty years; Harbor Master Doyle, knees wrecked by salt and weather; and Mrs. Bennett, who had arrived with a basket of rolls as if no decision could be made on an empty stomach.

Marley entered quietly, sensing the atmosphere thick

with purpose. She glanced once at Damien, who gave her the kind of nod that carried more weight than any sentence.

Miriam opened with no preamble. "Marley," she said, her voice low but clear, "we've been reading the charter page you and Damien uncovered. The one with Aurelia's name—'Beacon of the Grove.' It mentions another title, barely noted in the margin. *Custos Memoriae.* Keeper of Memory."

The words landed like a stone placed carefully, not dropped. Marley inhaled. The phrase hummed in her ribs as if it had been waiting.

Ruth Caldwell leaned forward, her hair a storm of white curls. "Aurelia held it first. We believe you should hold it now."

The room stilled. Marley looked down at her hands, the wax still faintly scented on her skin from that morning's candle-pouring. "Why me?" she asked quietly, not out of humility but because the question demanded an honest answer.

Harbor Master Doyle scratched his beard. "Because you've been carrying it already. The logbooks, the spiral, the Rite—you're the one who listens without rushing. Aurelia wrote, 'Memory remains where hands work.' That's you."

Damien's voice came steady, grounding her. "She doesn't have to decide tonight."

"No," Miriam agreed. "But the town has to offer. And we are offering."

Marley's throat tightened. Keeper of Memory. It was not a crown—it was a ledger, a trust, a discipline. To hold names, to pass them on, to catalog not only artifacts but the breath that gave them weight. She thought of her aunt lighting wicks in the back room, of Aurelia's journal resting now in the Chapel's east chamber, of the Circle's faces reflected in the Mirror Room glass. Keeper of Memory meant holding not only objects but the unglamorous threads that tethered the town to its truest self.

"I accept," Marley said softly. Then louder, steady: "I accept, but not alone. If Aurelia had a Circle, then so must I. This cannot be one person's charge. Keeper of Memory only works if it's shared."

A murmur of agreement traveled the table.

Damien leaned forward, his hands folded over the notebook he hadn't yet opened. "Then I'll take the first part of that Circle. I'll digitize the journal, the Rite, the logbooks. I'll make them accessible—preserve them so a spilled cup or a careless hand won't undo what was entrusted." His eyes met Marley's. "You hold the memory. I'll help carry it."

The elders nodded, satisfaction softening their faces. Miriam wrote a single note in her ledger: **Keeper of Memory—Marley Waters, with Circle.** Then she closed the book, sealing the decision not in ink but in practice.

Afterward, in the square outside, Mrs. Bennett pressed the basket of rolls into Marley's hands. "A Keeper must feed people," she said matter-of-factly. "It's part of the job." Marley laughed, but her chest was still trembling with the weight of what had been asked and what she had said yes to.

Damien fell into step beside her, his voice low, steady, protective. "We'll do it together," he said. "Every scrap, every carving, every note. Nothing will stay buried."

And Marley, Keeper of Memory now in more than name, nodded with a new steadiness. "Then let's begin."

THEY BEGAN IN THE LIGHTHOUSE, because the headland had been the heart from the start. Damien brought crates, gloves, and the portable scanner Pollard had insisted on lending despite its temperamental battery. Marley brought her ledger and the cloth embroidered with the Circle's initials, laying it across the keeper's desk as if to remind the room that the work was not just about cataloging but about lineage.

The first artifact was humble: a brass compass worn smooth at the edges, initials A.W. faint on its lid. Inside, the engraving glowed faintly under light: *Guided by light and green flame.* Marley wrote its entry carefully:

Artifact 001 — Compass of Aurelia Ward. Inscription: "Guided by light and green flame." Provenance: Antique dealer, confirmed by logbook reference. To be housed in archive.

Damien photographed each angle, his movements precise. "We'll upload scans to the town's archive once the council approves the digital framework. Everyone should see this compass, not just us."

Next came the charter fragment, its edges fragile but ink still bold. Marley placed it gently onto linen. Damien scanned it at the highest resolution, watching the words appear pixel by pixel. "Aurelia Ward. Beacon of the Grove."

They worked steadily, speaking less as the rhythm set in. Candle remnants, shards of lens glass, the ceremonial bowl, the embroidered cloth, Aurelia's medical journal—all passed through Marley's hands, recorded in her precise script, and into Damien's lens for preservation. Each entry added a stitch to the fabric of Brookwood's reclaimed memory.

At noon, they carried the work to the bridge. Under its beams, Marley collected weathered carvings of spirals long overlooked as idle graffiti. She copied them into the ledger, noting their alignment with moon phases and dates of repair. Damien photographed the stones, marking them with chalk for later cataloging. "People thought these were vandals," he said, crouching to trace one spiral with his gloved hand. "Turns out they were guardians leaving policy."

From the bridge they walked to the grove, where the remnants of Aurelia's gatherings still whispered in the soil. Hazel met them there, handing Marley a packet of pressed leaves she'd collected years ago. "I didn't know what they were for," Hazel admitted. "But I knew better than to throw them away." Marley identified lavender, rosemary, and nettle, each one present in Aurelia's journal. She wrote: **Artifact 014 — Pressed herbs from the grove. Matches ritual entries in Aurelia's book. Source: Hazel, Moon & Morrow.**

By dusk, their ledger had grown to twenty entries. Damien closed the scanner, weary but satisfied, and Marley tied the ledger with a ribbon her aunt had once used to bundle candle wicks.

"This is only the beginning," she said, exhaustion humming through her bones but steadied by purpose.

"It's already a foundation," Damien answered. "The Circle left the pieces. We're building the table they meant us to eat at."

The beam lit across the water, steady, its rhythm now echoing the chant that had woven into Damien's dreams: Keep. Illuminate. Carry. Mend. The work of memory had begun to take shape not as preservation only but as community inheritance.

THE FOLLOWING WEEK, the Chapel east chamber transformed into Brookwood's first community archive. The long oak table now held Aurelia's journal in its protective box, the compass in a clear case, the charter fragment framed under glass. Linen-covered boxes lined the shelves, each labeled with clean lettering: *Bridge Carvings, Grove Herbs, Keeper's Logbook, Spiral Candles.*

The elders arrived first to bless the room with their presence, not ceremony. Ruth Caldwell brought a list of students she planned to bring for lessons on "reading artifacts like you read novels." Eamon Hart leaned on his cane and muttered, "Never thought I'd live to see the day the lighthouse taught us law instead of tide." Evelyn brought biscuits, because archives, like revolutions, run best when fed.

Marley stood at the head of the table, the title *Keeper of Memory* newly written into the ledger. She felt the eyes of the town not as pressure but as trust. "This archive belongs to all of us," she said. "It isn't a secret cupboard. It's a table. Everything here will be cataloged, digitized, and preserved so that memory remains where hands work."

Damien stepped forward, holding the laptop now housing the first scans. "Every entry will be accessible through the town library's site. The Circle's history will not live behind velvet ropes or whispered folklore—it will live here, in the open, where it can't be erased again."

Applause was not Brookwood's style, but nods rippled like tide. Miriam Merrick wiped her glasses and spoke softly. "Aurelia would be pleased. Not that you've honored her, but that you've fed the town with her memory."

Later, as the townsfolk drifted away, Marley and Damien remained in the chamber. They stood before Aurelia's journal, now resting under glass. Marley whispered, "Keeper of Memory. It's more than I thought I could hold."

Damien placed his hand near hers, not on it, the way

they had learned. "You're not holding it alone. The Circle never was one woman. And now it isn't either."

She breathed, the steadiness of the title settling into her bones. Keeper of Memory—yes, but also witness, scribe, and servant. Not to Aurelia alone, but to Brookwood, to her aunt, to Sophie, to the generations yet to walk the spiral.

Together, they turned off the chamber lights. The green vial in its case glimmered faintly, catching the last shard of dusk through the window. The lighthouse pulsed beyond, steady and constant.

The legacy had been reclaimed—not as relic, but as living trust. And Marley, Keeper of Memory, knew this was only the beginning of what they were meant to pass on.

29

RECLAIMING THE FLAME

The summer solstice came dressed in light that lingered like a guest reluctant to leave. Brookwood had always marked midsummer with some form of gathering—sometimes a dance in the square, sometimes only the lighting of a few extra lamps—but this year carried an undercurrent none of the elders could dismiss. Something older had been remembered, and memory had a way of insisting it be carried forward.

The council had issued no formal proclamation, but word spread by the quiet means Brookwood preferred: Evelyn passing rolls with a whispered reminder, children chalking spiral patterns on the cobbles, Hazel placing hand-poured lanterns in the shop windows, Pollard printing a single sheet without byline that read: **Midsummer Walk. Sunset. Bring a flame. Bring your memory.**

By dusk the town square was alight not with electricity but with anticipation. Families arrived carrying candles tucked into mason jars, hurricane lanterns polished from attics, and even one small kerosene lamp that had belonged to a fisherman's grandmother. Children carried their flames with both pride and solemnity, as if each wick were more than a light—it was a charge.

Marley stood at the fountain's edge, the vial of green flame cradled in her palms. Its glow, muted in daylight, brightened as the sun sank toward the horizon. She wore no ceremonial robe, only her simple linen dress, but the way the light caught on the glass made her look like a figure lifted out of a story told too long to be false. Keeper of Memory—she felt the title settle around her shoulders as naturally as her aunt's shawl once had.

Damien stood beside her, not in front, not behind, holding the lantern that would be used to rekindle the restored beacon. He had spent the morning checking the lens, the wiring, the spiral carving at the base of the tower. Everything was ready, but even readiness could not blunt the tremor in his chest.

Miriam Merrick cleared her throat. "Brookwood," she said to the assembled crowd, her voice carrying without strain, "tonight we walk. From the square to the headland, each with a flame. In spiral, as the Circle taught. And when we reach the tower, we will let the flame that has been kept pass forward, so that the beam may keep us still."

The murmurs hushed. Marley lifted the vial. Its green glow reflected in dozens of eyes, dozens of glass jars. She spoke only one sentence: "One must hold the light. One must pass it on."

The walk began.

Children led, weaving into a loose spiral that widened as more joined. Their candles bobbed like fireflies, tracing curves across the square's stones. Behind them came families, elders, shopkeepers, fishermen, schoolteachers—each carrying a flame, each falling into the rhythm of the spiral without rehearsal. Damien watched as the pattern spread, and for a moment he thought of the dream chant: *Keep. Illuminate. Carry. Mend.* It was happening here, in bodies, without instruction.

Marley walked at the spiral's center, the vial steady in her hands. She felt Aurelia's presence as more than memory —it was as though the town itself had become the Circle. Each step forward was an act of reclamation, not of relics but of inheritance.

When the spiral had wound itself tight, Miriam gave a nod. The children unspooled first, circling outward, their path now turning toward the road that led to the headland. One by one, flames lifted, a river of light flowing through Brookwood's streets. Windows opened; hands waved; some joined spontaneously, carrying kitchen tapers or lanterns long unused.

The headland loomed ahead, the lighthouse waiting like a sentinel who had been patient far too long. The road climbed. Breath came harder, but no one faltered. Damien glanced back once from the rise: the sight stole his words. A spiral of light winding out from the square, curving into the road, rising toward the sea. A town, luminous and alive, refusing to forget.

At the lighthouse gate, Marley paused. She lifted the vial again. The crowd fell into reverent silence. The green flame shimmered against the twilight, answering the sky's deepening indigo. She looked at Damien, and in that look was the passing of trust. He nodded. Together, they stepped inside.

The community waited outside, the flames forming a spiral around the tower's base. From above, if one could have seen, it would have looked as though the lighthouse rose from a galaxy of fire, stars drawn down into mortal hands.

Inside, the work of centuries waited to be mended.

THE KEEPER'S quarters smelled of wax and salt, as they always had. Damien placed his lantern carefully on the desk while Marley set the vial at the spiral carving's heart. The green glow seemed to seep into the lines of the etching, tracing the grooves like veins filling with light. For a moment, the spiral pulsed—then steadied, alive again.

"Are you ready?" Marley asked softly.

Damien nodded. "This isn't just mechanics. I know that now." He adjusted the lantern's wick, then lifted it, his hands steady as a man who has been asked to do something not just important but necessary.

They climbed the stair. Each turn of the spiral felt like the movement of history itself, winding upward, carrying them toward the beam that had guarded more than ships. Marley held the vial close, its light brushing the walls, casting shadows that looked like hands guiding them on.

At the lantern room, the great lens waited, polished to clarity, its prisms catching even the faintest light. Damien set the lantern down, opened its glass, and looked once at Marley. She uncorked the vial. The green flame flickered, alive but contained, its glow unlike any fire he had ever seen —soft and fierce all at once.

He dipped the wick of his lantern into it. The flame caught instantly, leaping gold-green, a marriage of earth's ordinary fire and Aurelia's remembered light. The lantern blazed. He lifted it with both hands and stepped to the beacon.

The moment his flame touched the restored wick of the beacon, the entire room brightened. The lens flared, prisms scattering green and gold across the glass walls. The beam ignited with a roar that was not mechanical but elemental, as if the lighthouse had exhaled after a century of holding its breath.

Outside, the town gasped as the beam swept across the water, not white but tinged with the faintest green, a color no storm could claim, no fog could mute. Children cheered, elders wept, fishermen crossed themselves or whispered thanks in words older than they knew they knew.

At the base of the tower, the spiral symbol carved into stone began to glow faintly, traced in green fire. It pulsed in rhythm with the beam—three short, two long, the code that had haunted Marley's nights. Only now it was not a riddle but a declaration: *We are here. We remember.*

Marley placed her hand near the stone, not on it. "Aurelia," she whispered. "It is kept."

Damien stood beside her, chest rising with a breath that felt like release. "And carried forward."

They descended slowly, the light spilling down the stairwell ahead of them. When they emerged, the town erupted —not in noise alone, but in the sound of relief, of recognition. Flames lifted higher, children dancing in the spiral they had formed, their candles glowing like stars fallen into mortal reach.

Miriam Merrick stepped forward, tears bright in her eyes. "Brookwood has its flame again," she said. "Not just for ships, but for us all."

Marley shook her head gently. "Not ours alone. It belongs to every hand that will carry it after us."

Damien took her words into his chest as a vow. The community cheered again, their flames steady, their voices rising into a song improvised from memory: fragments of hymns, shanties, lullabies. The headland became not a promontory but a stage where the town remembered itself in chorus.

The lighthouse beam swept the horizon, and the sea answered with light of its own—moonrise lifting, silver crown meeting green flame. For a moment, even time seemed to bow.

THE SPIRAL of lanterns wound tighter around the lighthouse as the night deepened. Children ran in loops, their parents too moved to scold them. The beam turned, green-gold, steady, marking each sweep as a heartbeat the town could count on.

Marley stood at the base, still holding the vial—empty now, but glowing faintly as though memory had imprinted itself in the glass. She looked out over the crowd: Hazel laughing as she held Pollard's arm, Mrs. Bennett handing out biscuits she had somehow smuggled up the hill, Ruth Caldwell with a line of students writing in notebooks by candlelight. Each one part of the Circle, whether they knew it or not.

Damien came to her side, his shoulders squared not from duty but from belonging. "We did it," he said, his voice hushed despite the celebration.

"No," Marley corrected softly. "We remembered it. And that's harder."

He smiled at that truth. Together, they walked a small circle of their own, weaving between families, greeting each person, each child, each elder. Keeper of Memory was not a title to sit on a shelf; it was a practice lived in steps, in greetings, in making sure no one left unfed or unseen.

As the spiral of candles began to unwind, families returning to their homes, Damien led Marley back inside the tower. At the keeper's quarters, they paused. The spiral symbol glowed faintly still, as though the stone itself had learned to breathe again. Marley laid the empty vial beside it.

"Let it rest here," she said. "Where it belongs."

Damien nodded. "And tomorrow, we catalog it."

She laughed softly. "Of course you'd say that."

He shrugged, eyes warm. "Memory needs its lawyers."

They climbed once more to the lantern room. The beam swept out to sea, steady, constant. Damien adjusted a knob, ensuring the rotation would hold. Marley stood at the glass, watching the town's lanterns twinkle on the path below as families walked home, still singing.

"Keeper of Memory," Damien said, his voice quiet but firm. "The Circle chose well."

Marley turned to him, her eyes glinting in the green-gold glow. "The Circle chose us all."

They stood together in silence, watching the beam mark its rhythm. For the first time in years, the lighthouse was not only a guardian for ships—it was a beacon for a town that had learned to carry its memory openly, a flame reclaimed not as relic but as legacy.

And as the night deepened, Brookwood kept its vow. The light stayed on.

30

THE LIGHT STAYS ON

They climbed without ceremony, because ceremony had been satisfied last night. This was the evening after the midsummer walk, the day when the body catches up to what the town has done. Bread had been eaten, lanterns rinsed and placed upside down to dry on windowsills, children put to bed early with stubborn glittering eyes. The Chapel east room smelled of linen and ink and a readable ambition. Someone—Pollard—had pinned Sophie's rule sheet more square than it wanted to be. Miriam's tiny plaque under the window, burnished brass with a single word—**HOME**—sat so modestly it changed the temperature of the room by half a degree. The archive had found its pace. The town had found its pulse.

They took the headland stair together, not to perform anything, just to sit in a place that had learned, as they had, what work feels like after the applause goes home. Damien carried a thermos and two enamel mugs. Marley carried the journal in its box, not because it needed more hours of being read, but because some objects settle best when they are allowed to watch the thing they swear to.

At the fourth turn, both of them paused, the way you pause to acknowledge a point in the body that has healed and knows it. Near, not on. The air there, always a degree cooler, pushed across their wrists like a cat forgiving someone it had once judged.

They reached the lantern room at the hour when the glass understands it is no longer the subject. The beam already worked, steady and certain, taking its three short, two long, and the pause that is never empty—just where the room inhales. Outside, the river adjusted its shoulder into the ocean. Far below, town windows performed their own choreography of on and off.

Damien poured coffee that tasted faintly of smoke and the metal it had borrowed its heat from. He set one mug by Marley's hand and sat, back against the inner wall, long legs extended, the kind of posture that says a man believes he is allowed to be comfortable in a sacred place. He had learned that here.

"Well?" he said, after the kind of silence that deserves to go first. "How's our town?"

"Walking a little taller," Marley answered. She put the journal box on the floor between them, not on the pedestal —never on the pedestal—and rested her palm on the lid as if she were smoothing the sheet of a sleeping thing.

"Union rules," Damien said. The joke had lived long enough to become a blessing.

"Sophie hung her star wheel near the sign-in book. She's pretending to be bored by everyone asking her to point out Deneb. She loves it. Miriam started the Tuesdays by reading the paragraph about nettle and iron to the high schoolers and then made them all eat a slice of steak. Public education at its finest."

"Whitaker sent me an email with four adjectives and no

commas," Damien said, satisfied. "That is how I know we are winning."

The beam swung across the water. The green stitched into it had grown thinner in daylight, had learned modesty, but at dusk it returned—just a breath of color, not the kind that demands spectacle, the kind you notice if you have been taught to pay attention at the right bar in the waltz.

He would never stop thinking of the chant. Not because it was dramatic—because it was useful. *Keep. Illuminate. Carry. Mend.* He had used it this morning to dry plates. He had used it at lunch with Sophie when he nearly tried to make a speech and instead handed her the syrup. He was using it now, the metronome under his ribs. He said none of that aloud. Some rhythms do their best work when you don't brag about them.

Marley watched the beam and tried to let herself be as still as it was. Being Keeper of Memory had looked, yesterday, like carrying a glowing vial. Tonight it looked like sitting with a man you trust enough to let the hour live exactly as long as it wants to. She flexed her hand once, just to feel her pulse find the same count as the light. She had not slept much. The body asks for explanation when the town remembers too much in a day; she had offered it soup and a nap and a list of names instead. The list had worked better than the nap.

"Ruth Caldwell told me she's adding a unit to eighth grade history called 'Things the town forgot on purpose,'" she said. "The kids are apparently electing a committee called The Footnotes."

"God bless the middle school," Damien said, not ironically, and they smiled, too tired to give their cheer more volume than a breath.

Down below, the spiral carved in stone at the stair's base

had held its faint glow all day like a bruise you are secretly proud of. The archive had received five new contributions: a ledger from a barbershop, three pressed herbs in waxed paper, the corner of a map with a spiral doodled in the margin, and a letter that began *I haven't known what to do with this* and ended *please keep it where it belongs.* The east room had made room. The Circle got louder without raising their voices.

The lantern room hummed. On one shelf, the compass rested in its case. On the table, a copy of the Rite waited under a cover weight shaped like an oak leaf—Pollard's compromise between utilitarian and tender. Out on the water, a skiff moved without hurrying. He thought of Harbor Master Doyle muttering his approval and threatening to buy a green filter for his porch light so he could "join the party without falling in the river." He had promised to write a policy against porch light filters and had delivered the policy in a loaf of bread.

This room had witnessed storms and apologies and a grown man learning to stop using skepticism as a pair of mittens. It had seen a woman take a title that could have turned her into someone pretentious and watched her turn it into a chore list. It had seen a town walk uphill in a shape that reminded itself how it had been kept. It had seen his late wife kiss a baby's ear. It had seen him not tell anyone that he had seen it. It had watched them both decide, without conference, to let love be honest work.

"Tell me the sentence again," he said, softer than the glass could carry. "The one for tonight."

"In a minute," she said. She looked out at the dark stitching itself together. "Let it arrive on its own."

They drank coffee and said nothing. The beam worked.

The town breathed. A gull insulted a rock. The hour did its arithmetic.

WHEN SHE WAS READY, she reached down and lifted the lid. The journal had learned to be at home in this box quickly, which is what happens to an object when the room it lives in has been told the truth. She opened to the last page, because even practical people are allowed to prefer the part where the book knows how it's going to end.

Her thumb found the corner, the way it had yesterday and the day before. The script was Aurelia's, the precise, unfussy hand of a woman who would have despised fonts. Marley could hear her aunt in the line. She could hear Miriam's steady breath, Pollard's clearing of the throat, Hazel's chair scrape, Ruth's whisper to a child to write this down even if you don't know why yet. She could hear the Mirror Room's glass shifting its weight toward her shoulders. She could hear the town's feet on stone steps, heading up to a room they meant to meet halfway.

She read aloud, not as performance, as invitation. "May all who bear witness find truth in the light."

The beam turned. The words did not echo. Echo is for stone and cathedrals. The sentence made itself available instead, the way a door's latch yields to a person who has learned the trick. It allowed itself into the hour.

"Again," Damien said, not because he had not heard, because he wanted to see if the second time felt more like now.

She read it again. "May all who bear witness find truth in the light."

He nodded. There are phrases you tape to a refrigerator; there are phrases you teach children; there are phrases you do not let the council edit. This was all three. He looked at the beam as if it were a colleague. "Permission to carry that into meetings?"

"Permission granted," she said, Keeper and friend.

He tilted his head, thinking, and then—because he had learned to say what he was actually thinking instead of what he had trained himself to pretend he was thinking—added, "Jackie would have liked that line. She hated when piety got vague." He smiled a little. "She liked kitchen-table truth."

"We built a table," Marley said. "We added chairs."

They let the sentence sit between them like bread at supper. He felt how it spoke to all the rooms at once: the Mirror Room (memory, not shadow), the east archive (truth in the light, not the spotlight), council chambers (witness is not gossip), the headland stair at the fourth turn (bear witness to yourself catching your breath and not letting shame interrupt the count). It spoke to a child with a star wheel who drew the triangle wrong and learned that wrong shapes can still lead you home. It spoke to a man who knows how to write policy and now knows when to put the pen down.

"Let's inventory the day," she said, because even reverence needs a list before it can relax. "We have the journal, now under glass. We have the compass. The bowl. The cloth. The fragment. We have the vial resting by the spiral. We have the reading room hours posted and the rule sheet at kid-eye height. We have Pollard's humidity discipline and Ruth's lesson plan and Miriam's Tuesdays and Mrs. Bennett's biscuits. We have the harbor master's grudging blessing. We have Whitaker's adjectives. We have Sophie's crown on a string."

"And we have the beam," he said.

"And we have the beam," she agreed.

He felt something uncoil in him at that, some last strand of habit that wanted to argue with obvious kindnesses. He let it go. He was tired of pretending to be cleverer than light.

They spoke about the listening session—the way a man had stood up and said the apothecary once left nettle on his doorstep and that after he drank the tea he had stopped yelling at his children; the way an old woman in a hat had said she had avoided the lighthouse because she had thought ghosts too expensive and now understood the house was for the living; the way three teenagers had asked if it was "allowed" to form a club to copy the recipes by hand, and Miriam had said not only allowed but paid if they'd read aloud every fifth page.

"Lydia would like all of this," Marley said, and her mouth smiled at the idea of Lydia pretending to be annoyed by children who do not push chairs in. "Joan too. Eliza especially."

"Aurelia," he said.

"Aurelia," she repeated, and the name did not make the room bigger or smaller; it only made the edges truer.

Below, the town lifted its own lamps as if trying to catch the last opportunities to be outdoors. He could hear a saxophone down by the Chapel—the musician who had dreamed the waltz playing a version whose tempo had been told to slow down by the headland wind. He could hear the bell that never rings unless the building wants to cough. He could hear himself exhale without noticing when he had started.

"Say it once more?" he asked. He did not apologize. He would never again apologize for asking to hear a sentence he meant to memorize by muscle.

She did. "May all who bear witness find truth in the light."

He didn't say *amen*. He said nothing. Saying nothing is a kind of agreement when the room is doing all the work. He reached for his mug and found it already empty, which is how he knew he had been listening correctly.

They closed the book and left it open inside themselves. She slid the lid on. He did not hurry the strap. They set it down, a box in a room, not a relic, not a threat.

Down on Main, the placard in the Chapel window—**BE KIND, BE IN TIME**—bowed twice, a draft doing its duty. The print shop lights clicked off in sequence. Hazel's candles in the shop windows burned down into the crescent of themselves and showed off the stubborn discipline of wicks. The fisherman's porch light didn't turn green. The harbor master was keeping his dignity a little longer. That was fine. Everyone gets a turn at the pause.

He looked at Marley the way you look at a person you've agreed to meet in difficult rooms for the rest of your life. She looked back with the absurd, serene confidence of someone who has learned what to do when a town becomes heavier: add chairs. The world had not become easier. It had become honest. He could do honest.

"Ready?" he asked, though for what he didn't say.

"Yes," she said, and that was enough.

THEY DID NOT PLAN IT. Plans have a way of embarrassing moments that agree to appear on their own. They just sat and received the dusk like a letter opened with clean fingers. The beam made its seam. The words they had just read did their new job and did not look over their shoulder to check if anyone was keeping score.

She put her hand on the floor beside the box and left it there, palm open, a posture that looks like prayer and is actually rest. He put his hand near—habit is a fine thing when it serves—and felt the small ache in his forearm the way you feel a tooth you've stopped grinding. He set his hand down, then, the final quarter inch, the way you set down a tool you intend to use again.

Fingers touched.

Nothing happened, which is to say everything happened very quietly. No breath caught theatrically. No eyes closed for effect. No swear of forever burst out of a man who has learned the more dangerous noun is tomorrow. Their hands rested. The room made room around that fact like water does around a boat it approves of.

She watched the glass. He watched the line where her wrist met his. The beam turned. Three short. Two long. Pause. The green held its place like a stitch you can't see unless you know what you're looking for. They sat inside that stitch and declined to be impressive.

"This is what stillness feels like," she said at last, smiling without showing it off.

"We might survive this," he said, tone dangerously close to light.

"We already have," she answered. "Now we have to fail at it a while and get better."

He nodded, grateful for someone who treats tenderness like a craft and not a test. He let his thumb shift—barely—so that it meant *I am here* and not *I am afraid*. She let her fingers answer *good*.

They talked about what they would do next, but not because lists satisfy anxiety—because lists teach love to behave in public. Finalizing the digitization plan. Scheduling Miriam's Tuesdays on the library's page. Teaching the Footnotes how to cite oral histories with respect. Asking Ruth which shelf is best for facsimiles that wander into children's backpacks. Conspiring with Pollard about an exhibit titled **Seven Stations** with no mannequins, only hands-on tables. Writing the smallest possible plaque for the lighthouse: **Keep. Illuminate. Carry. Mend.**

He would draft the stove rules for the east room because somebody would bring a crockpot and you can't have humidity in a room where old paper is trying to be alive. She would write the caption that made people cry and then admit it felt good. They would ask Harper to stand at the door and say hello to everyone by their first name, because heaven requires a harbor master. They would remind Whitaker that adjectives cannot be archived. They would deliver biscuits to the volunteers because Mrs. Bennett had to sleep sometimes. They would measure chairs. They would bring wastebaskets. They would live here.

He told her, because the hour had permitted confessions all week, the one he had been saving for a quiet evening: "I used to think the point of light was clarity. Now I think it's fidelity."

"Both," she said. "But fidelity first. Clarity can be brutal without a promise under it."

He let that adjust him. "Fidelity," he said again, trying it on his tongue, and the word looked back at him with the face of steady work.

"Say the four," she said, to calibrate the machine that is a man who wants to do good and has been trained to be useful.

He did. "Keep. Illuminate. Carry. Mend."

They didn't need to add "eat," but they did it anyway. "Eat," he said, apologetic and joyful.

"Eat," she agreed, union rules extending to the heart, and they both laughed enough to remind the room it housed humans.

He told her about Sophie's drawing from the listening session—stars connected in lines that made new constellations, none of which could get anyone lost so long as you read the captions: **This one points home even if you disagree.** She told him about the note found under the shop door after the walk: a scrap from a grocery list with seven initials written between *eggs* and *soap.* They did not value these things less for being small. They valued them more for knowing where to sit in a pocket.

The lighthouse kept its rate. The room did not ask them to move. He thought, for an unserious second, of asking the beam to turn itself off so he could watch it relight and prove to himself that faith has respect for switches. He did not. He kept his hand where it was and let the light have its job.

In the Mirror Room below, the circle of fragments, dark for the night, remembered scenes it would show to others later, when asked correctly. In the archive, the journal rested. In the Chapel, someone—Miriam, probably—straightened the guest book and drew a line after today's names, as if to reassure tomorrow it would be allowed to begin again responsibly. In kitchens, someone salted a doorstep out of habit, not fear. On porches, someone told a child a story about a woman in green and forgot to call it a story. On the river, two lights passed each other like greetings exchanged without needing to be converted into opinion.

He breathed and realized he trusted evenings again. That was new. That was not nothing. He had thought evenings were where doubt lay down next to you and asked questions out loud. Now they were where work braided itself into peace.

"Truth in the light," he said, borrowing the sentence as casually as a cup. "It's a good rule."

"It is," she said. "It demands witnesses, not winners."

"Then we should ask the light to keep witnesses," he suggested.

"It already does," she answered, amused. "That's what the room is. That's what you are. That's what I am."

"And that's what the beam is," he agreed.

They watched one more sweep. He wanted to count, but he didn't. He let the light count them. He let the room give them back to themselves. He let his hand remark on the dignity of being allowed.

The door below creaked, a friendly sound. Footsteps on the stair—slow, respectful. Sophie appeared in the hatch like an apparition who had had a glass of milk. She took in their hands, their mugs, the journal box, the beam, the hour. "Is it okay if I sit?" she asked.

"No is holy," he said automatically, grinning.

"Yes," Marley said, because this was that sort of house.

Sophie sat on the other side of Marley and set her star wheel on the floor. "I named the pause," she announced. "It's where you breathe."

"What's it called?" Damien asked.

She rolled her eyes. "*The Pause.*" Children are gods at naming.

They sat three. Light and green stitched the beam. Somewhere behind them history stopped performing and started sleeping. Somewhere ahead of them history woke early and put on work clothes. He did not look ahead. He did not look back. He looked here.

Marley, Keeper of Memory, placed her free hand over the journal's lid and spoke the last line one more time, not as an incantation, not as a bow, just as a sentence that did its job: "May all who bear witness find truth in the light."

She did not add *amen*. He did not add *so be it*. Sophie did not add a flourish. The beam took the sentence and folded it into its sweep without asking for acknowledgment. The town, below, continued its effort to be decent. The sea asked nothing and gave everything.

They held hands in stillness, finally, not to make a claim but to keep a promise that had been waiting for bodies to be ready. Their connection did not feel like thunder. It felt like an archive with the right humidity; like a ledger you can read in anyone's handwriting; like bread that proves; like a waltz played at the correct speed under a summer window. It felt like a future that could bear weight because the past had been told the truth. It felt like Brookwood.

The beam turned. The room did not fail. The night learned its lesson. The light stayed on.

EPILOGUE: THE WINTER BELL

The first frost had not yet set, but the air carried that thinness, that clarity, that only late autumn can bring. Brookwood's streets had settled from their summer of lanterns and songs into the hush of early dark. Shop windows burned with amber light, candles replaced by oil lamps against the lengthening nights. The lighthouse still pulsed, steady and green-tinged, a sentinel that had outlived its own prophecies. But now the town's gaze was turning inland, toward another keeper of memory: the bell tower rising above the Chapel.

Marley walked there alone, scarf pulled tight against her throat, journal tucked under her arm. The beam swept behind her, its rhythm now as natural as her pulse. Keeper of Memory—that role had rooted itself in her days: cataloging, reading aloud, teaching children how to hear between words. But tonight, her steps were drawn not to the archive but to the bell.

It had always rung. For births, for deaths, for solstice walks, for weddings that stitched families together with sound. The bell was not merely an instrument—it was

Brookwood's own lungs. Its voice had carried through storms when radios failed, its toll had gathered mourners when ink could not reach. Eighty-eight years since it last fell silent.

She touched the Chapel door. A stillness answered, not the simple stillness of night, but a silence heavy with absence. She knew before stepping inside.

The rope hung slack. The bell had not rung that evening for vespers. People had gathered anyway, waiting for the chime that never came. Some had murmured about rust, others about wind. But Marley, standing beneath it now, knew better. Objects remembered. And this silence was memory refusing to move.

Damien entered quietly, as if summoned not by her letter but by the same instinct that had pulled her here. He carried no books tonight, no lantern—only his presence, tall in the shadowed hall. "It didn't ring," he said, confirming the truth she already held.

She nodded. "For eighty-eight years, it has never missed. Not once. Until now."

They stood together in that hollow quiet, listening to what had not been said. Marley felt the weight of her new role press differently here: Keeper of Memory was not just about light and flame. It was also about silence, about vows that had been left to rot beneath ceremony.

Damien touched the rope, lifted it, then let it fall. No echo. No sound. Only the echo of what should have been. He turned to her, eyes shadowed but steady. "It's not broken," he murmured. "It's refusing."

She exhaled, steadying herself. "Then we have to ask what vow it's holding hostage."

Their hands brushed briefly as they turned toward the stair that spiraled up to the bell. Neither pulled away. The lighthouse had taught them touch could be both anchor and promise. But beneath that touch, questions stirred: how far their hands could travel together before the paths of duty and love bent in opposite directions.

The bell loomed above them, waiting.

By lantern-light, the bell looked older than the lighthouse itself. Bronze darkened by decades, its lip etched with tiny nicks from storms and years of resonance. Around its crown, faint letters gleamed: **"Veritas in Silentio."** Truth in stillness.

Marley brushed the inscription with her glove. She had never noticed it before, though she had passed beneath this bell her entire life. Keeper of Memory meant reading not only words in books but the sentences carved into metal and stone. And this one, tonight, demanded attention.

Damien leaned on the railing, watching her with that mix of admiration and unease he had never learned to disguise. "Stillness reveals truth," he translated softly. "That was Aurelia's language too."

"She wrote it in light," Marley said. "And here it's written in sound—or the absence of it."

They both stood still, listening. The bell's silence was not emptiness—it vibrated, a held note waiting to be released. Marley closed her eyes, and in that hush she almost heard it: faint laughter, the echo of footsteps on the stair, the sharp intake of breath before vows spoken. And then, absence—a wedding that had not happened, a name that had never been called to witness.

Her eyes opened. Damien was watching her, not the bell. "You heard something," he said.

"Not words. A space. A missing piece." She turned back

to the bell, her fingers trailing the inscription again. "A forgotten bride."

He frowned, not at her intuition but at what it meant. "Then this isn't mechanical. It's memorial. The bell remembers a promise broken. And it won't ring again until we find out who was left standing in silence."

The phrase hung between them. Marley felt the tug of two currents: the call of the archive, of piecing together lost vows, of restoring Brookwood's memory yet again—and the call of her heart, tethered more each day to Damien's steady presence, his willingness to follow her into storms of truth. But with each step forward, she wondered: would his path always align with hers? Or would his roots, his daughter, his town obligations draw him where she could not follow?

The bell, patient and unyielding, offered no answer— only silence.

Below them, the town slept, unaware that the absence of a chime had already opened another chapter. Above them, the beam swept, steady, as if to say: one vow at a time.

They descended the stair slowly, carrying with them the silence like an artifact. Outside, the square lay washed in moonlight, its cobblestones silver. Marley held her scarf tighter, as though words unsaid were colder than frost. Damien walked beside her, close but not touching, each lost in thought.

At the fountain, she stopped. "Do you ever wonder," she asked, her voice low, "whether choosing to hold memory means choosing not to hold anything else?"

Damien turned, the question striking closer to bone than any artifact could. "All the time," he admitted. He looked at her fully, the man who had once brushed everything aside now learning to confess without armor. "I wonder if being Keeper of Memory means you'll leave when I need someone to stay. I wonder if my roots—Sophie, this town—will keep me here when you're called elsewhere."

Her heart tightened. She wanted to say the words that would mend it, to promise the lighthouse beam would always align with the bell's silence. But Keeper of Memory meant truth first. And truth was: she didn't know.

"We don't have to answer tonight," she said softly. "Stillness first. Listening first. The truth will speak between the memories."

He breathed, then nodded, accepting her answer because it was the only honest one. His hand brushed hers once more—no grip, no claim, only the reminder that they were here, still.

From the bell tower behind them, silence stretched. From the lighthouse ahead, the beam swept across water, steady as ever. Between them, the town of Brookwood slept under both silence and light, unaware that its next mystery had already been awakened: a vow broken, a wedding lost to memory, a bride no one remembered.

And Marley, Keeper of Memory, and Damien, her steady counterpart, would have to decide—not only how to solve the silence of the Winter Bell, but how to carry each other through it.

The bell waited. The light stayed on.

AFTERWORD

A Reflective Legacy

The Brookwood Mysteries begins, as so many stories do, with silence.

It was the silence of a bookshop whose shelves held more than novels—the silence of Clara's vow, of words written in margins, of echoes that could only be heard when someone dared to listen. Marley stepped into that silence not as an intruder but as an inheritor, though she did not yet know it. *The Bookshop Secret* showed her—and us—that history breathes through the most ordinary doors, waiting for hands brave enough to turn the lock.

From there, the path winds into resonance. *The Bridge of Echoes* carries voices across time, testing whether past promises could be trusted in the present. Each echo reminds Brookwood that memory is never idle—it insists, it demands, it shapes. Marley and Damien began to realize that listening was not passive but covenant: if they carried the echoes, they must also answer them.

The Lighthouse Prophecy shifts the gaze outward, to signals cast against darkness. It asked: what do we guard, and what do we guide? In that season, the town learned that prophecy is less prediction than mirror. The light did not foretell what must be—it illuminated what already was: a community standing on the threshold of its own forgotten story.

The Winter Bell gives voice to stillness. A bell that should have rung but didn't, a vow that had been broken, a bride whose absence echoed for decades. Silence again—but this time charged, asking whether absence could be as loud as sound. Marley and Damien discover that love and loss, entwined, toll not as ending but as call.

And finally, *The Hidden Grove* reveals itself as culmination, not simply continuation. The stones, the spirals, the ledger, the seed—all mysteries unfolded into memory, and memory unfolded into inheritance. What began as secrecy becomes community. What began as whispers becomes vows. What began as one woman's step into a bookshop becomes an entire town's covenant with its own roots.

Brookwood's Legacy

The mysteries are not puzzles to solve, nor riddles to conquer. They are invitations—to listen, to remember, to rise. At every turn, Brookwood asked its people a single question: *Will you keep what was entrusted to you, not as possession, but as promise?*

Marley answered yes. Damien answered yes. The townsfolk, hesitant, divided, afraid—they too answered yes.

And so the series does not close on a solved case or a quiet conclusion. It closes on a circle, still widening. Children's hands pressing seeds into soil. Elders whispering names into bark. A grove alive with bloom and resonance.

The mysteries of Brookwood will always remain, not

locked in secrecy but alive in inheritance. And so, the circle holds:

We remember. We root. We rise.

Brookwood Mysteries
    Book 1 - The Bookshop Secret
    Book 2 - The Bridge of Echoes
    Book 3 - The Lighthouse Prophecy
    Book 4 - The Winter Bell
    Book 5 - The Hidden Grove

ABOUT THE AUTHOR

Jordan Jace is a Pacific Northwest author whose mysteries and heartwarming tales are set against stunning landscapes. With a deep connection to the PNW region's natural beauty, Jace infuses each story with the magic of misty mountains, lush forests, and tranquil coastlines. Jace believes that joy can be found in the smallest moments and the most unexpected places. When not writing, Jace is exploring the world, seeking inspiration in every corner for the next unforgettable story. Discover more at visionsinprint.com

9 781967 657506